JIM DITCHFIELD

Published by Odyssey Books in 2016

www.odysseybooks.com.au

A Cataloguing-in-Publication entry is available from the National Library of Australia

ISBN: 978-1-922200-42-6 (pbk)
ISBN: 978-1-922200-43-3 (ebook)

Cover design: Karri Klawiter
Cover photo: State Library of Queensland Collection

Nursing Fox

1

*Number 1 Australian General Hospital, Heliopolis, Cairo,
Friday, 25 February 1916*

Lucy studied the young man on the stretcher. He'd been stoic as she'd changed the dressing on his stump, not a single grumble or complaint, although it must have been painful when she removed the old bandage. The wound was healing well without any sign of the gangrene that had infected the first amputation, and the doctors had closed the flaps two days earlier. As she'd cleaned the wound she'd admired the neat sutures, and hoped that she'd be as professional after she'd completed her doctor's training, but that would have to wait until the end of the war.

As usual she'd struggled to keep the site sterile, but despite her efforts, she'd been unable to prevent dust settling on the wound.

The *khamsin* had been blowing for over a week, the searing wind stirring up dirt that penetrated every crevice. The marquee wards gave no protection and in an effort to provide a more hygienic environment the ablutions room had been converted into a dressing station, but the door and windows were poorly fitted so that even in that tiled concrete building the *khamsin* dominated and the air was filled with swirling sand as fine as talcum powder.

She hadn't seen the man before and she checked his record card. AIF—10 Batt. 3 Bde. Anzac.

'What happened to your leg?' It was the seventh question she'd asked, but so far the man had not spoken. He'd stared at the ceiling as if he were a spectator and not the major player in the tiny drama.

'Frost bite. One foot was too far gone to save.'

Lucy had known the answer before she'd asked. It was in his notes, but it had been another attempt to open the conversation.

'That's a relief.' She raised her eyebrows. 'I was beginning to wonder if you'd lost your tongue as well as your leg. Where did it happen?'

'Gallipoli.'

She became serious. 'I thought that was over. I thought we'd pulled out of Gallipoli at the end of last year.'

A smile crept across the soldier's face, but it turned into a grimace of pain before it had fully developed. A few seconds passed before his breathing steadied and he said, 'Sorry, Sister. Didn't mean to be rude, but I was wondering what the future holds… It is over. At least the fighting is.' He sighed, then lapsed into silence again.

'I've heard it was bad. What was it really like?' If she could get him to talk he might begin to feel better.

'Bad… It was bad, all right. A bloody fiasco. A bloody blood bath. All those men killed and we achieved nothing.' The soldier paused, staring across to the door where another patient was being carried in. 'Eight months I'd been there. I landed with the first wave at the end of April, but it was the cold that did for me. We'd no decent clothes, and the rain and blizzards were killers. I was lucky. Some poor buggers froze to death and others drowned when their trenches flooded. My platoon was getting ready to move down to the beach, a couple more nights were all we had left. I'd been looking forward to being somewhere decent for Christmas. Bugger of a Christmas present.'

'Where did they operate, Lemnos?'

'No, we skipped Lemnos, hundreds of us. They brought us straight back to Gypo Land. I ended up in a hospital at Alexandria. After they'd taken my foot off they sent me down here.' The soldier eased himself onto his right elbow. 'Everything seemed fine for weeks, but then the leg turned bad, so they had another go, above the knee this time. The doc says they have it under control now, and my condition is satisfactory.' He pursed his lips and closed his eyes, and Lucy saw his hands clench. 'Satisfactory… It might be satisfactory for him, but it's not satisfactory for me. Sorry, Sister, it's not your fault.'

'That's all right. I can understand how frustrating it must be. How's the fresh dressing feel?'

He frowned. 'A bit easier, but it's still sore and the stump's itching like mad. Always does when the dressing's been changed. Drives me insane.' His eyes closed and he snatched a breath, his face creased with pain. After a few seconds he relaxed. 'The damn leg hurts more now than it ever did before they took it off. It wears you down. I can't help wondering how I'll cope when I'm back in Civvy Street. How will I earn a living?'

'Won't you have a pension?'

'Pension? I suppose, but it'll be a pittance. I'll have to get a job, but what the hell will I be able to do with only one leg?'

For a moment Lucy could think of nothing to say. She'd seen so many men who'd have the same problem. Some would never adjust, and this man had been set back twice. If she could give him a bit of hope it may help.

'I understand how you feel, but there's nothing anyone can do to bring your leg back. I wish there was, but they're doing marvellous things with artificial limbs these days, and you're young. You'll walk again, and it won't take long before you're back doing what you used to do.'

'That's easy for you to say, Sister, but you've still got two legs.'

'True, but my father hasn't. He lost a leg in the Boer War, but most of the time people who don't know him have no idea.' Lucy watched the soldier's face relax. 'You look a determined sort of bloke. I reckon you'll do the same.'

'You're not bulling me are you, Sister?' the man asked. 'You wouldn't raise a bloke's hopes unfairly?'

'It's the truth. You'll be right, just keep positive. It'll be hard at times, but I think you'll do it.' Lucy gathered the soiled dressings and said, 'The orderlies will be along in a minute to take you back to your ward. Which one are you in?'

'One of the marquees at the front of the building, the one at the end near the gate. This *khamsin*'s a bugger though. How long's it going to go on for?'

Lucy shrugged. 'I don't know. It's early this year and some people say it could be at least another month. I hope it doesn't last much longer, it would be good to see the sun again.' The orderlies appeared and as they carried the man away she called after him. 'I might pop by this evening to see how you're getting on.'

'You haven't time to waste with idle yacker, Paignton-Fox. There are other patients in need of attention.'

Lucy swung round at the sound of the voice, wondering how long Matron Morgan had been in the dressing station. Much older than the other nurses, the large woman dominated the room. She'd been a matron at the Sydney Hospital where, so they'd been told, she'd insisted on instant obedience. She hadn't changed. Her attitude was reminiscent of the strict discipline Lucy had experienced during her training, but she hadn't expected to find the same dogma in the Army Nursing Service. It was as if the matron had been soured by life and resented the younger women.

One of the nurses had worked under her in Sydney and described how they'd installed a time clock. The nurses had to record the times they went on and off duty, and even when they returned to their quarters after an evening with friends or family. She'd introduced the others to the matron's nickname, Morgan the Moron.

'I've just finished dressing his wound, Matron. I had to make sure he has no infection.'

'You've been taking far too long over it. In future simply concentrate on your own work and don't interfere with the doctor's.' Sweat ran down the matron's face, collecting dust like a magnet attracts iron filings. Her bosom heaved as if she'd been running. 'The reason you're here is to attend to the patients' medical needs, not to flirt with them. If I catch you wasting time again you'll be disciplined.' The matron lumbered out of the room, her face suffused with vindictiveness.

Lucy stared at the matron's retreating back. What's wrong with that woman? Doesn't she have any compassion? She dumped the soiled dressings, glanced at her watch and washed her hands, muttering to herself.

She made her way across to the dining hall, still puzzling over the matron's attitude. Surely she could see it was only an attempt to lift the man's spirits. He'd find life difficult with only one leg and a little encouragement could make a big difference. Her dad must have felt like that before he met Dorothy. She'd nursed him in the hospital at Bloemfontein after he'd lost his leg. They'd married when he was due to be repatriated to Australia and she'd returned with him to his cattle station, Aughton Park, in the Northern Territory.

It was Dorothy's devotion to her father that inspired Lucy to take up nursing. Her encouragement had been an added incentive. It was to please her that she'd studied so hard during her training and as a result had been offered a place at medical school to train as a doctor. Dorothy had been ecstatic and her encouragement had become almost an obsession.

Another seven years' study was a daunting prospect, but as Dorothy pointed out, it was a rare opportunity for a woman. Lucy was determined to do well. It would be a way to repay her stepmother for the care and devotion she had lavished on her father. Although he was a strong character, without her help and knowledge he would have taken far longer to recover.

After his initial objection her father had refused to try to influence her when she had joined the Army Nursing Service, saying it was her choice, and he'd back her whatever her decision was. In contrast, Dorothy had been so disappointed.

Now that she'd thought of her father and Dorothy, memories of her embarkation leave flooded back.

Aughton Park, Northern Territory, Australia,
Monday, 21 September 1914

Lucy woke to the jingle of a bridle. She stretched as the smells of her childhood drifted through the open window: wood smoke, sweet grass and cattle. For a few minutes she lay, still sleepy, reliving her memories, then she threw the sheet back. As she sat up, she searched unconsciously for the two Bagust Heelers that had always rushed to her side when she left her bed, but Chaos and Mayhem had died during the first term of her nurses' training. That's the problem with dogs, she thought, they never lived for long, although sixteen was a good age. She'd been crawling when they'd been puppies and they'd grown up as her devoted companions.

Chaos had gone first, but Mayhem followed after a few weeks of pining, as if she couldn't face life without her lifelong mate. She missed them still and for a moment struggled to control her emotions, then the happy memories overcame the sadness. They'd been good years.

She moved to the window and stared across to the yards where two Aboriginal stockmen were mounting up. For a moment she wondered what was different about the cattle station, then she realised she could see only about thirty horses in the home paddock. They needed over one hundred for the musters. In this country the musters were hard work so a stockman would change horses three or four times a day, and each horse had to be spelled for three days between the days it worked.

This was the first morning of her leave. She made her way along the passage to the kitchen marvelling, as she always did, at how well her father had built the homestead using virtually nothing but dirt from anthills. It was always so cool, thanks to the thick walls and high ceilings. Dorothy and her grandmother brightened the place, and kept it filled with flowers from the garden they tended together. They worked tirelessly to keep the home spotless, the Aboriginal housemaids helping with the heavy chores.

She paused, unnoticed at the kitchen door, trying to store the memory away. Her father sat at the head of the long table, Dorothy on his right, and her grandparents at the bottom. A place was set at her father's left, her place. They were in animated conversation.

A cast iron stove had been fitted into the stone fireplace. The stove was new since she'd last been home, and Betsy One was filling the teapot from the built-in boiler at the side.

She watched the Aboriginal woman with affection. Her hair was more grey than black these days, but her back was still straight. She'd never been fat, but now she was so thin that Lucy wondered if she was ill.

Betsy One looked much older, but she realised with a start that they were all older, except for Betsy Two. Lucy thought back to the incident. Betsy Two had been younger than she was now when her mother—her natural mother—killed her. That had been a bad time and she pushed the memory aside, deciding to pay her respects to Betsy Two later in the morning.

Betsy One looked up. 'Lucy. Piccaninny Lucy…'

She smiled at the pleasure that flashed in the old woman's eyes. When she'd arrived home the previous evening Betsy One had been in the Aborigines' camp so they hadn't seen each other.

Lucy had been five when her mother had died just a few months after the trauma with Betsy Two, yet Betsy One had cherished her with no animosity. They'd grown close, the difference in the colour of their skins immaterial. It was as if she found that caring for a child as a surrogate daughter had helped her come to terms with losing Betsy Two.

'No more piccaninny, Betsy One,' she said.

Betsy One shook her head and patted her chest. 'All time Piccaninny Lucy this fella.' She placed the teapot on the table, rushed to Lucy and clasped her in a hug.

'Betsy One, all same strong fella. Are you trying to squash me? I can't breathe.' Lucy gave the old woman a kiss then eased herself free, holding her at arm's length and saw the tears trickling down her face. Betsy One pushed herself out of Lucy's grasp and dashed from the room, as if embarrassed by her show of emotion.

'Lucy, come and sit down,' Charlie Paignton said, patting the chair on his left, his face wreathed in a paternal smile. 'How did you sleep? You look well. It's so good to have you home, even if only for a short while. The station's not been the same with you away. How long before you have to be back to Adelaide?'

'Give me a chance, Dad. I'm not going back to Adelaide.'

'But your place at medical school. What about that?' Charlie turned to his wife. 'You know more about this than I do, Dorothy. If she's not going back to Adelaide, where will she go?'

'I don't know, unless they've transferred her to Melbourne or Sydney. Or perhaps she's landed a place overseas.' Dorothy leant across the table, her eyes bright with anticipation. 'Where are you going, Lucy?'

'I am going overseas, Mum. I've joined the Australian Army Nursing Service.' Lucy watched horror spread across her father's face. She wondered if it would have been better to have told him quietly while they were alone, but it was done now, and Dorothy may help her to explain. She must have had a similar reaction from her parents when she joined the Australian Nursing Service of New South Wales, and gone off to the Boer War.

'The army? But we're at war. There'll be shooting. You could be injured or… There'll be men.'

Lucy reached across the table and took his hand. 'Yes, Dad, and they'll be wounded. They'll need someone to nurse them, just like you did when you met Dorothy.' She saw her father glance down to his leg. 'That's where I'll be needed, Dad. That's where the troops will be.'

'I thought the minimum age for a nurse to enlist was twenty- five,' Dorothy said. She bit her bottom lip and looked as if she was about to burst into tears.

'That's not true, Mum. You have to be between twenty-one and forty and unmarried. Some married nurses were so keen to enlist they said they were single.'

Dorothy took a deep breath and pursed her lips, frowning, her eyes locked on Lucy's face. 'But if you go off with the army, what will happen about your place at medical school? I had such high hopes when I got your letter. It was not something open to us when I was nursing, and it will be such a shame to waste all your hard work. You can't give it up.'

'Don't worry, Mum, everything's arranged. Because I've joined the Army Nursing Service they'll hold a place for me until I return, and the experience will be good grounding. I think I'll learn a lot of practical stuff.'

'Thank goodness. I thought for a moment that you'd abandoned the dream of being a doctor,' Dorothy said with a sigh. 'You'll get plenty of experience with the army, and be expected to do things that women are never be permitted to do here in Australia. It'll be hard work and for long hours, but it'll be real nursing. You'll have a head start when you return to your studies. I'll be so proud when you qualify.'

'I won't allow it. Not the army,' Charlie said. 'I forbid it. I'll never give my permission.'

'Dad, I'm twenty-two,' Lucy said and squeezed his hand. 'I don't need your permission. Anyway, I've already signed on. I have to do my bit to help. I'm posted to Number 1 Australian General Hospital and we sail from Sydney on November 28.'

'But you'll come under fire.' Charlie reached down and stroked his knee where his wooden leg was strapped to his stump. 'You could be wounded.'

'That's nonsense. The hospitals will be well back from the fighting. She'll not be in the front line, Charlie,' Dorothy said.

'Charles, Lucy's a grown woman. I don't like it any more than you do, but if that's what she wants to do, you can't stand in her way. I'm proud that my granddaughter will be doing something to help the boys who get wounded,' Marion Paignton said.

Lucy smiled at her grandmother as her grandfather leant forward, wagging his finger like a schoolmaster admonishing a pupil. 'Your mother's right, Charles. We know how you feel, but remember how determined you became when we tried to prevent you coming to Australia. Lucy's old enough to know her own mind. She's not a child anymore, so don't make the same mistake we did.'

Lucy joined her friend, Vicky Bright, who was already at a dining table, one of fifteen arranged in three rows beneath the ventilation ducting in what had been the restaurant of the racecourse. She placed her plate down, reached up to adjust the punkah-louvre, and raised her face to the stream of tepid air.

'Have you heard?' Vicky blurted out before Lucy had time to pull her chair back.

'Heard what?'

'We're being transferred to Number 2 AGH and then we're off to France.' Vicky rushed on without giving Lucy time to reply. 'If we get leave we might be able to see Paris.'

Lucy laid her knife and fork down. 'I've heard that the men over there are having a bad time. Worse than Gallipoli by all accounts. I think we'll be too busy to visit Paris, and it won't be like it was before the war.' She turned to glance out of the window at the swirling sand. 'I'll not be sorry to leave this dust behind. Any news about when we're due to sail?'

'I've no idea, but Matron Kenny's at that end table, she might know,' Vicky said, pushing her empty plate aside. 'I'm going to get a cup of tea. Would you like one?'

Lucy nodded and resumed eating.

Vicky returned and as she slipped into her chair she said, 'We leave some time during the last week in March. Tubs wouldn't give me the exact date. I'll tell you this for nothing, I'll be glad to see the back of the damn flies and these *khamsins*.'

'Perhaps she doesn't know herself,' Lucy said and took a sip of tea. 'I heard the First and Second Anzacs have already left. That must be why we're being sent. Now Gallipoli's over there won't be as much work here. I wonder what France will be like.'

2

British XVIII Corps, front line, Arras,
Tuesday, 14 March 1916

'I can see why the French couldn't capture that hill,' Adam said. He was standing on the fire-step of the trench, staring across no man's land towards Vimy Ridge, the highest escarpment in the crescent of hills that formed a natural barrier to the north-east of Arras.

'They tried a few times, but they lost so many men they lost their enthusiasm.' Sergeant Crawford reached inside his shirt and scratched at the bites in his armpit. 'Bloody chats. We've been back in the front line less than a day and already they've made themselves comfortable. The little sods are making up for lost time.'

'At least they're always pleased to see you.' Adam dodged as the sergeant threw a playful punch. 'So now it's our turn to take a stab at it, is it?'

'Don't give me lip, Hayward.' Sergeant Crawford grinned. 'How would I know? I've heard that Fritz has been digging a lot of tunnels. The Frogs have been at it as well, but Fritz went deeper. They've been setting mines under each other's trenches.' The sergeant joined Adam on the fire-step to make room for a party of sappers. 'We're doing the same. That's what these chaps are for. I just hope there isn't a mine under this trench.'

'So that's what all these Royal Engineers are about?' Adam pointed to the sappers who were still filing along the trench.

Sergeant Crawford nodded. 'That's right. There are several companies of the bastards ferreting about down there. But it's not just the British; there are tunnellers from all over the shop, Canada and Australia. Some Kiwis too, so I heard.'

When the sappers had passed, Adam leant his rifle against the wall of the trench, sat in the entrance to a dugout, and watched the sergeant stand on a sandbag on the fire-step to peer over the parapet. Sergeant Crawford was a slim man, about five feet seven, three inches shorter than he was. He was always smart and Adam wondered how he managed to keep so clean, despite the mud.

The sergeant stepped down and joined him at the dugout's entrance. 'The buzz is they've found some caves and are using them to get down below Fritz. Apparently there are dozens of caverns. They're making them deeper and joining them up so the shells can't reach us.'

'That'll be good,' Adam said with feeling, but his attention was on the last of the sappers as he disappeared round the corner of the trench. 'They're a bit small for digging tunnels. You wouldn't think they were strong enough to work underground.'

'Don't underestimate the Bantams. They're tough little buggers, miners from the north of England. Hundreds of the poor sods.' The sergeant pulled a packet of Woodbines from his pocket. 'Fag?'

'Thanks.' Adam took the offered cigarette and lit it from the sergeant's match. 'How do you know?'

'While we were out of the line I was talking to a chap from Battalion HQ. He reckons the plan is not just to dig the normal tunnels for mines, but also to excavate huge chambers connected to the reserve areas so that people can come and go without being fired on.'

'That'll be an improvement.' Adam thought about the times they'd moved to and from the front line while being shelled. 'They could bring the meals up that way too.'

'They'll not need to bring meals up. According to that chap they've got cookhouses, and other things too, machine-guns and mortars included.'

'How big are these darned caverns?' Adam asked. Disbelief was strong in his face. 'Mortars underground? You sure about that?'

Sergeant Crawford stepped up to the fire-step and surveyed no man's land for a short time, then moved back to the lower section of trench. 'That's what the chap said, and he seemed to know. They have light railways down there too.'

'Who? Fritz or us?'

'Us, of course. I don't know about Fritz, but he's probably done the same.' He reached inside his shirt to scratch his armpit again. 'Oh, that's better,' he sighed. 'These little bastards are driving me batty.'

'Do we get to ride to work now they've gotten railways?' Adam asked, grinning. 'Are the seats padded?'

Sergeant Crawford returned his grin. 'You'll be lucky. The railways are only for the important stuff, like ammo. Why do you think they issued you with boots? You might get a ride back after you've been wounded, but don't bank on it.'

'Wounded? What aren't you telling me, Sergeant? How will I get wounded in the tunnels?'

'What do you think the machine-guns are for? There's already been some fighting down below. I think Fritz had a bit of surprise to find us there and not the Frogs.'

'I don't like the thought of fighting underground.'

'I'm with you. I don't fancy it either, but that's what that chap told me.'

'That's not the only place there's fighting. Look up there.' Adam pointed to a German biplane firing at an observation balloon. 'Isn't that an Albatros?' he asked.

'If you say so. I'm no expert on these aeroplanes.'

More stabs of flame shot out from the plane and lines of light marked the trajectory of the bullets. Two black specks leapt from the gondola of the balloon moments before it erupted in flames. They were halfway to the ground before a pale hemisphere appeared above each of them.

'There's another bastard,' Sergeant Crawford said and pointed to a second German plane that was diving and firing at the two observers who were floating below their canopies. 'And that's three more.' He became excited and pointed towards the three new arrivals. 'Bastards. Shooting at helpless men.'

Adam looked to where he was pointing. Three different biplanes were diving from the thin clouds. One peeled off and turned towards the plane that had fired at the balloon, but the other two converged on the plane that was targeting the two men. 'They're ours. Brits.'

The British planes closed and their machine-guns spewed streaks of tracer rounds. The German plane veered away, but smoke was streaming from the forward fuselage. Flames flared from the engine compartment as the port upper wing crumpled. The lower wing collapsed too, and the plane began to spin as it fell. The two British planes followed it down until it hit the ground. They began to climb again and turned towards the other Albatros, but the pilot had abandoned the fight and was heading back to German territory. The third British plane rejoined them and they flew off along the line of the remaining balloons.

As the planes moved away Adam said, 'They're those new Nieuport 17s that have just come into service.'

'How do you know they were British and not Froggies? I couldn't make out their markings,' Sergeant Crawford said. 'All these bloody aeroplanes look the same to me.'

'They had Lewis guns above the upper wings. The French use Vickers fitted on the fuselage.' The sergeant looked sceptical, so Adam continued. 'I keep up with airplane developments. That's what I'd really like to do—fly. If I'd thought about it I'd have tried for the Royal Flying Corps instead of the Infantry, but I was so mad at Ma's death I didn't stop to think.'

'How come you know so much about aeroplanes?'

'Aeroplane, I thought that's what you said. I've never heard that before. We just say airplane. Why do you English have to be different?'

'Don't ask me. That's the way it is. But you didn't answer my question. Where did you learn about aeroplanes?'

'When the Wright brothers made the first powered flight I was twelve years old and it grabbed my imagination. I began to read about airplanes, everything I could get my hands on. In January 1910, just before my twentieth birthday, there was an international air meeting organised at Los Angeles, and Pa took me for a birthday present. Fliers from all over the world, over forty of them, were at Dominquez Field. I think I must have asked everyone to take me flying. One of them agreed to take me up the next morning, but when I looked for him he'd disappeared. His plane had gone too.' Adam looked wistfully at the Nieuports as they left the scene. 'I had a good look at the airplanes though and one flier let me sit in his cockpit. That really fired my imagination. I can still remember the excitement. That's the way to fight. Flying must be magic.'

'Whatever… but you saw what happened to that Fritz,' Sergeant Crawford said, and nodded to where the German plane had crashed.

'It has to be better than all this trench digging and charging into machine-gun bullets across a strip of darned mud.' Adam was still staring at the planes, which were no more than tiny silhouettes as they closed with the horizon. 'As for living in holes in the ground, that's for worms.'

'Maybe you're right, but that pilot is just as dead as any of our mates who died in the trenches.' Sergeant Crawford shuddered and became thoughtful. 'It's an awful way to die if you ask me. I'd sooner have my feet on the ground.'

AIF, Second Australian Division, Anzac, Rouen,
Wednesday, 29 March 1916

'John, the commanding officer wants to see you at once,' the company commander said when Sergeant Mitchell presented himself at the tent that had been set up as the company office.

'What's he want to see me for? I'm not in the rattle, am I?' John asked.

'Not that I'm aware of. You've not been up to mischief, have you?' the company commander said, a broad smile on his face. 'There's only one way to find out what's on his mind, but it won't hurt to tidy up a bit before you present yourself. Don't be too long. He says it's urgent.'

'We've only just got off the train, sir,' John said. 'I haven't even had time for a meal yet, never mind get cleaned up.'

'I know that, and so does the colonel.'

As John made his way across to the battalion headquarters he passed the sergeant cook. 'I'll have a meal ready for you when you're organised,' the cook said. 'Do you know where the cook house is?'

'Show me.'

The cook pointed along a paved path. 'Down there about one

hundred yards. On the left. It'll only be a Maconochie stew. That's all I can organise in so short a time, but it'll be hot, so I don't want any wasted.'

'I'll do it justice, don't you worry about that.' John hurried on, the creases in his weather-beaten face accentuated by his scowl as he wondered why the CO wanted to see him. Everyone seemed to know he'd been summoned, even the cook, and he became irritated, but it was best not to keep the CO waiting when he said something was urgent. He increased his pace.

The adjutant met him at the door to the station waiting-room that had been commandeered as their temporary headquarters. The adjutant knocked and, on the CO's command, 'Come,' he led John into the room.

John marched up to the desk, halted and stood to attention, his back ramrod straight, emphasising his five feet eleven. He saluted.

'Good man,' the CO said and acknowledged his salute as the adjutant moved to stand by the door. 'At ease, Mitchell.'

John relaxed.

The CO picked up a signal from the blotter in front of him. 'I've just heard about a party of Australian nurses. They're due to land at Marseilles on 1 April, then they'll entrain for Rouen, like we did, but I'm not happy about them making the journey unescorted. You know as well as I do how chaotic it was, and I don't want our Aussie girls being left to fend for themselves at the food stops.' The CO paused and lifted his head.

'The first of April? Is someone having a go, sir?'

The CO flashed a fleeting smile. 'This is no joke, Mitchell. Those girls will need someone to take care of them. I want you to take twenty men. You're to escort the nurses throughout the trip and make sure they don't have to fight for their food, or anything else come to that. You'll probably find objections from some of the base-based wallahs, so use your discretion. If a senior officer tries to countermand my orders, refer him to me, but my orders are paramount. If you have to use your rifle, do so, but I'd prefer you didn't shoot anyone.'

'Righto, sir. Do you have any particular men in mind?' John

asked. After serving in the trenches with the CO throughout the Gallipoli fiasco, John knew exactly what he thought about base-based wallahs, particularly the senior officers who issued orders for attacks that were impossible to achieve. Then there were the support troops who failed to supply the right equipment when it was needed. He knew it wasn't always their fault, and so did the CO, but it had been hard to forgive when the Turks had been making life difficult.

This sounded just up his street and it had to be better than whatever the rest of the battalion would be doing.

'You know the men better than I do, Mitchell. I'm not interested in their parade ground ability, but choose men you can rely on. I don't want any nervous Nellies getting trigger-happy. I suggest some of the men who were with us at Gallipoli. By the time you have them together and organised there'll be a meal ready for you, but time is of the essence. I want you back here with your men in forty-five minutes for your written orders and travel passes. You can collect the ammunition at the same time. I've organised one hundred rounds for each man. Your train is scheduled to leave in an hour. Any questions?'

'No, sir.'

'Good man. I have no idea where we'll be when you get back, but you'll find us. I'll leave instructions. Away you go.'

Bloody hell, nursemaid to a mob of nurses. This was a real turn up, John thought as he hurried back to the company area. How lucky to land a job like this. He made a mental list of the men he'd take. It wouldn't be a good idea to tell them what's involved, or he'd be swamped with volunteers.

Marseilles, Saturday, 1 April 1916

Lucy leant on the rail of the *Braemar Castle*, examining the quay as the ship approached it, her skirt fluttering round her legs, her nurse's hat clutched in her hand. She huddled in her cape as the cold wind fretted at a few strands of hair that had come loose from her bun. Absentmindedly she brushed them from her face.

'Marseilles,' she breathed the word quietly and slowly. 'So this is France.'

The *Braemar Castle* crept towards the quay, aiming for a gap between a lighter and a dirty cargo ship. Now that the engines were stopped the deck was free of vibrations for the first time since they'd left Egypt, but the ship moved so slowly that Lucy wondered if it had sufficient momentum to carry it to the quay.

Vicky, leaning on the rail at her side, said, 'At last. I thought it would be exotic, but it's filthy. It's as dirty as Alexandria.'

'What did you expect? It's the docks. They're never exotic and it won't be exotic where we're going either,' Lucy said. She paused, thinking about the work ahead. 'I wonder what the hospitals will be like.'

'Goodness knows. Big tents, I guess, if Egypt is anything to judge by.'

'I suppose that'll be right. Big tents, full of wounded soldiers, all needing nursing.' Lucy thought back to the *khamsins*. At least they wouldn't have those hot winds and dust, but she wondered about tented wards in European weather. 'That will be bearable in summer, but what will it be like in winter?'

Vicky shrugged. 'Whatever it's like, I expect we'll be busy.'

Lucy examined the dock. Five horse-drawn wagons were lined up at the far side of the quay, the first being loaded with sacks that were lowered in nets from an opening high in a warehouse wall. Other wagons passed along the dockside in both directions. Three men, one of them dark skinned, rolled barrels towards the lighter tied up ahead of the space that the *Braemar Castle* was slipping into. Ahead of the lighter a team of men, stripped to the waist, balanced wicker baskets of coal on their shoulders as they hurried up a gangway of another ship. Their torsos were black with coal dust, and they reminded her of a stream of ants. Once the men had emptied their baskets they turned, ran down a second gangway and across the quay, where they disappeared into a wide doorway. From the other side of the doorway another stream of men appeared with full baskets to join the line at the up gangway.

'What's that stench?' Vicky asked. 'It's revolting, worse than gangrene.' She shuddered and pointed down. 'I hadn't expected that.'

Lucy looked to where Vicky pointed. The water between the dock and the *Braemar Castle* was thick with flotsam, and directly below she saw the bloated carcass of a dog.

The reek of putrid flesh was strong, and seemed to intensify as she stared at the carcass. For a moment she thought she was going to retch, but she looked away and the feeling passed. The flash of a light line caught her attention as it flew across the void between the ship's bow and the quay, where a soldier grabbed it. Four companions joined him and they began to haul it, and the hawser it was tied to, across the gap. As soon as they'd dropped the eye splice of the hawser over a bollard, the deck party on the *Braemar Castle*'s foredeck drew in the slack and made the hawser fast. The officer in charge turned to the bridge and raised his hand. Lucy heard the ring of the engine room telegraph and at once the ship began to throb. A surge of water boiled at the stern to swirl forward along the ship's sides. The rush of water forced the flotsam towards the bow, sweeping the dog's carcass clear. The hawser became taut and the gap between the ship and the dockside narrowed as the ship began to creep backwards. Less than a minute later, after another ring of the telegraph, the engines stopped and the vibrations came to an end.

The *Braemar Castle* drifted backwards and the stern moved in towards the quay. Lucy glanced up at the bridge, only a few feet ahead, where she could see the captain on the wing, watching the gap. He moved back to the centre of the bridge and after another ring, the propellers churned water again, which this time surged out astern, but the engines stopped after a few seconds and the ship became stationary. It was just inches from the stone wall of the quay and the party at the stern deck lowered another hawser to the wharf. Other crewmembers dangled rope fenders in the gap between the dockside and the ship. She watched the crew work quickly to secure two more hawsers, one leading from the ship's stern to a bollard on the quay near the bow, the second from the bow towards a bollard near the stern.

Lucy glanced back to the bridge where the captain stood looking pleased with himself. He should be pleased, she thought. He's just berthed a six thousand-ton hospital ship as gently as a mother placing her new born in a cradle. She thought back to the trip from Australia to Egypt and the trouble they'd experienced with the docking at Trincomalee, even with two tugs helping to manoeuvre the ship alongside.

'I wonder what France will be like. I'm looking forward to seeing the country. All that time in Egypt and I never got to see the Pyramids,' Vicky said. 'We were so close, but we may as well have been on the moon.'

'From what Matron Kenny told us I think we'll be far too busy coping with the wounded to see much of France,' Lucy said.

'How does Tubs know that?'

'She wouldn't make it up,' Lucy said with a shrug. 'She's probably been told things in confidence. All she told me was that the fighting has been heavy.'

'You're probably right, but it can't be worse than Egypt. I'm not sorry to leave all that sand.' Vicky pulled a face. 'The weather got me down.'

'That's two of us,' Lucy said. 'And all those flies. Up your nose so you couldn't breathe, in your eyes, and when you went to dress a wound…' She suppressed a shudder. 'It was revolting. I wonder the wounds healed at all.'

'I think you had it easy,' Alex Spence said.

Lucy turned to the plump nurse who had joined them at the rail. Like Lucy and Vicky she clutched her hat in her hand. 'Hello, Lex. You're not still rabbiting on about how bad things were for you.'

'But it's true. We had it much worse in Salonica. The insects, millions of them. Millipedes, scorpions, you name it we had it. Spiders, some as big as a fist.' Alex wrinkled her nose. 'It was awful. Pour a drink and a thousand flies would be vying for a place on the rim of the cup. Before you knew what was happening you had a cup full of fly corpses. Even though last winter was so cold the insects were just as thick.'

'Don't start again. You've told us already, Lex,' Vicky said. 'Many times.'

'But it's true, and it was so hot in summer. I've never experienced anything like it.' Alex pulled her cape tighter round her shoulders.

'That's because you come from Melbourne,' Lucy said and laughed. 'Forget it. It's all behind us now. Say g'day to France.'

'France. I've read so much about Paris, I wonder if I'll get to see it.' Alex was on Lucy's left, drumming her fingers on the rail as if she was impatient.

Lucy turned to her, trying to keep her amusement from her features. 'See Paris? You'll be lucky. In case you've forgotten, there's a war on.'

'But we'll have to go through Paris as we go north. I've checked it out. Surely we'll be able to see something of the city. I would like to see the Eiffel Tower.' Alex became thoughtful, then in a quiet voice she said, 'And I might be able to see Len.'

'Who's Len?' Vicky asked.

'My fiancé.'

'You're a dark horse, Lex. I didn't know you were engaged. What unit is he with?' Vicky asked, then added, 'He is an officer?'

'What's his rank got to do with anything?' Alex said.

'If he's not an officer and the matron finds out, you'll be in trouble. You know we're not allowed to fraternise with the other ranks.'

Alex looked up, her eyes flashing with anger. 'How do they think regulations are going to stop someone falling in love? He's a private, so I'm not going to take any notice. Anyway, we were engaged before we volunteered. I'm sure Tubs wouldn't say anything.'

'Perhaps not, but the Moron would,' Vicky said. 'You be careful.'

Thank goodness she didn't have that complication, Lucy thought. 'I agree with Lex.'

'But we're officers,' Vicky said. 'We can't walk out with just anyone.'

'Why not, for goodness sake? Who decided about these regulations? How dare they dictate with whom we should make friends? It's as if they have a breeding programme. That's what Dad does on the station. He selects the cows he wants to mate with the pedigree bulls, but I'm not a cow. It stinks of the British class system to think the officers are better than the other ranks,' Lucy said.

'But they're gentlemen,' Vicky said.

'Balderdash,' Lucy said with scorn. 'There's no correlation between rank and being a gentleman. I'll choose my own friends. I'm not going to take any notice of rubbish dreamt up by a mob of old fogies.'

'That's what I think too,' Alex said. 'And if I get the chance for leave I'll see Len. I don't care about stupid regulations.'

'Don't get your hopes up about leave, Lex, and I don't think we'll be going through Paris. From what I've heard Fritz is knocking at the gates. They'll probably take us round to the west,' Vicky said.

'Where did you hear that?' Lucy asked.

'Everyone's talking about it.'

'That's news to me. I'll bet it's just another rumour. The last I heard was that they were attacking Verdun, but they'd come unstuck, and the French are hitting back,' Lucy said.

'Where's Verdun?' Alex asked.

'Way to the east. It must be well over one hundred miles from Paris,' Lucy said. She was about to comment at Alex's ignorance, but checked herself. Both Alex and Vicky had gone to state schools and left at fourteen. She'd been so lucky to have a private tutor. She smiled, remembering Mr Brunton.

He'd been the tutor to Lord Barter's son in England, and because Grandfather had been the estate steward, Lord Barter had permitted Dad to share his lessons. When Lord Barter died the tutor had lost his cottage, as had many estate workers, including her grandparents, and Dad had brought Mr Brunton and his wife, Marie-Louise, out to be her tutor and governess at Aughton Park. Mr Brunton was a gentle old man who was sixty-two when he arrived and saw no reason to adapt his lessons, so had taught her the subjects he would have taught a boy, concentrating on maths, science, Latin and the classics. Marie-Louise was French and had taught her European geography and French. The usual girls' subjects—sewing, embroidery and household tasks—had been left to Grandmother. Lucy had been thirteen when Mr Brunton had contracted Blackwater fever and Dad had sent him to Adelaide to recover, but he died.

Marie-Louise gained a teaching position at the prestigious St Peter's Girls School in North Adelaide, and suggested that Lucy was enrolled to complete her schooling. Charlie bought a house on Kingston Terrace, a short walk away, and Marie-Louise cared for Lucy for the next three years while she attended the school. It was this education, possibly more than her good results during her nurse's training, that resulted in the place at medical school.

'But they've been shelling…'

'Why aren't you nurses wearing your hats?' The authoritarian voice came from behind them.

They turned and Lucy saw Matron Morgan looking furious. 'It's too windy, Matron. We'd lose them.'

'Oh, it's you again, Paignton-Fox. I should have guessed you'd be involved.' She glared as she examined Lucy from head to toe, as if trying to find more faults with her appearance. 'You all know the regulations about being properly dressed in public. If it's too windy get back below at once or I'll have to discipline you all.'

'We just wanted to see what France was like,' Alex said. 'It's all new.'

'This isn't a holiday jaunt, Sister Spence. We're here to do a job, not to be idle sightseers. Now do as you're told and get below at once.' Matron Morgan glared at the three nurses, then stormed off.

'Why is the Moron always so miserable?' Alex asked as they made their way to the nurses' lounge. 'I've not come across that sort of attitude since I was in training. Thank goodness Matron Kenny is in charge and not her.'

'That's why she's miserable,' Vicky said. 'I was talking to a Medical Corps sergeant in the registry before we left Heliopolis, and he told me that the Moron had applied to be the senior matron. She thought that with her experience she'd be automatically put in charge, but Matron Kenny got the job. The Moron's forty-two, you know, a lot older than Tubs. I think she's venting her anger on us.'

'But she's all right with some of the nurses,' Alex said.

'She has her favourites. The ones who suc—'

Lucy interrupted, 'Look at the time. We'll have to get our skates on or we'll be late at our disembarkation station. That'll really give the Moron something to whinge about.'

3

Hotel Jean D'Arc, Marseilles, Monday 3 April 1916

'Hurry up, Lex. We'll miss the train if you don't get moving,' Vicky said with irritation. 'What's holding you up?'

'I can't find my other shoe.'

'This one here?' Lucy asked as she dragged a shoe from under a bed and tossed it across the room to Alex. 'Get yourself sorted out before Vicky dies of apoplexy. We do have to get a move on.'

The three nurses hurried along the corridor to the stairs. As they passed the door to Matron Kenny's room they heard the two matrons arguing.

'I want Paignton-Fox in my group. She's too full of her own importance and needs to learn a bit of discipline. You're too easy with her.' Matron Morgan's voice was raised.

'What's that all about?' Vicky asked.

Alex put her finger to her lips and stepped across to the door.

Lucy shrugged and whispered. 'I've no idea. I hope Tubs doesn't agree.' She frowned. If the Moron was in charge, it would be a miserable journey.

'The arrangements have been finalised and I'm not about to change them. Paignton-Fox is in my party and she's staying in my party,' Matron Kenny said. 'Why are you so insistent that she's put under your supervision?'

'Someone has to teach her her place.' Matron Morgan's voice became louder. 'She's a bad influence on the other nurses. A dose of strict discipline will bring her in line.'

Lucy clenched her fists as her anger grew. She could imagine how the Moron would impose discipline.

'Don't raise your voice to me. It's obvious that you dislike her, but I'm not prepared to permit discrimination in the way any nurse is treated.' Matron Kenny's voice was still controlled. 'I've noticed how you are forever disciplining some nurses without valid reason. It has to stop. We'll discuss this further at Rouen.'

'What do you mean by that?' Matron Morgan snapped.

'I would have thought that was obvious. I'll not permit favouritism or vindictiveness in your attitude to the nurses. Now please go, you've made me late.'

'Who do you think you are?'

'I told you not to raise your voice to me, Matron,' Matron Kenny said. 'I'm in charge and we'll do things my way. Unless you improve your attitude I'll have you dismissed. Now get out.'

'You'll have me dismissed? You don't have the authority. If you had my experience you'd know better…'

'Get out.' Matron Kenny's raised her voice for the first time. 'At once.'

'I'm going to tell the Moron what I think of her,' Lucy said and reached for the doorknob.

Alex grabbed her hand. 'Not a good idea. Let Tubs deal with it.'

Vicky took her other arm. 'Come on, Lucy, we have to go.'

Together they urged her along the corridor to the stairs. 'Thanks. You're right,' she said as they left the hotel. 'I'd have made a fool of myself.'

No one spoke as they hurried to the station.

South of France, Monday, 3 April 1916

'I'm freezing. I never thought I could be so cold.' Lucy hunched in her cape, rubbing her hands together and stamping her feet in an attempt to generate some warmth.

'It's the damp,' Vicky said. 'It makes it seem colder than it is. And I'm so hungry.' She moved further under the canopy. Lucy and Alex followed her, away from the drizzle that the wind was drifting across the platform. They were in the first party of nurses travelling north with Matron Kenny. The rest of the nurses, another fifty, would follow with Matron Morgan in charge.

The nurses had climbed down from their train and were now gathered beneath the canopy like a mob of sheep in a market pen. Lucy, Vicky and Alex stared towards the concourse and the fracas at the food trolleys. The other forty-seven nurses stood in small groups, all watching the scrummage for food.

Five porters' trolleys were lined up near the gate to the platform. British and French soldiers surrounded them, the men pushing and shoving. Steam rose from an urn at one end of each trolley and, as the men fought to reach the food, the nurses caught glimpses of large platters piled with sandwiches and rolls.

'This is ridiculous,' Lucy said. 'How are we meant to fight our way through that mob? If I'd known it was going to be like this I'd have bought something at that patisserie we passed on the way to the station.'

'Aren't you girls eating?' A deep male voice with an Australian accent came from behind.

Lucy swung round with a start. The bloke who'd asked the question was a spare man with a weathered face, three stripes on his right arm and medal ribbons on his tunic. Rain dripped from the brim of his felt hat. A squad of soldiers clustered behind him. They all looked as if they could do with a shave—so did the sergeant. Every man's uniform was dishevelled and dark with damp, but all their rifles gleamed.

'What chance do we have to get any food with that lot hogging it all?' Vicky said.

'So when did you girls last eat?'

'We've had nothing since last night, and not much to drink,' Lucy said, glancing back to the melee at the end of the platform. 'We were given a list of places where we'd get a feed, but the train rushed through the first couple without stopping. Now it has stopped we've no hope. These blokes don't seem to care that we're women. By the time they've finished there'll be nothing left.'

The sergeant looked at the crowd at the nearest trolley and pursed his lips. 'Bloody Pommies and Froggies. That's it. They ain't going to push our Aussie sheilas around. Dump your kit lads. Fall in with your rifles and jump to it. We've a job on.' Within seconds the men had assembled in two ranks.

'Keep your eyes peeled for our kit. This won't take us long,' the sergeant said, a grin threatening to split his face. He turned to face his men. 'Now it's time to do what we were sent for. See that food cart?' He pointed to the nearest trolley. 'That's our objective. Capture it, and bring it back here. These nursing sheilas haven't had a bite to eat all day. If anyone tries to stop you, you know what to do.'

They set off at the double, charging into the surging crowd, swinging their rifle butts. The Australians forced a break in the throng of men and surrounded the trolley.

Two minutes later they were back, four men at the shaft, the others forming a protective arc behind it. A French soldier wearing an apron over his uniform ran after them, protesting and gesticulating wildly. The men pulling the trolley came to a halt under the canopy by the nurses and the French soldier tried to push his way towards it, still protesting.

The sergeant grabbed him by an arm and dragged him close. 'Look, Froggie, I can't understand a word you're saying, so piss off.' He pushed the soldier away violently, and the man fell to sprawl on his back in a puddle. He clambered to his feet, and for a moment he looked as if he was about to become aggressive, but when two Aussies stepped towards him, he fled.

'I don't know what we've got for you girls, but come and help yourselves.' The sergeant swept his arm towards the trolley and the nurses crowded forward, selecting sandwiches and rolls, and pouring tea from the urn, which had a methylated spirits burner beneath it.

Lucy was on her second roll when she saw the French soldier returning in the company of an overweight English officer. She lowered the roll as they reached the Australian soldiers.

'What do you men think you're doing? Who's in charge?' the officer asked. He had a crown on each epaulette and his eyes flashed with anger.

'I am, mate.' The sergeant stepped forward, his rifle held across his body with his finger on the trigger. 'What's your problem?'

Lucy was surprised at the belligerence in the sergeant's voice. He hadn't saluted, or even called the officer 'sir'.

For a moment the officer was speechless, then he recovered. 'Who do you think you are?' He examined the sergeant. 'Your uniform is a disgrace. What regiment are you from?' He paused as if summoning courage before he repeated, 'What do you think you're doing?'

'We're Aussies, mate, and we're obeying orders.' The sergeant glared at the officer, the challenge unmistakable. 'This is a food halt isn't it? These ladies have had nothing to eat since yesterday and those ignorant pigs wouldn't let them near the cart, so we brought the cart to them.'

The officer's mouth dropped open and apprehension spread across his face. 'You've no authority to commandeer a food trolley.'

'My CO gave me all authority I need,' the sergeant said. 'If this food halt had been properly organised it wouldn't have been necessary for us to commandeer a cart. With a little discipline, those pigs would have had to wait in line. It's ladies first where I come from.'

Half the nurses had re-boarded the train, but the remainder had gathered behind Lucy, Vicky and Alex and were watching the confrontation with wide eyes.

The sergeant glanced at the swarm of British and French troops crowding round, turned his back to the officer and faced his men who had formed a ring, protecting the trolley. 'Fix bayonets,' he barked.

Twenty Australian bayonets flashed and locked onto the rifles with loud clicks, and the men turned the blades towards the troops who faced them.

'Load with ten rounds.'

Each man placed the butt of his rifle against his groin, pulled the bolt back and pushed two chargers of ammunition into his magazine, before closing the bolt again.

'Take that trolley back to where you found it,' the officer said. 'At once.'

The sergeant swung round to face him. 'Take it up with my colonel. He ordered me to ignore people like you.' He turned back to his men. 'Safety catches on. I don't want any accidents.'

Some of troops began to melt away as the officer stepped round to the front of the sergeant and repeated, 'Take that trolley back.'

The sergeant looked at the officer with contempt. 'I've told you, I'm obeying my colonel's orders. If you'd been doing your job, I wouldn't have had to do this.'

'You're on a charge, Sergeant. Insubordination. You talk to a superior officer with respect and call him "sir".'

'Spell that C-U-R, do you?' The sergeant cocked his rifle. 'Tell the rest of these bastards to clear off.' He jerked his thumb towards the few men remaining under the canopy.

'Who do you think you are to tell me what to do? You'll respect my rank.' The officer's face was bright red and his lips trembled. Lucy wondered if it was due to anger or fear.

'How many times do I have to tell you? I'm obeying orders, and if you won't tell them, I will.' The sergeant faced his men. 'Extended line, forward march. Clear the platform.' As the Australians stepped towards the remnants of the onlookers, they shrank back and the sergeant said, 'Piss off, all of you. Take your hook. Imshi, or whatever it is in, Froggie, before I get annoyed.'

The major watched, speechless, his face redder than before, his lips still quivering and his eyes enormous. Finally he managed to say, 'You can't do this. I'll have you arrested.' He fell silent, casting glances over his shoulder. 'I'm an officer. I demand respect.'

'Haven't you noticed? I've already done it.' The sergeant stepped to one side and examined the flash on the major's upper arm. 'Service Corps? You want respect?' His voice dropped to a whisper. 'You have to earn respect.'

'You'll hear more of this,' the major said and scurried away, waddling along the platform like an overweight pigeon.

The sergeant turned to the nurses and introduced himself. 'John Mitchell, Australian Imperial Force, 2nd Australian Division, 1ANZAC.' A smile split his weather-lined face. 'I really enjoyed that. When the colonel heard that some Aussie nurses were coming from Egypt, he sent us along to take care of you on the journey. That's only fair. It'll be your turn to take care of some of us soon enough.'

'Thank you for your help, but won't you get into trouble for speaking to an officer like you did?' Lucy asked.

'It won't be the first time, but I'm not worried about that pompous ass. I was only doing as I'm told, looking out for you. We saw how things were a few days ago. We should have been down to meet you when you disembarked, but as you may have noticed, travel's a bit chaotic. Sorry we're late.'

'A bit chaotic,' Lucy echoed his words as she watched the major disappear through a door at the far side of the station concourse. 'He wasn't very happy. He is a major, even if he is in the Service Corps. He'll be causing trouble.'

'Trouble? Johnny Turk gave me trouble, but I survived. This is nothing to worry about. That fat major's got Buckley's. My colonel expected something like this. How many of you?'

'Fifty, plus Matron Kenny,' Lucy said.

'That all? It's not as many as the colonel thought.'

'Don't forget the girls with the Moron,' Alex said. 'They'll have the same difficulties.'

'Of course. How could I forget her?' Lucy said and turned to Sergeant Mitchell. 'There are another fifty-one following tomorrow.'

'We didn't know there were two parties. That makes it complicated. I'll have to change our travel passes, and I'll need to speak to the lady in charge. Where's your boss?'

Lucy pointed to the far side of the concourse. 'Matron Kenny's over there. She went to find the transport officer.'

The sergeant set off towards the concourse and the three nurses climbed back into their compartment.

'Talking of the Moron, it was great to hear Tubs putting her in her place this morning,' Alex said.

'How do you think I feel? I wasn't happy that she wanted me in her party. That would not have been fun. It's as if she hates me. I don't know what I've done to upset her, but she's been like it since I joined.'

'She's jealous. It's because you'll be going to medical school when we get back home,' Vicky said. 'I've heard her say that because you're going to be a doctor you think you're better than anyone else.'

'That's not true, but she'll have seen my Service Certificate. My medical school entrance place is on that.' Lucy frowned and turned to Alex. 'I never expected anything like this.'

Rouen, Friday, 7 April 1916

'We're so glad we found you, Sergeant,' Lucy said. She had walked, with Vicky and Alex, from their hotel to the military camp to find the Australian soldiers who'd escorted them north.

'Thank you,' Vicky and Alex said in unison as soon as Lucy had finished speaking, their faces wreathed in smiles.

'Thank you?' the sergeant asked. 'For what?'

'For taking care of us, Sergeant,' Lucy said.

'It was my pleasure, but don't stand on ceremony. You sisters can call me John. That's who I am. John Mitchell, stockman, ringer, general jack-of-all-trades. Now soldier.'

'You look like a stockman,' Lucy said. She shivered and pulled her cape tighter against the wind.

'That's what I am… what I was. I've done a bit of droving in my time, but I prefer station work. Before I joined up I was head stockman at Gidgealpa, north of SA. Wish I was back there now instead of this place, but needs is must. I'll be back like a shot as soon as we've dealt with Fritz.' John cupped his jaw in his hand, and half closed his eyes. 'Why did you say I look like a stockman? What do you know about stockmen?'

'Dad owns a station in the Northern Territory. We get white ringers coming through with drovers from time to time, but our stockmen are all Aborigines.'

'Well I'll be buggered. Cattle? What's the name?'

'Nothing else but cattle in the Territory. The station's called Aughton Park. It was run down when Dad took over the lease in 1892, but it's a bonzer place now.' Lucy smiled, remembering the games she'd played with her Aboriginal playmates. Although she'd never realised at the time, they all had a serious side, and that had stood her in good stead as she'd grown older. 'It's where I grew up. I love life on the station.'

'Know what you mean. I've never been to the Territory. Kept meaning to, but something always cropped up.'

'Sergeant Mitchell?' A staff sergeant hurried across to them with two lance corporals trailing behind him.

'That's me. What can I do for you, mate?' John said as he turned towards the newcomer.

'Military Police, and I've been warned about you, so don't give me no trouble. I have orders to place you under arrest. And call me Staff Sergeant when you speak to me.'

Lucy examined the staff sergeant. His uniform was immaculate, the creases in his trousers looked sharp enough to cut down trees, and the toes of his boots reflected the afternoon sun like a lawyer's brass door-plate. Around his right bicep a dark blue brassard displayed the crimson letters 'MP'. His peaked cap, sheathed in a scarlet cover, was incongruous against the drab khaki of the rest of his uniform. She compared the smart staff sergeant to John Mitchell, whose uniform was rumpled and stained, and had a feeling that when it came to the crunch, John would be the better man.

'What the hell are you arresting me for? I'm a bloody Aussie, mate, and you're a Pommie. Different bloody army.' Lucy noted that John ignored the other man's rank and couldn't help smiling.

The staff sergeant must have chosen to ignore the omission as well. He said, 'You know very well what for. I've a warrant here to arrest you for insubordination. We may be in different armies, but it's the same military law. We can do this easy and you come along with me with no fuss, or we can put the manacles on you. As you like.'

The two lance corporals were big men, each holding an entrenching tool handle in his right hand, tapping the steel ferrule at the head of the shaft in his left palm.

Lucy saw John Mitchell eye the two men, then he shrugged. 'Is this that fat Service Corps major?'

'I've no idea who made the charge out,' the staff sergeant said. 'All I know is I have orders to arrest you.'

'Then we're coming too. We were witnesses,' Lucy said. 'Where are you taking him?'

'That's not your business, Sister,' the staff sergeant said. 'This is an army discipline matter and no concern of you nurses.'

'Oh, but it is. We were there. We saw exactly what happened. If you won't tell us where you're taking him, we'll just have to follow you.'

'We saw everything,' Vicky said. 'If Sergeant Mitchell hadn't got a trolley for us, we'd have had nothing to eat.'

'That's right,' Alex said.

'You don't have to worry about me, Sisters. I can look out for myself,' John said, his eyes sparkling.

'You knowing where he is can't hurt, I suppose,' the staff sergeant said. 'It's Battalion Headquarters.' He pointed to a large building at the far side of an open square. 'We're in the Hotel de Ville, first floor. He'll be up before the colonel on tomorrow morning's defaulters' parade. The CO's office is straight up the stairs when you enter and turn right at the top.'

'What time's that?' Lucy asked.

'Goodness. You girls want to know everything.' For a moment Lucy thought the staff sergeant was about to refuse, but he said, 'Starts at 0800 hours. Goes on until it's finished.' He tapped John on the shoulder. 'Come on, Sergeant. Let's get it over with.'

4

Service Corps Headquarters, Rouen, Saturday, 8 April 1916

'Sir,' the adjutant said to the CO. 'We have twenty-two Australian nursing sisters in the corridor. They say they're witnesses in the case of Sergeant Mitchell.'

The CO, a lieutenant colonel, sat behind a simple table with papers in neat piles on the top. Other than the table and a couple of chairs the room was devoid of furniture. Several wooden boxes were stacked against the right hand wall. Above the boxes pristine rectangles gleamed in contrast to the faded paint of the rest of the wall, where notices or posters had protected the paint over the years.

'I've seen nothing in the documentation about witnesses. Australian nurses, you say?' The colonel sat back in his chair and frowned. 'In that case we'd best hear his charge first. The nurses are due out of here this morning.'

Sergeant Mitchell halted and saluted. His uniform had been sponged down and pressed, but the bloodstain on the right arm of the tunic was still obvious above his sergeant's stripes. So was the sewn up tear around it. The adjutant read out the charge, then a description of the events.

The colonel locked his eyes on John's face. 'How do you answer?' he asked.

'Just obeying orders, sir.'

'What orders?' The colonel glared at John as if he suspected he was lying.

'They're in my pocket, sir. Permission to remove them?' The colonel nodded and John pulled a creased piece of paper from a breast pocket, which he handed to the adjutant.

The adjutant unfolded and smoothed the paper and passed it to the colonel who read it quickly. 'This says you and your party are to render assistance, as necessary, to the sisters of the Australian Army Nursing Service. How did being insubordinate to a British officer constitute rendering assistance?'

'The girls, I mean the sisters, had had nothing to eat for a day and the food halt was chaos, like a pub brawl. Froggies and Pommies… sorry, sir, Brits, fighting like mangy dogs to get to the carts. The sisters had no chance and they were hungry. We had to do something. We couldn't allow a rabble to stomp all over a bunch of sheil… ladies.'

'Food had been provided for everyone on the train,' the colonel said.

'That may be so, sir, but the food stops weren't organised. The sisters didn't have no chance with that mob pushing and shoving. That's not the way to treat ladies. We'd been ordered to render assistance, so we went and got a cart. What else could we do? If we'd waited there'd have been nothing left.' John went on to explain what had happened.

'That's no excuse for insubordination. You should have explained.'

'I tried to, sir, but that fat major wouldn't listen.'

The colonel lowered his head to read the charge sheet. 'It says here that you threatened the major with a loaded rifle. You cocked it and threatened him.'

'It weren't possible. It's true, I did cock it, but it weren't loaded,' John said.

'It says here you'd ordered your men to load with ten rounds. The major saw them do it.' The colonel sat back and John saw him examining his battledress tunic.

'That's true, I did order the men to load, but I didn't do so myself. I had no ammunition in my rifle.'

'You were still threatening a superior officer. When you cocked your rifle he thought it was loaded,' the colonel said.

'A real soldier would have noticed.' John tried, but was unable to keep the scorn from his voice. 'The sound's different when you push a round up the spout.'

'That's still no excuse for insubordination. The major was in charge of the food halt. You should have gone to see him and made arrangements for the sisters to have a special trolley.' The colonel returned to studying John's tunic.

'I told him I had orders, but he wouldn't listen, sir. The platform was a total disaster. I had no option. There weren't time for anything else. If I'd gone to find the major I don't think he would have acted. Even if he had, all the food would have been scoffed and the nurses would have still gone hungry.'

'I can see there's merit in some of the things you're saying, Sergeant, and you have a point, there was some urgency, but I can't condone your disrespect for an officer. I do, however, accept that your intentions were honourable, but there are procedures to follow.'

'There were no procedures, sir, the station was a shambles. All it needs is a bit of discipline, everyone in line and taking their turn. That way everyone will get a fair go.' John leant forward and lowered his voice. 'Where I come from it's ladies first.'

The colonel had relaxed and the sternness had left his face. 'And where do you come from, Sergeant?'

'Australia, sir. Nowhere particular, but the last station was Gidgealpa.'

'What and where, pray, is Gidgealpa?'

'How can I say? It's a cattle station, sir.' The colonel frowned and John realised he didn't understand what a station was. 'It's like a big farm, sir. About half the size of England, but just full of cows and bulls, except most of them ain't bulls no more, they've been cut. There are about eight to ten thousand head all up in a good year.'

The colonel lifted his head, his eyes full of interest. 'Half as big as England?' He raised his eyebrows. 'That's a big place. And it's just cattle? Don't they do any arable farming at all?' he asked.

'Arable, sir? What's that?' John asked.

The colonel sat back, his face suffused with surprise. 'Cultivation,' he said. 'Ploughing and growing crops. Australia is a big exporter of wheat and you're telling me you don't grow cereals.'

'Shit no, sir,' John said, failing to keep the disbelief from his voice. 'Not where we are. The wheat properties are much further south. It's far too dry at Gidgealpa, it's desert. That's most of the time, but it can flood, then you can't move for water.'

The colonel scratched his right ear. 'Sounds like a funny old country to me. You didn't say where this Gidgealpa is.'

'Sorry, sir. About thirty days, maybe thirty-five, by horse, north from Adelaide. Pretty damn close to the centre of Australia. It's a long way from anywhere, but we know how to treat ladies.'

The colonel sat back, raising his eyes from John's tunic. 'I see you have the Distinguished Conduct Medal. Where did you earn that?'

'Gallipoli, sir. And bar.' The colonel seemed impressed by the DCM and John began to relax.

'I see, awarded the DCM twice.' He became thoughtful and pursed his lips. 'If this report is correct, Sergeant, I should place you in custody to await a court-martial, but before I do anything else, I'll hear what the sisters have to say. Wait outside please.'

As John left the office he felt relieved. The colonel seemed a fair-minded bloke who was prepared to listen. Perhaps it hadn't been necessary to play the unschooled colonial, but it was too late to change.

Forty-five minutes later John was called back before the colonel. 'The sisters confirm your story, and I've been in contact with your CO. He thinks highly of you. All I can say to you is case dismissed. Next time be a bit more diplomatic.'

'I don't know what diplomatic means, sir. It's not a word we use when mustering cattle.'

'Get out, Sergeant.' The colonel sounded harsh, but John saw the glint of amusement in his eyes before he lowered his head to examine the next case.

As John hurried down the stairs he thought, that's a turn-up. There's at least one decent officer in the British army.

Rouen, Monday, 10 April 1916

The second party of nurses had arrived and the Number 2 Australian General Hospital was up to full strength. One hundred sisters assembled on the racecourse where the British Number 12 General Hospital was already established. They had provided overnight accommodation, but there was insufficient room to set up a second hospital in the same grounds.

The nurses were herded onto buses and driven from hospital to hospital, but each was at full complement with no spare accommodation or facilities for additional staff. They returned to Rouen late in the afternoon where Matron Kenny stormed into the headquarters.

Over an hour later she returned and addressed the assembled nurses. 'Until the army can arrange a suitable location for our hospital, we're going to be divided up between four British establishments. Three are to the east in the Pas-de-Calais region, Boulogne, Étables and Frévent. They are not far back from the front line. The other is to the west, at Le Havre. I'll do my best to keep you with your special friends, but I can't make any promises. So please form into four parties. I hope it's not too long before we're back together in our own hospital.'

'After the shambles of the food halts, this doesn't surprise me,' Lucy said to Vicky as they boarded the coaches to be taken to hotels for the night. 'I only hope the fighting units are better organised.'

Rouen, Friday, 26 May 1916

'Bloody cattle trucks,' Lofty Mathews said, the disgust strong in his voice. 'Can't the bloody army give us decent carriages to go to war in?' He drew himself up to his full six feet three and scowled, glaring along the line of identical vans standing at the platform.

'What did you expect, mate? We are no better than cattle in the eyes of the generals.' Edward Haslar stepped forward and peered at a notice painted at the side of the doorway of the van. 'What's this mean?'

Lofty didn't answer, so he called to Sergeant Mitchell who was standing by the doors of the next van. 'Hey, Sarge. What's this mean?'

'What's what mean, Ted?'

'This. *Hommes 40 chevaux 8*,' Ted said. He pronounced *chevaux* as '*chevox*'. 'Lofty here don't know, and neither do I.'

'That makes three of us,' John said after he'd studied the words. 'Muscles, come here,' he called to a private who was fussing with his pack further along the platform. 'You went to school, didn't you? Tell us what this means.'

'Of course I went to school, Sergeant,' Hughie Sampson said as he joined them. He bent forward, examining the painted words as if he was short sighted, then stood back to review them from arm's length. He shook his head. 'No bloody idea. It's not English.'

'I know that for Christ's sake. If it was English I wouldn't have to ask. It has to be Froggie. I thought everyone in Adelaide could speak Froggie.' A lieutenant walked past as he spoke and John grabbed his arm. 'Do you know what this means, sir?'

The officer glanced at the notice and laughed. '*Hommes*, that's men and *chevaux*, that's horses.'

'*Chevaux*?' Ted said. 'So that's how you pronounce it. Why can't the Froggies speak English?'

'It would make life easier, but they're French, so it's *hommes quarante, chevaux huit*. That's how many they allow in the van, forty men or eight horses. So now you know where you stand in the scheme of things. Time to get aboard. No more than forty men to a van, remember.' The officer laughed again and moved off as they threw their packs into the van and clambered after them.

'That'd be right,' Lofty said as he sat on the floor. 'One horse is worth five men. Just as well the bloody horses can't fire a rifle. We wouldn't be here if they could.'

'Pity they can't to my way of thinking,' John said as he dropped alongside Lofty and leant back, stretched his legs and began to roll a cigarette. 'I'd be happy not to be here.' He glanced up. 'At least we've a roof over our heads.'

'Why are we going to Étables, Sarge?' Ted asked as Don Knowles joined them.

'Training before we move up to the front.'

'What? More bloody training. How much training can a bloke absorb?' Lofty said. He struck a match and offered it to John before lighting his own cigarette. 'We've trained till I'm sick of it. What are we going to learn this time round?'

5

Number 15 CCS, South-east of Hazebrouck,
Saturday, 27 May 1916

Lucy stepped back from the operating table and eased her shoulders as the Royal Army Medical Corps orderlies carried the patient away. It was 0400 hours and she'd been working in the operating theatre with the English doctor since 0800 hours on Friday. The only breaks had been about fifteen minutes for lunch and another fifteen minutes for dinner, with a hurried snack at midnight.

'Is that the last, Doctor?' she asked.

He shook his head and pointed to the entrance where four orderlies were carrying another wounded man into the theatre.

The doctor had been a senior surgeon at St Thomas' Hospital in London before the war, but now he was a major in the RAMC and operating in a casualty clearing station less than two miles behind the front line.

'I told you to call me Malcolm. Surgeons are usually called mister in England, but I think Mr Rigby is a bit formal under these circumstances, and I can't get used to being called sir by a lady. I'd prefer Malcolm to doctor.'

'Sorry, I keep forgetting.'

Malcolm's face lit in a smile and his eyes twinkled. 'Don't worry about it. We're all in the same boat here.'

They fell silent as he stitched a ragged gash in the man's shoulder. When he'd tied off the last suture Lucy dressed the wound and stood back so the orderlies could take the patient to the recovery tent.

'This is the last man, sir,' one of the orderlies said as they picked up the stretcher.

Malcolm turned to Lucy and said, 'Go and get your head down. We've four hours respite. You look all in. I know I am.'

He was right, she felt drained. While she'd been working she hadn't noticed her tiredness, but now she struggled to keep her eyes open. 'What's been going on, Malcolm? Do you know?'

'From what I hear in the mess, it's a stunt at a place called Fromelles, just up the road. Carnage. Your Aussie blokes took the brunt of the casualties. Their objective was the Sugar Loaf Salient, but it seems that the Boche had prior warning. As you've seen, we've had a lot of wounded. Numbers 12 and 50 CCS have dealt with just as many. Go and get your head down.'

There will have been a lot of deaths too, Lucy thought as she stepped from the marquee that was their operating theatre. She hunched down in her cape, pulling the collar closed against the rain, and set off along the mud-greased duckboards, keeping her balance with difficulty.

Without the duckboards she would have been knee deep in the morass. It was as if nature was annoyed with the war and was deliberately making life difficult for the combatants, but at least the mud didn't get blown around.

The night had been hectic with three patients dying on the table, and the bright sun did nothing to lift Lucy's mood as she made her way to the tent she shared with Vicky. Now that she no longer had to concentrate on her work, the events of the night crowded her mind. All these wounds. During the night they'd performed four amputations, one arm and three legs. How many men would return to Australia with missing limbs?

She stopped and turned, surveying the canvas hospital. So many men disabled, and her thoughts moved back to Heliopolis and the man who'd had the double amputation. He'd been so despondent, but at least she'd been able to give him hope for a little while. It would be the same for the men who'd lost their limbs during the night. She wondered how they'd cope when they returned home. Some men never came to terms with being crippled, unlike her father. He had adapted so well that occasionally he'd use his disability to his advantage.

She smiled and continued towards her tent, thinking back to her embarkation leave.

Aughton Park, Northern Territory, Australia,
Monday, 21 September 1914

The breakfast dishes had been cleared away, but the family was still at the table talking when Betsy One came back into the kitchen. She was leading a young Aboriginal boy by the hand. He gazed about the room in awe.

'Soldier fella, little big mob white fella, ask where bin boss, *Mullaka*.' The boy's words came out in a rush.

'Where are they?'

'Breaking yard, *Mullaka*.'

'What are soldiers doing here, Charlie?' Dorothy asked.

'Horses. I heard these jokers were in the district mustering horses for the army, but they're not having any of mine.' He reached down to rub his stump. 'They're taking all those they think are more than a station needs, but what would the army know about cattle work? They're paying of course, but it's a set rate and station owners have no say. It makes no difference how good the horse is. If they refuse to sell, they're served with a requisition, but as we've no spare horses, we can't help them.'

Charlie stood, grabbed his walking stick and hurried to the door, Dorothy at his heels. He reached for his hat and they left the house together. Lucy hurried to catch them, wondering about the horses. She knew there had to be more than those in the paddock.

'Dad, what's happened? Where are all the horses? I thought it was strange when I couldn't see Monarch and Princess last night. Surely you'd have told me if they'd died.'

Charlie stopped, examining three horses that were grazing close to the fence. 'Don't say anything, Lucy. We don't have any horses for sale. There's no way I'll allow horses I've bred to be used in a war, it's inhumane.' He turned to Dorothy and said, 'I mean that. Not one word.' He set off again, limping across the yard.

Lucy hid her smile and gazed fondly at her father as he hurried on—the station horses were like children to him, especially those sired by Monarch. There was a special bond between that stallion and her father.

He was a burly man, not overly tall, but powerful with muscle. His hair and beard were showing the first streaks of grey, particularly the beard, but it wasn't very noticeable against his fair hair. Unlike many men of forty-four, he was still fit and wasn't carrying any surplus flesh, despite his artificial leg. She was so proud of the way he'd adapted, as if losing his leg was nothing out of the ordinary. Riding or walking, he could go on all day, working harder and longer than most men half his age. Normally his limp was hardly noticeable, but today he was hobbling, his limp more pronounced than she'd ever seen it.

'Is your leg playing up, Dad?' she asked as she hurried to catch up with him.

Charlie winked at her. 'It'll be fine just as soon as these blokes have left.'

An officer stepped away from the squad as they approached. Behind him Lucy could see a sergeant and five men leaning against the rails of the breaking yard beside their tethered horses. The officer was a slim man with broad shoulders. His uniform—khaki tunic, riding breeches and leather riding boots—was immaculate and enhanced his physique. His Sam Brown belt glistened in the morning sun.

'G'day. Lieutenant Quentin Denison, Australian Army Veterinary Corps.' He held his hand out and Charlie took it.

'Charlie Paignton. What can I do for you, Quentin?'

'I'm on a buying mission. We need remounts for the war effort. How many can you spare?'

'You're out of luck, I'm afraid. We don't hold a big mob, just what we need for the muster each year. That's all we have.' Charlie indicated the horses in the paddock.

Lieutenant Denison examined the horses, half closing his eyes against the glare of the sun. A minute passed in silence, then he said, 'You must run a lean operation. I can only see about thirty or so. I'd have thought you'd need more horses than that.'

'We manage. There's no point in carrying more. We've too much poison weed, so we have to be careful. We used to lose a lot of horses to that walkabout disease when we had a large mob. Now we keep all the horses in this paddock. We've cleared it of the poison weed, but that's the biggest mob we can handle until we've fenced another area.' Charlie led the lieutenant across to the wire fence where he leant forward, supporting his weight on his stick.

Dorothy took Lucy's hand. 'We'll wait here. Let the men get on with things.' They were about five feet behind the two men. 'We can still hear what they're saying.'

'That walkabout disease is a terrible thing. You feel so helpless. I don't want to see any more of that, not in my horses.'

'I have to agree with you, but this is an interesting way to deal with it,' Lieutenant Denison said as he examined the horses. 'I'd have thought the paddock wasn't big enough to keep the grass up to so many.'

'You're right,' Charlie said. 'This is only part of it. We've divided it halfway, you can't see it all from here. We spell them to give the grass time to recover. There are some years when we have to bring grass in towards the end of the dry, but I prefer to do that than have to shoot the poor buggers. That's all you can do when they get that walkabout.'

'And there are no horses in the other section?'

'No. Go and check if you like.'

'That's not necessary.' The lieutenant studied the horses. 'These look to be fine beasts, Mr Paignton. You should think about breeding. That stallion is magnificent; he'd give you some beautiful foals. The army will take all you can supply.'

'We need good horses. They work bloody hard when we're mustering, but I'm not interested in breeding for market. I'm a cattleman, and I'm not getting into horses, especially with all the poison weed about. I've enough to give me the replacements I need. Stick to what you know is what I say.' Charlie scuffed at the dirt with the toe of his boot, then turned to the lieutenant. 'People say the war will be over by Christmas, so what will we do then? Even if it goes on a bit longer most of the mares would be pregnant and we'd be short for next year's muster. It'll be two or three years before the foals are big enough to do anything serious. The army won't want them till then.'

'Think about it. Could be worth your while. And this is every animal on the station?' Lieutenant Denison raised his eyebrows as he reached over the wire and patted the shoulder of a mare.

'I've plenty of cattle, but these are the only horses, and I need every one of them. Can't help you. Sorry about that.'

The lieutenant became thoughtful then he shrugged. 'Well, if you haven't got them, we can't take them.' He turned and started towards his men, then he stopped to allow Charlie to catch up. 'What happened to your leg?'

'Boer War, Elands River. A shell made a mess of my ankle and the surgeons took the leg off. Could have been worse.'

The lieutenant looked back at the horses. 'I've read about the Boer War. If I remember rightly that Elands River was a blood-bath, but I can't recall the details.' He fell silent, as if deep in thought, and eased his shoulders. 'Got to be on my way. If you don't have any horses there's no point in me hanging around. I can see you need all those in that paddock, so I won't requisition any. By my thinking you should have more to give these a break during your musters. One could go lame easy enough in this country.' He pointed to the north. 'Is that the track to Timber Creek? We've a mob waiting there for the steamer.' Charlie nodded and the lieutenant called for his men to mount up.

Lucy, Dorothy and her father watched until the soldiers disappeared at the first bend. 'I don't think he believed you, Dad. He knows more than he's letting on.'

'I think you're right. He's not as green as he's cabbage looking,' Charlie said and grinned. 'He's spot on about needing more horses for a muster. I should have thought it through better than I did, but I was in a rush.'

'So, where are the horses?' Lucy asked.

'That pocket down the river, the one we use when we're brumby mustering. Tomo's taking care of them. If they'd headed in that direction he'd have moved the mob long before they reached them. There's no point in bringing them back for the moment. There's plenty of feed, and we don't need them here. They can stay there until the army's left the district.'

'You don't trust them, do you?' Lucy noticed her father was no longer limping.

Charlie shook his head. 'I underestimated that young officer. He knows more about mustering cattle than any army vet I met in South Africa, and he must know that's the track to Timber Creek. He'd have had to come in that way. I'll send some boys out to watch until I'm certain they've gone.'

'Why are you so determined not to let the army have any horses?' Lucy asked. 'They'll get them from someone else.'

'I can't do anything about that, but they won't have any of mine. I know each one of those horses, and I can't forget how one of them saved my life on that drove down into Western Australia in '97.'

'I thought you said that was Monarch?'

'I think it was, but I'll never be completely sure. It makes no odds, I'll not allow any of my horses to be subjected to the treatment that those in South Africa received. Poor dumb animals had no idea what was happening. Elands River was the worst I remember.' They had reached the breaking yard where Charlie stopped, leant back against the rails and reached down to ease the straps at his knee. 'We had fifteen hundred head of stock. A mixed mob, cattle, horses and mules. Every single beast dead, shot to pieces by artillery. Sometimes there'd be twenty or thirty killed by one shell. The poor horses were tethered, the mules too, lined up for the slaughter. I'd have sooner let the Boers have them than see them butchered like that. I know logic says destroy the enemy's assets, but how could they do that to innocent animals? Cruel so and sos.'

Charlie composed himself. 'But it wasn't just Elands River.' He straightened up and moved away from the rails. 'That's why I don't want you going off, but as your grandmother says, you're a grown woman.'

'So she is, Charlie. We can't stand in her way. She'd never forgive us,' Dorothy said and looped an arm across his shoulders. 'The hospitals will be a long way from the front, just like we were. She'll be safe enough. The Germans won't be firing on hospitals, they're civilised.'

'I know she'll be behind the lines, but it's hard for me to accept.' He frowned and peered across to the house as if deep in thought. Then he said, 'I won't stand in her way, but you're wrong about the

Krauts. I don't trust them. They're too much like the Boers.'

'Thank you, Dad.' Lucy gave him a hug and kissed his cheek. 'This is something I have to do. I couldn't live with myself if I did nothing while men of my age are fighting for our country. I know you'll be worried, but I'm only doing what Dorothy did, and if she hadn't been in South Africa, you'd never have met her.'

'You can hit below the belt, young lady. I'll worry about you. We both will.' Charlie's eyes closed and Lucy could see he was struggling to control his emotions, but he quickly recovered. 'You're our only child, but it's your life. I think it's time to tell you why you don't have any brothers or sisters.' He glanced to Dorothy who smiled her encouragement and he took a deep breath. 'The shell that smashed my leg did other damage. Bits of shrapnel in all sorts of places. One piece meant I'd never father any more children. So you take good care. Promise me.'

Lucy fought back the tears until Charlie wrapped his arms about her. As he stroked her back she became calm and asked, 'How did you feel about it, Dorothy?'

'I guessed long before the specialists confirmed it, but I kept it to myself. I hoped, but…' Dorothy sighed. 'There are some things you can't tell a man, no matter how much you love him.'

'She nursed me, remember. She'd seen the damage.' Charlie broke off, breathing deeply and blinking. 'You're very precious to me, to Dorothy as well. You're her daughter too, even though she didn't give birth to you. Don't ever forget that.'

Étables, Monday, 29 May 1916

'Shut that bloody racket,' Lofty called and pulled the blanket over his head, but to no avail. The bugler was only halfway through Reveille when a sergeant flung the door of the hut back with a crash.

'Shake a leg. Everyone out. Fall-in in five minutes, PT rig. Come on, chop-chop. Hop to it.' He disappeared back through the door leaving it wide open so that a bitter wind swept into the hut.

'Hup… Hup… Hup…' called the corporal PT instructor as they

jumped on the spot, their arms rising and falling in time to his chant. 'Hup… Hup…'

'Hup yours too, mate,' Lofty said. 'How much bloody longer do we have to keep this up?'

'Keep your mouth shut, Lofty, for Christ's sake,' Don hissed. 'If the bastard hears you he'll keep us here all morning.'

'That would be better than another route march. That bloody pack gets heavy. All bloody yesterday morning. It wouldn't have been too bad if the roads had been half decent. I can march with the best of them if I have to, but I was knackered by the time we were back,' Lofty said. 'This is a piece of pudding in comparison.'

After breakfast the company assembled at the front of a hut with the legend, GAS CHAMBER, emblazoned over the door. A staff sergeant instructor explained about the respirators, which had just been issued.

'Get it right,' he said, waving his finger in warning. 'You've got six seconds to get your respirator on and adjusted. Remember, we're using the real gas and if you don't do it proper, it's curtains.' He drew his finger across his throat for emphasis.

Everyone took his words to heart.

'First platoon inside the chamber,' the staff sergeant said once he was satisfied that everyone had fitted his respirator correctly.

Lofty had to think about his breathing and make a conscious effort to drag air into his lungs through the filter on the mask. It was the same when he exhaled. While it wasn't difficult, he hoped he'd never have to perform any physical work while wearing the respirator. He noticed the others in the platoon were also labouring to breathe.

The hut was small, barely room enough for one platoon at a time. It was just an empty shell, walls devoid of windows, with a low roof. The door shut behind the last man, leaving just two electric light bulbs casting a dim light. As his eyes adjusted Lofty could make out rags that were jammed into the joint between the walls and roof. More rags had been stuffed into cracks in the planking of the walls. He heard a faint hiss, and guessed gas was being piped into the hut and wondered for a moment about the staff sergeant's words. He had to be trying to scare them. Not even the army would use real gas to train their men.

After ten minutes in the gas chamber they were ordered to remove their respirators before the door was opened. By the time they were outside their eyes were streaming and they were coughing, gasping for breath. As they recovered the staff sergeant said, 'That shows you how effective the respirators are. Don't worry, you won't die, it was just tear gas.'

'It might be just tear gas, but I'm dying all the same,' Lofty said.

Despite Lofty's cynicism they were all still alive at lunchtime. In the afternoon they practised hop-overs and bayonet drill.

'Anyone would think we'd never seen a bloody trench,' Lofty said as they made their way back to their hut. 'At least Johnny Turk wasn't taking pot shots at us.'

'Some of us haven't climbed out of a trench before. Not for real, that is,' Hughie Sampson said. He was one of the new reinforcements who'd been drafted in to fill the gaps when the unit was withdrawn from Gallipoli. 'I need the practice. I don't want to bugger up when it comes to the real thing.'

'Don't worry about it, Muscles. You'll be jake,' Lofty said. 'We'll take care of you.' He was about to say more about the horrors of real hop-overs, but he could see Muscles was just a boy. 'How old are you?' he asked.

'Eighteen. I'll be nineteen in November. Guy Fawkes Day.'

That's if you're still alive, Lofty thought, but he kept silent.

The next morning started with more physical jerks. After breakfast they trooped along, a platoon at a time, to a deep trench that was reinforced with sandbags. An opening, about two feet wide, formed a gun slit in the sandbags and was guarded by a staff sergeant.

'Good. Gather round and pay attention. What I'm about to teach you can save your lives,' he said and glared at them. He was bouncing what seemed to be a small pineapple in his hand.

'That'll make a bloody change,' Lofty said. 'Most of the things we've been taught here are likely to get us killed.'

'Good. I like a comedian in the squad. Makes the lecture more interesting. Pay attention though, 'cause if you don't, this will get you killed. This here is a Mills grenade, a new type of hand grenade, which we also call a Mills bomb.' He continued to bounce the grenade as he talked. Then without warning he tossed it to Lofty. 'Here, catch.'

Lofty was startled, but automatically his hands closed round the grenade. He recovered his composure and examined it. A ring fitted through the eye of a split pin that passed through a pair of wings, cast integral with the iron body, and held a curved lever against the body of the grenade. A safety device, he realised. He'd have a bit of fun. See if the joker had a sense of humour. He began to fiddle with the ring.

The squad was concentrating on the staff sergeant, except for Don Knowles, who watched him and frowned. He winked and Don winked back.

The staff sergeant was becoming impatient. 'Come on, you blokes, we haven't got all day. Gather round and pay attention.' He glanced towards Lofty. 'That means you too, my comedian friend— Don't pull that pin out!' he screamed. He'd paled and was no longer looking superior. 'Stop that, you bloody idiot. Pass the bloody thing back. It's fused, ready to fire.'

'What, this split pin?' Lofty said. He checked that the curved lever was trapped under his palm, poked a finger through the ring and pulled so the pin came clear of the first wing. 'It's a bit stiff, isn't it?'

'You'll kill us all, you bloody idiot. Push it back.' The staff sergeant stepped towards Lofty, who pretended to struggle to push the pin home, chuckling as he did so. Finally he squeezed the splayed halves of the split pin together, pushed it back though the hole in the wing and held the grenade out towards the staff sergeant.

'Here, take it. If it's so dangerous, you shouldn't have given it to me before you'd shown me how to handle it.'

The staff sergeant grabbed the grenade, relief flooding his face as he examined the pin. 'Any more tricks like that, Aussie, and you'll be up before the colonel. Your feet won't touch the ground.'

He returned to his position by the gap in the sandbags, breathing deeply. 'Very bloody funny.' He took another deep breath then grinned. 'You really are a comedian. Good. This here is a Mills grenade, number five, mark three. Don't ask me what happened to the numbers one to four or marks one and two, 'cause I don't know. And I couldn't care less. This is the latest design, and I reckon it's brilliant. You can see it's grooved, like a bar of chocolate, so when it explodes everyone gets a little piece. Don't you think that's democratic?'

No one laughed and he scowled before he continued.

'Glad to see you're paying attention. You throw it like you'd bowl a cricket ball… You have heard about cricket in Australia, haven't you?'

'You could ask Victor Trumper or Clem Hill, staff,' Lofty said. 'They could teach you how to play cricket. Monty Noble knows a bit too, especially about bowling.'

The staff sergeant stared at Lofty in silence for a moment, then he smiled and said, 'I'll give you that, Aussie. They're pretty good on a cricket pitch, but unlike cricket this isn't a game, so pay attention. Even Monty Noble would only make about thirty yards, but the fragments can travel up to eighty. So if you're in the open, as soon as you've thrown it, you drop, flat to the ground. If you're in a trench, duck down behind cover. Any questions?'

No one had any questions and he scowled again. 'I've never known such a disinterested squad. Maybe this will spark your interest. Get into line and come forward one at a time.'

As each man reached the gap in the sandbags the staff sergeant showed him the target: an empty ammunition box, about thirty yards to the front, with cardboard boxes on stands set in a ring around it.

'They're the enemy,' he said. 'Watch carefully.'

He pulled the safety pin from the Mills grenade, and showed them how he was holding it, glaring at Lofty. 'It's safe enough as long as you keep this curved lever hard against the body. Okay?' A few of them nodded and he reached out behind his legs, his right arm straight, holding the grenade low to the ground. His left arm pointed skywards, also straight. 'Stand by,' he said and whipped his arm up to hurl the grenade through the gap. 'Take cover.'

The explosion was followed by whistles and whines as pieces of shrapnel flew through the air. Smoke drifted above the spot where the ammunition box had been, but that had been blown aside. So had three of the cardboard boxes.

'Nice throw, staff,' Lofty said when they trooped forward to examine the damage. 'You got four of the bastards.'

The staff sergeant opened his mouth as if he was about to say something, but he snapped it shut without a word. They returned to the trench where the staff sergeant picked up a cut-away Mills grenade.

'This split pin that our comical friend was fumbling with keeps the curved lever in position.' He showed the grenade to each man. 'When the pin is removed, this spring forces the striker down and the lever is flung clear. So, when you pull the pin, make sure you cover the lever with your hand until you throw it. Any questions?'

A few men shook their heads.

He then removed the base plug from a real grenade and demonstrated how to fit the fuse. 'If you're throwing it by hand, you use a short fuse, just four seconds, but they can be fired from a rifle using a ballistic cartridge.' He showed them the cup that clipped onto the muzzle of a Lee-Enfield .303, and the powerful ballistic cartridge. 'It goes a lot further when fired from a rifle, so the fuse you use then is seven seconds.'

By the time they'd all armed and thrown one grenade the forenoon was shot. He dismissed them with a final admonition to remember to take cover as soon as they'd hurled a bomb.

'That was a lot of fuss about not very much,' Muscles said. 'Half a dozen times to show us how to fit a fuse and pull a split pin out of a couple of holes. We could have done the whole damn lot in an hour.'

'Don't be too hard on him,' Lofty said. 'That was a valuable lesson. When we next hop-over for real, I'm going to have a bag of these Mills bombs. I can see they'll be bloody useful to sort out Fritz in his dugouts.'

'You've changed your tune, Lofty,' Muscles said.

'When you've been around a little while you'll learn there are times to take the piss and times to be serious. Listen to me. Get yourself a bag of these Mills bombs before the next stunt.'

6

The Somme, Monday, 10 July 1916

'Hayward. Anyone seen Hayward?' Sergeant Crawford bellowed as he entered the barn they were using as a billet while they were resting. They were recovering from nine horrendous days in the front line. 'The company commander wants to see him urgently.'

Andrew Stanley and another man raced into the yard to where the ablutions block had been set up. A short time later Adam appeared at the double, breathing heavily, his blond curls still dishevelled and damp.

'Get your equipment together and come with me,' the sergeant said. 'You're getting your wish. A pilot has just landed in the field behind company HQ. His observer has been wounded and it was the quickest way to get him to a casualty clearing station. He asked for a volunteer to take over and, as you're the only bloke to know about aeroplanes, I've given your name to the company commander. He wants to see you before you leave. You're going to be flying.'

'Me… Flying…' Adam stared in disbelief at Sergeant Crawford. 'You mean… You wouldn't be kidding me?'

'That's what people do in aeroplanes, as I understand it. Come on, get your bloody feet moving. We haven't got all bloody day.'

'I've organised for your sergeant to send your gear on,' the pilot said as they hurried towards the plane. 'One of the damn Lewis guns jammed, which is why Joseph copped it, but it's been cleared.' He stopped and turned to Adam. 'You do know how to handle a Lewis gun?'

'Of course I do.'

The pilot grinned and said, 'Just pulling your leg. What's your name?'

'Hayward,' Adam said. Now he was about to take his first flight he was apprehensive.

'Not your surname. Your first name. I'm not one of those plum in the mouth blue-blooded snobs who call each other by their surname as if they're not Christians.'

'Adam. What's yours?'

'Clive,' the pilot said, then he quickly ran through the procedures. 'I'll try not to make any sharp manoeuvres, but sometimes it can't be helped. You'll need to hang on, especially when you're firing the guns. I don't want you dropping out on me.' He lifted a leather coat from the forward cockpit and handed it to Adam. 'You'll need this. It can get a bit nippy up there. Sorry about the holes, it's Joseph's.'

Adam took the coat and stared at the congealed blood around the holes. He felt sick and grimaced.

Clive pulled a handful of cotton waste from the cockpit and handed it to him. 'Wipe off what you can. When we get back to base I'll fix you up with a new one. You'll need these too.' He handed a leather helmet and a pair of goggles to Adam, pulled on his own flying helmet and turned towards the plane.

The double-breasted coat was too large and as Adam pulled it on he thought about the blood encrusted holes, hoping there'd be no more when they landed. He studied the plane while he fastened the buttons.

It was huge, the lower wing at shoulder height and the upper wing as far again above that. A truncated nacelle was fitted between the two halves of the lower wing, with the propeller at its rear. The struts connecting the two wings were massive, but whether this was normal or not Adam had no idea. He couldn't remember what they were like at the Air Meeting.

The nacelle housed the pilot's cockpit ahead of the engine. The observer's cockpit, his cockpit now, was exposed in the nose. He guessed he'd be glad of the leather coat. An open structure of four longitudinal struts reached back from the wings, like the frame of a box kite, making the tailplane appear to be an afterthought.

As Clive climbed into the cockpit he said, 'Okay, Adam. First job. Swing the prop.'

Adam went to walk towards the nose, but pulled up short then turned to continue to the rear of the wings. 'For a moment I forgot it was a pusher,' he said. 'Royal Aircraft Factory F.E.2b, isn't it? Who's the builder?'

Clive's head shot round to examine Adam, but all he said was, 'Ransomes, Sims and Jefferies. Damn good plane too.'

Adam reached up and took hold of the tip of the propeller and gave it an experimental tug to see how hard it was to turn. He set it horizontal and grabbed it with two hands. 'When you're ready,' he shouted.

'Go,' Clive called and Adam pulled down on the propeller with all his strength. The engine gave a cough, then hesitated, so that Adam thought it had failed to start. Then it coughed again and began to run smoothly, but so loudly that he clamped his hands over his ears.

He ran to the front, clambering over the cockpit coaming as Clive opened the throttle and the plane began to move. They taxied to the end of the field and turned into the wind. He gripped the side of the cockpit, fighting the blast of air and his rising alarm. Despite all his reading about flying, he was unprepared for the reality. They rushed towards the trees at the end of the field. Sitting at the very front he'd be the first to hit them and the flimsy nose would be no protection. His grip on the coaming tightened. The plane surged forward, bouncing hard enough to lift him from his seat, with the ground flashing past seemingly just inches below. He searched the cockpit for a strap to fasten himself in, but then he remembered Clive's words. He'd hang on all right.

The bouncing stopped. Adam felt heavy, and he held his breath as the nose tipped up. They were airborne with the trees far below them. The air filled his mouth distorting his cheeks, so he closed it. I'm flying, he thought.

He checked the forward Lewis gun. It was mounted on a tubular support to allow it to swivel over a wide arc. Hell, he thought, he'd have to stand to reach that. One glance at the rearward facing machine-gun, another drum-fed Lewis gun, made his stomach lurch. It was above the upper wing so he'd be almost out of the cockpit before he could reach that gun.

As the plane climbed Adam began to relax until Clive tapped him on the shoulder. When he turned, Clive leant forward and shouted,

'Check the guns. A short burst. Make sure they're both okay.'

Adam gripped the tubular support as he climbed to his feet and wedged his knees against the coaming, bracing himself. One hand at a time he transferred his grip to the forward gun. The wind tugged at him, as if trying to wrench him free, but he tightened his hold on the gun and concentrated on aiming and getting used to the swivel arrangement. After firing a couple of short bursts he turned and stepped onto his seat, but he had to stand on the coaming to reach the rear gun. He didn't linger, firing only a three-round burst, before he stepped back and dropped to his seat.

'We'll soon be at ten thousand feet,' Clive called. 'Keep your eyes peeled. I don't want any fighters creeping up on us. I'll keep an eye on the Boche on the ground.'

That's a long way to fall, Adam thought. He turned to find that his view behind was partially obscured by the massive wing struts, and the wide wings made another blind spot almost directly above.

They flew south. The view ahead was perfect and below he could see the British trenches zigzagging across the pockmarked ground. To their left he could see the German lines, in places less than a hundred yards from the British. A German reserve trench was about four hundred yards further back, connected to their front line by narrow communication trenches.

From this height it was not possible to make out the detail of the tangles of barbed-wire he knew rimmed both sets of trenches. He shuddered, thinking of the nights he'd worked, trying to remain silent, screwing the pickets into the ground and stringing the wires along them.

Flooded shell holes stretched across no man's land with not one square inch of earth undisturbed and Adam's enthusiasm for flying returned. This was much preferable to slogging through mud, fearful of the shells and bullets.

Nothing was moving below, but that would change as soon as darkness fell. Occasionally a shell exploded, throwing up great plumes of earth and flame. At this height the sound was little more than a muted pop, but down below the blast could be loud enough to burst eardrums. He thought about the barrages he'd tried to sleep through and wondered about his mates in the platoon. For the moment they were in reserve, but it wouldn't be long before they were back in the line and in a dugout somewhere, each man hoping he wouldn't be the victim of a Fritz shell.

Directly below them he could see an enormous crater and he heard Clive shouting. As they maintained course an eruption rent the ground with a plume of earth and smoke, and about thirty seconds later the sound of the explosion reached them. The earth settled and Adam could see the crater that had obliterated over fifty yards of the German trench.

Clive screamed, 'Got it,' and Adam turned to see him shouting into the microphone of a wireless, but his voice was overpowered by the sound of the engine. Clive grinned and gave him a thumbs-up, then pointed excitedly to the ground. Moments later another huge explosion ripped more of the German trench apart.

For a few seconds Adam studied the new craters, thinking of the sappers he'd seen in March and empathising with the men who would be injured and bleeding, but when he resumed his scrutiny of the sky he saw three planes climbing from behind the German lines. They were in silhouette, but he recognised their single wings instantly and turned back to Clive, jabbing his fingers frantically in the direction of the enemy flyers.

'*Fokker Eindeckers*,' he yelled, wondering if Clive could hear him.

Clive leant forward and called, 'Hang on…' The rest of the words were lost in the air stream, but immediately the plane banked and turned towards the three monoplanes.

The F.E.2 began to dive, gathering speed. Adam stood, steadied himself and gripped the spade handles of the Lewis gun, his knees jammed against the cockpit coaming. The wind slashed at his cheeks and he was grateful for the leather helmet and coat, and especially the goggles.

The planes closed rapidly, with Clive aiming the F.E.2 at the leading Fokker. Adam could see tracer bullets from the German planes. Most fell short, but a few whipped past their nose. He took aim and fired a burst in return, but the plane lurched and automatically his grip tightened, spoiling his aim. The German plane swung away, but

Clive didn't follow. Instead he made a small change in direction to line up on the second Fokker and Adam could see the flashes as the enemy fired. He waited, keeping the German plane in his sights. The Fokker turned away, exposing his lower surfaces. Adam made a guess at the allowance for their speeds, squeezed the trigger and let loose a long burst as he traversed the machine-gun. His tracers crept forward along the fuselage of the Fokker towards the cockpit and the fuel tank. Flames flared, to grow and spread to engulf the pilot's head. Adam's magazine ran out of ammunition as the German pilot leapt from his cockpit and the Fokker lurched to one side, beginning to spiral downwards.

By the time he'd replaced the magazine, Clive had lined up the F.E.2 with the third Fokker. Adam fired, but his tracers fell short and the plane turned, heading for German territory, slowly losing height. The first Fokker was ahead of it, but Clive turned toward the British rear without giving chase.

It was only as Adam settled down in his seat that he realised he hadn't felt any fear during the action, but now his hands trembled and he grabbed the coaming in an effort to steady his nerves. He noticed that his hands were freezing. If he was to fly again he'd need gloves.

They were flying low and he was able to make out the details of some artillery emplacements. The men manning the guns waved furiously and made the thumbs-up sign. He waved back and felt better.

Number 15 CCS, South-east of Hazebrouck, Monday, 10 July 1916

A flash of flame less than fifty yards from the casualty clearing station was followed immediately by a loud explosion that hurt her ears and Lucy flinched. The sound of the gun subsided to be replaced by the background rumble. Another explosion followed a little further away. The flash illuminated a huge gun with two large springs beneath the barrel. The towering wheels were fitted with flat plates, arranged on pivots around the rim to prevent the gun sinking into the mud. That would have been one of the new howitzers, the ones they'd developed to blast the Fritz trenches, but why did they have to put them so close to a hospital? She thought of the stories she'd heard about the German artillery concentrating counter-fire onto these guns once they discovered their location.

Beyond the gun she could see other flashes brightening the dawn as more guns spewed their share of explosives towards the Germans. Flames flared in the distance, illuminating the German positions.

She slipped and stumbled along the duckboards, wondering how she'd sleep through the noise of the guns and the explosions of the shells. She wearily removed her clothes and hung them on the hook at the central pole. Her shoes were filthy with cloying mud, which coated her hands as she loosened the laces, but she was too tired to do more than wipe them, and slipped into bed without washing.

It seemed as if she'd hardly closed her eyes when a persistent shaking penetrated her exhaustion.

'It's time, Lucy,' Vicky said.

The two nurses dressed and headed back to the wards. 'How many more?' Vicky asked, and pointed to a field ambulance where stretcher-bearers were carrying wounded men into the reception marquee. Other stretcher-bearers were taking patients from reception to the dressing tent as quickly as the clerk could record the men's details. Some wounded were being carried to the pre-operations tent, but more wounded were arriving than were being carried out.

The nurses' tents were on a slight rise and Lucy could see the CCS laid out with precision. The theatre was beyond the pre-operations' marquee, with the recovery marquee at the far side. Three lines of tented wards had been pitched across the compound, with the orderlies' and stretcher-bearers' tents at the end, as far from the nurses' accommodation as possible. Lucy wondered how anyone could think that separating the men from the nurses in this manner would prevent romantic liaisons. And how futile. Everyone she knew was so tired that an amorous dalliance was the last thing on their minds.

She looked back to the reception tent. 'You wouldn't realise that so many of these cases need emergency surgery. A wounded man won't be going anywhere so why can't they record his details after his surgery? A man could bleed to death while the clerks are filling out their forms.'

Vicky didn't respond. She stared at a party of stretcher-bearers who were unloading wounded men from three more field ambulances. 'This stunt must have been terrible,' she said.

Lucy and Vicky hurried past the reception tent, picking their way carefully, wary of slipping. As they passed the entrance to the pre-operations' marquee they saw doctors making the first examination of the new patients, deciding their treatment. Vicky turned off for her ward and Lucy moved on to the theatre where she joined Malcolm. He was bending over a wounded man on the operating table.

The man was still conscious, but covered in mud. He was prone on the table, his face black from the explosion of a shell. Lucy hurried to dress in her overalls and scrub her hands before she turned to the patient. She washed as much mud as she could from around the field dressing on his head and began to remove the blood-soaked bandage.

Malcolm asked, 'Where's your home? And don't tell me it's Australia, I know that.' He read the man's field medical card.

'Dimboola. It's a country town in Victoria, Doc,' the man said.

Lucy was still unwinding the bandage from the man's head and added, 'It's north-west of Melbourne, Mal…' She gasped at the sight of the piece of shrapnel lodged above the patient's left ear.

Malcolm too flinched, but he kept his voice calm as he bent to examine the wound. 'How do you feel?' he asked.

'My head aches a bit, but it's not too bad. My back's sore and my leg's hurting. See if you can make it a Blighty, please, Doc. I've had more than I can take of this shelling.'

A RAMC orderly finished cutting away the man's trouser leg and Lucy turned her attention to cleaning that wound as the orderly reapplied the tourniquet and the bleeding slowed to a trickle. The right leg was shattered below the knee. Slivers of bone and scraps of khaki cloth mingled with the mangled flesh.

After a quick glance Malcolm turned to the soldier. 'Don't worry. You'll get to Blighty.'

'Thanks, Doc. I feel better already. That stunt was bad, worse than any I've been in.' He fell silent for a moment then he said, 'I'll be no trouble.'

The man's breathing steadied as he succumbed to the anaesthetic. Lucy cut away the large field dressing from the right side of his back, swabbing the blood as it began to flow freely. Malcolm raised the flap of flesh that had been partly sliced from the man's muscles. Slowly he shook his head, as if doubting the evidence before his eyes.

The orderly cut away the rest of the man's tunic and shirt and Lucy could see more shrapnel wounds. Four deep ragged cuts ran across the left of his back, two of them had pieces of steel protruding from the flesh. Two more wounds were in his left buttock. 'He said nothing about these,' she said.

Malcolm examined them quickly. 'Shock. With the pain from his other wounds he probably didn't know he had them. I was worried about that head wound, but it's not as bad as I thought. We'll attend to that first, then I'll see what I can save of his leg. With a bit of luck I might be able to leave his knee intact.'

After he'd amputated the leg and sewn up the flap of flesh on the man's back, Malcolm probed into the other wounds. The shrapnel he'd removed from five of the wounds ranged in size from a farthing to a penny, but one piece in the buttock was deep and he abandoned his probing. 'We've too many cases waiting to spare more time for this chap. They can tidy him up back at base. While I'm attending to this buttock wound will you start closing those on his back, please?'

Lucy, taken by surprise at his words, became nervous. He wants me to finish the surgery, she thought. 'But Malcolm, I've never closed a wound before.'

'You've seen me do enough and I'm fully confident in your abilities. We'll save many more men if you attend to the minor wounds while I work on those more serious. There's no need to be nervous, you're a very competent nurse.' Malcolm smiled at her and squeezed her hand. 'Don't worry, you'll be fine.'

She was about to start stitching the first wound when Matron Kenny appeared and ordered her to wear her steel helmet and have her respirator close by. 'Now don't forget. If you hear the gas alarm you've only got six seconds to get your respirator on and properly adjusted, and get your own mask on before you see to the patient.'

As she placed her helmet on her head Lucy realised that the German bombardment had moved and shells were now landing close to the casualty clearing station. 'I didn't think I'd be nursing in a tin hat. Blast those guns,' she said under her breath, remembering the howitzers only a few yards outside the perimeter.

Her nervousness disappeared as she concentrated, and in what seemed no time she had put in the last suture in the last wound. She applied a dressing and stepped back, sighing with relief. Immediately two orderlies lifted the patient onto a stretcher and carried him across to a support rack near the entrance to the marquee. She looked round at the other five operating tables. Four orderlies were carrying another wounded man from the pre-operations' tent as Malcolm rejoined her. The orderlies placed the stretcher at the end of the line of new patients and crossed to the man Lucy had just attended to. They covered him with a waterproof sheet before they picked up his stretcher.

'These men are so stoic. How old do you think he is, Malcolm?'

'Nineteen, according to his card.'

She carried the instruments across to the steriliser and was halfway back to the table when she was thrown forward by a hot blast. Something heavy crashed into her head and she cannoned into Malcolm. They fell against the operating table, which collapsed, and they ended on the floor. Shell fragments whistled over their heads and the blast of an explosion drowned out all other sounds.

As the noise of the explosion diminished, Lucy struggled to her knees to find Malcolm bent over her. It was unnaturally quiet as he helped her to her feet. She took a couple of tottering steps and his arm wrapped around her shoulder, steadying her.

'Are you all right? Are you hurt?' he asked as he led her across to a chair that one of the orderlies had brought, and began to examine her.

'I can't hear properly,' she said.

Malcolm repeated his questions, speaking louder and pronouncing the words carefully.

'I'm dizzy. My neck's sore. So's my head, and my ears are ringing.'

She pressed her hands against her temples, her eyes closed. She reached a hand higher. 'Something hit me and my tin hat has gone. Can anybody see it?'

'Here it is,' the orderly said and handed her a steel helmet with a large dent in the crown. 'I'm not surprised your ears are ringing. Mine are too, but that clout on the head will have made yours worse. My God, you were lucky. But it did its job, didn't it?' The orderly nodded at the helmet and grinned, his eyes twinkling. 'Make a good souvenir and a great story to tell your grandchildren.'

She was still dazed as she placed the helmet on her head and the dent hit her skull before the headband settled. Immediately she whipped it off. Gingerly she reached up and rubbed the area where the helmet had touched. She could feel a growing swelling that already seemed huge. 'I can't wear that helmet,' she said. On the outside, at the bottom of the dent, a scrape of bare steel showed where the shrapnel had hit and she could see how the crown had been forced in. 'Look at this. No wonder my head's sore.'

'I'll get you another,' the orderly said and rushed away.

'The orderly's right. You were lucky, Lucy,' Malcolm said as he finished his examination. 'Apart from that lump on your head I can't see any injuries. You stay in that chair where I can keep an eye on you. We still have work to do so as soon as the theatre's sorted out one of the other sisters can work with me for the rest of the night.'

Lucy glanced around the operating theatre. The marquee was riddled with holes and the entrance was in tatters, the canvas draped across the ground. Two soldiers were cutting the material away as another party was erecting new poles to support the replacement. More soldiers were shovelling soil into a crater.

Inside the marquee the orderlies had been busy reorganising the tables and cupboards, and setting up the lamps again. She watched an orderly pick up the bucket that stood under their operating table and place it upright beneath the drain. Another orderly was spreading sand over the pool of blood that had spilled from it. At the far side of the theatre, the surgical teams had returned to their patients as if everything was normal.

'I can't sit here, Malcolm. I need to be doing something to take my mind off what happened. The boys up in the line carry on in these conditions, and so can I.' The barrage was less intense, but still heavy, although it had moved away from the casualty clearing station. 'What about our patient?'

'He bought it, I'm afraid, and three of the orderlies too. The fourth one got away without a scratch.' Malcolm paused, staring over to the chaos where the exit had been. 'The shell landed right amongst them.'

Lucy looked again at the entrance, no more than ten yards away and shuddered. If that shell had carried… She stood motionless, staring at the frenzied activity until two orderlies carrying a stretcher passed her and she recovered. 'They've put another man on our table, Malcolm. Once I'm doing what I came for I'll be right,' she said and stood. The dizziness had passed and she felt better, although her head throbbed.

7

The Somme, Monday, 10 July 1916

Adam followed Clive towards the mess hut, thinking of the devastation the mines had caused. Somehow it seemed underhand, but he remembered Sergeant Crawford saying that Fritz was doing the same and his sympathy died.

'You looked pretty cool during that fracas,' Clive said as they entered the hut. 'And your first time too. We could do with more people with that sort of nerve. How would you like to transfer to the Royal Flying Corps on a permanent basis? They've just asked for more volunteers and I'm told they've abandoned the requirement for a ticket.'

'What's a ticket?'

'A civilian pilot's licence, issued by the *Federation Aeronautique Internationale*. It restricted recruiting, and the instructors didn't take any notice of it anyway. Would you like me to recommend you?'

Adam couldn't believe his luck. 'Oh yes, I'd like that. Thanks.' How fortunate he'd mentioned his interest in airplanes to Sergeant Crawford. Flying had been more exhilarating than the action in the infantry, yet because things had been happening so quickly, he hadn't been so scared.

His thoughts drifted back, recalling the terror of his first action.

Festubert, Artois, Saturday, 15 May 1915

A mortar shell exploded behind their partly dug trench and instinctively Adam ducked below the rim of the excavation.

'*Minenwerfers*,' Sergeant Crawford said as they tentatively raised their heads again. He was digging alongside Adam. 'It's too bloody late when you hear the bang. Let's get this bloody trench deeper.' More shells began to rain down and they resumed their efforts, digging furiously, piling clods of earth along the rim on the German side of the excavation. All the men in X platoon were working with equal zeal.

The barrage faded and they paused to catch their breath with the short trench about four feet deep. Adam peered over the mounded earth and across the shell devastated ground towards the German positions. He could see a small party of about a dozen grey-clad troops moving across an open rise behind the German lines. They were trailing wires as they made for the trenches. Signallers, he realised, but they must have a death wish. As he reached for his rifle a machine-gun to his left opened up and several of the Germans dropped. The rest rushed forward, more of them falling as other British machine-guns joined in. Adam took aim, but before he could fire the sergeant's hand closed round his, forcing his finger from the trigger.

'Leave Fritz to the machine-guns, Hayward. This trench is more important. Fritz is building up to something, and now they know we're here they'll give us a bit of stick.'

Adam continued to watch as the remaining Germans raced for their trench, but not one cleared the open stretch of ground. 'What the hell is this place called, anyway?' he asked as he resumed digging.

'Festubert,' the sergeant said.

The *minenwerfers* and artillery shells began to fall in increasing numbers, as if in response to the shooting of the signallers, and the digging men picked up their pace. They worked in pairs in their own section of trench, deepening it until they were able to stand upright without exposing themselves. Only then did they begin to lengthen the hole.

Adam and Sergeant Crawford were working in a fire bay, a 'U' shaped loop of trench with the open end facing back towards their own rear. Other men worked in more loops to Adam's right and left. As the diggers completed the fire bays they began to excavate traverses from the ends of the loops, cross trenches that connected the fire bays into a continuous crenellated system.

He'd learnt a lot about trenches in the three weeks since he'd joined the company. The staggered arrangement protected the occupants against the blast from a shell landing further along the trench, and from enfilading fire if the Germans overran a section of it.

He'd learnt a lot about digging them too.

The artillery barrage had petered out by midday, but a light rain began falling before the sergeant was satisfied that the trench was deep enough and stood the men down, leaving lookouts to watch the German positions.

A carrying party arrived with hayboxes of hot stew, which was no longer hot, but Adam didn't care about the lack of heat. It was the first warm meal he'd had for two days. By the time he'd finished eating the light was fading. He picked up his spade with resignation and joined Mark Johns and Andrew Stanley excavating a dugout at the side of the trench.

'I feel like a troglodyte living in these holes in the ground,' Adam said as they deepened the dugout and began widening it to form the living chamber.

'Aren't you used to it? I thought all you Americans lived in caves,' Andrew said without pausing in his digging.

Adam ignored him. He was getting used to the jibes of his Limey companions, and was untroubled by them. It was a sign he'd been accepted.

'You'll be glad enough to dive in when the shrapnel starts flying,' Andrew added. He loosened the soil and threw it back to Mark, who shovelled it through the entrance to Adam. In turn, Adam threw it onto the parados, raising the mound at the rear of the trench.

'Hayward. Come here.' It was Sergeant Crawford's voice. 'Leave that and get your gear on. You've drawn the first patrol.'

'What patrol, Sarge?' Adam asked, leaning his spade against the side of the trench and stepping across to the sergeant.

'Along to the Indian battalion, on our left. The company commander wants to know their dispositions. I'd just like to know where the hell they are.'

'I didn't know we had Indians with us. What are they doing over here?' Adam asked.

'Fighting for the Empire of course,' Sergeant Crawford said. 'What the hell do you think they're doing?' He paused, then chuckled and shook his head. 'These aren't your bloody Red Indians, you idiot. These are the real MacKay, from India, the country in Asia. They're part of the Empire, but I wouldn't expect a Yank to know that. You're to tell them that HQ says Fritz will pay us a visit, probably at first light, so they're to keep alert.'

Adam bristled, but before he could think of a suitable reply he noticed the grin on the sergeant's face. Another jibe, he realised and held his tongue, wondering how long it would be before the teasing ended.

'How do they know that?' he asked as he settled the straps of his ammunition pouches on his shoulders and buckled his belt. He picked up his rifle, checked that he had a round in the chamber, and that the safety catch was on.

'Prisoners. Off you go, and don't get bloody lost.'

Adam set off in the half-light, forcing his way through the digging men, but he soon abandoned the trench, climbing out over the mounded parados and making much better progress. He'd covered about fifty yards when a flare rose from the German trenches, bathing the night in a growing white light. He had no time to drop, but his training kicked in and he propped, standing as rigid as a statue, feeling exposed and vulnerable. Movement would give him away, but provided he remained still it was unlikely he'd be seen. He screwed his eyes tight shut, but as the brilliance of the flare waned he cracked them open and examined the scene through slitted lids. Shadows lengthened and raced across the shell-broken ground that was no man's land. He could see no activity at the German trenches, but they wouldn't be using flares if they were about to attack.

He found the Indians and delivered his message to a major in their forward headquarters. The major was British, and Adam noticed that most of the officers were British. Once he'd been briefed about their dispositions he hurried back along the rear of the trench. It was dark now, and parties of sappers were erecting barbed-wire ahead of the trench. Every time a flare rose, they flung themselves to the ground, taking cover as best they could, but as soon as it faded they were again working furiously. Adam aped their actions, diving to the ground with total disregard for his comfort. He'd never been this careless of the knocks and bruises during training, but training had never carried the same urgency.

The return took fifteen minutes, but he made it safely and reported to Sergeant Crawford. He told him to report to the company commander who sent him on to battalion headquarters with a note to reinforce his verbal information. It was two in the morning before he was back. Andrew and Mark had made the dugout large enough to stretch out and were asleep. He spread his blanket and joined them. The dugout needed deepening, but they could work on that during the day, if they were still here.

It seemed he hadn't even closed his eyes when artillery shells began to explode around their position. He yawned, rubbed his eyes and asked, 'What time is it?'

No one knew. It was not yet dawn, and exploding shells were throwing up plumes of earth in front of and behind the trench. A shrapnel shell exploded in no man's land, a few yards ahead of the new wire. Bits of steel splattered into the parapet and instinctively Adam ducked.

'Back in your dugouts,' Sergeant Crawford shouted as he rushed along the trench. 'That means everyone not on watch. Fritz won't be coming until this lot's over.'

The sky was beginning to lighten when the bombardment stopped and the order sped along the trench. 'Stand to.' It was loud in the silence that had descended.

Adam, Andrew and Mark rushed to stand with their rifles pointing towards the German positions. Adam could see no movement, but to his right the stutter of Lewis guns shattered the silence and flames stabbed out as rifles joined in support.

White flares overcame the remaining darkness to expose the attackers flitting from shell hole to shell hole. The platoon worked the bolts of their rifles like machines, pouring a blanket of rapid fire at the attacking Germans. The noise of gunfire blotted out all other sounds and the smell of hot oil and cordite filled the air. Adam coughed as the acrid fumes irritated his throat and he tried to wipe the taste from his lips.

'Fix bayonets,' Sergeant Crawford called and there was a momentary slackening in the firing as the men complied. A moment later he called, 'Watch to the left. Fritz is switching his attack.'

More flares lit up no man's land as effectively as a noon sun, but the attack was over. Adam could see the Germans racing for their own lines. The platoon encouraged them with rapid fire.

In the new dawn a sergeant gathered five men for a patrol along the line of the trench. It was full daylight by the time they returned.

'Fritz never made it through the wire,' Andrew said as he rejoined Mark and Adam.

That may be true, Adam thought, but the platoon had still lost half a dozen killed and twice as many wounded in the barrage. This was on top of the casualties they'd sustained from Fritz's stick grenades during the attack.

He studied the grey-clad figures littering no man's land. Fritz must have suffered many more. As if to reinforce his thoughts, a low moaning, interspersed with a few non-English words, came from a short distance ahead of their newly erected wire. At the far side of no man's land, German stretcher-bearers appeared and began working across the ground, taking wounded men back to their own lines, but they left many more in the mud. The moaning intensified, building to a scream followed by a short silence before it began again.

'Why can't they take the poor bastard back?' Mark said, glaring at the stretcher-bearers. He grabbed a spade and began to dig furiously at the dugout, but when the man moaned again he flung the spade aside and crossed the trench saying, 'What are we going to do about that poor sod?'

'Bugger all we can do. Leave him to his own people,' Sergeant Crawford said.

'We could shoot him,' a man said.

'No bloody way,' Sergeant Crawford bellowed and turned to the man, his face livid. 'We'll have no more of that nonsense. If we start shooting the Fritz wounded, they'll retaliate. Do you want to be responsible for that? Leave him for their stretcher-bearers.'

About mid-morning the moaning stopped, but it turned noon

before a German stretcher party reached the British wire and the wounded man. After a brief examination they rammed the man's bayonet into the ground, using the rifle as a marker, then moved on with their stretcher empty.

'Pull out?' Mark echoed Sergeant Crawford's words. 'We had a hell of a job establishing this hole, and now you say we're pulling out. Why, for Christ's sake?'

'A relief's coming up,' the sergeant said. 'We lost too many men and we need to regroup. So get your kit together and be ready to scarper come dark. We don't want to lose any more.'

Relief was the right word, Adam thought. His first action and his heart was still racing. He'd be relieved all right.

It was the middle of the night and the German barrage had opened up before the three mates filed into the communications sap and away from the trench they had dug only three days earlier. Work on the sap, the trench leading from the front line to the rear, had stopped before it had been fully excavated, so they moved at a crouch.

'Hey you blokes, put a bit of a hurry-up on,' Mark called to those in front.

'Keep quiet,' Sergeant Crawford growled. 'Any more talking before we're clear and I'll put the bastard on a charge.'

A flare rose from the German lines as the platoon moved on. As the flare faded it was replaced by a star shell that hung in the air to illuminate the whole field and the German artillery fire increased. The earth around the sap seethed as high explosives raked the soil, and shrapnel shells filled the air with screaming balls.

They hurried round a corner and Andrew ran into the back of the sergeant. The company had bunched up at the end of the trench. The next stretch was shell-torn open ground bereft of cover. They were about six hundred yards from the front line, but it was at least another half a mile to the refuge of the British reserve trench. An order came to wait until the barrage slackened.

'Thank Christ for that,' Sergeant Crawford said. 'I wouldn't fancy that open ground with this shit landing all around me.'

That made two of them, Adam thought. Such an intense barrage could only mean one thing. He turned and said to Andrew, 'Fritz will be a bit surprised to find the new boys all fresh and ready to give him stick.'

'He should keep his ammo for his stunt,' Andrew said. 'It's stupid to waste it on blokes going out.'

'Waste it? You'll be lucky. Just keep your fingers crossed he doesn't land one in this sap,' Sergeant Crawford said.

He'd hardly finished speaking when a high explosive shell landed behind them, at the far end of the communications trench, and they were engulfed with the acrid stench of explosives. The bends deflected the blast so it had little force by the time it reached them. More shells began to fall nearby as the barrage became heavier. Another shell exploded in the sap, closer than the previous one.

For a moment Adam was deafened, but the convoluted layout of the trench again deflected the worst of the blast. As his hearing recovered he could hear Mark having a go at the sergeant.

'Why don't you keep your big mouth shut, Sergeant? Fritz has enough ideas of his own without your suggestions.'

Adam peered cautiously around the bend of the sap as the star shell began to drop. Above the German trenches he saw an observation balloon. 'Those Fritz observers must be able to see straight into this sap.'

The information was passed to the company commander. Half a dozen sentries were posted and the rest of the company huddled down, each platoon keeping to its own small stretch of trench. They dozed, despite the barrage, but were jolted alert when silence replaced the bedlam of the shells. The order to move came at once, each platoon waiting until the one ahead was halfway across the open ground before it set off on its own frantic race.

Adam, Andrew and Mark were the last to start for the rear, shepherded by Sergeant Crawford. There should have been more men ahead of them and Adam wondered how many had been lost. Daylight brightened as they left the shelter of the sap and they were in full view of the observers in the balloon. The German artillery opened up, blasting the open ground. Five spurts of flame erupted from the earth a few yards ahead and pieces of flying shell whistled overhead, but it was too late to dive for cover. The seconds they saved by not flinging themselves to the ground were invaluable.

They swung right and shrapnel shells burst close to where they would have been if they hadn't turned aside.

'With me,' the sergeant screamed and they were lucky to dodge more shells.

Following Sergeant Crawford's lead, they scrambled across the scattered logs of a corduroy road. The shell-torn road was strewn with the putrefying bodies of horses and mules and littered with wrecked wagons and equipment. The shell holes bore testimony to the ferocity of the barrage and human body parts could be seen amongst the carnage. Adam gagged on the stench and was glad to leave the wreckage behind, but he could see that other men had not been successful in suppressing their nausea.

The barrage was lighter, and they were less than fifty yards from the reserve trench, when Mark screamed. Adam and Andrew rushed back to him as he fell to his knees. His hands clasped across his guts and he gasped, blood spewing over his spread fingers. His face had lost its colour and his eyes were glazing. A stench of faeces filled the air and a grey-purple sausage hung over his hands.

Adam was the first to reach him. He was bent double and vomiting when Andrew joined him.

'Pull yourself together, man.' Andrew crouched and placed his fingers on Mark's neck.

'Is he dead?' Adam asked as he stood and wiped his mouth.

'If we don't get him to the aid post quick-smart, he will be,' Andrew said as another shell exploded near them. 'Give me a hand. Grab his other arm.'

They hoisted him across their shoulders and staggered for the trench as fast as they were able.

Friendly hands helped them lower Mark into the comparative safety of the trench and a party of stretcher-bearers raced up. By the time they joined them in the trench the bearers were shaking their heads. 'It's too late for us, mate,' one of them said. 'His troubles are over.'

Support lines, Artois, Monday, 17 May 1915

Adam and Andrew had finished their meal and were sitting, drinking tea, at the top of steps leading down to a dugout when Sergeant Crawford squatted down at their side.

'We're pulling out to a rest area to reform and build up our numbers,' he said.

Andrew disappeared without a word.

'We've lost a lot of men,' Adam said, looking along the trench. 'Do we know how many yet?'

'The platoon is down to twenty-three. We're lucky. Other platoons have lost many more. The whole company can only muster ninety-five. We should have a new batch of reinforcements in about a week. They'll be green, so it'll be up to you blokes to look after them and teach them the ropes.'

Green, Adam thought. He was green himself three days ago. He'd been lucky. So had the rest of the men who'd made it. 'Twenty-three out of fifty,' he said. 'And with nothing to show for it. All those men dead and Fritz is still there.'

'That's what soldiers do for a living,' Sergeant Crawford said. 'Put their lives on the line. Kill or be killed.' He became thoughtful then continued. 'A lot of good men caught it, but we achieved our objective and we're still holding it. All up we, that's the Brits and the Indians, had about sixteen thousand dead or wounded...' He drew a deep breath. 'Some may be prisoners, but that's no better as far as I'm concerned.'

Andrew reappeared with a mess tin of tea.

'I'll be back shortly,' Andrew said as he handed the mess tin to Sergeant Crawford. 'Things to do.'

'Thanks,' Sergeant Crawford said as he took it, then he turned to Adam and said, 'Hayward, I've been puzzled ever since you joined the platoon. What's a Yank doing in the British army?'

'My mother was English,' Adam said. 'We were over visiting her parents in Sheringham, Norfolk. We come over every other year. It was the end of January, the twentieth, and my grandfather took me to the pub. Said he wanted to share a pint with his grandson, but Ma and Grandmother stayed home.' He paused and breathed deeply for a few moments. 'While we were at the pub a Zeppelin came over and dropped some bombs. Ma and Grandmother were dead when we arrived back. I joined the army the next day.'

'So that's why you're here… I'm sorry… This must be your first stunt.'

Adam nodded.

'You did well, Adam.'

'Thanks, but it's Andrew and Mark who should have the credit. They looked out for me. And now Mark's dead.'

'Nothing we can do about that. Don't dwell on it. Stick with Andrew—he's been around since this game started. He'll teach you all you need to survive… You can't be much more than three weeks or so out of training.'

'Four, but I'm not alone,' Adam said.

'Keep your head down, Adam.' Sergeant Crawford stood, threw the dregs of his tea away and handed the mess tin to Adam. 'Give this back to Andrew. I've got to get back. Get all your equipment together and be at the HQ dugout in half an hour.'

8

Pozières, Wednesday, 26 July 1916

'What's going on, Sarge?' Lofty asked. 'It's been too quiet. They must have something planned for us.'

The battalion was in the reserve trenches known as Sausage Valley, about a mile back from the village of Pozières. Little remained of the village, which had been shelled by both the British and the Germans since 19 July. The 1st Australian Division had captured it on the 23rd, but the ridge behind it that dominated the surrounding country was still in German hands.

John laughed and asked, 'Where the hell have you been, Lofty? Didn't you hear Fritz shelling fit to bust his gut? He's been at it all day.'

'That was over at Pozières village. Nothing for us to worry about. I heard last night's attack was a fizzer and I've been waiting for Fritz to pay us a visit. What I'd like to know is when it'll be our turn.'

'That's two of us, Lofty. Maybe I'll find out at 1800 hours at the CO's briefing.'

'Sergeant Mitchell,' a runner called. 'Signal from the company commander.'

'Here,' John said and held out his hand. He read the signal and smiled. 'A meal's coming up at 1700.' He glanced at his watch. 'Get your battle order organised first. Then make your way down to that communications' sap. That's where the cooks will be. I'll see you there.'

At 2330 hours a guide from the 1st Division found them, and John gave the order for the platoon to move out. Lofty cursed to himself as they squelched through the mud in the darkness, but he was grateful that the moon was on the wane and its crescent wouldn't show until the early hours of the morning.

He was in the lead, following the guide, with Don just inches behind. Ted and the other old hands moved along in silence within touching distance of each other, their only means of communication. They knew how important it was to approach the line as quietly as possible.

Their platoon had been brought up to strength with six of the new reinforcements, and for them this was their first time in the front line. They were equally silent.

'You blokes come behind and watch us carefully, and no bloody talking. Do exactly as we do,' Lofty had explained to them before they moved off, and he was pleased to see they'd taken notice of his admonishment—or was it because they were too afraid to make a sound? He knew they'd be scared; that was natural, only an idiot wouldn't be. They'd be striving not to show their fear. That too was natural. He'd belaboured the importance of silence like a schoolmaster lecturing a class of recalcitrant children. It was better to be thought an old granny than be caught in a hail of Fritz machine-gun bullets because some new chum didn't appreciate the need to make no noise.

The relief moved on, lifting their feet high to clear the mud that had once been a road, the slurp as their boots cleared the glutinous ground the only sound in the blackness. At times Lofty stumbled against soft obstructions, the bodies of dead horses or mules. Occasionally the stench of rotting meat was strong when he lumbered into an older carcass, and he held his breath, struggling to control the heaving in his stomach. Poor bloody animals, he thought. What harm had they done to anyone? Other obstructions were less yielding and he felt his way past shattered limbers still attached to the guns, or wagons that were littering the edges of the road.

They were approaching the halfway point when the Germans opened up with an intense bombardment onto the line they were moving towards. There was no need for silence now and the guide increased his pace. Lofty hurried to keep up. Flashes lit the sky. They'll light us up too, Lofty thought, and wondered if there were any saps running back from the line.

'Now that's what I call a welcome,' Ted called. 'Who told Fritz we were coming?' He laughed, but Lofty realised it was more to release tension than because he thought his joke was funny.

'Down.' The urgent cry came from Don, and Lofty heard the sharp crack from behind the platoon.

He threw himself forward as the sound of an explosion reached him, followed by the splatter of shrapnel balls and bits of shell casing hitting the ground. 'Bloody whiz-bangs,' he shouted across to the new men as more explosions followed. Earlier, he'd done his best to explain about the whiz-bangs, but his words had been far short of the reality. He knew that some of the men had thought he'd been exaggerating.

Larger, slower shells droned overhead, but they fell with heavy crashes well to their rear.

The shelling moved away and they clambered to their feet, except for one of the new reinforcements. He sat up, moaning softly, and when Lofty crossed to him he found him clutching his left thigh trying to stem the blood from a jagged wound. Quickly he bound the leg with the man's field dressing.

'Stay here,' he said. 'The stretcher-bearers will be along soon. They'll take care of you.' He hurried back to the lead.

The ground ahead was lit by the exploding shells, the earth heaving in eruptions of flame and noise, and he grew cold. That was the position of the unit they were to relieve.

As they neared the line Lofty coughed on the acrid fumes that drifted from the shell holes they passed. They were no more than fifty yards from the trench when the guide sank onto one knee and pulled Lofty's hand.

'Down here,' he said. 'This sap leads to the line. They know you're coming. I'll stay and make sure the others follow.'

Lofty dropped into the communications trench without a word. He didn't blame the bloke for not wanting to get closer to the carnage, and wished he could stay at the end of the sap too, but there were other Aussies who needed relief.

Pozières, Friday, 28 July 1916

The German barrage had been heavy throughout the day, and the Australians had worked hard with spades, repairing and improving the excavations. They crouched low and pressed against the wall of the trench each time they heard an incoming shell. When a shell did land close they were peppered with mud laced with fragments of rubble. Sometimes the explosion threw up human body parts, but it didn't pay to think about that. At other times the blast flew harmlessly over the top of the trench, but some shells created havoc, ripping the trench apart and killing and maiming men. Even the men not injured would be deafened and incapacitated by coughing until the acrid fumes had subsided. They coughed too on the brick dust that drifted into the trench each time a heavy shell pulverised more of the shattered village. Throughout the day the battalion had lost a steady toll of men to the shelling and snipers.

Lookouts watched the ground to their front, peering cautiously through gaps in the sandbagged parapet, hunched down in their steel helmets. Every fifteen minutes fresh sentries took their turn on watch. They were equally cautious. Each man knew that to expose himself was to provide a target for a sniper or to invite the Germans to open up with their Spandaus.

As the daylight faded John Mitchell stared up at the two lines of German trenches on the ridge. British guns had pounded them all day, so Fritz would be as shattered as they were, he thought, but they could bring up fresh men from behind the ridge. At least the wind had prevented the Germans using gas.

'Can you see the bastards?' he asked. When Lofty shook his head he added, 'Neither can I. I'm not looking forward to tonight's stunt.'

'You mean there are some you do look forward to?' Lofty asked. 'And here's me thinking you had sense.'

'You know damn well what I mean,' John snapped. He was tired and not in the mood for light-hearted banter. 'This is going to be a tough nut to crack. That's as heavy a barrage as I can remember, anywhere. Fritz must be determined to keep the ridge.'

'Ours must have been as heavy,' Lofty said. 'It hasn't slackened for one minute. It's a wonder the barrels of the bloody guns haven't melted.'

John stepped back, his foot slipped and he stumbled, grabbing at the trench wall for support. A piece of metal protruded from the floor of the trench. He bent to pick it up. It was firm in the dirt and he had to loosen the earth around it before he could get a good grip. He struggled for a few seconds before a clod of earth gave way as the metal came free. It was attached to a piece of mouldy leather. He wiped the earth from it to reveal an embossed metal double-eagle, the remains of a German helmet. He recognised the badge.

'Prussian Guards,' he said under his breath. The badge would have been attached to one of their leather *pickelhauben*.

His attention moved to the ground leading to the slopes of Pozières Ridge. Littering the open space were dozens of grey-clad bodies of the enemy. Strewn with the bodies were *stahlhelms*, their new coal-scuttle steel helmets. There were also khaki shapes to show where the Spandaus had added their toll to the deaths.

Too many khaki shapes.

It was no wonder the 1st Division had abandoned the attack. Tonight it would be their turn, and it was a daunting prospect.

He wasn't surprised that everyone was subdued. They'd prepared for the hop-over, checking their weapons and loading magazines for the Lewis guns. They had extra bandoliers of ammunition for their rifles and a second water bottle. They'd checked their respirators, and filled their battle packs with rations. Men who'd cadged a second field dressing stuffed it into the pocket of their tunic with their other dressing. Each man had been issued with a spade. John picked up his and grimaced with distaste as he placed it with the rest of his gear, knowing that he may be pleased to have it later.

The company commander had briefed them on the forthcoming stunt at 1430 hours. After that most of the men had spent a couple of hours writing home. For some it would be their last letter.

About an hour after dusk a carrying party arrived with containers of Maconochie stew. It was cold, but they were hungry. The tea that had come with it was also cold and tasted of petrol, but they drank that too. They'd learnt not to be fussy.

At about 2300 hours John came along the trench with the company commander who, as always before a stunt, was carrying a stone demijohn in a wicker basket, a gallon of Service Rum Dilute. He stopped at the dugout where Lofty, Don and Ted were resting.

'If anyone doesn't want their SRD, I'll look after it for them,' the company commander said. After the howls of protest had died he shrugged. 'I'd better have an issue anyway.'

The men lined up and he splashed a generous measure into each mess tin. He stepped back after pouring the last issue. One of the men hadn't come forward. 'What's wrong, Hobbs? Where's your mess tin?' he asked.

'Don't drink alcohol, sir.'

'You don't? Well your bloody mates do. Get your mess tin. Your mates can take care of it for you. They'll be grateful.'

Hobbs found his mess tin and the company commander poured another generous portion. 'I'll have my share now.' When he handed the mess tin back the level of rum was noticeably lower. 'Here you are, lad. Pass it round.' He looked at the rest of the men. 'Don't be greedy. It's just a mouthful each. And don't forget to say thank you.'

The company commander beckoned to Sergeant Mitchell. 'What's wrong with Hobbs?' he asked in a whisper.

'He has religion,' John said.

'Oh dear. What's he like as a soldier?'

'He's a good man. Reliable. Never any problem and his religion doesn't stop him shooting Fritz. I wouldn't mind another half dozen like him,' John said.

'I can see there'd be advantages,' the company commander said and laughed. He moved on to the next dugout, but John lingered. The company commander's voice echoed along the trench. 'If anyone doesn't want their SRD, I'll look after it for them.' A stream of protests greeted this. 'Worth a try. Never mind, I'll have my ration while I'm here. It's getting chilly.'

John turned to Lofty. 'The bastard's had a nip at every dugout. 'He'll be pissed as a newt before we hop-over.'

'I don't blame him,' Lofty said. 'I wouldn't have his job if you paid me. Stuck out in front on his tod, it's a quid to a bloater he'll attract all Fritz's attention. You'd need to be pissed.'

Too bloody true, John thought, then said, 'Remember, we hop-over at 0012 hours, on the dot. Get your gear ready and make sure everyone has plenty of bombs.' He hurried after the company commander.

The hop-over went according to plan, but the rest of the stunt did not. The Germans were determined, well prepared, and their wire was mostly uncut by the British bombardment. The attack had been called off at dawn, and a much depleted unit had retreated to Sausage Valley to reorganise. Three more of the new reinforcements were missing.

'Why the hell did they send us in?' Lofty said. 'We didn't have near enough men and that barrage should have been heavier, a lot heavier.'

'I hear we're to have another go tomorrow,' Ted said.

'Thanks for the good news, mate,' Lofty said. 'I like to have something cheerful to look forward to.'

A runner appeared. 'Sergeant Mitchell?' John stood and crossed to him. 'The CO wants to see you at the double, Sergeant.'

'What's the CO want me for?' John asked. The runner shrugged and they set off together.

When he returned twenty minutes later, John removed his tunic and cut the stripes from his sleeve. Lofty and Ted watched in silence.

Don said, 'Shit. I'd have thought you'd been too busy with Fritz to have time for mischief.'

John said nothing, but he rummaged in his pack and found his housewife. Then he pulled a small package from his pocket and began to sew a cloth star on one of his epaulets. No one spoke while he worked. When he finished he donned the tunic, which now had two stars on each shoulder.

'Good on yer, mate,' Lofty said. 'Congratulations, sir. So that new lieutenant bought it?'

John nodded.

'Poor bastard,' Lofty said. 'His first stunt.'

The group fell silent until Don said, 'I'd sooner it was you than a fresh-faced wanker who knows nothing about what goes on.'

A stream of congratulations followed from the rest of the platoon, then Ted said, 'I suppose we'll have to put in a request in triplicate before we can speak to you now that you're an officer.'

'Too bloody right you will,' John said with a grin. 'Stand to attention and salute. And it's SIR when you do speak to me from now on. Don't you forget it.'

'Of course not,' Ted said, grinning back. 'Would you like me to lick your boots while I'm at it, cobber?'

Thiepval, Tuesday, 26 September 1916

Adam could see the British attack on Thiepval Ridge was still in progress and he thought about the comrades he'd left behind in the infantry. Several tanks, the new weapon the British Army had developed, lay abandoned, strewn across the ground. By all accounts the tanks were not very reliable, but when they worked Fritz was paralysed with fear. The infantry would be grateful for that small compensation.

He was grateful he'd left the footslogging behind.

A reconnaissance plane, a F.E.2b of the Royal Flying Corps, was flying over no man's land directing artillery fire. A German Albatros dropped from the clouds to attack the observer. Adam opened the throttle and eased the stick forward, revelling in the build-up of speed as his Nieuport 17 closed with the enemy plane.

He swept down from above and behind the German, diving in the pilot's blind spot. The dive compensated for the speed deficit of the Nieuport and, like a hawk homing in for the kill, Adam closed with the enemy who was concentrating on the reconnaissance plane. He saw his tracers hit the fuselage of the Albatros behind the wings and eased back on the control stick. His bullets began to strike further forward. Splinters of wood flew from the streamlined fuselage and, as the German pilot turned to check behind, his plane veered to the right. The pilot turned back, frantically trying to correct the swing, but he slumped forward in his cockpit, the Albatros rolled, and began to lose height rapidly.

'Got you, Fritz,' Adam called in jubilation. The observer gave a wave in thanks and continued on his patrol.

Adam followed the stricken plane down until it hit the ground behind the British trench. As he pulled back on the control stick he saw three Albatros above him, the first beginning a dive. Flying so low he was vulnerable to the more heavily armed enemy and desperately needed height. He opened the throttle and began to climb, keeping a careful watch on the German plane. The Nieuport had gained about five hundred feet before the Albatros opened fire with a long burst. Adam jinked right, pushed his stick forward and, as the Nieuport curved over in a dive, he throttled back and reversed the stick. The Albatros overshot and was now ahead of him, and Adam snapped a short burst. Moments later he saw a flash of steam at the right of the engine compartment.

That must be a new pilot, he thought, as he began to climb again. The German turned for his own territory. With two more enemy sitting on his tail Adam couldn't give chase. Again he jinked away from the streams of bullets they were pouring towards him. They too overshot and in the brief respite he levelled out and drew his Lewis gun down to replace the magazine. His plane had been hit, but a quick instrument check showed that everything important seemed to be functioning. When he glanced over the side of the cockpit he was alarmed to see oil creeping back along the port fuselage. He checked the oil gauge again and saw that the pressure was holding.

He turned to search for the two remaining German planes. They were a little below him, climbing at full power, but heading in the direction of the German lines, which were now some distance away. He swung his Nieuport after them, diving at a shallow angle to gain speed. He was still at the limit of his machine-gun's range when he fired a burst at the lower of the two, but it was wide. He corrected his aim and after a second burst he was rewarded with smoke streaming from the German's engine, and the plane began to lose height. The last Albatros was now beyond the German trenches. Below him, to his right, Adam could see the small town of Bray and to his left lay the front lines. It was time to make for the airfield and have the source of that oil leak investigated.

As his breathing steadied he became aware of pains in his right arm, and his hand slipped on the control stick, which was slick with blood. While he'd been focused on the fight he hadn't realised he'd been hit. He turned west, heading for Corbie, but he began to feel light-headed and dizzy, and had to force himself to concentrate. It wasn't far to the airfield, so all he had to do was hang on until he was on the ground. It would take just minutes after landing to get to one of the casualty clearing stations. That's if he made it, and he wondered which would fail first, him or the Nieuport.

He eased back on the throttle until the plane was barely above stalling speed, hoping it would reduce the oil leak, and checked the instruments. The oil pressure was still holding, so with luck he'd not have to make an emergency landing. His shoulder and arm had stiffened, but the pains had diminished to a dull ache, except when he moved. He was still light headed and his vision blurred. He shook his head and his vision cleared, but the plane was pointing too far south.

He corrected his heading and glanced down to no man's land.

A few minutes later he found that he'd drifted off course again and he dragged his mind back to his flying. He was overjoyed to have at least one, possibly two, enemy planes to add to his score. If he was allowed the second kill, he would only need one more to bring his tally to five.

It was a good result considering his minimal flying training. His thoughts wandered back to his transfer. Due to the shortage of pilots, the army had released him with alacrity. He'd been flown to England to begin his training within three days of the Royal Flying Corps requesting his transfer. Just eleven days later he'd completed his flying course and returned to France. When he'd joined the squadron in late August, he'd had just fifteen hours solo, but he'd survived. Others had not been so fortunate. Of the six new pilots to join the squadron with his intake, only two of them were still alive, him and a second lieutenant. Now he'd been wounded.

He forced himself to concentrate and checked the oil pressure. It was beginning to drop and he was having difficulty focusing.

The plane skimmed the trees, clearing their tops by inches, and flying slower than the manual said was possible, but somehow it hung in the air. Another stand of trees came up, but he was too low to clear them and swung round to port. The plane responded slowly. His starboard lower wing clipped the foliage and Adam saw fabric peeling back from the leading edge. He lost focus, but moments later his vision began to clear and the airstrip appeared as a hazy stretch of graded ground ahead. The oil pressure gauge showed zero and he cut the engine. More speed was washed off as he lined up with the runway, but without power the Nieuport was sluggish. The plane dropped rapidly, closing with the ground too fast. He hauled back on the stick, but the plane did not lift. It bounced heavily, and after a second bounce it slewed to the left and tilted. The port wing-tip caught on the grass and the plane spun.

Number 5 CCS, Corbie, Tuesday, 26 September 1916

Lucy, Vicky and Alex were taking the opportunity for a rest before they went on night duty. Over half the medical officers had been transferred to the Somme at the end of the Fromelles stunt, and the Australian sisters had moved with them. For the moment the CCS was quiet, but they knew that a new stunt was taking place at Thiepval, and they guessed they'd be busy soon, probably for some time. The Battle of the Somme was expected to drag on for weeks.

Lucy, Vicky and Alex watched a dogfight overhead.

'Four Fritz. Look at those black crosses on the wings. They make me shiver,' Lucy said. 'I think the other one is ours.' She pointed to the planes that were jousting for supremacy not far above the CCS.

Vicky said, 'It is. Can't you see the circles on the fuselage?' They fell silent, watching the fight. As the German planes turned away Vicky said, 'Oh, good'o, he got two of them. There was another one of ours as well, but he didn't do anything.'

'I noticed that too,' Alex said.

'Mail up ladies,' an orderly called as he joined them and handed out their letters.

'Why didn't that plane help the other one?' Vicky asked and pointed to the slow flying plane that was now returning.

The orderly looked to where she was pointing. 'They only use that model for observation these days. It's an old design and too slow for fighting. Do you know where Matron is?'

One by one they finished reading and began to talk excitedly about the news they'd received.

Lucy noticed that Alex was unusually quiet. 'What's wrong, Lex?' she asked.

'Len. He's in the front line, or he was on the second of July, when they captured Fricourt. Goodness knows where he is now. You know how many wounded were brought in.' Alex wiped her eyes and folded the letter, pushing it carefully into her pocket.

'I heard it was over fifty thousand,' Vicky said, and gasped when Lucy kicked her. 'That hurt.'

'What do you know about anything, Vicky?' Lucy said, glaring at her friend who was rubbing her shin. 'Of course he's still alive. All those men were casualties before July first.' She turned to Alex. 'Cheer up. If he was at Fricourt, he can't be one of them, Lex. You'd have heard if he'd been injured.'

'His mother's down as his next of kin. If he's been killed they'd tell her, not me.' Alex fumbled with her pocket and pulled the letter out again. 'He says they've been practising with tanks. What are they?'

Lucy was pleased to see Alex was calmer. 'I'm not sure, but I've heard they're big trucks with thick steel bodies so Fritz can't stop them with bullets. I think some of them have machine-guns. If he's with tanks he'll be fine.'

'I hope you're right,' Alex said. 'Len said a lot of men have gone down with trench foot from standing in the mud all the time.'

'I thought they had oil to stop that,' Vicky said. 'Whale oil, isn't it?'

'What good does anyone think oil will do?' Alex asked.

'They put it in their boots and rub it on their feet to make them waterproof,' Vicky said. 'If he gets trench foot, at least they'll bring him out of the line. He'll be safe then.'

For a moment Alex stared wide-eyed at Vicky, then she said, 'I don't believe that load of baloney. My feet are waterproof without rubbing oil in.'

'Why don't you write and let him know you're here? One of the men taking supplies to the front should be able to get a letter up to him,' Lucy said. 'He does know you're over here?' Alex nodded and

Lucy continued, 'He'll be worried about you. What's his surname?'

'Devlin. I'll do that. I didn't know he was so close. My letters have been going all the way back to England. So have his. Do you think I'll be able to get to see him?'

9

'It looks like we'll be busy later, but they've brought no one in yet,' Malcolm said as he turned towards the post-operative ward. 'Come with me, Lucy. I have to check that pilot we took care of yesterday.'

Busy again, Lucy thought. She closed her eyes and flinched, as if she'd been physically assaulted. More mutilated men. There had been so many that she should be inured to the injuries by now, but how could anyone fail to be moved by the appalling wounds? She realised that the men they saw were the lucky ones and her despair increased. The doctors and nurses did what they could, but for so many men their lives, like their bodies, were in tatters.

Many died in agony before the stretcher-bearers reached them. She shuddered. Some died on their way to the CCS… Yet others would have been better off if they had died. Then there were those whose injuries were not physical, but the CCS could only pass them back to the base hospitals. It was not equipped to treat mangled minds.

'Where was it this time?' she asked. The thought of the stream of wounded men being brought into the theatre throughout the night increased her despondency. She was usually exhausted at the end of each night's duty, but despite her weariness, the horrors of the operating table disturbed her sleep. She rubbed her eyes, a futile attempt to wipe the tiredness away.

'Pozières, not far from here. Your chaps did well and I hear there are recommendations for a couple of VCs. They took the village, but were unable to capture the ridge that overlooks it. The fighting is still going on for that, and I hear the casualties are high. That's on top of more than the five thousand men you lost at Fromelles.' Malcolm stopped in the centre of the duckboards, folded his arms and his head drooped. 'And we're supposed to be civilised. Sometimes I despair of the things I see. Such valour. Such suffering. Such a waste of lives. Take that poor bloke in July. We'd saved his life, but for what?' He sighed. 'At least he knew nothing about it.'

Malcolm lifted his head. 'I have this terrible image of the families who've lost sons, husbands, fathers. Their lives have been ruined too, perhaps more than those killed. The only good thing to come out of it as far as I'm concerned is that you are getting more experience than you ever would at medical school. In time that will pay dividends, but the price... While it's still quiet I'd like you to perform some more complicated procedures under my supervision. When the rush is on we'll do what we did at Number 15.' Malcolm reached for her hand and squeezed it. 'You'll make an excellent doctor.'

More complicated procedures, Lucy thought, as they resumed walking. Each time she'd prepared for a simple operation she'd been nervous, but once she started to work her fears subsided. Already she was performing surgery that she'd only read about under normal circumstances.

'How are you feeling, Adam?' Malcolm asked as Lucy checked his record card. His temperature was up slightly, his pulse rate was elevated, his blood pressure a little low and his hands cold, which was not surprising considering the amount of blood he'd lost.

'I'm sore all over, and I'm so weak that I couldn't manage a spoon this morning. The sister had to baby-feed me, but I'm breathing, which is the main thing.'

'That's the way to take things. Keep positive and you'll recover more quickly. You're doing all right and you'll soon be back to normal, but you'll be hobbling around on crutches for a few weeks.'

Adam seemed unconvinced. He gently rubbed his shoulder, then he tapped the plaster on his left leg. 'What happened? I can't remember.'

'You crashed on landing,' Malcolm said. 'By all accounts you're lucky to be alive.' He turned to the ward sister. 'If you want to take care of that patient,' he pointed to a man who was vomiting into a bowl at the far end of the marquee, 'Sister Paignton-Fox can attend to the dressings here.'

'Will I be able to fly again, Doctor?' Adam asked.

'It might be a little while, but once that plaster is off your leg there'll be nothing to stop you. The other wounds are not serious. Now we've got you stable most of your pains will be from the bruises. From what I hear you made a real mess of your plane, so that won't fly again, but you'll be fine. In a few days you'll be able to go back to your unit. As you're not in the trenches the MO at your base can take care of you.'

Lucy had removed the dressings from his shoulder and arm while Malcolm had been talking, and now he bent to examine the wounds. 'These are coming along nicely. No infection. A few weeks and all you'll have will be a couple of scars to remind you. I'll be along to see you tomorrow.'

He said to Lucy, 'I'll see you in the theatre when you've finished here.'

As she wrapped a clean dressing on Adam's shoulder she said, 'You really can't remember the crash?'

'I remember coming in to land, but don't remember anything else. I was weak as a newborn, and dizzy, thanks to this.' He touched his shoulder. 'I think I must have blacked out. I'd been in a dog fight and was bleeding all over the shop.'

'A couple of friends and I watched a dogfight yesterday. One of our reconnaissance planes was in trouble and a British pilot came to his rescue.'

'That could have been me. I was over this way and I did look after a reconnaissance plane that Fritz was attacking.'

She finished dressing his shoulder and began to redress his arm. 'Where are you from? I haven't heard an accent like yours before.'

'It's American. Dad's American, and I grew up over there.' He paused then said, 'Mother was English, but she was killed in January last year. We were over visiting her parents in Norfolk and had stayed on after Christmas. A Zeppelin came over and…'

'I'm sorry. What about your father?'

'He'd already gone back to the States. He had to get back to work.'

'Did you learn to fly in America?'

'No chance. We couldn't afford to go flying. I joined the army after Ma was killed, but managed to transfer to the RFC.' Adam went to sit up, but gasped. Once he'd regained his composure he continued. 'Sorry, the shoulder hurts when I move. I've been interested in airplanes since the Wright brothers left the ground, but I never thought I'd be flying. I'm very lucky to be a pilot.'

'I still find it amazing that men are flying about in the sky. That British pilot tackled four Fritz and brought two of them down. When the other two saw what had happened they made off.'

'I did tackle four Fritz and there were no other pilots in this area, so that has to be me. I'd have given chase, but those Albatros are faster than my Nieuport, so I wouldn't have caught them. Just as well I suppose… You said I brought two down. Are you sure about that?' Adam asked.

His eagerness came as a surprise. 'Yes,' she said. 'They both crashed. I don't know where, but it wasn't far away. What's so important about that?'

'Thank you. Thank you. That's the confirmation I need. It brings my tally to four. One more will do it.'

Lucy frowned, wondering why he was so excited. 'Calm down. Just lie still. Don't get so wound up. What do you mean by one more will do it?'

'That's my fourth. I only need one more and I'll be an ace,' Adam said, and lifted his head from the pillow. 'You need five kills to be an ace.'

Lucy turned away to hide her expression. She hadn't thought of it before, but shooting down planes was just another way to kill people. While Fritz was trying to kill our boys, it was only right we'd retaliate, but how could this man get so excited about shooting down planes? He was like a small boy with a stamp collection. He only needed one more. One more kill. She shuddered as she remembered how the Fritz plane had burst into flames as it fell.

Number 5 CCS, Corbie, Friday, 29 September 1916

Lucy had just joined Malcolm in the theatre when two orderlies rushed in with an unconscious man on a stretcher.

'Accident, doctor. He fell under a train,' one of the orderlies said as they lifted the man onto the operating table.

Lucy flinched when she saw the extent of the man's injuries. Both legs were severed, the right at the knee and the left at the shin. His right hand was crushed, his face was blanched and his pulse was almost indiscernible.

After a brief examination Malcolm called across to one of the other surgeons. 'Colin, I need your help. This man's lost too much blood. He'll never survive unless we give him a transfusion.'

Lucy looked up in surprise. Transfusions were complex operations and she wondered how Malcolm planned to go about it.

Malcolm turned to the orderly from Colin's team. 'See if you can find a donor. One of the walking wounded in reception will be the best bet. Quick as you can, please.'

'A transfusion? That's a hell of a procedure, Malcolm,' Colin said as he joined them. He was a captain in the RAMC.

'Not a direct transfusion. That's too complicated,' Malcolm said. Then he turned to the orderly in his team. 'Graham, I need eight syringes, four cannula needles and saline solution. At the double, please.'

'So what do you intend?' Colin asked.

'We'll use the syringe-cannula method, but it'll still need three of us. You, Lucy and I.'

Lucy felt her excitement surge at the thought of helping with a blood transfusion. They had touched on them during her training, just a short lecture about the procedures a few doctors were pioneering in England and America to transfer blood directly from a donor to a patient, but she hadn't expected to be involved in one at the CCS. This would put her streets ahead of the other students at medical school. She might even know more than the lecturers.

The orderly returned. 'We only had six syringes, sir. All twenty cc.'

'We'll have to manage.'

'I've never heard of the syringe-cannula method,' Colin said.

'It's simple, but we have to be quick or the blood will clot. What I need you to do is draw the blood from the donor's artery and pass it to me.'

The volunteer donor was hurried into the theatre. 'This table, please,' Malcolm said and directed him to the operating table that had been positioned at the side of the patient. 'Get your tunic off and roll up a sleeve.'

'What if it's the wrong blood group?' Colin said. He sounded sceptical.

'There's no time to check, so that's a chance we have to take. He'll be dead if we do nothing. Get that cannula in his arm and start to draw blood.' He turned to the nurse who was part of Colin's team. 'Keep a check on the patient.' Then he said to Lucy, 'Your job is to flush the syringes. Get them in the saline as soon as I've emptied them.'

He inserted a cannula into the patient's vein and waited while Colin filled the first syringe. He passed it to Malcolm who connected it to the cannula and began to inject the blood into the patient. As soon as the syringe was empty he passed it to Lucy. She was flushing it with the saline solution before Colin had filled his second syringe.

She placed the cleaned syringe on the tray as Colin connected the third syringe. Again she took the empty syringe from Malcolm and began to flush it.

'How's the patient?' Malcolm asked the nurse.

'He's cold. His blood pressure is still falling and his pulse is weaker,' she said.

Malcolm frowned.

They worked rapidly, injecting twenty ccs at a time. They became quicker and Malcolm had connected the sixteenth syringe when the nurse said, 'I can't feel a pulse and his breathing has stopped.'

Malcolm straightened up, checked the patient and shook his head. 'That's it, Colin. He's gone.' He beckoned to a couple of order-lies who hurried across with a stretcher.

As they carried the dead man away, Colin withdrew the cannula from the donor and the nurse applied a pad and bandage to the puncture.

They stood there for a moment in silence before Colin said quietly, 'I can't help thinking it's for the best. What sort of life would he have had with no legs and only one arm?'

'It would have been difficult for his family too, but it still hurts to lose a patient,' Malcolm said and scowled.

'Where did you learn about this method?' Colin asked.

'I met a surgeon a year ago at the Number 2 Canadian CCS, Major Robertson. He's had a fair bit of experience with the syringe-cannula method and published a paper in the *British Medical Journal* a short while ago. You didn't see it?'

Colin shook his head.

'I'll look it out and let you read it.'

'Could I read it too, please?' Lucy asked.

Malcolm nodded. 'Of course you can. I think everyone should read it. Now we've done it once, I think we should use it on some of the casualties in the moribund ward when we're not flat out in the theatre. Robertson said he'd used it to good effect with men who would have died without his intervention.'

'So, what went wrong? Mismatched blood, do you think?' Colin asked.

'Probably. It's a pity we didn't have longer to cross-check. If we could test everyone when they were brought in, it would be a help.' He shook his head. 'But it wouldn't be practical when there's a stunt on and that's when it would be most beneficial.'

'Why can't they check everyone's blood group beforehand?' Lucy asked.

'Go on,' Malcolm said. 'What are you proposing?'

'When they join the army they have a medical and there's plenty of time then. Every man's blood group could be stamped on their name tags. That way it would always be available.'

'Excellent idea. I'll recommend it in my report, and make sure the senior officers are aware that it's your suggestion.'

Number 5 CCS, Corbie, Wednesday, 4 October 1916

Leonard Devlin... Devlin? The name seemed familiar, but Lucy had seen so many names. She abandoned the attempt to place it and concentrated on removing the splinter of shrapnel from the man's back.

The rush after the battle for Thiepval had slowed, but men were still being wounded by the German shelling. Others had been days in the rain, lying in shell holes, too injured to move without help, and so covered in mud they could be mistaken for lumps of dirt. Leonard Devlin was one of those.

When the stretcher-bearers had found him they had thought he was dead and were about to reverse a rifle to mark his position when he opened his eyes. He'd been too weak to call out or move, but they'd noticed his blink. To the annoyance of the sergeant clerk, the stretcher-bearers ignored the reception tent and brought him straight into the theatre.

She secured the last dressing in place and, as the orderlies carried him out to the post-operative ward, her mind switched back to the man's name. Where had she heard it?

By the time she returned from placing the instruments in the steriliser there was a new man on the operating table.

'Right, your patient, Lucy. How are you going to tackle the surgery?' Malcolm said. He was standing at the far side of the table. She examined the wound and talked through the procedure she'd decided to use.

'Good,' he said, his face showing no emotion. 'Get on with it then.'

Lucy's nervousness evaporated as she lowered the scalpel to make the first incision. She extended the puncture that the scrap of shell had made so that she could more easily remove the piece of steel and make a more detailed examination of the wound. Carefully she fished all the scraps of embedded material from the flesh, and it seemed no time before she'd completed the operation.

The name Leonard Devlin was still fretting at her memory. She had a few minutes before the midnight meal would be ready and made her way to Number Three post-operative ward. When she reached his bed he was surprisingly lucid.

'How did you get wounded?' she asked as she pulled up an empty box and sat at his bedside. He'd been given a bath and was in clean pyjamas. There was no sign of his mud impregnated uniform. That was so full of holes he would need a new one, and burning was the only way to get rid of the lice—*chats* the men called them.

'I was in a carrying party and we got thumped by Fritz. We were taking a hot meal up to the front, but those hayboxes are heavy so you're a bit slow. They make it difficult to remain rock still when a flare goes up. As soon as Fritz sees you he dumps a load of shells. It happens all the time, and it's not unusual for someone to get clobbered. This time it was me.' He started to struggle to lift himself off the mattress, but Lucy restrained him.

'Lie still, just rest. You'll be staying in the casualty clearing station for a few days.'

'Which one is it, Sister?' he asked.

'Number Five.'

'That's the one Lex is in. Alex Spence. She's my fiancée.' Again he tried to turn over, but only managed to twist onto his uninjured side before he collapsed back on the bed. 'I never knew she was here until she wrote to me last week. Do you know her? Can you tell her Len's here, please?'

'I knew your name was familiar. We're friends. Of course I'll tell her you're here, but not until we go off duty. She won't be able to see you until then.'

Len renewed his struggles to lift himself from the bed. 'I want to know she's okay. I know she'll want to see me.' He seemed drained by his efforts to move and collapsed. 'Please, Sister.'

Naturally Lex would want to see him, but there was no urgency. 'Of course I'll tell her, but not until the morning. You won't be going anywhere.'

'Thank you, Sister.' He closed his eyes and Lucy watched as he fell asleep. He was older than most of the men, many of whom were little more than boys. She checked his card, twenty-eight. That was about three years older than Lex.

They had cleared the backlog and the operating theatre was quiet. Lucy decided to check those of her patients who were still at the CCS. A hurricane lamp shed a dim light across the ward when she entered and she saw Adam Hayward sitting up in bed. Overhead she could hear the drone of aircraft.

'They're Benz. I'd recognise the sound of those engines anywhere,'

Adam said when she reached his bedside. He screwed up his eyes in concentration. 'I didn't know Fritz came over during the night.'

Lucy glanced at her watch and said, '2200 hours. He's spot on time again.' As she finished speaking an explosion shattered the stillness. It was quickly followed by four more, but they were all some distance away. 'It sounds as if he's attacking Number 21 tonight.'

Adam glared at the roof of the marquee. 'What, the CCS? He's attacking a hospital? He can't be.'

'He's been over every night for the last couple of weeks, either 21 or us. Always the same time.' She paused at the sound of more explosions. 'We think it's the same plane every night.'

'I'll sort him out as soon as I'm back with the squadron,' Adam said. 'I'll teach the so and so to bomb hospitals.'

'Most likely we'll have moved on by the time you're fit,' Lucy said. She reached out to touch the plaster on his leg. 'It'll be a while before you're flying again. Can't your mates do something about him?'

The drone of the engines faded as the plane flew on. 'We had no idea. Why didn't someone tell us?' Adam concentrated again.

'I don't know why you haven't been told, but we've been too busy with wounded men to worry about planes,' Lucy said.

'You say he comes every night?'

'Always at the same time. He returns early in the morning. You could set a clock by him.'

'Every morning? What time?'

'0200 hours, almost to the second.'

'Is there a phone I can use?' Adam asked. She nodded and he said, 'Can you show me where it is? I have to talk to my CO, to organise a welcoming party.'

'I'll get a couple of orderlies,' Lucy said. 'They'll take you over to the signals unit.'

'Can't you put the lights out when he's overhead? They'll make you an easy target.'

'This is a hospital. How are we going to take care of the patients without lights?'

'Yes, of course. I see the dilemma, and the lights will help us as well as Fritz.' Adam tried to swing his legs over the edge of the bed, but collapsed and clutched his shoulder. 'That's painful. How about chasing up those orderlies? The sooner the CO knows about Fritz, the more time he has to get organised.'

Lucy watched as Adam was carried off to the signals' tent, then continued her round of the post-operative wards. It was 2220 hours when she found Len lying on his side with Alex holding his hand and talking her head off. She turned round as Lucy joined them.

'I can't believe it, Lucy. He's safe.'

Lucy simply smiled at her and said to Len, 'How do you feel?'

'Bonzer, Sister. Bonzer… How come it was you and not one of the docs who took the shrapnel out?' he asked.

'Lucy's going to be a doctor after the war,' Alex said before Lucy could reply. 'The doctor she's helping is a top surgeon in London and he's teaching her about surgery. She's getting lots of experience.'

'She'll do that all right,' Len said. 'It must be bedlam when there's a stunt…' He cocked his head, listening, and peering to the roof of the marquee. 'That sounded like one of Fritz's bombers.'

'It was,' Alex said. 'Fritz comes over every night.'

Len's mouth fell open, then he said, 'Where are our flyboys? Why haven't they sorted him out?' He was becoming agitated and Alex tried to calm him, but failed. 'You girls shouldn't be here, not so close to the line. You could be killed.'

'No one told them, so they knew nothing about it,' Lucy said. 'One of the men in another ward is a pilot. He's talking to his CO right now, trying to arrange a welcoming party for Fritz when he returns at two o'clock.'

'I'll bet he's pleased to be here and not hopping off to get into a dogfight,' Len said with a smile. 'I know I would be. Those bombers are bristling with guns.'

'He's not pleased at all.' For some reason Lucy felt she had to come to Adam's defence. 'He was all keen to have a go himself, but he's laid up in bed. He's got a broken leg and a couple of bullet wounds. It'll be some time before he's flying again.'

A vehicle drew up and she peered out through the door. She could see bearers lifting stretcher cases from the rear of a motor ambulance.

'I have to go,' she said and tapped Alex on the shoulder. 'And you should be in your ward, Lex. They're bringing in more wounded.' Another motor ambulance drew up as she was speaking.

Number 5 CCS Corbie, Monday, 16 October 1916

'We're relocating next week, Lucy,' Malcolm said as they were cleaning up after their last operation. 'The fighting will ease off during the cold weather and Number 21 will be all they'll need here. We're moving to Albert so we'll be closer to the new front.'

Lucy was drying her hands, but she paused at Malcolm's words. 'Will that mean more shelling?' she asked.

Malcolm nodded.

She frowned. 'I was hoping that we'd seen the back of that. It's been so quiet since the airmen brought down that Fritz bomber.'

Number 5 CCS Corbie, Thursday, 19 October 1916

'How's Len getting on, Lex?' Lucy asked. The three friends were sitting together eating dinner.

'He's being transferred to Number 1, General Hospital at Rouen,' Alex said. 'I've asked Tubs for leave.'

'Did you have to give a reason?' Vicky asked.

'I told her I wanted to see my fiancé who was recovering after being wounded. She says she'll let me know this evening.'

'Does she know he's a private?'

'She'd have to be blind not to know, the way Lex has been mooning around him while he's been here,' Lucy said. 'It's plain as a pikestaff.'

'I don't care. If he'd been left in that shell hole any longer he'd be dead. I'm terrified what will happen when he's recovered.' Lex wiped her eyes. 'I wish he didn't have to go back to the front, but I know he has to, so I want to be with him as much as I can.'

'Here she is,' Lucy said as Matron Kenny entered the mess and came across to their table.

'Your leave's been approved, Lex. The CO wanted to know his name, but as you hadn't put it on your leave request, I couldn't tell him. He didn't press the point.'

'It's Len De…'

'Don't tell me,' Tubs said. 'That way I can deny any knowledge without telling lies.' She smiled and crossed to the serving hatch.

Aughton Park, Monday, 27 November 1916

Charlie's fingers fumbled as he tore at the envelope. It was much thicker than normal so she couldn't have been busy when she wrote it. He left the rest of the mail unopened on his desk and hurried to the house, calling as he went into the kitchen, 'Dorothy. A letter from Lucy.'

Dorothy rushed through from the lounge, with Marion and Arthur Paignton following more sedately.

'She's attached to a casualty clearing station at a place called Corbie. I wonder where that is.' Charlie glanced at his father.

'I'll get that map you had sent up from Adelaide,' Arthur said and hurried from the room.

'What does she say? Is she well? Safe?' Dorothy asked. 'Does she need anything? It must be getting cold over there now.'

'The hospital is about ten miles back from the front.' Charlie raised his head. 'Ten miles. That's not very far. They'll still be in range of the German guns.'

'Surely they'll not fire on a hospital?' Dorothy asked.

Charlie frowned, remembering what his solicitor had told him about his son who'd been wounded at Fromelles. If he told her the truth she'd be beside herself with worry, and he didn't want that. He was worried enough for both of them. 'You're probably right.'

'What else does she say?' Dorothy asked.

'They've been busy. A lot of men were wounded at a place called Poz…' He held the letter towards her tapping the word Pozières with a finger. 'I don't know how you pronounce it. She's still working in the operating theatre with that English surgeon… Hey, look at this.

He's teaching her surgery. She's performing operations. She's doing a doctor's job. The surgeon discovered she's going to medical school after the war, so he's helping her gain some practical experience.' His mind flooded with pride. Lucy, performing surgery.

'Let me see.' Dorothy snatched the letter from his hand. She read in silence for a few moments. 'He sounds a real nice man. She'll be way ahead when she starts her studies.' She lowered the letter, sighed and said, 'Aren't you glad you didn't stop her?'

'How could I even think of trying to do that?' Charlie smiled, remembering their disagreement. Knowing she was under fire added to his pride as well as his worries.

'You were being a father, Charlie. Like most fathers, she's still your little girl.' Dorothy draped an arm round his shoulders. 'It's natural, but you had the sense not to stand in her way.'

Arthur had returned and had been poring over the map as they'd talked. 'Here it is,' he said. 'It's due north from Paris, not far from a big place called Ami… something, Ami–ens.' He found the scale at the bottom of the map and measured the distance by spreading his fingers. 'This scale's in those French distances, kilometres. It's about one hundred. You had all that schooling with Lord Barter's son. What's that in a real measurement, Charles?'

'I'll need a pencil and paper.' They all fell quiet, waiting while Charlie worked it out. 'Just over sixty miles,' he said.

'That's a fair hike. She won't be wandering off to live the high life in Paris then,' Arthur said.

'Arthur. You know Lucy's not like that.' Marion Paignton stared at him in horror. 'Lucy's a good girl.'

'I'm not serious, Marion.' Arthur's face was full of contrition. 'I know she won't be being flighty. She'll be too busy with her nursing. Anyway, from what the papers say there's not much high life in Paris these days.'

Dorothy turned back to the letter. 'One of the patients is an American. He's in the Royal Flying Corps. She's put in a fair bit about him, but I suppose that's natural. He was one of the first men she operated on. What's an American doing fighting on our side? I didn't know they were in the war.'

'They're not, but I've heard some of them have joined the British army,' Charlie said.

She read on. 'There's more to it than the operations. She hasn't said as much, but I think she's rather taken with him.'

Charlie frowned, then he saw the disapproval in her face. 'Don't look at me like that. You know how I feel about Americans.' Dorothy's words had reminded him of Lucy's mother. She'd been an American and had turned out to be a bundle of trouble. Even after she'd died she'd caused him anguish.

'I understand, but you can't interfere. She's a grown woman and her natural reaction will be to resist any pressure you put on her. Let it ride and it'll most likely blow over.' Dorothy finished reading and handed the letter back. 'Sorry, I was so excited… I should have let you read it first. She's your daughter.'

'She's our daughter.' Charlie hugged her. 'You've been everything a mother could be. Far better than her natural mother. I couldn't have brought her up without you and Lucy knows and appreciates it. She loves you.' He thought back to Emma. How could a mother expose a child to the scenes that Lucy had told him about? 'She's your daughter as much as mine. Don't ever forget that.'

10

Adam eased forward and reached down to massage his left leg as he levelled out at five thousand feet. Each time he'd flown since he'd returned to duty, he'd felt twinges of pain where the break had been. He reached into his pocket, caressed the bullets from his wounds and thought of the nursing sister who'd removed them. His arm and shoulder still ached if he over-worked them, but that reminded him of her too. With a sigh he dismissed the thought. This was not the time for romance. What could he offer a girl? Tomorrow he might be dead. He forced himself to concentrate on flying. If he didn't keep focused he'd be dead today.

It was six months since his crash, and three months since he'd been flying again. Whether it was the cold at the altitude he flew or some other reason, he had no idea, but when it was quiet he noticed the pains. This last week though, it hadn't been quiet. That new Albatros D.III that Fritz had introduced had created havoc. The performance of that V Strutter was intimidating.

For the British pilots it was no secret that the Royal Flying Corps had lost one hundred and thirty-one aircraft during the first week of April. Some were calling it 'Bloody April', and he'd heard that the life expectancy of a new pilot was a mere eleven days. That could be true, he thought, so many of the replacements failed to return from their first sortie. But with fourteen confirmed kills to his credit he was well established as an ace.

It was the way Fritz flew in his *jasta* groups that was the big trouble. While one of the formation would attack a slow-flying reconnaissance plane, the rest would remain high, ready to pounce like a pack of wolves on any British pilot coming to the observer's defence. What irritated him most was that the *jasta* configuration was copied from the British squadron organisation.

Adam felt vulnerable on his own, but with all the losses of the previous week they were short of planes and he was flying a solo patrol over the ground battle. Again he checked the sky, and was relieved to see no German machines. With a clear sky Fritz had nowhere he could take cover, but neither did Adam. He might be an ace, but if a *jasta* found him he'd be unable to fight off six or more enemy. When he glanced to the west he could see the clouds beginning to move in.

Below, the attack was being pressed home by Canadian and British troops. They'd started at 0530 hours and fighting was still fierce in places. Poor bastards, he thought, but at least they'd had a decent barrage to soften up the Fritz defences. The shelling had been continuous since 20 March, but since 2 April it had become heavier, as if in reprisal for the losses in the air. A whole week of non-stop shelling, yet Fritz was still resisting.

A quick check of his instruments showed he was getting low on fuel. As he turned for the airstrip a flash of light in the distance caught his attention and he pulled his plane into a climb. The other plane was too far away to make out if it was an enemy or not, but he had no intention of taking unnecessary risks. The Sopwith Pup could out-climb most other planes, but not that V Strutter. It was important to gain height.

As the Pup rose Adam kept careful check on the other plane. It was climbing too, and on a course that would intercept his. After a couple of minutes he could make out the black crosses on the wings. A Fritz flyer, and alone. That's too good an opportunity to ignore.

Ten minutes later Adam was at twelve thousand feet. He had no doubt now that the plane was an Albatros D.III. It was still below him by a couple of thousand feet, but his climb had slowed and the German pilot would soon erode his advantage. 'So you want a fight, Fritz,' Adam said. 'Well, let's just see what you make of this.' He checked the sky again, but could see nothing of a *jasta*.

He turned towards the German and levelled out. The V Strutter was still climbing when he put the Pup into a dive. The German began firing, but Adam waited until the Albatros was about five hundred feet ahead. He missed and the enemy turned to dive after him as he shot past.

The German closed as Adam pulled out of his dive. The Pup was three knots faster in level flight and he could have outpaced him, but Adam wanted his fifteenth kill. There was a risk, but the Pup was so easy to fly and the manoeuvre had always worked before. It was a tactic that he'd based on his infantry training. Even the best marksman tended to shoot high when firing downhill, and he couldn't see why the same reasoning shouldn't be true for a pilot in a diving plane.

In the mirror he saw the flashes from the twin Spandau machineguns. He jinked right and opened the throttle, tightening the turn. The Albatros swept past and was now below him as he completed the manoeuvre. It pulled out of the dive and began to climb, trying to follow him, but it couldn't match his tight turn. He continued until he brought the German plane directly ahead.

He opened fire and saw his tracer bullets strike the fuselage. Immediately the V Strutter began to dive. 'Got you, Fritz. You're number fifteen,' he said, and followed it down as it rapidly lost height. Both planes were flat out, but at twelve hundred feet the Albatros pulled out sharply from the dive and Adam followed. As he lined up to fire again, the left lower wing of the German plane twisted and began to splinter, and the upper wing began to break up too.

Fifteen. Adam was pleased with himself, but he felt vulnerable flying so low and eased the Pup into a climb. The cloud was closing in again and he flew towards the sanctuary it offered.

He'd gained a thousand feet and was still climbing when he saw the flash of tracers over the nose of the Pup. He glanced over his right shoulder to see a D.III diving at him from behind, a little to the right. Another D.III was also closing in from behind, but to the left. Regardless of which way he jinked, he'd put himself closer to one of them. Bullets hit his upper wing, but as far as he could see they passed through without damaging anything structural. More bullets whistled past his head. These two Fritz had done this sort of thing before, he thought, and he realised he'd be lucky to survive.

As he put the Pup into a dive he caught a glimpse of another plane, also diving towards him, but from his front. His dive would take him below it, so he'd be a sitting duck, but that was a risk he couldn't avoid. He opened the throttle and no more bullets were finding his machine. In the mirror he could see the D.IIIs falling behind, but he could see nothing of the new plane.

Adam pulled out of his dive, swinging to the right and checking behind as he did so. 'What the…' One of the D.IIIs was spinning out of control. For a moment he was tempted to follow the flaming plane down, but with the other German fighters still around it would be risky, and he'd nothing to gain, so he began to climb, searching the sky.

The cloud had thickened, heavy with more snow. As he approached its base a plane dropped from the dark mass and Adam swung the Pup to meet it, his heart pounding as he tried to line it up in his gun sights. He hesitated when he saw it was a triplane, then, as it turned, the British roundels on the fuselage came into sight.

Relief flooded through his body. One of the Royal Naval Air Service machines. They converged until he was flying alongside the newcomer. The naval pilot waved and gave the thumbs-up. Adam replied and for a few minutes the two planes flew side by side. As they peeled off he made a note of the triplane's number.

He turned for his airfield to refuel and rearm, and to have that punctured wing checked before he flew another patrol. When he had the chance he'd drop in to Chipilly and buy the pilot a drink.

Number 5 CCS, Bray-sur-Somme, Thursday, 12 April 1917

'Your chaps have been in the thick of it again, a place called Bullecourt. Awful casualties,' Malcolm said as Lucy joined him in the theatre. 'It's been their worst day of the war.'

'They always seem to be in the heaviest fighting,' Lucy said as she began scrubbing up.

'Your fourth brigade had over two thousand casualties, and the twelfth about half that. But it's not just the Australians. The Canadians have overrun Vimy Ridge, but now they're under constant shelling and taking a beating. Our chaps have fared just as badly and the snow is making things worse.'

'It's as if the men are unimportant. You'd have thought the generals would have learnt from Gallipoli,' Lucy said.

'I don't think they have. Those at the top are all old school and most of them don't seem to understand modern warfare. We need a few more leaders like your John Monash. Unlike the senior staff, he's not constrained by tradition.'

'Surely someone could make them see sense,' Lucy said, drying her hands. 'What about all the advisers?'

'That's not something I can comment about,' Malcolm said. 'Junior officers have to be careful what they say to generals.'

'Well, I'm not intimidated by their rank. If they ever come round here I'll tell them a few things.'

Two orderlies brought a wounded man to the operating table and Malcolm bent to begin his examination. Again he left the less serious wounds to Lucy's ministrations, but the abdominal injuries were particularly complex and she had to assist him.

Throughout the night the Gotha bombers had been overhead, but this time their target had not been the CCS. Lucy examined the marquee wards as she made her way across to the nurses' tents. Most of the tents and marquees had once been white, but now they were painted in splashes of green, brown and a yucky yellow, to make them blend in with the ground. Some of the camouflage had been improved by daubs of mud. A few marquees were plain khaki-drab, but she could see that these attempts to hide the hospital had failed. Even the snow had not helped, but perhaps it would be worse without the splodges of paint. Her gaze moved on to the white circles with the Red Crosses that had been painted over the camouflage on the roofs of some of the wards. It was not something she'd noticed before. No wonder the German pilots could pick them out in the dark.

A battery of guns, large howitzers, had been moved close to the CCS during the night. They were a covered by nets with dull coloured material woven through the mesh in another attempt at camouflage. It would make no difference, Lucy thought. As soon as they began firing, Fritz would try to find them.

Flame vented from the muzzle of the nearest gun as it fired and she flinched at the sound of the discharge. The earth at her feet trembled as if it too was fearful of the consequences. It would be difficult sleeping today.

Lucy made her way along the duckboards with seven other sisters, heading for their night's duty. Everyone was tired. Although the howitzers had moved away at noon, the German gunners had continued shelling the area and several shells had fallen in the CCS compound.

Overhead she heard the drone of the bombers. She stopped with a couple of other nurses to stare up into the sky at the moving pattern made by the beams of searchlights as they probed the blackness. The searchlights were attached to an anti-aircraft battery about a mile from the hospital.

More anti-aircraft guns opened up to add to the noise. One searchlight found a Gotha bomber and the others followed to latch onto the plane. Shell bursts added to the illuminations, but the plane moved steadily on. Most of the searchlights moved away to seek their own bombers, but two stayed with it as it droned on with shells exploding around it.

'The archies will have it now,' Vicky said.

Was that excitement in her voice? Lucy wondered. Or was it fear?

The flash of an exploding shell erupted ahead of the bomber and its nose tilted down. The plane fell away from the searchlights, but still the anti-aircraft shells peppered the sky. Flames defeated the darkness, lighting the fuselage of the Gotha, as fire licked back from the nose, and the plane twisted. Moments later it exploded, shooting a ring of smaller fires through the night sky like a huge firework.

Another bomber was caught in a searchlight beam and Lucy saw small black objects fall from it. The plane began to dive, making no attempt to escape from the probing light. Anti-aircraft shells ringed it as it flew down the shaft of light with small stabs of flame spurting from its nose. It continued down the beam, apparently untouched by the anti-aircraft shells. More flames stabbed from its nose and the plane disappeared into the night as the searchlight failed.

Two orderlies stepped round them and Lucy became aware of the bombs falling in the distance. 'We should hurry,' she said. 'The day shift needs relief.'

Several bombs exploded close by as the sisters began following the orderlies in single file. A high-pitched whistle made Lucy look up and she tripped, falling forward into Vicky, and they tumbled into the mud at the side of the boards in a confusion of flailing arms and legs. A bomb exploded ahead of them as they hit the ground and Lucy felt a hot blast tug at her uniform.

As she struggled to her feet she could make out a crater where, only moments before, the two orderlies had been walking. Muted screams cut through the ringing in her ears and she turned to see a sister climbing to her feet at the side of the walkway. The lamp that one of the nurses had been carrying was sitting on the duckboards, still upright and still alight. Lucy grabbed it and held it high. Four shapes lay in the mud and she hurried over to them. The first sister was dead, and so was the sister lying at her side. Their uniforms had been torn into tatters and were red with blood.

Agnes, the third sister, was groaning and trying to sit up. Blood was streaming from her shoulder, spreading across her apron. Vicky crouched down and after checking her shoulder she turned to Lucy and asked, 'Do you have a dressing?'

Lucy removed her apron, which was plastered with mud along the front. She tore free the two flaps that wrapped round her back and folded them into a pad. With Vicky's help she placed the pad over the gaping wound and secured it with the shoulder straps.

'I'm going to see if I can find Annabelle. She was at the end of the line,' Lucy said. 'I'll take the lamp.'

Annabelle was lying unconscious on a piece of undamaged duck-board. She was breathing and had no obvious wounds. 'We need stretchers,' Lucy called.

'I'll see what I can find,' Vicky said, but she hesitated, staring at the crater and the shattered duckboards.

'There's no need. People are coming.' Lucy pointed to a lamp moving towards them from the direction of the wards and called out,

'Two sisters are wounded.' She realised she hadn't seen the orderlies who had passed them and added, 'Two orderlies are missing as well.'

The German bombs had missed the theatre and the wards, and within five minutes Malcolm was removing the shrapnel from Agnes's shoulder. Annabelle was concussed, but otherwise uninjured, and had been taken to a ward for observation.

The field ambulance unit that shared the compound with the two CCS hospitals had received a direct hit, but fortunately all the men were out bringing wounded from the front. The bomb had destroyed the workshop with one ambulance that was being repaired, and the petrol dump had been set alight. It had burned out in an hour.

All night they had worked frantically, receiving fifty wounded at a time, alternately with Number 48 CCS. It was Monday evening before the rush of wounded slowed and they were able to relax for short spells.

With the influx of wounded reduced, a single CCS could cope with the work. Number 5 had been given a twenty-four hour break while Number 48 handled the casualties. They'd swap roles the next day.

Lucy couldn't sleep and crossed to the recovery ward to see how some of her patients were coping. This was the part of the work that was most rewarding: to see the men gaining strength and know that in part it was due to her.

She stopped at the bedside of a young man whose left leg was in plaster and his right arm swathed in bandages. He was just a boy and she wondered if he was old enough to be shaving. She'd removed seven pieces of shrapnel from his arm two nights earlier while Malcolm had removed a large piece of shell casing from his head, which was now embalmed with bandages.

'How are you feeling?' she asked.

'Nay too bad, Sister,' he said in an accent so thick she had difficulty deciphering the words. 'Ah can'a think how Ah'm not deeded. Ah was damned lucky Ah reckon. Me chums, does you know what happened to them?'

'I'm sorry, I can't say, but I can have a look at the admissions records. If they're here I'll let them know where you are. They could be in the other CCS,' Lucy said. 'Who are they?' She leant across and rearranged his pillow.

'Thanks, Sister, that'll be tops.' He gave her their names and closed his eyes, wincing with pain, then he asked, 'Could you do something else for me, please?'

'Of course, if I can. What is it?'

'Will you write to me Mam? Tell her Ah'm fine. Ah can'a do owt wi' this hand.' He raised his right arm. 'Ah knows 'er worries all the time, but Ah couldn'a stay home wi' all me chums joining up.'

Lucy found a pad of writing paper and a pencil, and returned to his bedside with a chair. 'Where do you live?'

'Durham,' he said, and gave her the address. She furrowed her brow, trying to remember her geography, but couldn't recall anything about Durham. The boy must have seen her puzzlement. 'Up in north-east, Newcastle way. Geordie land.'

'Newcastle. That's nearly in Scotland isn't it?' she asked.

The boy nodded. 'Where do you live, Sister?'

'Australia.'

'Australia… And you've come all this way to help men like me. Eh, that's reet gradely. What do you think on it?' the boy asked.

'I've not had much chance to see anything except the inside of a hospital, but I don't like this war,' Lucy said and frowned. 'Oh, and I've had more than my fill of mud.'

'Me neither. Din'a like the war Ah mean, but we have to stop Fritz. They're bad-uns that lot.'

'What am I going to tell your mother without worrying her more than she is already?' Lucy asked. 'I'll have to tell her you've hurt your hand. If I don't she'll wonder why you're not writing yourself, and worry that you've copped a lot more.' Which was true, she thought.

'Weel now. Do that, Sister, but don't say owt about me head or the shrapnel. You can tell 'er Ah've broke me arm, but Ah'm all reet. Tell 'er Ah was larking about and fell off a lorry. 'Er'll believe that.'

Lucy blinked back her tears. He might be just a boy, she thought, but he's a real man. She wondered how many other mothers, wives and sweethearts were being told lies to allay their fears for their men.

It had been a quiet night, apart from the bombers, with few new casualties, and most of the medical staff had been able to snatch a few hours' sleep. They'd eaten breakfast and Lucy, Vicky and Alex walked back to their tents.

'John Mitchell,' Lucy said, surprise strong in her voice. 'What brings you here?'

'Hello, Sister. I'm looking for one of my men, a bloke called Ted Haslar. He was wounded when Fritz recaptured a trench at Bullecourt.' John looked expectantly at each of them in turn. 'You don't know where I'll find…' A shell burst outside the compound and cut him off. 'Bloody hell. You girls shouldn't be here,' he shouted. 'Doesn't Fritz know this is a hospital?'

Lucy turned to her companions, her question unspoken. They shook their heads, equally silently. 'Sorry, we've not heard of him. Come on, we'll take you across to reception. If he's here, they'll know where he is,' Lucy said, and set off with John at her side, Vicky and Alex trailing behind.

'I see you're an officer now, John. Congratulations,' she said.

'Thanks. They made me up at Pozières last July.'

'What rank are you?' Alex asked.

'Lieutenant. Can't you see these two stars?' John asked and stooped, leaning to his left and tapping his shoulder.

'Is that higher than a captain?' Alex asked.

John laughed. 'I thought you nursing sisters were all officers.'

'We are, but I still don't have a clue about these army ranks,' Alex said. 'Before I joined the nursing service, I thought sergeant was the highest rank in the army.'

'You're not far wrong with that,' John said and laughed again. 'If it wasn't for the sergeants the army would grind to a halt. They make sure everything's organised correctly. The officers are all too busy feeling important. That includes me these days.'

Alex blushed then said, 'All these stars and crowns get me confused. No one's ever explained them to me. I feel foolish not knowing.'

'It's easy,' John said. 'The officers start at second-lieutenant—one star, then lieutenant—two, then captain—three, then major—he has a crown, they're the common ones, after that you have lieutenant colonel, colonel, then the big brass… generals and blokes like that.' After a short pause he said, 'You'd know them with no trouble. They'd have a mob of other officers fussing over them.'

'We're here,' Lucy said, and led them into the reception tent.

'Haslar,' the clerk said as he ran his fingers down a list of names. 'Yes, here we are. Abdominal, two days back. Try the recovery wards, sir.'

'Good on you, cobber,' John said, and the clerk's head shot up. John took Lucy's arm and steered her towards the entrance. 'You'd better lead on, Sister.' He grinned. 'I still haven't got used to the rank. It'll take me a bit longer yet.'

The smile of the duty sister faded at John's request. She pursed her lips, then said, 'He died last night. He's being buried at 1100. You don't have much time if you're to get to the cemetery for the service.'

After a quick goodbye, John made off. Vicky and Alex started back towards their tents, but Lucy said, 'While I'm over by the wards, I'll just check on one of my patients. I'll see you later.'

The bed was empty and Lucy went to find the ward sister.

'Who are you looking for this time?' the sister asked.

'That young boy. The one I was talking to yesterday. I wrote to his mother for him. He wanted to put her mind at rest. He must have lied about his age, he's no more than a schoolboy. No wonder his mother worries about him. With those wounds I think he'll be sent to Blighty. At least he'll be out of this for a while.'

The ward sister blinked and wiped her eyes. 'That boy's out of this forever. He didn't make it through the night. Delayed shock, the doctor said. You're right about him lying to join up, he told me he was only seventeen.'

Lucy sank to the edge of a bed. 'Poor little soul. I wish I could get that letter back. I'll have to write to his mother again.' She hurried from the ward, fighting to keep calm, but her thoughts were in disarray. What was she going to say to the poor woman?

11

Number 61 CCS, Edgehill (Ypres), Thursday, 7 June 1917

The earth vibrated so fiercely that bottles and boxes fell from the shelves in the dispensary. For a moment Lucy thought a shell or a bomb had landed near the ward, but it must have been a huge bomb. It was the best part of a minute before she heard the noise of an explosion, so it had to have been miles away. Despite the distance it was still loud. She hurried into the recovery ward, worrying about the patients.

As she passed along the beds she checked her watch: 0311 hours. Halfway along the ward a small man was struggling to sit up and she stopped to help him. His head was swathed in bandages. So was his shoulder.

'You should be resting,' she said as she arranged the pillows at his back. 'Get some sleep. It's the best thing for you.'

'Nay, lass, I couldn'a sleep now. They've done it then?' He was so excited he had difficulty getting his words out. 'That's reet gradely. I never thought we'd get it finished.'

It was over a minute before Lucy managed to calm him. 'Done what?' she asked. 'What did you think you'd never finish?'

'Mines. We've been tunnelling under Messines Ridge. Digging like moles for more than a year. Tunnels all o'r shop. It was busier than Piccadilly Circus. Three bloody layers of them. At times we'd find we were near a Fritz tunnel, then we'd set off a camouflet and close it down. He'd do the same to us at first, if he had the chance, but we got to be better than him. We set all these bloody great mines. Twenty-one of the buggers.' He grabbed her hand and pulled her closer. 'So they've been and gone and done it. Ooh, I'm reet glad.'

Lucy couldn't help but smile. He was like a young boy who'd been given the birthday present he'd been dreaming about. 'Just what have they done with these mines?'

'Blown Messines Ridge to smithereens, and Fritz with it, that's what. Twenty-one mines we set. Twenty-one. You heard them. You felt them. That's what woke me up. It would have woke Fritz too. He wouldn't have known what hit him. Somat like four hundred and fifty tons of Ammonal explosive. Over one million pounds of the stuff. A lot of blokes thought we were wasting our time. They were so sure Fritz would find them. Ooh, I'm reet glad they were wrong. It would have blown him sky-high all reet, and saved a lot of lives. Reet deep we went, under all t'other tunnels and Fritz never knew owt about owt.' The man snuggled back under his blanket and she rearranged his pillow again. 'He'll know all about it now though.'

'You've been working on them for a year? That's a long time.'

'Aye, it is that. We did a good job too. Those tunnels are magnificent, and there were men from all o'r world working in them. Australia, New Zealand, Canada. Then there were us from England. A lot of us from the mines in Yorkshire, Lancashire, Geordie Land and some from other places. You wouldn't believe what we have down there. Railways, barrack rooms, huge big kitchens, ammo dumps, workshops and stores of all sorts. We even have hospitals, but no pretty nurses. Just a lot of Medical Corps blokes. I didn't fancy them.' The patient grinned up at her. 'It's not the same being treated by a bloke. Give me a pretty nurse any day, Sister.'

Lucy chuckled and said, 'Less of that flannel. I can see you're getting better.' She examined the man more closely, then checked his record card. Ten stones four. 'I would have thought you'd need to be bigger to dig tunnels, it must be hard work.'

'That's what the army thought in 1914, Sister. They wouldn't have us then. Too small to be a soldier, see. All of us were less than five three, that was the minimum height. But they changed their tune quick smart when they wanted people who knew about mining. We were big enough then all reet. Every man Jack on us came from coalmines, at least the English did. I don't know about t'others. Oh, we were big enough then all reet. We were the men for the job. Don't you think no different.'

'Sorry,' Lucy said. 'I didn't mean it critically. It's just I expected…
Oh, it doesn't matter.' She went to move away, but the man grabbed
her hand again and pulled her back.

'That's all reet, Sister. Fritz thought the same. Sometimes he'd
break into one of our tunnels, or we'd break into his. Just by accident, like. Then it was on, a proper battle. The only difference was
we used spades and pickaxes mostly. We had machine-guns and
rifles, but spades and picks were better and we already had them
in our hands. Being small was useful then.' The man's face glowed
with pride. 'Those spades are nasty, especially after being sharpened
by months of digging. Well, it's all o'r at last. Ooh, I'm reet glad.'
The man grinned up at her. 'There'll be a few sore heads in Fritz's
trenches reet now, and a lot who'll never have a sore head again.'

The patient relaxed and lay back. Lucy was pleased to see he'd
calmed.

'Are they our guns that have opened up?' he asked.

She became aware of the background rumble of guns, which she
hadn't noticed as she'd concentrated on what the man was saying.
After listening for a while she said, 'You're right. You can hear the
sound of them firing, then the shells exploding in the distance.'

'Good on the gunners. That'll keep Fritz on the hop,' the man
said. 'The charge will be going in now. I'm glad I'm not part of it, but
I wish I could see it.'

The casualties started coming in at midday, and by the time Lucy
was back on duty there was a steady stream of wounded. Malcolm
had been transferred to 61 CCS and, as the Australian nurses' rede-
ployment had been postponed, he'd requested that Lucy was transferred with him until Number 3 Australian CCS was re-established.
He'd been promoted with the move and was now a lieutenant colonel, although he'd refused to transfer to an administrative role and
was still performing surgery.

'That was some explosion they set off this morning,' he said as he
joined Lucy in the operating theatre. 'Nineteen mines demolished
Messines Ridge.'

'Nineteen? I was told they'd set off twenty-one.' Lucy laid out the surgical instruments at the side of the operating table. 'One of the tunnellers is in the recovery ward and he was telling me all about it.'

'They did set twenty-one, but two of them were in the wrong locations. The nineteen that did go up shattered the Boche trenches. They shattered the nerve of those men who survived too.' For a moment Malcolm covered his face with his hands, then he continued. 'Awful business. They estimate that the Boche had about ten thousand killed, many of them buried alive, but better them than our chaps.' He completed fastening his overalls and stepped across to the basins to scrub up as two orderlies carried their first patient of the night to the operating table.

'That's a lot of men. How can they know so soon?' Lucy asked.

'When our men reached the Boche trenches, they found the survivors totally bewildered, deafened by the blast and wandering around aimlessly and so demoralised they just blurted everything out. It was like herding a flock of sheep. Their senior officers gave us the numbers of the men manning that section of the line, and no one escaped.' Malcolm moved back to the operating table as the anaesthetist placed a mask over the man's face. 'The Boche had heard we planned an attack and had brought up reinforcements. They had about ten thousand dead, and almost as many captured. I suppose a few got away, but eighteen thousand Boche were eliminated.' The orderlies moved away. 'We've work to do, Lucy.'

Messines, Thursday, 7 June 1917

At 1130 hours the tank lurched forward. John Mitchell followed at the head of Number 2 section. The other sections in his platoon, Number 1, about twenty yards to his left, and Number 3, to his right, were each protected by their own tank.

John was pleased to see that the men in each section were strung out in single file in perfect artillery formation, a couple of paces apart. They began to climb towards Messines Ridge, the tanks leading the small groups of men like teachers shepherding children into a classroom.

They had reached halfway to the crest when the German guns opened up and the hillside sprouted plumes of dirt and dust. It was a mixture of whiz-bangs from the field guns and high explosive shells from the 210-millimetre howitzers that were searching for the tanks. John didn't know which he feared the most.

He checked his other sections. Number 3 was still strung out in artillery formation, but Number 1 had bunched up. All but two of the men were from the new reinforcement with no experience, and the corporal was young too, only recently promoted. John would have preferred a more seasoned man, but they had lost too many NCOs and it was not his choice. Why the CO permitted the promotion of such inexperienced soldiers was a mystery, but those who survived their first couple of stunts usually made good leaders.

'Keep them as they are. Don't let them close up. I'm going to sort out Number 1,' he said to the lance corporal of Number 2 section, shouting to make himself heard. He was even younger than the corporal in Number 1, but at least he had Lofty to show him the ropes. Lofty and Don would have made good NCOs, but for some reason they shied from promotion like unbroken colts from a farrier.

John had covered less than ten yards when he heard a shell and dived into a hole as it exploded behind the tank in a flash of yellow and red flames. When the fragments stopped flying he raced on, but of Number 1 section only two men still lived. One man had a scrap of shell in his arm. The other was unhurt, but dazed.

'With me,' John shouted, then stumbled, coughing from the acrid fumes. He recovered and grabbed the dazed man's arm, leading him back towards Number 2 section. The wounded man hesitated until John screamed at him, 'You too, Archer. Come on.'

They reached Number 2 section as the tank that had sheltered Number 1 erupted with a roar of flame and dirt. Internal explosions rocked the stricken vehicle as its ammunition added to the destruction. It lurched to the left, spun round and slithered into a shell hole.

In the few minutes John had been away, Number 2 section had closed with their tank. When he moved to the head of the section he could smell the exhaust fumes.

'Keep your distance,' he called as he slowed and forced the men to fall back until he could no longer smell the exhaust. It was a pity to lose the close protection that the tank provided, but the fumes could kill as effectively as machine-guns. He'd been told that the dangerous gases had no smell, which was a worry and he dropped further back. By the time they walked clear of the barrage, John was hoarse from repeatedly calling, 'Down.'

Most of the company reached the top of the ridge and were still in formation. To his right John could see a huge crater. He guessed it would be close to two hundred yards in diameter and at least twenty or twenty-five feet deep. At each side of it, for one hundred yards or more, the enemy trench had been obliterated. John hurried past the gaping void, stumbling occasionally as the loose ground slipped under his feet. Dead Fritz without a visible wound lay everywhere. Others had had limbs torn off, their wounds black with congealed blood. Some had been buried only to be torn from the earth by the barrage that followed the mines.

Already the rim of the crater was pockmarked with smaller craters from the bombardment the British guns had laid down as the first wave pressed home their attack. He hurried over the churned-up ground, across the remnants of the captured trench, and started down the eastern slope of the ridge, but without the protection the tanks had provided.

The German artillery fire intensified and the Australians began alternately diving into shell holes and dashing forward. Machine-guns began to fire and men began to drop, but the rest pressed on until they reached the white tape that was the assembly point for their attack. They flung themselves prone, taking cover as best they could.

John dashed across to Archer. 'How do you feel?' Archer was struggling to tie his field dressing across his arm. Blood was still flowing from the wound, bright red against the dull khaki of his sleeve. 'Here let me have that,' John said and fastened the bandage firm. 'How do you feel?' he asked again.

'I'll be jake, sir. It'll take more than a bit of a cut arm to put me out of it.'

'Good man. Keep with Two section,' John said. The wound was

more than a bit of a cut, but he was pleased with Archer's attitude. He crawled away to check Number 3 section. Before he was back to his position an order passed along that their attack had been postponed and they were to return to the newly captured trench. More men dropped before they reached safety.

The survivors barely had time to catch their breath before a lookout shouted, 'Fritz is coming. Stand to.'

John joined the men lining the parapet, grateful that he'd kept his rifle. Across the open ground to his front he saw a mass of grey-clad Germans advancing.

'Come on you Fritz bastards,' he called as he opened fire. He reloaded and resumed firing, oblivious to everything except his rifle and the advancing Germans.

The Germans' line thinned and faltered in the overwhelming fire from the rifles and Lewis guns, but a second line rose to follow it. That too thinned, but it pressed on and was joined by a few survivors from the first wave. The Germans continued, losing men as they advanced. They were less than twenty yards away before their nerve failed and they turned to race back towards their own positions, many of them falling before they reached their trench.

John led the remnant of his platoon, twenty-four of the original fifty men, back to the starting line. The white tape was in disarray and difficult to make out. They were just yards from it when German shells began to fall and they dived for cover.

Ten minutes passed like ten hours before the British creeping barrage began and the cry came, 'With me. Charge.'

The charge proceeded in a series of rushes from one hole to the next. Men were hit and dropped, but the charge continued. Their objective was in sight, but a machine-gun opened up from directly ahead and they were forced to dive into a shell hole. The machine-gun was less than fifteen yards from their hole and it was impossible to move without drawing the gunner's fire.

John checked the men in the hole with him: Lofty, Don, Muscles and Archer—who had lost his helmet and was staring wide-eyed at the German trench from behind a clod of earth.

Archer pulled a Mills bomb from a pocket and placed it on the rim of the hole, then removed a second from which he pulled the pin. Before John had time to call out and stop him, Archer knelt, exposing his upper body, and threw the bomb. Immediately he grabbed his rifle and the first grenade, and was on his feet, racing for the machine-gun. It was seconds before the machine-gunner reacted and fired a long burst, but Archer raced on and hurled the grenade as the other exploded. The gun fell silent, and Archer still ran forward.

'With me,' John yelled and was on his feet as Archer jumped down into the German position. They reached the trench as a German officer raised his pistol towards Archer, who was about three feet from him, but Archer's bayonet was in his guts before he could pull the trigger. Both men collapsed, Archer on top of the German. When John pulled Archer clear, he saw his stomach was a mess of blood and mangled flesh.

'*Kamerad. Kamerad.*' Half a dozen Germans rushed from a strong point, their hands raised. Lofty herded them against the trench wall as Muscles tossed a Mills bomb into the dugout they had just vacated.

Len Devlin tossed a second grenade and screamed, '*Kamerad* this between you, Fritz.'

In seconds the prisoners had been searched and pointed towards the rear positions.

John hurried along the trench to check how the rest of his platoon had fared.

Two Germans staggered out from a second dugout, one bleeding from his head, the other clutching a bleeding arm. Muscles tossed a grenade down the steps, waited for the discharge, then dashed into the dugout.

He re-emerged herding an officer ahead of him. 'Found this bastard cowering in the dugout. I had to prod him a bit with my bayonet.' He grinned at Lofty and pointed to the right sleeve of the officer's tunic, which was saturated in blood. The man cradled his arm, and blood dripped between his fingers.

'I not surrender to private,' the officer snarled.

'Is that right, you mongrel?' Lofty said. 'Please your bloody self, but if you won't surrender I'll just have to fucking kill you.' He raised his bayonet so it was pricking the man beneath his chin. 'Do I cut your bloody throat or would you prefer me to pull the trigger?'

'*Kamerad*,' the officer screamed and raised his arms. As soon as they'd removed his pistol and searched him, he scrambled over the rim of the trench, hurrying to join the other prisoners.

'Thanks, Lofty. I've more important things to do than get involved with an arrogant bastard like that. Take charge here, I'll be back as soon as I can,' John said. Just forty-nine men held the company's section of trench. John was the only officer. For a moment he felt awed with the responsibility, then his training took over and he found a signaller who had just set up a field telephone.

John reported to the CO, requesting fire support. It was five long minutes before the first shell landed on the German lines, but it was the harbinger of the barrage.

The signaller called to him that the CO had no reinforcements and had ordered him to withdraw at the earliest opportunity as he expected the usual counterattack. John looked back over the ground they'd crossed and saw their wounded still struggling to get back. Some of those who could walk were helping their mates, and stretcher-bearers were collecting the more serious cases.

'Tell him I'll hold Fritz off as long as possible to give the wounded a chance. And I need that barrage as intense as they can make it,' John ordered the signaller.

He sited the three remaining Lewis guns to give overlapping arcs of fire, arranged the riflemen evenly spaced along the trench and distributed their remaining Mills grenades.

As the barrage intensified Germans appeared from their trench and began to advance. 'Fritz is on his way. Tell the CO,' he yelled at the signaller. 'Tell him we need shrapnel, as much as they can give us.'

John hurried along the trench, giving encouragement, watching the progress of the German attack. 'Wait. Let them come,' he said as he passed the men. 'Leave it to the Lewis guns until my order.' It was better to allow Fritz to close before the riflemen opened fire. He knew how they felt; he wanted to take a shot himself.

More Germans joined the massed advance as shrapnel shells began to burst over their heads. At the sight of the shrapnel ripping through dozens of men and adding to the carnage, John felt sickened. But better Fritz than them.

The leading Germans were less than one hundred yards from the wire when he heard '*Attackieren*', and they broke into a shambling charge.

'Open fire,' he called and joined in, but after firing three quick rounds he stopped. It had relieved some of his tension, but his job was to direct and not become embroiled in the fight.

His riflemen were firing rapidly now, a continuous cacophony of sharp cracks adding to the rattle of the machine-guns. With each man capable of firing over thirty aimed rounds a minute the lines of Germans were thinning rapidly.

The leading attackers had closed to just fifteen yards, but not one of them advanced an inch further. Those behind went to ground in whatever shell holes they could find. It had been less than a minute since the Australian rifles had fired their first shot.

'Rifles, hold your fire,' John shouted. The rifles fell silent and he called, 'Get ready with bombs. I'll throw the first then let them have it. When they bolt the Lewis gunners can give them the gee-up.' John raced along their position repeating his order. There were only forty-one men still fighting fit, four walking wounded, one who'd need a stretcher and three more dead. Just forty-one… The company had been two hundred and fifty strong when the stunt started.

The three Lewis guns were keeping the Germans pinned in the shell holes and John ran back, pulling the pin from a grenade as he went.

'Stand by,' he called as he judged he was about central. He aimed at the nearest shell hole and hurled his Mills bomb. Thirty-eight grenades flew into the air following his and Germans leapt from their holes, racing towards their own lines. Germans further back saw their comrades running and joined in the rush.

'Keep firing,' John ordered, then crossed to the wounded men. A man had found a stretcher and John ordered the three other walking wounded to help him. 'Get that man back quick as you can.' He glanced at his watch. 'We'll give you five minutes. I can't promise more.'

There was no sign of another German attack. John waited. As he watched the British shells tearing the German trench apart, the memory of Archer's charge intruded. His sacrifice would have saved many lives.

The five minutes he'd promised turned into six, then seven as he made his way along the trench organising the men into four parties who would withdraw in turn. They might be pulling out, but he was determined they wouldn't run. It would be an orderly withdrawal with one party moving back at a time while the others gave covering fire. He found the signaller who handed him the field telephone and he explained to the CO what he was doing. 'Give me another ten minutes of the barrage. That's all I need, sir.'

'You have it,' the CO said. 'Good luck.'

Number 61 CCS, Edgehill, Sunday, 10 June 1917

'That's the lot for now, Lucy,' Malcolm said, massaging his spine. 'What a night. It's sixteen hours since we came on duty. I'm knocked up. You must be too. Why don't you grab a bite to eat then go and get some sleep?'

'I'm not hungry, Malcolm, but sleep sounds good,' Lucy said.

After she'd cleaned up and placed the instruments in the steriliser, she left the operating theatre and headed towards the nurses' tents. As she passed the last ward she heard low moans and opened the flap to check inside. The marquee was crammed with stretchers, each one loaded with a wounded German prisoner.

'Water,' one of the men near the door gasped. 'Water.'

'Orderly,' she called and hurried inside.

Another man grabbed at her skirt and half rose, resting on one elbow. His left leg was bandaged along his thigh.

'Two day,' he said when she stopped and crouched down at his side. 'Two day. No thing. Not have water. Not have food. Not have medicine. Mans die.' He sank back on the stretcher.

An orderly rushed into the ward and Lucy said, 'These men need water. Can you organise it? They've had nothing for two days.' She wondered about the two days, but it was irrelevant.

'Good God. A ward full of Fritz. Bugger them.'

'Fritz or not, they're wounded men. How can you expect the Germans to take care of our wounded if we don't look after theirs?'

'Sorry, Sister. You're right. Leave it with me. We've been too busy with our own wounded and didn't know they were here.' The orderly raced out as another two entered.

'Start getting these men into reception. I'll find the doctors.' Lucy hurried back to the operating theatre to find Malcolm and the other night surgeons were still there, relaxing with a bottle of brandy.

After Lucy explained about the German wounded, Colin, the surgeon who had helped with the transfusion, stood and said, 'We'll take care of this, Malcolm. You people get to bed. You too, Sister.'

'There are fifty-three of them, or there were. You'll need everyone's help,' Lucy said. 'They're in a bad way, so we've no time to waste. The more people helping, the more men will survive. I'll stay. It's why I joined.'

'Even though they're the enemy?' Colin raised his eyebrows.

'Enemy? I suppose they are, but they're wounded men who need our help. They'll be no threat.'

'Good for you, young lady. We'd better get on with it then.'

'They're being taken into reception for assessment, but the MO isn't there,' Lucy said.

'In that case we'll do the assessing ourselves,' Malcolm said. He turned to Colin. 'Can you see to that? Send the worst cases in first.'

Sixty minutes later Lucy watched the last wounded German being carried to the hospital train. She swayed with fatigue. The team of eight surgeons had performed forty operations in forty-five minutes. Most were straightforward shrapnel extractions, but others were amputations. Thirteen of the Germans had either been dead in the ward, or died before they'd reached the operating table. Some of the forty still living would soon join them, but most of them would live.

'This time you will go to bed,' Malcolm said as he came up behind her. 'And I don't want you checking in any wards on the way to your quarters. Promise?'

'I promise,' she said with a tired smile.

It was evening when Lucy woke and most of the marquees had been struck. 'I'd forgotten we were scheduled to move today,' she said to Vicky as they made their way to the nurses' mess. 'I'm still impressed at how quickly they can move a hospital, when you think how long it takes to build one under normal circumstances.'

'We're not going with them,' Vicky said. 'We're to go to Abbeville to Number 3 Australian CCS.'

Alex was sitting with three other nurses when they joined her. 'Do you remember that pilot you patched up when we were at Corbie last year?' she asked. Lucy nodded and Alex rushed on, 'He's back. He's been shot again. They've left the ward he's in until the last. He was a bit weak after the surgery and the doctors wanted to give him as much time as possible before they moved him.'

'That American? Is he all right?' Lucy asked.

'He'll be fine. It was just straight forward bullet wounds this time, nothing complicated.'

Lucy finished her coffee. 'I think I'll go and say hello.' She tried not to hurry as she left Vicky and Alex sitting at the table. She didn't want them to get any ideas, and tried to convince herself it was just professional interest. Even so, she remembered his blue eyes and his mop of curly hair. At the time she'd wondered how he managed to get away with keeping it so long.

'How are you feeling, Adam?' she asked as she pulled up a chair at his bedside, automatically straightening his blankets and tucking them in.

Adam opened his eyes and blinked. It was the nurse who'd removed the bullets the last time he'd been in a CCS. Although he'd thought of her often, he'd never expected to see her again, especially not like this. He didn't even know her name. 'Hello, Sister. Will you be looking after me this time?'

She smiled and shook her head. 'You're being shunted off to a base hospital. The train's waiting now.'

'Do you know which one?' Adam asked.

'Sorry. No idea. It'll depend on which has the beds. Most likely it will be Étables. That's fairly close and they have several hospitals there. I heard that a pilot called Adam Hayward was in this ward all shot up, so I thought I'd say hello before you were sent away.'

'What's your name, Sister? You know who I am, so it's only fair I know who you are.'

'Lucy. Lucy Paignton-Fox.'

'I still have the bullets you removed. I take them up every time I fly. They're my good luck charm.'

'Not much of a good luck charm.' She picked up his chart and shrugged. 'We usually throw them away.'

Adam eased himself back against the pillows. 'How come you gave them to me if they're normally thrown away?'

'They were the first bullets I'd removed from anyone. I couldn't keep them, but I thought you might like them.'

'So I was the guinea-pig? I don't know what to make of that.' He saw her frown and added hastily. 'You did a good job.'

Two orderlies appeared at the side of the bed. Adam was surprised to see the rest of the ward had been cleared while they'd been talking. 'It's time we took him away, Sister. The train is about ready for the off,' an orderly said and bent to help his mate transfer Adam to a stretcher.

'You didn't say where you were going, Lucy. I'd like to write,' Adam said as the orderlies lifted him and started towards the door.

'Number 3 Australian CCS, but I don't know where we'll be,' Lucy called as they carried him through the door.

He'd find her, Adam thought, and relaxed.

'So this is where we say goodbye, Lucy,' Malcolm said. 'I shall miss you. It will seem strange working with another nurse.'

'I shall miss you too, Malcolm. You've taught me a great deal.' Lucy was close to tears. She'd grown comfortable with Malcolm and she'd have to start from scratch to get to know another surgeon. That's if she was assigned to the operating theatre in the Australian Casualty Clearing Station. She could be in one of the wards, and after months of working with Malcolm, she wouldn't like that. 'I hope I'll be able to continue with theatre work. I feel I'm doing something positive to help the patients.'

'That's because you are,' Malcolm said. 'It's not for everyone, but you have an aptitude for it. When do you leave?'

'Tomorrow morning, at 0730. They didn't give us much time to get ready,' Lucy said.

'It's the way it is in war. Do you know which way you're going?'

'First to Abbeville, but we don't know where we'll end up. We're to join Number 3 Australian.'

'You'll do well. And good luck with your studies when you get back to Australia.' Malcolm took her hand in both of his. 'Goodbye, Lucy. Write and let me know how you get on. Here's my home address.' He pulled a small card from his breast pocket. 'If you get to England after the war, you'll always be welcome.'

Lucy hugged him and kissed his cheek. When she drew away she read the address on the card and said, 'I will write and I'll take you up on that invitation. You'll always be welcome in Australia too.' She pulled a notebook from a pocket and wrote her address, ripped out the page and gave it to him. 'You'll find it somewhat different to London.'

12

Calais, Sunday, 29 July 1917

Officers began leaping from the train before it had come to a stop, all racing towards the transport office at the end of the platform. Matron Kenny hesitated as she climbed down from the carriage. 'I was told I had to be smart to beat the rush, but I never expected anything like this. How am I going to fight my way through that mob?'

The Number 3 Australian Casualty Clearing Station was being established at Brandhoek, close to the front line, but so far only twenty sisters and Matron Kenny had been released from the British hospitals they'd been attached to. The others would join them over the next weeks.

'You'd think officers would have more manners,' Matron Kenny said, glaring at the melee. 'I wish I knew which trains we should catch. Then I wouldn't have to face this chaos.'

'We need John Mitchell. He'd sort them out now he's an officer,' Lucy said. She was the only sister paying attention.

Matron Kenny was still glaring along the platform. 'But he's not here, is he? I don't know why they couldn't have given me all the papers before we left Abbeville. I suppose it's secrecy, but I hate being treated like some irresponsible child.'

Lucy could see the matron's irritation building, but getting angry wouldn't help. It wasn't the fault of the officer in charge at this station. 'I don't think it's anything to do with secrecy. It's more likely that no one in Abbeville knows what trains are available in this sector. The transport officer here will be the only one who has that information.'

The matron sighed, but began to relax. 'I guess you're right.' She pursed her lips, glowering at the officers. 'There's nothing for it, I'll have to go and face the scrummage.'

A few minutes later Lucy said to Vicky, 'I thought Tubs would be ages. I wonder why she's coming back so quickly.'

Matron Kenny rejoined them, a broad grin creasing her face. 'The transport officer called me forward as soon as he saw me.' She turned to stare back along the platform. 'He's still convalescing from wounds and appreciates the work we do. We're to change trains for Hazebrouck and he handed me more sealed orders. Our train's not in yet, and he's not sure exactly when it'll be here, but he thinks it'll be at least an hour. I suppose we'll eventually reach Brandhoek. Perhaps they'll tell us where that is once we arrive.'

Hazebrouck was as chaotic as Calais, and it was some time before the matron received the new orders. From Hazebrouck the sisters went to Abele.

'So you finally got here,' the transport officer said when Matron Kenny and Lucy reached his office. 'The train you should have caught left over two hours ago so now I have to find somewhere for you to spend the night. Where the hell I'm going to accommodate twenty-one women I've no idea.'

'I'll thank you not to swear. I've no wish to cause you grief, but my orders were to report here for more instructions,' the matron said. 'That is exactly what I've done, so please be civil, even if you don't like the situation. It's not my fault the train was late.'

The officer fell silent and opened the sealed orders, made a note of a number, pulled out another envelope from a tray on his desk and removed a signal. 'Sorry, Matron. I'm snowed under here, as you can see. I won't be able to get you away until tomorrow and we've nowhere suitable for women to spend the night. This came earlier this afternoon.' He tapped the signal. 'Number 3 ACCS is not even close to being ready for you. Excuse me. Now you're here I'll have to make more phone calls.'

'We're not happy about it either,' Lucy said. 'We're being passed around like a parcel. Is there anywhere we can we get something to eat?'

The officer cast a harassed glance to the two women. 'Can't help. The field kitchen that we'd set aside had to move on. Sorry again. You'll have to use your initiative until I can find some accommodation for you. See if you can find something in the town. If you can be back here in thirty minutes I might have been able to make arrangements.' He spun on his heels and crossed the office to slump into the chair behind his desk. He picked up a telephone hand piece from the top of a khaki painted box and wound furiously at a handle on the side.

'Thank you very much,' Matron Kenny said under her breath as they left the office. She turned to Lucy. 'There must be a café somewhere near here. It wouldn't have cost him anything to give us directions.'

Lucy glanced round. The train they had arrived in had moved out, leaving the station silent apart from an occasional bang as something heavy was dropped. The transport office was the only part of the concourse being used. All the other offices had their windows and doors boarded up. The roof had been torn apart and she could see steel beams poking from the walls. Over a roped off section, other girders hung precariously from the damaged structure. A burst of laughter echoed across from the next platform where a party of British troops were offloading wooden boxes from a covered rail van onto a couple of flatbed trucks.

'There are four Tommies over there. They may know where we can get a feed,' Matron Kenny said. She took Lucy's arm, leading her from the office. Vicky and Alex joined them and the rest of the sisters trailed behind.

Further along the platform Lucy could see another party of Tommies rolling large drums from an open rail wagon onto another truck. A large no smoking sign leant against the wagon they were emptying. A couple more trucks were waiting in line for their turn to be loaded.

'Do you know where we can get something to eat?' Matron Kenny asked when they reached the four men.

The soldiers stopped and straightened up. 'Not a clue around here, love,' one man said. He was a corporal with a dirty bandage wrapped round his forehead. His battledress jacket was torn and stained where mud had impregnated the material. He glanced at the boxes they were unloading and a smile spread across his face. He beckoned to the privates, then said to the nurses, 'I think we might be able to do something for you ladies though. We can't offer much, but it'll be better than nothing.'

The first man joined him, the two others a pace behind.

'Got your Froggie tin opener?' the corporal asked.

'You know damn well I have.'

The corporal's smile broadened. 'These boxes are full of cheese. If one fell off the lorry I bet it would split open, and these ladies are hungry.' As he was talking he worked one of the boxes to the edge of the flat tray and it fell, landing on a corner. The wood splintered and a tin rolled out.

The private grabbed it and read the stencilled wording. 'You were right, corp. Cheddar cheese.' He fished in his trouser pocket and pulled out a small folding tin opener.

While he set about opening the tin the corporal said to the other two privates, 'The boxes on that other lorry are biscuits. Go and get a couple.'

'They'll be missed, corp,' one of the men said.

'So what? We only loaded. No one told us to count them.' He turned to the matron and said with a wink, 'Grub's up, ladies. Compliments of the army. Sorry there's no caviar.' He opened his clasp knife and handed it to the matron. 'You might find this helpful.'

Another train came to a halt with a hiss of steam a couple of platforms away. Troops began to disembark and the station was filled with the shouts of men.

The sisters had all grouped behind Matron Kenny. 'You've been real gentlemen, which is more than I can say for some of your officers. Thank you,' she said as the sisters began to slice the cheese. 'You won't get into trouble, will you?'

'Trouble? Not us, love. Fritz is the only one to give us trouble, and he's just as likely to blow this lot sky high before it reaches the front.' He opened another tin as he spoke. 'What you don't eat now take with you. That's the only way you can guarantee you'll have something later.' He ripped another board from the box and began to hand tins of cheese to the nurses. 'Those in charge couldn't organise a bag off in a bro… Sorry. Slip of the tongue. You forgets how to talk to ladies when you're in the front line.'

Lucy suppressed a grin and saw Matron Kenny struggling to stifle her smile. Before the matron had recovered she said, 'We understand. Thank you for your help. This is the only food we've had all day. What about you? Don't you want any for yourselves?'

'Thanks, love, but we're old soldiers. We know our way around. We can always scrounge a feed. Oh, and you'll need this.' The corporal pressed his clasp knife into the matron's hand. She examined it for a moment then frowned. 'To open the tins. The opener on it isn't as good as his Froggie thing, but it works okay. Keep the knife. I'll get another from the QM when I'm back in the unit.'

'Old soldiers?' Vicky said to Lucy as they moved towards the office, following the matron who had gone ahead. 'He doesn't look a day over nineteen.'

Lucy stopped and glanced back to the soldiers who had resumed emptying the rail wagon and loading the trucks. 'They'll grow up quick. A year out here must be like ten in civilian life. Nineteen will be old, but so many of them don't live that long.' She thought of the young boy for whom she'd written the letter. 'I wonder if they'd have volunteered if they'd known what it was like.' She stepped aside to avoid a porters' trolley being wheeled along the platform by a couple of privates.

'Like us, you mean?' Vicky asked as they hurried to catch up with the rest of the party.

'In a way, yes. At least we're doing something positive, and we have a bed to sleep in. Not like those poor souls. All they have is a hole in the ground.'

'A hole in the mud more likely,' Alex said.

'You're getting all philosophical, Lucy,' Vicky said. 'They're young and it's an adventure. Nothing would have put them off.'

Half an hour later Matron Kenny returned from the transport office. 'Gather round, girls.' When they'd settled in a semicircle she continued. 'The area where they're setting up our CCS is being shelled constantly, which is why they've not been able to get it ready for us.' A murmur rippled through the nurses and the matron waited until they were quiet. 'They're sending us to a British CCS until the morning. A convoy of ambulances will be along shortly. That's all I can tell you for the moment.'

'What about this new push at Arras, Matron? Did they say anything about that? I heard some of our Anzacs will be taking part with the Canadians,' one of the nurses said.

'Where did you hear that?'

'Everyone's talking about it.'

'Well, no one should be talking about it. And I don't want any of my nurses spreading gossip like that. If there is any truth in the rumour, we don't want Fritz getting wind of it,' the matron said.

'Is that why they're setting up our own CCS?' Vicky asked. 'So we can take care of our own men?'

'They say the bombardment will begin in a few days,' the nurse who'd mentioned the push at Arras said.

Matron Kenny glared at her. 'I've just told you, none of this loose talk. Next time you hear anything of this sort, tell whoever it is to keep their mouth shut. It's our blokes' lives they're putting at risk. Now no more of this gossip. You're worse than a mob of galahs.'

It was dark before their transport arrived. Lucy, Vicky and Alex scrambled into the same ambulance as Matron Kenny. The canvas top extended to the windscreen, but the sides, also canvas, ended behind the front seats. There were no doors. At the rear, racks for stretchers ran along each side above wooden bench seats. They were the lead vehicle in a convoy of six.

Their driver was a small cheerful man who whistled as he wove his way through the mess of traffic, but for most of the time his whistling was lost in the noise of the engine and bangs and crashes as the ambulance jolted along the corduroy road. Lucy shivered as the wind whipped through the open doorway. Masks had been fitted over the headlights, making them barely powerful enough to illuminate the obstructions and damage. The spatters of mud covering the windscreen made it even more difficult to see, but the driver seemed to avoid the obstacles by some sixth sense. They were forced to stop by a team of Chinese labourers who were working furiously to replace the logs of the corduroy, hurrying to repair a stretch of road destroyed by the enemy shelling. The traffic banked up behind them in a log-jam of its own and it was fifteen minutes before they cleared the damaged section.

'Gets worse than this closer to the line,' the driver shouted, swinging the wheel to the left to avoid a large box. 'Sometimes it's all you can do to keep moving.'

'How close are we?' Lucy asked. She peered through the mud-splattered windscreen at a flare that was slowly descending. As it faded the night to their right was lit up by flames from the muzzles of guns. They were firing so rapidly that the flash of their discharges merged into one continuous line of light. In the distance the explosions of the shells were more dispersed. Some shells were low, and the screech as they flew overhead penetrated the noise of the vehicle, but to Lucy's surprise she was not afraid. She felt detached, a dispassionate observer of a nightmare.

'The CCS I'm taking you to is about three miles back. Others are much closer. Which one will be yours?' the driver asked.

'Number 3, Australian,' Matron Kenny said.

'I may as well tell you, you'll find out soon enough,' the driver said and wrinkled his nose. 'It's less than a mile from the line.' He fell silent as he pulled out to overtake a horse-drawn gun and limber. Once he was clear he continued. 'That's close to the fighting all right. I think it's too close.'

'We need to be close. The earlier we receive the patient the more likely he is to survive,' Matron Kenny said and braced herself as the ambulance swerved to avoid another shell hole and the smell of cordite drifted into the ambulance. 'These roads wouldn't improve a wounded man's chance of recovery.'

When they arrived at the British CCS Matron Kenny said to Lucy, 'Come with me, Sister Paignton-Fox. The rest of you stay here.'

They were greeted by the CO who was accompanied by a flustered and angry English matron who said, 'I don't know why they sent you here. I've nowhere I can put you, not even for a night. We're overflowing with wounded. They should have telephoned before sending you on a wild goose chase. I suggest you go on to Number 3. If they're still not ready when you arrive, you'll be able to help them get organised.'

'Do you need help here?' Matron Kenny asked.

'Thank you, but our own nurses can cope.' The matron was calmer. 'More people would be a hindrance, particularly as you won't know where anything is.'

They passed the entrance to a marquee as they made their way back to their vehicles. In the light from the opening Lucy could see bearers unloading stretchers from a motor ambulance. Large white circles on the sides with bold red crosses defeated the intent of the khaki paintwork, although the mud that covered the vehicle helped to subdue the brightness.

'No room at the inn,' Matron Kenny said to the driver when they reached their ambulance. 'I don't blame these people. Just look at the wounded. That's where their priority lies, so we'll do as they suggest. Do you know the way to where Number 3 is being set up?'

'Too right I do. I've been driving these roads since 1914.' The driver hurried off walking along the line of ambulances, pausing briefly at the cab of each. When he returned he climbed behind the wheel and said, 'I'll get you to Number 3 if I die in the attempt.'

'We'd prefer you not to do that,' Matron Kenny said. 'We're going to be busy enough without you adding to the work load.'

Lucy chuckled. At least Tubs hadn't lost her sense of humour.

The driver laughed and pulled out at the head of the convoy. The road deteriorated and the traffic thickened. They moved over to pass a column of marching soldiers making their way to the front. In the darkness Lucy couldn't see their features, but they were all laden with packs, their rifles slung on their shoulders. A little later they eased over to pass six teams of horses pulling small guns and limbers.

As they slowed Lucy became aware of an eerie whistling overhead. 'What's that noise?' she asked, but the driver was concentrating and didn't reply.

When they'd cleared the guns he said, 'They're field guns, eighteen pounders. There's not usually as much movement as this on the road. They must be getting ready for a stunt.'

'Are they the guns that are firing? The ones making that screeching noise?' Lucy asked.

The driver shook his head. 'Those shells are from Fritz's big how-itzers, they fly way high. That's where they're landing.' He pointed to the flashes in the distance to their left. 'Fritz is giving Poperinghe a right pasting tonight.' After avoiding another shell hole he continued. 'The shells from the field guns are usually shrapnel. They're much faster. You can't hear them until they've passed, and then it's too late.'

A shell exploded ahead, not far from the road, but the driver ignored it. Lucy glanced across to Vicky and Alex, but all she could see were two silhouettes in the dark of the ambulance. For once Alex wasn't burbling on.

Another shell fell close to the road about three hundred yards ahead and Lucy saw several logs leap into the air in the flash of the explosion. 'Don't worry girls. That far away they won't hurt you,' the driver said. 'They make a mess of the road though. It's bad enough without Fritz rearranging the corduroy.' He lapsed into silence again, concentrating as they crept past the crater that the shell had made.

They arrived at Number 3 in the middle of a bombardment, to be greeted by the CO, a lieutenant colonel in the Australian Army Medical Corps. His face registered surprise. 'What are you doing here? We're way behind schedule, nowhere near ready for the nursing staff.' He turned to the driver and asked, 'Which way did you come?'

'By the south road, past Poperinghe, sir.'

'Do you have a death wish?' the CO asked. He stared past the driver towards the road they'd used. 'That road's closed. The Boche have been giving it a real going over all day. What the devil do you think you were doing driving on it?'

'Nobody told us,' the driver said. 'I thought it was a bit hairy, but if Fritz has been targeting it all day he's not done much damage. A few shell holes here and there, but mostly it's no worse than normal.'

'That may be so, but I'll not allow you to go back that way.' The CO beckoned to a couple of doctors who joined them. 'Show these drivers the way to Proven. One of the CCSs there will have beds they can use.'

'When will you be ready?' Matron Kenny asked. 'We've been

passed from pillar to post since we left Calais. I'm sure there's something we can do to help.'

'I sympathise, Matron, but you can't sleep in the mud. Proven is twelve miles back. You'll be safe there, and you'll be more use after a decent night's sleep. Excuse me while I use the telephone. I'll find someone to put you up until we're organised.'

He started towards a tent about twenty yards away. Matron Kenny chased after him.

'Before you go, sir, I've a letter for you from Lieutenant Colonel Rigby.' The matron opened her brief case and pulled out an envelope. 'He was one of the surgeons with the CCS we were attached to.'

The CO read the letter then asked, 'Rigby? Used to be with St Thomas' Hospital?' The CO's voice carried to the nurses and Lucy sat up at the mention of Malcolm Rigby's name. 'That's quite a recommendation from someone as eminent as Mr Rigby. I'll certainly act on his suggestion. We should encourage ability.'

It had turned 0200 hours before they reached the British Number 12 CCS at Proven, but the matron and four nursing sisters were waiting to welcome them. A meal was organised and, after they'd eaten, one of the British sisters led them to a marquee where beds were ready.

'Is this a ward?' Matron Kenny asked.

The sister nodded then said, 'We have nowhere else we can put you. It'll be okay for one night.'

At first Lucy lay unable to relax. Other sisters were also tossing and turning. In the distance the muted explosions were a constant rumble, but too far away to be disturbing and after a while she drifted off to sleep.

It was bright when she woke and the guns were silent. Most of the sisters were still sleeping, but a few were up and dressed. She joined them and they were escorted to the mess by one of the CCS sisters on day duty. Soon they were all up and volunteered to help, but their offer was declined. At 1400 hours they were told that the re-establishment of 3 ACCS had been postponed and that they were to be sent to a general hospital at Étables until the CCS was ready to accept patients.

'I feel as though I'm not wanted,' Lucy said as they boarded the charabanc that had been sent for their transport.

'You'd think they'd be falling over themselves to make use of our expertise,' Alex said. 'It's not as if there's nothing for us to do.'

In daylight the chaos on the roads seemed worse than they had the previous night. A constant stream of traffic was heading towards the front. Guns and limbers, some horse drawn, were interposed between buses packed with soldiers and small cars full of senior officers. Heavy-laden trucks struggled along the corduroy, their engines labouring as they jolted across the logs and planks. Some were fitted with racks packed with shells, others were loaded with boxes. Lucy could see their solid rubber tyres slipping on the muddy timbers, the wheels spinning as they forced their way past the slower moving guns.

Occasionally the sun broke through the clouds, but within seconds it had disappeared again, as if it was reluctant to shine on the devastation below.

The stench of blood, waste matter and rotting flesh was strong. In the darkness of the previous night, Lucy hadn't noticed it, but now it came in waves as the breeze wafted through the windows of the charabanc.

Khaki was everywhere. Squads of marching men hugged the edge of the road in silence. They followed their regimental bands, which were equally silent, as if they'd reached the limit of their musical repertoire. One party was made up of dark skinned men, apart from their white officers, all wearing the British Brodie helmet. Lucy wondered which part of the Empire they were from.

They were part of a line of empty trucks and damaged guns, which were making their way back from the front, threading through squads of trudging infantry. The soldiers, stumbling with exhaustion and with vacant staring eyes, took no notice of the reinforcements heading in the opposite direction. Ambulances, filled with wounded men, dodged the worst of the shell holes. British soldiers chivvied squads of German prisoners who trudged past with grim, strained faces that matched the grey of their uniforms. The guards held their rifles at the port, the muzzles above their left shoulders, bayonets fixed. It would only take a moment to swing them down towards the prisoners. Some of the bayonets were coated with a dark crust. Lucy noticed that the guards' fingers rested near the triggers and she suspected that the safety catches were off. Most of the guards sported blood-stained bandages. Prisoners and guards, like everything else, were caked with mud.

A few Belgian civilians walked in silence with the exodus. Some pulled small handcarts, others had even smaller carts pulled by dogs. In their arms they carried a few precious possessions. One or two carried nothing except a small child, their most precious possession of all. No one smiled.

Lucy looked away from the despair in their faces.

At the side of the road she could see the damaged vehicles that had been pushed aside to clear the path for traffic. Mingled with the wrecked machines were the mangled bodies of horses and mules. She remembered her father's story of Elands River and his determination that none of the horses from Aughton Park would be taken by the army.

'Thank you, Dad,' she said under her breath.

'What was that you said?' Vicky asked.

'Nothing.' She took a deep breath to compose herself before she continued and pointed to four dead horses still harnessed to a shattered limber. 'What have these poor animals done to deserve a death like this? What have they got to do with this war? They must be terrified most of the time.'

'I know it's awful, but they're only animals. It's worse for the men. They know they could die any day,' Vicky said. 'Don't waste your sympathy on dumb animals.'

'How can you say that?' Lucy said. She hadn't expected Vicky to be unsympathetic to the fate of the horses, and had to remind herself that her friend was a city girl who wouldn't have the same affinity for horses as she had. 'The men volunteered. These horses had no choice. It's wrong to subject any animal to these dangers.'

13

Dickebush Rest Camp, Monday, 30 July 1917

John watched the men emerge from the bathhouse. The new reinforcements gathered in nervous groups. The old hands, a mere thirty-three survivors, collected in a single party. They had a confidence and easy comradeship born of shared experiences, but they too were subdued. There had been two hundred and fifty men on the company strength before Messines. The survivors of the men who had been new before that stunt had passed their initiation and were now equals.

He was proud to be their leader, but his pride was overwhelmed by sadness. So many men were missing. Those who had fought on with their wounds had been taken to a CCS and it would be at least a couple of weeks before the first of them rejoined the company. Some would never be back. He crossed to the group of old hands.

'You're a bloody rabble. How the hell do you expect me to lead you into battle in that state?' His face was wreathed in a wide grin and he was wearing a new battledress. 'I'd be ashamed to let Fritz see you in those uniforms.'

'I see you've done all right for yourself,' Lofty said. 'How'd you bag yourself a new suit?' John simply smiled and Lofty continued. 'I see. One rule for the officers, but another for us. You don't have to worry though. We won't hold a grudge if you leave us behind when you next hop-over to say g'day to Fritz.'

'We've been together a long time now, Lofty. It wouldn't be friendly to leave you out of all the fun, but I don't want to be embarrassed. I'll see what I can do about some new clobber.' John beckoned to the company sergeant major. Warrant Officer Carter was new to the company, but he was a career soldier so should know what was required. However, the sergeant major still had to prove himself as far as John was concerned. 'Get on to the quarter master and arrange new uniforms for these men.' He indicated the thirty-three old hands. 'Just these scruffy sods. The new reinforcements are fine.'

Warrant Officer Carter came to attention and saluted. 'Sir.'

'At ease, Sergeant Major. We're not on parade now so there's no need for that bullshit. As soon as everyone is mustered we'll make our way back to the billets. They can have the rest of the day off. No one can say the old hands haven't earned it.'

John stepped back and watched as the sergeant major and the senior NCOs began to assemble the men into their platoons. All the NCOs were new to the company, and there were too few of them. Every one of the original NCOs had been killed or wounded and until the wounded men returned they'd be shorthanded. Only two officers had survived, himself and Lieutenant Leyton, who'd been clobbered by a chunk of shrapnel. Just how he managed to escape unhurt still surprised him, but there was nothing to be gained by dwelling on that. It was the way things were, and he was grateful. New officers were on their way to join them and he wondered what they'd be like, particularly the man who'd take over as company commander.

Number 3 ACCS, Brandhoek, Tuesday, 31 July 1917

'It'll be good to be back together again, and in our own hospital,' Lucy said as their convoy pulled into the compound at 1130 hours.

'They still can't be ready for us,' Vicky said. 'Just look at all those men, they're like a swarm of insects.' She looked at the teams digging a row of shallow circular holes. At a few of the holes, bell-tents had been erected. Other men were filling sandbags with the spoil from the excavations and building walls around the bases of the tents.

'I've never seen that before,' Lucy said. The reason for the sand-bags was obvious, but despite the logic she hoped she was wrong.

To their left, across a railway line, they could see five marquees. More men were raising another marquee at the far end of the row.

Further to their left, beyond a corduroy road, they could see similar frantic activity and on the right, at the far side of another road, ambulances were disgorging wounded at a CCS that was already operating.

Two officers, an Australian Army Medical Corps lieutenant colonel and a major in the British Army Service Corps, greeted them as they climbed from the trucks. Lucy recognised the lieutenant colonel. He was the CO who had sent them off to Proven.

'Good morning, Matron, sisters,' the colonel said. 'I'm pleased to see you ladies, but unfortunately, once again your accommodation is not ready.' He waved his arm, indicating the few bell-tents and the excavations. 'The theatre's not yet ready either. I can't understand why they sent you. Nothing's ready.' He turned to the major and asked, 'What have you organised?'

'We've arranged to use two of the wards as interim accommodation,' the major said. He turned to Matron Kenny. 'I'm sorry, but you'll have no privacy until we have the tents erected.'

'We'll be right, sir.' She turned to address the CO, but looked beyond him to the ward marques. 'We'll be fine in the wards. If they're good enough for the men, they'll do for us.'

'Sorry, Matron. I wasn't having a go at you. Just forgot myself for a moment,' the CO said. 'Please excuse me, but the safety of you and your sisters is just one more thing to worry about. We've been under constant fire since we arrived. They should have known at HQ; I've sent enough signals to appraise them of the situation. Well, you're here now so we'll just make the best of it. I'm not sending you away this time unless the situation deteriorates. If it does I'll have no alternative, and there'll be no arguments about that.'

'Has our baggage arrived?' Matron Kenny asked. 'It was sent on ahead two days ago. All we have with us are our small cases.'

The CO turned to the major, who said, 'We've seen no personal kit, but that's nothing unusual. If people don't keep it with them it often becomes misplaced.' He shrugged. 'I expect it'll turn up in due course.'

The matron pursed her lips. 'All our clothes are in that baggage. We've no clean uniforms, or anything else until it arrives.' She glanced up at the overcast sky. 'We'll probably need the mackintoshes before long.'

The major too looked up at the sky. 'I guess you're right, but transport is rather chaotic and ammunition has precedence above everything else. Your kit will be way down on the priorities. You'll have to make do with what we have for the men until your personal belongings arrive. I'll make enquiries, but don't raise your hopes.'

'Matron, I still have that letter from Colonel Rigby,' the CO said. 'I'll attend to it before we open for business.' He left them and walked towards an officer overseeing the men excavating the holes for the bell-tents.

'This way please, ladies,' the major said. He led them across the railway line and pointed to their right where wounded men were being lifted from two ambulances. 'Number 32 CCS. They've been up and running for days. On the left.' He swung his arm round. 'That's Number 44. They're in the same state we are. Those two smaller camps are the field ambulance units.' He indicated two identical arrangements of tents clustered around a central Nissen hut, one at each side of the complex. 'Since we lost one complete unit at Bray in April, we've taken to splitting the ambulance sections into smaller units.'

Lucy shuddered as she remembered the incident. She looked over to the line of bell-tents and recalled the CO's words '…under constant fire…'

The major noticed her interest and said, 'Digging the pits for your tents has slowed the preparations down, but the sandbags will protect you from shrapnel. It will take a direct hit to do any damage, but you won't be in them during a raid. We're excavating a shelter.'

'A shelter?' Lucy was surprised and frowned. They'd never had a shelter before. Was the CO over-reacting, or had the shelling been heavier than he was admitting?

'That's right. A bombproof shelter. It's almost finished. When it is you'll be safe from the Boche projectiles. We're not taking any risks with you ladies.'

'What about the patients?' Lucy asked. 'We can't run off and abandon them while we hide.'

'The men know the risks and they're used to being under fire,' the major said. 'We'll sandbag the wards as soon as we can, but it will be a while before we can get round to that.'

Lucy stifled a gasp. How could this man be so callous? 'Maybe the men are used to being under fire, but that's no reason to leave them,' she said, but the major ignored her. From the way he'd referred to them it was as if the men weren't human and had no feelings. She'd heard about officers like him from some of the wounded, but this was the first time she'd met one.

The major stopped at the first marquee. 'These are the two wards for your accommodation, this and the next one. While you're sorting yourselves out, I'll make sure that your dining arrangements are organised.'

A medical corps sergeant joined them and the major said to him, 'Issue some bedding to these sisters and see what you can do about greatcoats. Their kit has gone missing.' The major left them without another word.

The sergeant took them to the bedding store where he handed two blankets to each nurse. 'Afraid they're a bit grotty, but we don't yet have a laundry. Some of the equipment has gone astray and we're waiting for the Service Corps to sort it out.'

Most blankets were soiled with blood and mud. Some carried the remnants of other fouling. As she made her way across to the ward with Vicky and Alex, Lucy wrinkled her nose in disgust. 'I won't be sleeping under these. It can't be that long before our kit arrives,' she said.

'What else can we do?' Vicky asked.

'It's not cold at nights, so I'll sleep fully clothed, as if I was on a muster.'

Ypres, Friday, 3 August 1917

'Have a seat,' the colonel said. John lowered himself into the chair with caution. For the CO to ask a man to sit down in his office was unusual.

'Relax, John.' He froze. This had to be something serious.

Commanding officers didn't normally use a man's first name, at least not on duty. The CO was a fair man, but he'd never been this friendly before.

'There's nothing to be worried about,' the CO said. 'You've been promoted. As of now, you're Captain Mitchell and have command of 'C' company. Congratulations.'

'A captain, sir? I've not had the training to be a captain.' John fidgeted in the chair, beginning to sweat as panic set in. 'I don't know how to run a company.'

'I know your training has been limited, but it has no bearing on the matter. You were a senior NCO so you know how to handle men, and you can always refer to me on matters of military law. I need someone in charge who knows the ropes, someone with experience.' The CO jabbed his right index finger towards John. 'You know more than enough to get by as regards discipline and I can think of no one better to lead the men into action.'

'I don't know if I can do it,' John protested. It was one thing to be a lieutenant in charge of a platoon, fifty men at the most, but he'd always had the company commander to advise him. To be in charge of a whole company was quite different. He would be responsible for two hundred and fifty men.

'You've already proved you can do it.' The CO smiled as if he was trying to reassure him. 'When Captain Freeling was killed you stepped up and took command. You're the best man to replace him. You may not have had the formal training, but you've had the experience. That's what counts here. I'll organise more training, but it'll be a while before I can release you.' The colonel leant forward and continued. 'You're a good soldier, John. You'll be fine. The men look up to you. They respect you… I respect you.'

John frowned. 'But, sir, Lieutenant Leyton is senior to me. He'll be a bit put out. He's a career officer.'

'Leyton is too bloody young and he lacks the experience,' the CO retorted. 'If his nose is out of joint, he'll have to learn to live with it. It won't be the last time he'll have to accept that he's not ready for promotion.' The CO began to fiddle with his swagger stick, rolling it backwards and forwards across his desk. 'As a career man, he'll understand. He'll get his chance… if he lives long enough.' He sat back in his chair and fixed John with a scowl. Then he leant forward and his features mellowed. 'I know it's unexpected, and you're full of doubts, but the way you handled the withdrawal at Messines demonstrated your ability. The men appreciate how you took care to ensure the wounded had a chance to reach safety before you withdrew. Before you return to the men, have your third pip sewn on. My batman's outside. He'll do it for you. And it's time you had a batman of your own, so you can think about who that's to be while he's busy. Any questions?'

'Archer, sir. Have you had time to think about my report?'

'That's one of the reason's I've promoted you. You still care about your men, even though they're dead. I agree, it was an act of the highest bravery. I've recommended that his name be forwarded for a VC, but the decision's not mine.'

Number 3 ACCS, Brandhoek, Sunday, 5 August 1917

'I'm so tired,' Alex said and yawned as the sisters left the dining tent after breakfast. 'Those guns didn't stop all night.

'You're not the only one, Lex,' Vicky said. 'I couldn't get to sleep for ages. At least they've stopped now.'

'I can hear planes,' Lucy said and searched the sky. 'There they are. I think they're Fritz.' She pointed to four moving silhouettes approaching from the southern sky. The planes droned closer and dropped lower as they neared the CCS.

'They are Fritz,' Alex said. 'I can see the crosses. I've never seen anything so huge.'

A pair of triplanes appeared from the base of the cloud and dived for the bombers, which turned and headed back to the south with the triplanes in pursuit. The German planes returned four hours later, but they dropped their bombs several miles away and had disappeared before the British fighters turned up. They were back again at 2200 hours, as they had been every night since the nurses had arrived, and this time some of the bombs landed in the vacant compound next to where Number 44 CCS was still being constructed. Apart from a short burst of anti-aircraft fire they were unopposed.

The British heavy guns opened up at 0130 hours, laying down a barrage on the German trenches. Ten minutes later the German artillery replied and a few shells began to land in the compound.

For a while Lucy lay trying to ignore the clamour, but despite her exhaustion she couldn't sleep. She slipped from the bed and left the marquee. Across at Number 32's compound she saw a motor ambulance receive a direct hit while still offloading wounded men. Another shell exploded close to a ward.

Vicky and Alex joined her as the CO arrived. 'Where's the matron?' he asked. The three nurses led the way to her bed where the CO said, 'I want you girls to gather your kit. I'm sending you to Mendighem. Vehicles will be along in a few minutes.' He turned and hurried away.

A few minutes later he rushed back. 'You can't go. The Boche are shelling the road. Get yourselves down into that shelter.'

The shelling reduced at dawn, but it increased again at mid-morning and, as the nurses were eating lunch, a large shell exploded by the perimeter of the compound. The CO was agitated when he appeared.

'It's ridiculous to expose you to this shelling when there are no patients, so this time you are going.' He raised his hands at the outcry that greeted his words. 'I know. I know. You volunteered, but this is too much. Just look at yourselves. You've hardly slept since you arrived. It's all you can do to keep your eyes open and you'll be no help to anyone if you get killed. I'll broach no argument. Number 64 CCS will take care of you.'

It had started to rain during the morning and the corduroy road was greasy with mud and uneven where some logs had been replaced by planks. The truck skittered around shell holes as it rattled along and the sisters, sitting in the back, had to hang on to the framing that held the canvas tilt.

A fine spray of rain swirled in through a tear in the canvas at a front corner and Lucy tugged the collar of her greatcoat higher. She shivered, despite the thick material. The coat was too large, but she was grateful that she had it.

'This driver will kill us if Fritz doesn't,' Vicky said as the truck lurched and lifted a wheel during a violent skid. It recovered and raced on, swerving to avoid another hole, but it had to slow to plough through the mud at a section where the corduroy had been ripped away.

'Don't say that,' Alex said as the rear of the truck slithered sideways and she moved her grip to a stanchion. 'It's scary enough without you adding to my fears.'

'For goodness sake, the pair of you, stop whinging. You're like a pair of frightened schoolgirls. He's only trying to get us clear of the shelling,' Lucy said. 'Does anyone know where this Mendighem place is? I've been looking on my map, but I can't find it anywhere.'

'You won't,' Matron Kenny said. 'It's near Proven, but it's a made up name. There are several CCSs on the site. I think they're all British.'

The shelling eased as they moved further north and the driver slowed until he was driving at a more normal speed. They reached Number 64 CCS without incident.

The English matron was waiting to meet them. 'Oh, you poor dears. You look all in. There'll be a meal ready for you in fifteen minutes,' she said as the other trucks in the convoy pulled to a halt behind them.

The sound of the guns had faded to a faint background rumble and it seemed unnaturally quiet. Lucy was amazed at the contrast the short ride had made. Her nerves were on edge and she was so tense she wondered if she'd be able to sleep, but as soon as she'd eaten her tiredness took charge.

At breakfast Alex said, 'It's so quiet without the guns, almost unnatural. It's surprising what you can get used to.'

'That hop-over was cancelled,' Matron Kenny said. 'That's probably why our guns have stopped. It sounds as if Fritz has had enough too.'

Number 3 ACCS, Brandhoek, Friday, 10 August 1917

The sound of gunfire became louder as they neared the CCS. As the trucks pulled to a halt beside the line of bell-tents, Matron Kenny said, 'I think we'll be staying this time. It looks as if everything's ready at last. Stay here while I check.'

She returned a few minutes later. 'The CO will address us as soon as we've got ourselves organised. Our kit has arrived too, so find your things and get unpacked as quickly as you can. Report outside my tent in an hour.' She pointed to the bell-tent at the end of the line closest to the wards. 'Matron Morgan should be arriving with the rest of the sisters later this afternoon.'

'It's a pity the Moron didn't get lost,' Alex said. 'I'll not be happy to see her miserable face again.'

Each tent was set up in a shallow pit about two feet deep. The wall of sand bags ringing the excavation raised the protection by another three feet.

When they assembled the CO briefed them about a hop-over that was taking place. 'Conditions are atrocious,' he said. 'Deep mud, so the tanks can't support the men, and we're taking heavy casualties.'

Heavy casualties. It's always the same, Lucy thought, and wondered when it was going to end. The senior officers talked about casualties as if they were something abstract, even this CO who witnessed the injuries.

The CO finished his briefing and they were detailed off for their duties. Lucy was assigned to the operating theatre. When she reported, the surgeon in charge, a major in the Australian Army Medical Corps, took her to one side and told her she'd be working with him.

'I have the letter from Colonel Rigby. Welcome to the team, Sister Paignton-Fox.'

'What letter's that?' Lucy asked with surprise.

'Colonel Rigby has explained how you worked with him and recommended that you continue to be used in the same capacity. We would be fools to ignore his opinion,' the major said. 'What's your first name?'

'Lucy, Doctor.'

'I'm Robert Simmons, but call me Bob. We don't stand on ceremony here.' He winked. 'Come and meet the others while it's quiet. You'll know the sisters of course.'

Lucy rejoined the other sisters and they were introduced to the surgeons and the orderlies. When they were allocated their duties, Lucy found herself detailed for nights once again. She was pleased as the shelling seemed heavier at night and she'd become used to her everted existence.

Over lunch she discovered that Vicky and Alex were also assigned to night duties, both working in the surgical recovery wards, so they would probably be caring for the patients she'd helped on the operating table.

They had no patients in the theatre when Lucy started her shift at 2000 hours. She found that strange, particularly as the attack had been progressing all day. An hour later they still had no patients and she made her way to the reception ward.

'What can I do for you, Sister?' Lucy spun round at the brusque words. She hadn't expected to find the Moron on night duties.

'It's so quiet, Matron. I wondered where all the patients were.'

'What do you expect with this weather? The whole front is a sea of mud and the stretcher-bearers can't cope. Most of the men here are walking wounded, but the casualties are building. It won't be long before we'll be busy.'

Five wounded Chinese labourers were brought in as Matron Morgan spoke. Their stretchers were laid on trestles with their bags dumped beside them. The matron crossed to them as the orderlies began to remove their clothes. One man with a shell splinter lodged in his left shoulder protested vehemently, struggling and kicking at the orderly who had started to unfasten his tunic.

'Him no like take off clothes,' one of the other Chinese said. 'Him no take off clothes after come here, Flance.' The orderly had given up struggling with the man and stood back looking puzzled.

'We'll have to cut them off then,' Matron Morgan said. She glared at the man and beckoned to another orderly. 'Give him a hand. And you too,' she said to a third orderly who came rushing over. 'I'm not having this nonsense.'

Two orderlies held the man down and the third wielded a pair of scissors, slicing along the sleeves of the tunic and down the side. A nurse stood by the man's head trying to calm him. He was soon naked and an orderly rushed across to a bin where he dumped the man's clothes. He grimaced, brushing his hands together with vigour as soon as he'd released the bundle, as if wiping them clean.

'What's wrong with you, mate?' one of the orderlies holding the man down asked, then he stepped away from the stretcher.

'Vermin. His clobber stinks. I've never seen so many chats. Gives me the bloody creeps.' The orderly shuddered and the other man laughed.

A moment later the patient reached down to his bag. When he straightened up he had a large kitchen knife in his hand. He swung round towards the nurse, raising the knife ready to strike.

'Watch out,' Lucy called, and stepped towards the stretcher.

An orderly grabbed the man's arm and the other orderly twisted the knife from his hand. 'Forget about those bloody chats, come and help us tie the bastard down,' one of the men called.

'Where did he get that knife from?' Matron Morgan asked.

'He had it in his bag,' Lucy said.

'You still here, Paignton-Fox? If you can't do as you're told I'll have you reassigned to a ward where you'll do some real nursing. Get back to the theatre.'

When the Chinese were brought to the operating theatre, Bob claimed the man with the shell fragment in his shoulder.

'Why is he lashed down?' he asked as two orderlies placed the stretcher on the operating table. 'That's no way to treat a wounded man.'

'He attacked the sister while we were preparing him for theatre,' the orderly said.

Bob raised his eyebrows. 'Come on, man, I want the details,' he said. 'Why did he attack a nurse?'

Lucy was laying the instruments out on the trolley and explained what had happened. 'He's not very big, but he's strong, and he put up a good fight. That's why he's hobbled like a mickey bull.'

'We'll give him the anaesthetic while he's immobile in that case. He'll be quiet enough then. We don't want any ructions,' Bob said.

The Chinese had been taken from the theatre and there was a lull. The rain had stopped and the clouds had broken up, allowing a half moon to spread a fitful light over the camp. Lucy and Bob were taking a breather, standing at the door of the theatre when a *jasta* of German bombers flew over. They were high, heading north, veering towards the east.

'They are so big and there must be at least twenty of them,' Lucy said and looked at her watch. It was 2230 hours.

'They're Gothas,' Bob said. 'I think some of them might be the new GVs, but it's hard to tell in this light. I'd like to know where they've been dropping their bombs.'

His question was answered an hour later when the wounded began to arrive. There were so many injured men that the three CCSs were hard pressed to keep up with the inflow, each taking fifty cases at a time. The wounded were saturated, plastered with mud and so cold that they could have been dead. Often only a weak pulse gave the sisters in the resuscitation ward the indication that a man was still alive. Some of them had died in the field ambulances. Others died of their wounds as the nurses tried to revive them. The sisters and orderlies struggled to get the men out of their uniforms, cleaned up and into beds. As their pulses strengthened, if it was necessary, the patients were sent to the pre-operative ward to be readied for surgery.

When Lucy and Bob checked at the ward to get an idea of how busy they'd be in the theatre, they found one patient waiting for surgery who was stronger than most.

'Where did this happen?' Lucy asked.

'We were getting ready for a stunt against Langemarck when those Fritz bombers came over. There must have been a couple of dozen of the blighters. They gave us a right pasting,' the man said. He lowered his head to the pillow. When he opened his eyes again he said, 'Fritz caught us on the hop all right, no bloody messing about. Bang, bang, bang. We didn't know what hit us.'

The German shelling resumed and Bob and Lucy returned to the theatre. One of the first patients was the man who'd explained about the air raid.

'They'll be sending the ones with the best chance of survival first,' Bob said. 'It makes sense, they'll recover better, but blokes like this could last for quite a while and we could tackle someone who only had a slim chance of making it. We might waste a bit of time, but I think most of them would live with the necessary care. Nothing I can do to change the system, so the sooner we get this bloke out of the way, the sooner some of the others are given a turn.'

As the night wore on, the wounded from the stunt that had taken place during the day began to arrive and for the remainder of the night the staff in the operating theatre had no time to rest.

Lucy straightened up as the sister relieving her arrived. 'I'll be finished here in a couple of minutes.'

'My job, I think,' the sister said. She pulled another swab from the box and dabbed antiseptic on it. 'Go and get your head down. You look as if you need it.'

Shells were landing close to the CCS compound as Lucy made her way to the nurses' mess. Now she was off duty she was nervous and pushed her breakfast away half eaten. She hurried to her tent, keen to get into bed and have the shelter of the sandbags.

The shelling had stopped when she woke. She made her way to the mess for lunch where she found Vicky and Alex in a heated argument. 'What's going on?' she asked.

'This silly moo wants to go across to the front line and what's more she wants us to go with her,' Vicky said and began to cough. When she'd recovered she said, 'Going to the front is fine when the line's quiet, but not with all these shells flying about. She'll get herself killed. That's her privilege, but count me out.' She started to cough again and leant on a table with tears streaming down her face.

'Vicky, what's wrong?' Lucy asked and placed an arm round her shoulders.

'It's that Fritz gas. It's in the men's uniforms so you can't help breathing the fumes. I don't feel hungry anymore. I'm going to bed.'

'I'm worried about Vicky,' Lucy said as they watched her go. 'I'll give her a bit of time, but if she's still coughing when I get to the tent I'm going to find a doctor.'

They joined the queue and as they moved along the counter she said, 'Do you really want to go to the front?' When Alex nodded, she asked, 'Why, for goodness sake?'

'Len's battalion is there. I want to see him. It's not that far, so it won't take long. I just want to make sure he's all right.'

Lucy helped herself to vegetables. What could she do to make Lex change her mind? To oppose her directly as Vicky had done would achieve nothing. 'Do you know where his company is?' she asked. 'It's a fair way to the front, further than you think, and with all this mud it'll take ages. Then you have to find him. Vicky's right, it's not a good idea, Lex.'

'It's the waiting that's hard, not knowing how he is,' Alex said. 'I just want to see him.'

'You'll hear soon enough if he's wounded,' Lucy said. She took a deep breath and closed her eyes. She had only just stopped herself saying 'if he's killed'. 'Think of the women back home. They don't know what's happening to their men and there's nothing they can do about it except wait and pray.'

'But I do know what it's like here,' Alex said. 'That makes it harder.'

'It's not a good idea, Lex.' Lucy no longer felt hungry. 'I'm going to see how Vicky is, then it's bed for me. I think you should do the same. If you don't you'll be useless on the ward tonight.'

14

Number 3 ACCS, Brandhoek, Saturday, 18 August 1917

The explosion was close, and Lucy woke with a start. As she pushed the blanket back she heard thuds at the sandbags that ringed the tent. The silence that followed was soon broken by the faint shouts of men and women. Her heart raced as she climbed from her bed and poked her head through the tent flaps.

The day was bright with sunlight, but just a few yards from the line of tents a roiling mass of smoke rose from a crater. Fragments of shell protruded from the sandbags, and she coughed as acrid fumes snaked around the tent.

A couple of orderlies rushed past with a stretcher and she called out, 'Can I help?'

'Best thing you can do, Sister, is get down to the shelter,' one of the men called back.

Earth and flames shot into the air as another shell exploded somewhere behind the wards and the noise of the blast overwhelmed all other sounds. Ahead of the orderlies she could see another crater, and closer to the railway line the duckboards were in disarray.

Lucy stepped back into the tent and checked her watch. It was 1210 hours. That first shell had been so close. If it had carried a few more yards… She dropped onto her bed as she realised that some of the nurses, friends she knew well, could have been wounded or killed. She could have been killed… She took a deep breath. Other people may not have been so lucky.

Get into the shelter indeed. What did he think they were here for? Lucy glanced across to Vicky, who was still asleep, and she remembered how tired and ill she'd been when they came off duty. She wouldn't disturb her. With the tents sandbagged she was as safe in bed as in the shelter. Unless there was a direct hit, and that could happen anywhere in the hospital. She dressed and hurried along the line of tents and across the railway line looking for Matron Kenny. She found her in the reception tent.

'Can I do anything to help?' she asked.

'You can go back to bed, that's what you can do,' the matron croaked, her voice hoarse. She looked flushed and her eyes were red. 'We have plenty of people on the day roster.' The matron coughed and staggered, reaching out to grab the desk for support.

'Are you all right?' Lucy asked and moved to help her.

'Just do as you're told and go back to bed.' Lucy recoiled at the uncharacteristic harshness in the matron's voice.

As Lucy started towards the entrance the matron said, 'Lucy.' She stopped and turned. 'Thank you, but everyone has their own tasks.'

Lucy lay listening to the barrage as it moved to the east, away from the CCS, wondering if she'd be able to get back to sleep. Fifty minutes later the shelling ended abruptly, but she was still tense.

Alex rushed into tent. 'Lucy, I'm go—'

'Ssh,' Lucy hissed, pointed to Vicky and whispered, 'Don't wake her. You know what she was like when we came off duty.' She slipped out of bed, grasped Alex's arm and led her from the tent. 'What's wrong, Lex?'

'I've heard about this new stunt,' Alex said. 'The men they brought in during the night said there were lots of casualties. I can't stop worrying about Len, so I'm going to find him. I was hoping you and Vicky would come with me. It won't take long.'

'What? Go over to the line, now? Are you out of your mind?' Lucy asked, but she could see Alex was distraught, well beyond reason. A few yards away she could see a squad of men searching the ground around the shell crater. 'That's not a good idea, Lex. Just go back to bed.'

'How can I with all this going on?' Alex said. 'I'd only lie there worrying. I've got to see how Len is.'

Lucy was about to refuse until she saw that Lex was close to tears. 'How are you going to get there?'

'An ambulance driver has promised to take me. He'll be heading back as soon as he's discharged the wounded and refuelled.' She checked her watch. 'Please come with me. Any ambulance will bring us back.' Alex took hold of Lucy's hand. 'I've heard there's another stunt coming up and I just want to see him. Only for a minute.'

Lucy could see her determination, but had one last try to dissuade her. 'A minute or an hour, it won't help. If there's a stunt he won't want you around. You'll only get in the way.'

'I'm out of my mind with worry. Once I see he's all right we can come straight back. Please come. I'll go on my own if you won't.'

It was crazy to go to the front with all this activity, but Lex was a good friend and, if the positions were reversed, she wouldn't hesitate to help. 'You need somebody to make sure you don't do anything stupid,' Lucy said, wondering what could be more stupid than going to the front line right now. 'You're sure about getting back?'

'That's what the ambulance driver said.' Alex dabbed her handkerchief at the tears that were now running down her cheeks. 'Thank you.'

Lucy said, 'We'd better get moving if we're going to catch that ambulance. I'll get dressed.' She stepped back into her tent and Alex followed. Lucy saw that she was wearing her normal shoes. 'You'll need your gumboots. The sun might be shining, but the mud hasn't dried. You'll need your tin hat too, and don't forget your respirator.' She picked up her own as she finished speaking.

They headed across to the transport section where an ambulance was being refuelled. 'That's the one,' Alex said, and waved to the driver.

'How far will he take us?' Lucy asked.

'He'll drop us off near the regimental aid post. That's as close to the front as he's allowed to go.'

A man with his head bandaged walked back from the line. The mud caking his battledress was fresh. 'This bloke may know where the units are,' the driver said as the ambulance slithered to a stop.

'Do you know where we can find Len Devlin?' he asked when the man came round to his side.

The man started to shake his head, but stopped and raised a hand to the bandage. He began to sway and reached out to the ambulance, wincing as he recovered. 'I shouldn't have done that… Devlin… Len Devlin… Sorry, can't help you, mate. What's his unit?'

'He's with the Anzacs, in D company, Number 3 platoon, with

Lieutenant Mitchell,' Alex said. 'I know it's somewhere along this section of the line.'

'Captain Mitchell now. Yeah, over that way, past those stunted trees, about half a mile.' The man pointed to a shell-ravaged copse. 'Why're you asking?'

'Len Devlin's my fiancé,' Alex said. 'I want to make sure he's all right. Can you show us the way?'

'Not on your life. Not while Fritz keeps lobbing shells over. You'll get yourself killed, and if this Len bloke cares anything for you, he'll be frantic when he sees you.'

As if to emphasise his point a volley of shrapnel shells burst behind them, far enough away that they were in no danger, but both Lucy and Alex flinched.

'See what I mean,' the man said and turned to the driver. 'Take them back. You should know better than to bring a couple of women up here in these conditions. Damn bloody stupid.'

'I know, but they were going to walk all the way otherwise,' the driver said. 'At least that one would.' He jerked his thumb towards Alex. 'If you won't show them where to go, they'll go wandering off on their own and get lost. Christ knows what will happen then.'

The man glared at the two nurses in silence, his lips pursed as he considered his options. 'Bloody pig-headed women. I'm on my way out, looking forward to a hot bath and getting cleaned up when I reached the CCS.' He turned to stare back towards the front line. 'Bugger… okay, but you're to do everything I tell you. If I say drop, you drop, and I mean flat on the ground. No hesitation. Right down in the mud. The lower the better. Understand?'

Lucy and Alex nodded.

'I mean that. Everything, without hesitation, and I don't want any ladylike reluctance. Your life will depend on it.' He glared, examining them from head to toe. 'You'll be filthy.' He slung his rifle on his shoulder and set off across the mud.

They'd gone no more than a dozen paces before their skirts and mackintoshes were splattered with mud.

'See those holes?' the man pointed to a couple of shell craters about ten feet ahead. 'If I shout take cover, dive into the nearest hole.

They're the best place when Fritz opens up with his machine-guns. And keep your heads down.'

Lucy stared at the muddy holes with dismay. The man was trying to put them off, she thought.

'Do we have to?' Alex asked.

'Too bloody right we do,' the man said. 'This isn't a soddin' game of footy.' He started to shake his head again, but flinched, breathing deeply. After a few seconds he said, 'You chose a bloody fine time to visit the front line. Why don't we go back before Fritz sorts us out for good? Leave it for another time.'

'No. No. I'm not going back now I've come this far,' Alex said.

The man rolled his eyes then looked at Lucy, who shrugged. 'That's a—' He raised his hands as if surrendering, cocked his head and glanced up at the sky. 'Down. Drop,' he yelled and flung himself into the mud. Lucy did the same, but Alex hesitated. 'Bloody get down,' the man screamed. She heard an explosion as he scrambled to his knees and dragged Alex to the ground a moment before shrapnel pellets whistled over their heads.

'What did I tell you?' he shouted. 'If you won't do what you're told I'm off, and you'll be on your own. Come on, let's get to the trenches before Fritz opens up proper. And next time when I tell you to drop, don't bloody hang about.'

Lucy clambered to her feet and began to shiver as the damp seeped through her clothes. She was appalled at the state of her mackintosh. It was no wonder the men were smothered in mud when they were brought into the CCS.

They had covered one hundred yards when Lucy heard a whistle overhead and the man called, 'Take cover.' The urgency in his voice was clear, and he grabbed their arms, dragging them across to a shell hole with him. As they fell into the crater a gout of mud and a flash of flame erupted about twenty feet from their refuge.

The noise obliterated all other sounds and the earth trembled. Lucy felt the blast of hot gas on her face and snuggled deeper into the mud of the hole, coughing as the fumes from the explosion drifted over them. Almost immediately the man grabbed their hands and dragged them to their feet.

'How did you know to take cover?' she asked.

'You heard the shell, didn't you?' the man said and began to hurry. Lucy struggled to keep up with him.

'Was it that whistle?' she asked.

'That was it. It was a big gun. It was the sound that warned me. It's different with the whiz-bangs, you don't hear them until they've passed. The gas shells are different again.' He checked over his shoulder and Lucy turned to see that Alex was about six feet behind. 'Hurry up,' the man called. 'This isn't a stroll in the park for Christ's sake.'

They had covered five hundred yards with a few sporadic shells landing close, some of them whiz-bangs, and Lucy had stopped worrying about her mackintosh. She glanced across to Alex as they clambered to their feet after the eighth large shell. Her face was white where it wasn't splashed with mud, and her mouth was drawn tight. She'd be just as dishevelled, but she couldn't let Alex go on her own.

The shelling became heavier and the man said, 'Nothing for it now but to run for your life. It's going to be a real shindig.' He set off at a run and they stumbled after him, awkward in their gumboots. Lucy slipped and slithered, almost falling, but she managed to keep her feet and before she realised what was happening raised hands were helping her into a trench.

'What the hell are you doing here?' John Mitchell shouted. His voice was a snarl and his eyes flashed with anger. 'Fritz will be coming over any time and that's enough to be worrying about without a couple of women to look out for. Get into that dugout.' He pushed them towards a set of steps leading underground and followed them down. He turned to the men already in the dugout. 'Out. Use the next dugout. I want a word with these sisters in private. And don't say anything to the others or you'll be in the rattle.'

He waited until the men had climbed the steps. 'Are you out of your bloody minds? What the hell am I going to do?' He fell silent, deep in thought, then he said, 'Stay down here and keep out of the way until I tell you it's clear. I don't want the men distracted.' He turned to the man who'd led them to the trench who was sitting on the steps nursing his head. 'What happened to you?' Lucy saw John examining the man's bandages.

'Shrapnel, sir. Hurts like hell.'

'Then stay with them, and make sure they remain here or you'll be on a charge. And you'd better have a good explanation.'

'It's my fault,' Alex said. 'My fiancé is here and I was so worried I had to see him. He's Len Devlin. Lucy only came to keep me company.'

'You wanted to see your fiancé, so you come traipsing into a front line trench in the middle of a battle like some selfish child. You don't have the sense you were born with. As for you…' Recognition crossed his face. 'Lucy isn't it? You just came along to keep her company. For Christ's sake, what the hell were you thinking about? I would have thought you'd seen enough wounded men to realise the dangers.' The barrage was heavier now and John paused at the bottom of the steps. 'I can't send you back in this. Keep out of the way until things quiet down. I just hope Fritz doesn't pull a stunt. The last thing I need is a couple of dead nurses.'

As he rushed up the steps a dark grey shape raced across the floor, close to the wall, and disappeared into a corner. For a moment Lucy thought it was a cat, but then she saw the long scaly tail.

Alex stared wide-eyed at the corner where the rat had disappeared. 'What do they live on?'

'They get stirred up when there's a barrage going on, but the little sods get all over the shop when it's quiet, especially in no man's land,' the man at the steps said. 'They find plenty of meat out there.'

Alex gasped. 'That's awful.'

John had been gone a couple of minutes when Len Devlin rushed down the steps. 'What are you doing here, Lex?'

Alex flung herself into his arms. 'I was so worried. I had to see you were all right.' She began to sob.

'I was fine,' he said, caressing her, 'but what the hell do I do now? Lex, you shouldn't have come. It was bad enough knowing you were sometimes shelled at the CCS, but here…' He kissed her and wiped the tears from her cheeks as she calmed. 'I wish you weren't here.'

Corporal Lofty Mathews saw John Mitchell hurry along the trench towards him. Most of the men were in the dugouts sheltering from the barrage. He was one of the few on the firing step watching across no man's land. 'Was that a couple of nurses I saw?' he asked as John passed him.

'Never mind about them, Lofty, and keep it quiet. It'll be best if the others don't know they're here. Keep your eyes peeled and make sure everyone has a full magazine. Fritz is up to something.'

John passed on and Lofty heard him calling down to each dugout as he reached it, 'Fix bayonets and charge your magazine.' He wondered if the second part of the order was necessary, but John was only doing his job and some of the new blokes may have forgotten to check.

The German shells fell closer as the barrage began to concentrate on the trench and a large shell exploded in front of the parapet. Lofty crouched, pressing against the trench wall. He coughed on the fumes and raised his head again when the rain of dirt subsided, but ducked back immediately as a brace of shrapnel shells straddled the trench. Pellets zipped into the parados and parapet, but most whistled harmlessly overhead. As they cleared he peered over the parapet to see more shells carving holes in the ground around their wire. John was right, he thought, and watched the wire settle again, even more entangled than before. He was glad that for once it would not be him fighting through the barbs.

The shelling stopped abruptly and he heard John hurrying back along the trench urging men onto the fire-step, but most of them had vacated their dugouts before he reached them. A Lewis gun was lifted into position beside Lofty as the first grey-clad figures materialised at the far side of no man's land.

The machine-gunner opened up with long bursts and, as the enemy moved closer, the sharp cracks of Lee Enfield rifles blended with the stutter of the Lewis guns into one continuous cacophony of noise. Every man was firing his rifle as quickly as he could work the bolt and re-aim. Frequently a man would push a couple of chargers of ammunition into the magazine then continue the slaughter with barely a pause in his shooting.

The Germans were still coming, but there were fewer grey-clad forms. The first wave of the attack reached the wire where they were met by a volley of Mills grenades. Not one German reached the trench, but several of their stick grenades caused casualties. Now the men in khaki were fewer too and in the trench the stretcher-bearers struggled to cope.

The second wave had reached the wire. Some attackers had scrambled over their dead comrades to cross it and had reached the trench.

Lucy and Alex were applying a field dressing to a man's leg when Alex screamed and dashed away, leaving Lucy to finish wrapping the bandage. She paused and looked up in surprise to see Alex grab a spade as she ran towards a melee further along the trench.

'Lex, what are you doing?' she called. 'Come back.'

But Alex was already well along the trench, then Lucy saw Len Devlin struggling to ward off two Germans. He tripped and one of the Germans rammed a bayonet into his throat.

Everything seemed to be happening in slow motion. Lucy thrust the bandage tails into the wounded man's hand. 'Finish it yourself,' she said, and rushed towards her friend.

Alex flew at the Germans from behind, raised the spade and swung it down at an angle. The edge caught one German across his neck. The man's head flopped to the side as he slipped down to the floor, blood spraying over Alex and the second German. The man swung round and Alex brought the pointed blade up under his chin. He slumped, falling across Len.

Two more Germans appeared in the trench beyond Len, but they hesitated when they saw Alex. The bloody spade flashed again. The nearest man fell and the last turned, trying to escape, but he stumbled as Alex swung the spade and the blade sliced through his upper arm. Lucy was amazed at the force Alex was using. How could someone so small have so much strength?

Another German dropped into the trench behind Alex and drove his bayonet through her back, skewering her to the timber shuttering. For a few seconds he struggled, unable to withdraw the bayonet, then he pulled the rifle free, abandoning the bayonet, leaving Alex pinned to the wall.

Lucy was flung aside by an Australian corporal who ran past, swearing. 'You bastard, Fritz,' the corporal screamed and rushed at the German. 'Attack a woman, and a nurse at that. You're a heap of dog's turd.' The German swung round and raised his rifle, but he was too slow. The corporal drove his bayonet into the man's stomach and, in a frenzy, continued to ram the bayonet again and again into his body long after he was dead. The corporal collapsed against the trench wall, trembling and gasping for breath.

Lucy scrambled to her feet and rushed to Alex, who still clutched the bloody spade, but she could find no pulse. Len was sprawled on the floor of the trench beneath two of the Germans Alex had killed. He too was dead. She glanced round, but she could see no living Germans in the trench and tried to pull the bayonet from Alex's body, hoping to lower her, but it was too firmly embedded in the trench wall. Bile rose in her throat and she felt tears well… Alex dead. She took a deep breath, wiped her mouth and forced back her tears. There'd be time to grieve later, but now there were wounded who needed her help.

The corporal who had dispatched the German was still leaning against the wall of the trench, breathing deeply.

'Are you hurt?' she asked.

He shook his head. 'Just mad at those Fritz bastards. I can't abide men using violence against women.'

'They've turned,' came a shout. 'They're running. Give them a hurry-up.'

The corporal straightened up and sprang onto the fire-step where he began to fire his rifle, working the bolt furiously. The rifle fire increased and a few men threw Mills grenades after the fleeing enemy.

Through bleary eyes Lucy became aware of the extent of the butchery. If this was life for these men it was no wonder so many of them were in shock when they reached the CCS. For the first time she noticed the stench of voided bowels, mingled with a faint sweet smell.

She crouched to help a wounded man who was trying to tie his field dressing around his upper arm. When she'd secured the tails she asked, 'How do you feel?'

'I'll be jake, Sister,' he said. 'Check out my mate. He needs your help more than me.' He pointed to a man sitting on the floor of the trench a couple of feet away. He had a blank expression on his face, which was streaked with blood.

Lucy discovered a deep gash above the man's ear. The field dressing was inadequate, but it stemmed the worst of the bleeding. As she tied it off the man whose arm she'd dressed said, 'Thanks, Sister. I'll get him to the aid post. There's another bloke who needs your help.' He pointed to a man lying on the fire-step with his hands clasped over his abdomen, then dragged his mate's arm across his shoulders.

She pulled the new patient's field dressing from his pocket, unfastened his tunic and pulled his shirt up to expose a gaping wound across his stomach. The dressing was totally inadequate, but it was all she had. She held it centrally over the wound with one hand and was trying to feed the bandage tails around the man's torso when a man asked, 'Are you all right, Sister? You're not injured?'

She glanced up to find John Mitchell watching her with concern. 'I'm fine, but I need more of these dressings. Can you get some for me? Quick now, it's urgent.'

John detailed a man to find the field dressings, and pulled his own from his pocket as two stretcher-bearers arrived. They produced a large dressing and Lucy stood back to allow them space to work.

'Thank Christ you're not injured. One dead nurse will take enough explaining,' John said.

Lucy stepped aside so that the stretcher-bearers could lift the man they had just bandaged onto a stretcher. A bundle of grey fur dashed along the fire-step, ran up the back of a man and jumped onto the parapet before he had time to react. As it disappeared she saw the long scaly tail and shuddered.

'That another rat?'

John nodded. 'There're hundreds of the buggers. The shelling drives them crazy. Hate the bloody things. Now I want you out of here, *toute de* bloody *suite*.'

'I'll go with these bearers. We need to get him to surgery as soon as possible.'

'Get a move on then. They can take you to the aid post and someone will see you to the advanced dressing station. From there cadge a ride in his ambulance.' He stepped away as if to leave, but turned back. 'It was a bloody stupid time to come into the line. The men have enough to worry about.'

Lucy glanced across to see that Alex had been lifted down and was lying on the fire-step. 'What about Lex?' she asked, pointing to Alex's body.

'She's dead. We've the living to attend to before we give the dead any thought,' John said. 'I'll get her body back to the CCS as soon as I can. Now get out of here.'

She followed the stretcher-bearers along the trench in silence. What was she going to say to Tubs?

The German shelling resumed as they made their way to the regimental aid post and the ground around the trench was a mass of flying dirt and shell fragments. The bearers were following a communication sap where they were protected from most of the flying shrapnel, but they had to tilt the stretcher to manoeuvre it round some of the corners of the traverses. At a new section, where the trench bypassed shell damage, the corners were still sharp and too tight to negotiate no matter how they held the stretcher. The bearer at the front turned to his mate and nodded. Without a word they clambered out over the parados to the exposed ground at the back of the trench. Lucy scrambled out behind them. A salvo of shells hit the ground near them, but despite the flying projectiles the bearers walked steadily, trying to minimise the jolting.

Lucy walked at the side of the stretcher, ignoring the shells that landed close, wishing she could relieve the man's pain. She was clumsy in her gumboots, and slipped on the muddy surface as she struggled to keep up with the stretcher. The patient relaxed and she called out, 'He's passed out. You can hurry now.'

The bearers continued at their steady pace, somehow avoiding injury as the shells exploded around them. As soon as they cleared the new section they dropped back into the trench. Now that Lucy had protection from the shrapnel, she realised that she'd been concentrating so much on the wounded man that she hadn't felt frightened while exposed. She began to tremble, but pulled herself together, following the stretcher, trying to see how the injured man was faring and thinking about the courage of the bearers. These men faced the same dangers many times a day, yet they hadn't hesitated to clamber into the open to get their wounded mate to the aid post.

They turned a corner and, to the side of the sap, Lucy saw the heavily sandbagged regimental aid post. They could only have travelled two hundred yards, maybe a bit more. She hadn't realised the aid posts were so close to the action.

As she passed through the doorway she noticed the rolled up blanket fixed above it. It was soaked and dripping. A gas blanket, she realised, which would have been saturated with caustic soda. She followed the bearers past a second blanket at the far end of the entrance tunnel and into a small chamber where they placed the stretcher on a pair of trestles.

The light was poor, despite four hurricane lanterns that hung from the roof. The musty smell of damp earth was strong, laced with that of disinfectant, but Lucy could detect an underlying rancid odour, which she guessed came from blood that had soaked into the earth floor. The sound of the exploding shells was muted, but the vibrations were more noticeable than on the surface.

The MO joined them as an orderly began to remove the dressing. 'What the hell are you doing here, Sister?' he asked. 'Never mind, but seeing as you are, you can make yourself useful, administer the tetanus antitoxin and stand by with the morphine in case he recovers. The orderly by the exit will give you what you need.' He pointed to a man working near another door opposite the entrance.

Lucy administered the injection and joined the MO as he examined the patient. An orderly had wiped most of the mud from the man's abdomen, but the flesh was still filthy. 'Can I help, Doctor? I work in the operating theatre, so I'm familiar with what's required.'

'That'll be good, but we don't have time for flash surgery. All we do here is patch the men up so they can hopefully make it back to better care.'

With her help the MO tied off the major vessels and stopped the worst of the haemorrhaging. They were soon finished and Lucy stepped back to give the MO room to apply a fresh dressing.

She examined the aid post. To her right was a set of racks for stretchers, which could be placed three high with curtains to screen them from the rest of the post. In the central section, as well as the trestles that the stretcher now occupied, she could see a row of benches. A couple of men sat waiting for treatment. On the opposite side, shelves and pigeonholes were filled with bottles, dressings and instruments. Two bunks were set up in a small compartment to her left and a second compartment was furnished with a single bunk and a table. That would be for the MO.

The MO straightened up from the patient and joined Lucy. 'This man's on his way to the rear as soon as the orderlies have finished, we can't wait with an abdominal injury. I'm sure you realise that.'

Lucy nodded.

'Which CCS are you with?' he asked.

'Number 3, Australian.'

'Good. You're going with him. It'll get you back to where you belong and it'll be useful to have a nurse to care for him on the way. It'll be rough going. The bearers will take him to the advanced dressing station so there's not much you can do during that part of the evacuation. That's about six hundred yards. From there a motor ambulance will take you back, so you'll come into your own then. Can you cope with that?'

Lucy nodded again. She was too nervous to speak.

'Right, my girl, time to clean up,' the MO said and began to wash his hands. Tell me what you were doing in the front line, but make it quick. I've other men to attend to.' When Lucy finished her explanation he shook his head. 'I'll never understand women. That was an extremely stupid thing to do. Your friend got herself killed because of it. Her fiancé too, probably. You were very lucky.'

'I'm aware of that, Doctor. It won't happen again.'

'I should hope not,' the MO said. 'Whom do you work with?'

'Major Robert Simmons.'

'I know Bob. He's a good mate, but I have a feeling your matron is going to be rather angry. I'll give you a note for Bob expressing my appreciation for your help. He might be able to intercede on your behalf. You're going to be in for a serious dressing down, and quite rightly too. What's your name?'

'Lucy Paignton-Fox. I couldn't let Alex come on her own, Doctor.'

'I suppose not, Lucy.' The MO scribbled a note, folded it and handed it to her. 'Good luck.'

The orderlies had completed the dressing and covered the patient with a blanket. The MO beckoned to the bearers who came over, lifted the stretcher down from the trestles and set off through the exit door.

Lucy followed them along the communication sap. The German gunfire was still heavy, but most of the shells were falling around the front line.

The advanced dressing station was a larger version of the aid post, built of curved corrugated iron embalmed in sandbags, but the bearers made straight for the ambulance parked on the corduroy road. Lucy climbed aboard and the ambulance moved off.

Even at the ambulance's slow speed the corduroy made for a rough ride. Lucy heard a German shell explode nearby and a piece of shell casing cut through the thin sheet steel of the ambulance body, narrowly missing her, ripping another hole as it disappeared through the opposite side. Shrapnel pellets rattled on the bodywork, raising a rash of pimples as if the ambulance had developed acne. She held her breath, hoping that they didn't receive a direct hit, thankful that it was not one of the older canvas-bodied vehicles.

The wounded man groaned as the ambulance swung round to avoid an obstruction. He groaned again and Lucy pushed open the small communication panel and called to the driver, 'Can you slow down? I need to give him morphine.'

'How slow?' the driver asked.

'If you can stop for a moment that will be good,' Lucy said. She prepared the injection as the driver braked and as soon as the ambulance came to a halt, she pulled the blanket away from the man's shoulder and jabbed the needle through the uniform into his upper arm. 'Okay. Away you go. I've finished,' she called. The driver accelerated away as if to make up for the time he'd lost, although it was no more than seconds.

The patient was glassy eyed, but his moaning had stopped and Lucy made a note about the morphine on the tag tied to his ankle.

When they reached the CCS, the doctors would need to know how much of the drug she'd given him, and the time of the injection.

She was relieved to be on her way back, but she wasn't looking forward to meeting Tubs.

15

Number 3 ACCS, Brandhoek, Saturday, 18 August 1917

Lucy entered the tent that was the matrons' office, but hesitated when she saw Matron Morgan sitting behind the desk, writing in a ledger. 'I'm looking for Matron Kenny. Do you know where she is?'

'She's ill,' Matron Morgan said, then lifted her head. 'Oh, it's you, Paignton-Fox.' She sat back, her eyes wide with surprise. 'You're filthy, a disgrace. Go and get cleaned up at once. You're on duty in…' she checked her watch, 'fifty minutes. I'll see you when you're presentable. What did you want to see Kenny about anyway?'

Lucy was tempted to leave without saying anything, but she had to report Lex's death. 'Sister Spence. She's been killed.'

'Killed? What do you mean, killed? How?' The matron raised her head, her eyes blazing.

Lucy stepped back at the aggression in her voice, but she steeled herself. After the trauma of the afternoon she wasn't going to be intimidated by this woman. 'We were at the front when a German attack came through.'

'At the front?' The matron's face flushed red. 'What the devil were you doing at the front?'

'Sister Spence was worried about her fiancé and she asked me to keep her company while she went to check that he was all right.'

For several seconds the matron continued to glare at Lucy in silence, then she said, 'I find that hard to believe, Paignton-Fox. I've warned you before, and now you're hiding behind a dead sister as an excuse for your own stupidity. Kenny's been too lax with you, but I'll not permit it. It's time you started to do some real nursing instead of making eyes at the surgeons in the operating theatre.' She fell silent, frowning, then said, 'I should suspend you from duty pending a discipline hearing, but we have too few nurses, so I'm assigning you to the surgical recovery ward. Now get cleaned up.' She glanced at her watch again. 'You've forty-five minutes before your duties start. I'll advise the theatre you've been redeployed. Report to me when you come off duty.'

Lucy staggered under the verbal onslaught, then she became angry. How could this woman make such unfair accusations? 'I've told you the truth, but you're so biased you wouldn't believe me whatever I said. You've never liked me.'

'How dare you speak to me like that? You've been a troublemaker since the day you joined, and now you're lying.'

Lucy clenched her fists and moved closer to the desk, but she hesitated, breathed deeply and left the tent. It would be futile to argue against such animosity.

She met one of the other nurses from the theatre as she made her way to the ward. 'Can you give this to Major Simmons, please? And tell him I've been moved to the recovery ward.' She gave her the note from the doctor at the aid post.

Lucy performed her duties automatically, ignoring the questioning glances of the other nurses, and only spoke when forced to do so. The sky was brighter, and there had been no new admissions for a while. She was turning off a hurricane lamp when she was startled by a male voice behind her.

'Not pleasant at the front, is it, Lucy?' She swung round to find Bob Simmons. 'Sorry about your friend, but at least you were able to do something useful. I have Roland's note. He was pleased to have your assistance. How do you feel?'

'I feel drained, Bob, but surprisingly, not physically tired.'

'I know what you mean, but you'll notice it later.' He took her arm and led her through the door out of the ward so they were alone. 'Why have you been moved from the theatre? You were doing so well. Is it because you went to the front?'

Lucy nodded and explained, 'Matron Morgan hasn't liked me since we first met.'

'And she wouldn't believe you?'

Lucy shook her head.

'Leave it with me.' Bob turned, but swung back. 'By the way, the man you brought out is recovering well. I thought you'd like to know.'

Lucy made her way to the dining room hoping to see Vicky, but there was no sign of her. After breakfast she made her way back to their tent. She could hear coughs as she neared it. When she entered, Vicky was red-eyed with tears streaming down her face and the backs of her hands were covered in blisters.

She had been carrying out extra duties in the acute gassed wards for the last couple of weeks.

'Why are you crying?' Lucy asked. This wasn't the time to tell her about Lex.

Vicky looked up in surprise and keeled over in a bout of coughing. When she sat up she wiped her eyes. 'I'm not crying,' she said, her voice barely audible as fresh tears trickled down her cheeks. 'At least, not the way you think. That new mustard oil gas that Fritz has is a shocker…' She broke off, coughing and gasping for breath. 'The gas is in the men's clothes and it gets down your…' She fell back on her bed in another spasm of coughing.

Lucy was about to ask why Vicky hadn't been wearing her respirator, but checked herself. It would be difficult working in one and bedsides, how would the patients react? They'd already been gassed and would be terrified.

After Vicky's cough subsided she struggled to her feet and steadied herself against her bed. 'I can't abandon them, they're in such agony despite the ointment, and some need the oxygen so badly.' She shuddered, took a single staggering pace then sat down, her hands over her eyes. 'I feel so useless. The men have burns and blisters everywhere and bathing them only relieves the pain for a few seconds. Now my eyes are burning I can understand how they feel. They're in agony. Some of them are hurting so much we have to strap them to their beds to prevent them harming themselves. The only thing that seems to help is the cocaine. It cuts me up when I hear them whimpering like injured animals, yet with normal wounds they are so stoic.' She began coughing again. When she recovered she said, 'My throat's so sore.'

With difficulty Lucy suppressed her panic and took Vicky's arm. 'You know what we were told. Come on, I'll bathe your eyes.' Vicky rose with Lucy's help, but immediately collapsed to sink back on her bed, coughing and gasping for breath.

'It's the MO for you, Vicky,' Lucy said. 'Up you get. Lean on me.'

'I don't need the MO. I'll be fine in a minute.' Vicky pulled away, wriggling backwards on the bed.

'Just look at the state you're in. You're no good to anyone. If you don't see a doctor you'll be as bad as the men you've been treating. Up you get.'

Lucy reached for her arm again, but Vicky evaded her outstretched hand, curling up and shaking her head.

'Don't be so stupid.' She had to do something to jolt Vicky out of her denial. 'I've just lost one friend through stupidity. I don't want to lose another.'

Vicky stared at her, her mouth slack and her eyes wide open. She leant forward. 'What do you mean, you've just lost one friend?'

'Lex. You know she wanted to go to the front. She was killed.' Lucy crouched down, folded her arms around Vicky and struggled to suppress her tears. She felt Vicky's arms creep round her waist and her grief overcame her will. For a few minutes the two nurses sobbed in harmony, then Lucy pulled away. Vicky was still in tears.

Lucy took a deep breath. 'Look, you can't continue breathing that gas, you'll be dead too if you don't get help. We have to look out for each other. I don't care what you say, I'm going for a doctor.'

She was back a few minutes later with one of the doctors from the acute gassed wards and two orderlies.

'I told you, I don't want a doctor. I don't need a doctor,' Vicky said, and was immediately wracked with coughing.

'I'll be the judge of that,' the doctor said. 'Lucy's done the right thing. Come on, let me check you out.'

Vicky's resistance evaporated and she allowed the doctor to complete his examination without further protest. 'This is more serious than you think, young lady. You'll need specialist care for several weeks, so it's base hospital for you.' He turned to the orderlies. 'That ambulance train is for Boulogne, isn't it?'

'Yes, sir. Number 13 General Hospital. It's due to depart in forty-five minutes.'

'Good. Get her on it, and make sure she's private. I'll speak to Matron and organise a nurse to travel with her.' As the orderlies hurried away to get a stretcher he turned to Lucy and said, 'Can you pack some clothes for her? I think it'll be seven weeks at least before she's back.'

'I'd like to go with her, doctor. We're mates and she'll feel happier with me than anyone else,' Lucy said.

The doctor frowned. 'You're on the night roster aren't you?' Lucy nodded. 'I understand you wanting to take care of a friend, but you look whacked. Matron can arrange for someone from the day shift.'

The doctor left and Vicky said, 'Thanks, Lucy. That would have been nice, but the doctor's right. I'll be okay.' She collapsed, coughing. When she recovered she said, 'Have you noticed that doctors talk about patients as if they can't hear what's being said? I'd never given it any thought before. What happened to Lex?'

'It's a long story and there's no time to tell you now. She'd dead, and so is Len. I'll write with the details, so let me know your address as soon as you're settled.'

The two orderlies reappeared with a stretcher and carried Vicky off to the train. Lucy was still packing her clothes when Matron Morgan appeared with one of the day sisters who began to help Lucy with the packing, then she set off for the train with the case.

As soon as they were alone, Matron Morgan said, 'I told you to report to me when you came off duty, Paignton-Fox. Why do you never do as you're ordered?'

'It was more important that I organised a doctor to examine Vicky than to see you. I don't see the point of talking to you. You'll never believe what I say.'

'That's the last straw. Short staffed as we are, I'm going to recommend that you're removed from duties for your unsatisfactory conduct and lies. You'll see the CO.'

'I'll look forward to that. I'm sure he'll be interested in what I have to say about you.' Lucy stepped towards the matron and raised her hand to push an errant lock of hair back from her face. The matron backed away, her face filled with alarm, and rushed from the tent without a word. 'Go find a shell hole and drown yourself,' Lucy called after her.

Number 3 ACCS, Brandhoek, Monday, 20 August 1917

John Mitchell, with Lofty, Muscles and Don arrived as the nurses were finishing breakfast. 'We've come for the funeral of the sister who died in the line on Saturday,' John said.

'You've wasted your time, Captain,' Matron Morgan said. 'We don't have her body, so we can't bury her.'

'It's in the ambulance, with her fiancé's. We thought her friends would want to say goodbye. They should be buried together, and better here than at the front where their bodies will be thrown up in the next barrage. We can't spare much time, so we'll get started on the grave. If you wouldn't mind making the arrangements for the service, we'll see you in the cemetery. Give us half an hour.'

The CO joined them as the nurses assembled round the wide grave and the men lowered Alex's body into it. Len's body was placed at her side as the padre intoned a prayer. Within fifteen minutes the grave had been filled and Lofty and his mates made their way across to the ambulance, which was waiting to take them back to the front.

'She was a brave woman,' John said, indicating the fresh grave. He had stayed with Matron Morgan. Behind the matron he could see the rows of white painted crosses, each marked with the basic details of the man in the ground. He ran his eyes over the markers as he would have done with a mob of bullocks. There must be five or six hundred, he thought. Five or six hundred men who'd never see their families again. And this was only one of the cemeteries that marked the site of each CCS. They'd be the only reminder of the suffering when the CCS moved on. He swallowed and blinked. At least these families knew what had happened to their men.

'She was a silly woman,' the matron said. 'She'd no business going to the front line with Sister Paignton-Fox. If she hadn't been so stupid she'd still be alive.'

'You might be right,' John said. 'She's dead though, so let's not have any harsh words. As far as I'm concerned she's a heroine the way she reacted. The men think so as well.' He turned and saw Lucy, who was in tears as she was led away from the grave by two nurses. 'That one too. She did a lot of good work with the wounded.'

'They had no business being there,' Matron Morgan said. 'It was stupid.'

John turned back to face the matron. 'I couldn't agree more, but they were there. They handled themselves well and the men were inspired.'

'So you think it would be a good idea to have a nurse in the front line?' the matron asked.

'Goodness gracious, no I don't. A few of the advanced dressing stations have a sister attached, but that's far too close to the fighting.' He stopped and surveyed the tents of the CCS. 'This is too close in my opinion.' He pointed to the shell holes that dotted the ground. 'You should be much further back, out of range of Fritz's guns.'

'Even if we were further back, the bombers would still reach us,' Matron Morgan said. 'We just have to put up with it.'

'Bastards,' John said under his breath and started after his men, but the CO intercepted him.

'Excuse me. Captain Mitchell, isn't it?' He held out his hand.

John nodded as he took hold. 'Yes, sir.'

'I realise you're in a rush to get back, but if you can spare a few minutes I'd like to ask some questions.'

'Certainly, sir.' It had to be about the death of the nurse and John wondered what was coming.

'Do you know why the nurses were there? I'd like an independent assessment, verbal for the moment, but if you could follow it up with a written report, I'd appreciate it.'

'Not a lot to it. The sister who died, Sister Spence, wanted to see her fiancé. She was worried about him. Sister Paignton-Fox came along to give her moral support.'

'Are you sure about that?' the CO said.

'Definitely. I tore them off a strip for arriving when they did. I feel bad about that now. They weren't to know Fritz was about to pull a

stunt. Sister Spence told me herself that she was the one who insti-
gated the visit. Sister Paignton-Fox tried to dissuade her.'

'That's all I need, but in writing. It could end up as evidence in a
disciplinary hearing.'

That set off alarm bells in John's head. 'Is Sister Paignton-Fox in
trouble?' he asked. 'She was only standing by her mate.'

The CO hesitated before he said, 'Not Sister Paignton-Fox, but
that's confidential. If you'd let me have your report at your earliest
convenience, I'll appreciate it. Just the facts, as you've told me.'

John glanced towards the matron who was making her way across
to the line of marquees. 'Best I do that while I'm here, sir. It won't
take long. I could be dead before I'm back in the line. I'll let my men
know I'll be a few minutes. They can find themselves a cup of tea.'

Number 3 ACCS, Brandhoek, Monday, 20 August 1917

'Thank you for coming so promptly, Matron,' the CO said as Matron
Morgan entered his office tent. It was 1830. He did not invite her to
sit.

'What's so urgent, sir?'

'I'm concerned about your handling of the death of Sister Spence.
Please explain the steps you took to investigate the incident.'

The matron bristled. 'Investigate? What was there to investigate?
It was obvious to me that Paignton-Fox had persuaded Sister Spence
to accompany her on a stupid jaunt. Paignton-Fox has always been a
prima donna and has been given too much leeway.'

The CO studied the matron before he said, 'If you had made
enquiries, you would realise that you are wrong. I have talked to the
ambulance driver who took them forward, and he assures me that
the person to request his assistance was Sister Spence.'

'That can't be true,' Matron Morgan snapped. 'The man must
be lying. I can't think why. Matron Kenny is far too lenient with
Paignton-Fox, allowing her to spend all her time in the theatre. She
has got above her status and thinks because…'

'Let me stop you there, Matron. Captain Mitchell confirms the ambulance driver's story. When he questioned the two nurses, Sister Spence admitted that she was the one to initiate the visit. Are you going to question the word of an officer?'

'He must have misconstrued what she said.'

The CO sat back, frowning. This was not developing the way he'd hoped, but from what he'd learnt during the day, he was not surprised. 'Matron, I have two totally independent witnesses who confirm Sister Paignton-Fox's account; neither has any reason to lie. It seems to me that you are allowing your personal animosity to influence your actions.'

Matron Morgan's eyes widened and she stiffened. 'What do you mean, my *personal animosity*?'

'During the day I have talked to all the sisters on duty and it is clear to me that you have favourites that you treat with consideration, and others whom, for some reason, you dislike. It is common knowledge that Sister Paignton-Fox is one of the latter. That is not an attitude that I expect in a person placed in authority. Impartiality is paramount. What have you to say?'

Matron Morgan frowned and said, 'I think you've been talking to the wrong people. Many of the nurses don't like me because I'm strict. They are given too much free rein by Matron Kenny and resent my discipline as a result.'

'You should remember, Matron, that the nurses are not children. They are all adults and volunteered for this dangerous duty. They should be treated with respect.'

The matron reached forward and began to pull a chair back from the CO's desk.

'I didn't invite you to sit, Matron.' Matron Morgan's mouth fell open, and the CO said, 'This is what you are going to do, immediately you leave this office.

'Number one—before the nursing staff take up their duties for the night, you are going to apologise to Sister Paignton-Fox and return her to her duties in the theatre. She's a great help to Major Simmons and we would be remiss in our responsibilities not to reward ability.

'Secondly—within one hour you will place a written request on my desk for a transfer to a base hospital, which I will support.

'If you fail to apologise to Sister Paignton-Fox, and your request for a transfer is not forthcoming, I will initiate the necessary action to have you removed from this CCS with a recommendation that you are never again placed in a position of authority. In either case, you will leave this CCS at 0830 hours tomorrow. Do I make myself clear?'

'You can't do that.'

'That is well within my powers, and with the written evidence I have gathered you will be lucky not to be discharged with disgrace. Dismissed.'

'You're like all the rest…'

The colonel raised his face and glared at the matron. 'I said, dismissed. You have just one hour to think about your course of action… DIS-MISSED.'

16

*Number 13, British General Hospital, Boulogne,
Wednesday, 5 September 1917*

The address was in Lucy's handwriting and Vicky eagerly tore open the envelope, wondering why the letter had taken over a fortnight to travel the fifty miles from Poperinghe. When she checked the post-marks she saw it had been across to England before being sent back again.

It started with concerns for her health before the news of the Moron's dismissal, then it moved to the details of Lex's death. She lowered the letter as her eyes filled with tears, which developed into uncontrolled weeping. Ever since Lucy had told her that Lex was dead, she'd wondered how it had happened, but she hadn't expected anything like this.

'Whatever is the matter? Can I do anything to help?' It was a male voice, refined, upper class English.

She lifted her head to see a tubby officer standing in the door-way of her ward. Her vision was blurred, but she recognised the patient from the ward next to hers. Captain Stewart was in the Royal Artillery, and like her, was being treated for gas poisoning. Too choked to speak, she thrust the page with the details towards him, and he stepped into her room to take it.

'A friend?' he asked when he finished reading.

A nurse joined them. 'What's wrong?' she asked and the officer passed the page to her, indicating the passage. She read it quickly and hurried out, only to return a few moments later with a glass of amber liquid.

'Drink this,' she ordered as she gave the glass to Vicky. 'Cognac. It'll calm you.'

Gheluvelt Plateau, Sunday, 23 September 1917

Adam eased the throttle further forward, revelling in the response from the plane as it climbed. He'd only been flying the Sopwith Camel for eight days, but already he had the utmost confidence in it. If he was shot down it would not be the fault of the aircraft.

The plane was as temperamental as a thoroughbred and needed the same careful handling, but he forgave it its idiosyncrasies and delighted in its sensitivity. It was the most responsive plane he'd flown. To starboard he could swing it round like a circus pony, but to port it was like a draught horse. He'd already exploited that vicious right turn, winning one dogfight because of it.

The twin Vickers machine-guns were a huge improvement. The Camel was the first British fighter to be so heavily armed. The guns were fitted directly ahead of the small windshield, synchronised to fire through the propeller, with fairings covering their breeches. They did look like humps, he thought. No wonder they named it Camel.

The altimeter moved past nine thousand feet and he checked his watch. Less than ten minutes since take-off. Below, on the Gheluvelt Plateau, he could see the new British trenches, just a row of disjointed slits that they'd established following their attack. Plumes of dirt and smoke erupted from the artillery shells that both sides were lobbing at each other.

In the distance he noticed the silhouette of a triplane, which puzzled him. He didn't know the navy were operating in this area, but he dismissed the triplane and levelled out at ten thousand feet to start his patrol, easing back on the throttle. He watched for movement of troops on the ground and enemy aircraft in the skies. Apart from the artillery activity, everything was remarkably quiet. Even the triplane had disappeared.

Behind the German lines he could see an observation balloon. It was too good a target to ignore and he turned for the east, but before he'd settled on his new course a stream of tracer bullets flashed past his head. He spun round to see the triplane diving out of a cloud.

He swung the Camel to starboard, drawing the stick back to counter the tendency of the plane to dive. As he turned, the triplane pulled out of its dive and banked, and the black crosses became clear on the fuselage. For a moment he thought it was a captured Sopwith triplane, but then he realised the tail and wings were quite different.

Hell… So Fritz had a new plane. Adam wondered how it would perform. He watched the triplane swing round in a tight turn. He guessed he was about to find out.

He began to climb and the triplane followed him. The Camel soared higher as he opened the throttle fully. When he checked he'd gained on the German plane, but far less than he'd expected. He eased out of his climb and turned hard to starboard to swoop down, but the German plane turned too. It was unusual for a German plane to be alone and he wondered about the others in the *jasta*. They wouldn't be far away.

They circled, neither able to turn inside the other as they slowly lost height. The triplane began a shallow dive and Adam followed wondering what the German was planning to do. His Bentley engine was screaming at maximum revolutions and slowly he reduced the distance between himself and his enemy. He fired a burst and saw his tracers straddle the tail of his opponent.

As he closed with the triplane he fired again. This time his bullets hit the leading edge of the upper wing. Another burst hit the engine nacelle and the triplane swung to starboard, exposing the side of the fuselage. Adam raked it with a long burst. The German pilot slumped and the triplane began to spin. Adam followed it down until he saw it crash, then he started to climb again, searching the sky for the *jasta*.

He'd heard nothing about this German triplane and had been surprised that its performance had matched that of the Camel. The sooner that information was promulgated throughout the Royal Flying Corps, the better.

For a moment he toyed with the idea of abandoning his patrol to report, but he could see no sign of a *jasta*. He'd complete his mission. A delay of an hour or so would make little difference to his report about the plane, but the information he could gather about German troop movements could be used immediately. And there was still that observation balloon to attend to.

Number 13, British General Hospital, Boulogne,
Sunday, 23 September 1917

Vicky was resting in the sun after lunch and lowered the novel she was reading as Captain Stewart walked along the patio. He was smart in his new Royal Artillery uniform. It was well tailored and disguised his burgeoning paunch. She enjoyed his company and had come to know him well in the five weeks she'd been in the hospital. His dry sense of humour had helped her recovery, from both the mustard gas and the shock of Lex's death.

'It's good to see you looking so well,' he said. 'How about coming for a walk?'

'I'd like that. Do you have anywhere in mind?'

'What about the beach?'

She took his hand, but once they reached the dunes he slipped his arm round her waist, his hand gently caressing her hip. She lifted it away, but a moment later it was back, and this time she let it stay, but took hold of it, restraining it.

The wind off the water was fresh, so after a short walk he led her into the shelter of the dunes where they sat. He drew her close and kissed her. She responded and laid her head on his shoulder. Moments later she felt his hand on her breast.

'No.' She sat upright. 'You're very forward, Captain Stewart.'

'Sorry. I was just feeling a bit down.' His wavy dark brown hair tumbled across his forehead and he looked like a chastened chubby schoolboy. 'I received my orders this morning. I return to the front on Saturday so I won't see you after Friday. I've no idea when I'll have some leave. I've enjoyed your company and had hoped that you enjoyed mine too.'

'I have, Captain Stewart. You're a charming gentleman, but I'm not that sort of girl.'

'I told you to call me Harry.' He fell silent for a moment. 'It can be distressing at the front when you see a member of your gun crew catch a shell splinter, or worse. It makes you wonder when it'll be your turn.' He sighed, and his lips clamped into a thin line. 'No point in dwelling on those thoughts. One has to keep one's wits sharp or one cops a packet, but being in command is a lonely job. The rest of the crew have each other to chat to, but the man in charge is on his own… I shall miss you.'

'We can write,' she said. He'd drawn her close again and his hand was back at her breast, but she made no effort to remove it.

'That's true, but a letter's not the same as physical contact.' He kissed her and she responded.

She felt him fumbling at the buttons of her bodice. The warmth of his hand had been pleasant and he would be risking his life in a few days. It seemed such a small thing to allow him to fondle her breasts, and she unfastened the buttons. As she stretched up to kiss him she felt his hand slip through the open material.

The best part of an hour had passed and Vicky sat up. It had been unintentional and she was surprised at how easily it had happened, but she had no regrets. It had been enjoyable, although she felt a little tender.

'We must get back or I'll be in trouble,' she said, and began to pull her petticoat down and straighten her dress. As she fastened the buttons Harry pulled her down and kissed her, but she broke free, clambered to her feet and finished straightening her clothes.

Polygon Wood, Wednesday, 26 September 1917

'Where is this blasted Polygon Wood?' Lofty asked. Two days earlier he had been promoted to sergeant, and now he was lying in a shallow excavation with John Mitchell, his section spread out at each side. It was one of a number of scrapes that they'd dug when they'd moved up during the early hours of the morning.

John smiled to himself. He could understand the emotions that would be coursing through Lofty's head. Lofty had finally suppressed his reluctance to be promoted and, thanks to his experience, his advance had been rapid. He'd hardly had time to sew on his corporal's stripes before he'd been made up to sergeant. As a private he'd done as he was ordered, usually after some light-hearted repartee, but now he was taking his responsibilities seriously. He'd be more aware than most that his men relied on him knowing exactly what their objectives were.

John glanced at his watch, wondering what had happened to delay the attack. It was 0410 hours and the sky was brightening. They'd been waiting for the order to advance for over an hour and he was feeling colder as the time passed. He studied the men he could see. Each man had a sandbag filled with Mills grenades slung round his neck and a second bandolier of rifle ammunition draped across his chest. Everyone was besmirched with mud. So much for all the spit and polish of training, he thought. He was in charge of a bunch of desperadoes, but he wouldn't have it any other way. One look at these blokes would be enough to scare Fritz to death.

To their right he could see a stark vista of gaunt tree trunks. Most of the trees that remained upright were devoid of branches, others were leaning at various angles and yet others were strewn across the ground like discarded matchsticks. Beyond the wood great spouts of mud were thrown up from the shells that straddled the German trenches.

'Blasted is the right word, Lofty,' John said and pointed to the devastated trees. 'That's it, Polygon Wood, or what's left of it. Fritz's trench is about one hundred yards beyond the far side.'

He could see that shells were finding their mark right along the German positions. The barrage was so heavy it was impossible to differentiate between the explosions. The German gunners were replying, but their shells were landing without any pattern.

'Fritz has no idea we're here.'

'I can't say I'm sorry about that,' Lofty said. 'If we keep quiet maybe he'll forget about us.'

In the growing light John raised his binoculars and examined the ground they'd have to cross when they went forward. 'I don't like the look of that mud. It'll be a long one hundred yards.' He passed the glasses to Lofty. 'Take a look.'

'At least it'll be a soft landing when we take cover, but knowing my luck I'll smash my head on one of those fallen tree trunks,' Lofty said as he passed the binoculars back.

A runner dropped beside John. 'The CO says the start time has been put back.'

'Seeing we were meant to go in at 0400, we'd managed to work that out for ourselves,' John said. 'What the new time?'

A flash of irritation crossed the runner's face. 'The first wave sets off at 0515 hours, sir. You're to follow as the second wave ten minutes later. The artillery will lift at the same time you start. He wants all company commanders for a briefing at the HQ in five minutes.'

'So we go in at 0525. Is that all?' The runner nodded and John said, 'That's a bastard, it'll be fully light.'

He checked his watch. 'You heard that, Lofty. We've an hour to wait. Pass the word to the rest of the company. I'm going to find out what the CO wants. Make sure there's no noise. We don't want to alert Fritz.' He knew that was unnecessary. After all these years, keeping quiet was second nature to Lofty, but reminding the new men of the need for stealth wouldn't hurt. It was strange how some sounds carried in a battle.

As John set off towards the headquarters he realised he was still calling Lofty by his nickname. He should start to use his rank, at least in front of the men, but it would take a while before it came naturally. It seems they'd been together for a lifetime.

Twenty minutes later he was back and moved along his company positions, reappraising each NCO of their objective. 'We're to pass through our first wave and take that new trench Fritz has established behind what is now his front line. The artillery will lift as we go forward. That should make Fritz keep his head down until we're established.'

The time crept to 0515 and the British barrage strengthened, bursting on the enemy wire and trench with a continuous blast of flame, noise and smoke. Red German flares shot up along the front and their shells began to focus on the line of men moving steadily forward, but their machine-guns were quiet. John knew the gunners would be sheltering in the dugouts, waiting for the British bombardment to end. Then they'd be in position, eager to set up their posts before the wave of attackers overran their defences. It wasn't a happy thought and even though he wouldn't be part of that action, it would be his turn soon enough. His mouth was dry and he longed to drink, but it was too early, and he knew it was nerves, not thirst. He'd need every drop of water later in the day.

The first wave passed through and closed with the German trench, but dropped to the ground short of it. The creeping barrage moved forward and the first wave were on their feet racing for the trench. They had to slow at the confused matrix of wire, which the shelling had failed to destroy. Machine-guns started to snarl and hand grenades exploded, adding to the noise and turmoil.

John leapt to his feet. 'With me,' he called and set off at a steady walk towards the enemy positions. Enemy high explosive and shrapnel shells were landing around them and men were falling, but ahead they could see the Germans abandoning their trench. The machine-gun fire had slackened too, and he hoped it was a sign that the first wave had been successful.

They passed walking wounded making their way to the rear, but could do nothing to help them. Some with calm faces limped along as upright as their wounds allowed; others shivered, their faces contorted with the pain of their injuries. At least they're walking, John thought. It wasn't far to the regimental aid post and then the dressing station, where they'd be patched up before being taken on to a casualty clearing station. He knew there'd be others lying in the mud waiting for the bearers to find them. Too many of them would drown before help reached them. Cowed German prisoners passed through the advancing men, blood stained, mud splattered and terrified, not a spark of fight left. They'd been assembled into small parties, each herded by a wounded Australian who called obscenities as he hurried them along.

They leapt over the captured trench to hurry after the enemy who were fleeing to their new position and into the barrage that was pounding it. They were so close to the retreating Germans that John hoped they'd shield them from the machine-guns. They were halfway to their objective when the German gunners opened up, firing through their own men. Many of them fell.

So did many Australians.

'Down,' John called and slithered into the morass of a shell crater. They were thirty yards from the German trench on which the British shells were still falling. The cold of the mud seeped through his sodden battledress and he shivered as he checked the men and saw the gaps in their ranks. Muscles was away to his left and further along the line; Don, lying in a shell crater, was wrapping a dressing over his forearm; but he could see no sign of Lofty. Dejection took hold for a moment, but he'd other men to think about and the barrage would soon lift. 'Bombs. On my order,' he called.

From over on his right he heard his order repeated. It was Lofty's voice and he breathed a sigh of relief.

The barrage moved on and machine-guns opened up, one almost directly to their front.

'Bombs,' John screamed. He counted the seconds after he'd thrown his own grenade. '…Two… three…' His count of four was drowned out by the first blast when the Mills bombs exploded and the gun fell silent. 'Go,' he called as the sound of the blasts died and he jumped to his feet. Germans were abandoning the trench, scrambling over the parados, making for their rear positions.

The trench was a shambles. Dead Germans lay strewn across the floor, twisted wrecks of grey-clad bodies like abandoned dolls, their uniforms torn and frayed, riddled with grenade fragments. Wounded men slumped against the trench wall, their eyes glazed, taking no interest in their surroundings. Scraps of other grey-clad bodies littered the trench and mingled with pools of glistening blood. The stench of evacuated bowels added to the chemical stink of Baratol, sulphur and phosphorous.

After a couple of minutes of furious bayonet work the remaining German resistance crumbled. Men worked in pairs, dashing along the trench throwing grenades into the dugouts as they reached them. German soldiers scrambled from a few of the dugouts with cries of *'Achtung. Kamerad.'*

The gunners hurriedly set up their Lewis guns while a few men re-sited the captured German Spandaus. John detailed half the men to harass the retreating enemy with rifle fire. Other men pulled sandbags from their packs and began filling them to build palisades around the Lewis guns. Yet others worked their spades furiously to improve the shattered trench. More sandbags were positioned to form improvised fire-steps.

The prisoners were assembled to be sent to the cages. Australian wounded chivvied them along as if they were blue heeler cattle dogs snapping at their heels. The uninjured prisoners helped their wounded comrades, carrying some of them in blankets, fully aware that the Australian stretcher-bearers would collect no Germans until their own men had been attended to. They hurried. They had already experienced the British barrage and would have no wish to be around when their own guns opened up.

German shells began to fall around the trench and a signaller rushed up to John. 'The CO wants to talk to you, sir. We've got a line laid.'

'Fritz is on his way!' The cry came from one of the sentries and John could see the Germans climbing from what had been their reserve trench, about five or six hundred yards away.

Before John had time to issue the order, the new parapet was lined with riflemen. He turned to the signaller. 'I'm too damn busy. The CO will be wanting to know the situation. You can tell him as well as I can. Fritz is counterattacking so make sure he knows I need that barrage increased. I'll be along to report as soon as I can.'

The Germans moved slowly, maintaining parade ground precision, but they were still too far away for accurate shooting.

'Hold your fire,' John called and heard the order being passed along the trench by the NCOs.

British high explosive shells were still pounding the area around the German trench and a few of the attackers fell, but the others closed up and continued their advance. John watched, ready to order firing to commence when they were closer.

The Germans had not reached the halfway point when the British shrapnel began to fall among them in an unceasing roar of flames and flying metal, as if a tap had been turned from a trickle to full flow. Gaps appeared in the precise line, which disintegrated completely as the attackers leapt into shell holes to disappear from view.

A German officer sprang from his refuge and organised his men. The attackers began to advance again, this time at the run, abandoning their former cohesion.

'You three.' John beckoned to three riflemen. 'When the officer reaches that stump, drop him.' He pointed to a tree trunk about two hundred yards ahead. 'Do you see it? That one with two torn branches low down on our left.'

John turned to a corporal. 'Pass the word. When these three start the ball rolling the rest of you commence firing. Good luck.'

He moved along the trench to check the Lewis guns. 'Hold your fire until the riflemen open up, then fire at will,' he said as he reached each position. All three gunners had ten full magazines, each holding forty-seven rounds. John hoped it would be enough.

He stepped onto the fire-step beside Hughie Sampson. 'How are you going, Muscles?'

Across the ground ahead the German line was thinning. Men were falling as the shrapnel wreaked havoc, but they were still advancing, urged on by the officer who had rallied them.

'Better than those poor bastards,' Muscles said, pointing to the attacking Germans. 'But you have to give them ten out of ten for guts.'

'No more than us,' John said. 'Don't get to thinking they're invincible.' He watched the advancing Germans dispassionately.

The German officer reached the stump and three rifle shots rang out. Before he'd hit the ground concentrated rifle and machine-gun fire opened up and more Germans crumpled. They still advanced into the fusillade of small arms fire, but they were leaderless, and as their numbers dwindled they began to take cover in the shell holes.

'They might be safe from our .303s, but that shrapnel will be sorting the bastards out,' Muscles said. His Lee Enfield still aimed in the direction of the Germans, his cheek on the stock and his finger ready on the trigger. 'They'll break any time now.'

'Just be ready for them when they do,' John said.

The order was unnecessary, but there were other men within earshot and it wouldn't do to show favouritism. John made his way along the company's line, checking the casualties. They'd paid a heavy price for this bit of land. He surveyed the ground they'd taken, measuring the distance with his stockman's eye. Half the company either wounded or killed, for about half a mile of disputed miserable mud. A worthless bit of rubbish, and they still had to sort out the remnants of the German advance. He'd take the Australian Outback any day. For a moment he wished he hadn't joined, but it wasn't all bad.

The army had given him confidence and he'd learnt things about himself. Things he'd never have known if he'd remained in Civvy Street. Good things. All he had to do now was survive.

John found the signaller's dugout and reported. He explained about the Germans' stalled attack and asked for more shrapnel to be sent over. 'We can't reach them with our rifles. We've taken a battering and I'm reluctant to lose more men in flushing them out. If there's enough shrapnel their position will be untenable. We'll catch them in the open when they break.'

He reported the butcher's bill, handed the phone to the signaller and made his way back to the fire trench. The ground seemed to boil as shrapnel pellets churned the mud. A German popped up from a shell hole and began running towards his own trench. Four others followed him, but before they'd taken a dozen paces they had fallen to the Australian rifles.

The other Germans fled, running from shell hole to shell hole, trying to work their way back. Most of them fell. Whether they were the victims of the shrapnel or the rifles, John didn't care. They'd be chary of mounting another stunt.

The Allies should be continuing the attack, John thought. For a moment he considered calling the CO and suggesting it, but when he looked round at his men he shook his head. They were far too few to press home their advantage.

17

Menin Road, Friday, 28 September 1917

Sergeant Lofty Mathews turned to examine the line of weary and mud-stained men behind him. He didn't have to count, he knew there was less than one hundred. The battalion had been relieved and his platoon was leading the remnants of their company out of the line to regroup and be reinforced. They'd earned their rest, he thought, and wondered how long it would be before they were back at the front.

A fresh British regiment moving up passed as they skirted Shrewsbury Forest. 'How did it go?' one of the men asked.

'You'll be right. Fritz used all his shells on us,' Don said. He had a blood-stained bandage visible below his steel helmet. It was grey with dirt.

'We feel bad about hogging all his attention. We told him you'd be disappointed if he didn't keep something back for the rest of you, but he insisted,' Muscles added. The sleeve of his tunic flapped open, exposing his filthy field dressing.

'Leave off,' the man who'd asked said, and moved on as the man behind him thumped him on the back.

It would take more than a few shells to shatter the spirit of these men, Lofty thought. But those few shells had been rather a lot. Even so, the Australians could still laugh and joke. Part of that was relief that they were leaving the carnage of the front line. He was proud to be one of them. Being a sergeant had made no difference to their mateship. They had accepted his new authority without rancour and he knew, from what he'd overheard, that they were pleased to have someone in charge whose ability they trusted.

He smiled, but it was fleeting and painful, and he wished he hadn't as the scab on his own wound split and he felt blood trickle down his cheek. He'd been lucky. Don had skewered the big Fritz as he thrust his bayonet at him and the German's blade had missed his throat. Now he sported a gash that ran up his left cheek from the side on his mouth to the top of his ear. Fortunately it hadn't caught the bone and was just a flesh wound, but it was impossible to bandage. It had been stitched at the regimental aid post, but he'd refused to move back to the CCS. He had a job to do and there were men with more serious wounds still in the line. It would leave a nasty scar though, and he wondered if it would queer his pitch with the ladies.

He glanced back at the men following him and his pride swelled. They might look a rag-tag bunch of no hopers, but they'd shown Fritz a thing or two, or four. He'd been a very surprised Fritz… and not for the first time. Even the elite of the *Kaiserheer*, the much-vaunted *Sturmtruppen*, had found they were a tough mob. Too tough for the arrogant storm troopers despite their bunched *stielhandgranates*, and the Fritz carrying that *flammenwerfer* had no chance against a volley from the .303s. Those who'd come against his company wouldn't be terrorising any other poor wretches. He glanced at the sleeve of Muscles's tunic. It didn't seem right that he'd have to sew it up. If his rifle had been damaged they'd soon give him a new one; why couldn't they do the same for a tunic? Lofty made a mental note to talk to Captain Mitchell.

The men in the new relief they passed were parade ground smart, their uniforms clean and their faces shaved. Poor sods, Lofty thought. By tomorrow they'd be more like the men he was leading out. He looked back at his platoon. Most of them sported dirty bandages like trophies. Their bloodshot eyes were sunk in their faces, which hadn't had a razor near them for a week, but every man refused to surrender to his tiredness.

They might look a rabble, but they'd do him, he thought. There'd be no better men in any army.

His gaze moved to the skeleton tree trunks they passed by. Whose stupid idea was it to call it Shrewsbury Forest? The bloody Pommies couldn't help themselves. They had to give Pommy names to everything, but it wasn't much of a forest now. Almost every tree was denuded of foliage, most of those left standing had even been stripped of their branches, but occasionally one had defied the devastation. They seemed indecent, sporting their leaves like some unfeeling harlot at a funeral.

How does that happen? he wondered. One tree escapes unmarked, yet others are stripped bare. It's the same with them—Muscles, Don and himself, John Mitchell too—had all escaped with nothing more than minor wounds, yet other men had died within minutes of arriving at the front. The Froggies had it right, '*C'est la guerre*'.

The track they followed merged with another and the traffic became heavy. They tramped on, often forced to step off the corduroy to give right of way to horse teams heading to the front with guns and limbers in tow. Motor trucks carrying supplies were also given priority, as were ambulances. Only right, Lofty thought. More units of fresh-faced reinforcements streamed past, many of them were hardly more than boys. A few men joked with them, but most peered straight ahead, refusing to meet the Australians' eyes. They'd be scared, Lofty thought, especially the younger ones. He knew how they were feeling.

Number 13, British General Hospital, Boulogne,
Friday, 28 September 1917

Vicky lay in Harry's embrace with her head cradled in his arm, his hand caressing her back. Their clothes were in disarray, bemired with sand.

'I shall miss you, Vicky. These last six days have been wonderful and I'll be lonely back with the guns,' Harry said as he pulled her close.

'You will write as soon as you know where you are?' Vicky said as she freed herself from his embrace and sat up.

'Of course I'll write. Just as soon as I have the address. I do love you.'

'I love you too, Harry.' She reached across and kissed him. 'I'm surprised your address is not the same as it was,' Vicky said when they drew apart.

'I'm posted to a different battery. If mail's delivered to the wrong unit it often goes astray. It'll be better to wait until I have the correct address, my darling.'

Surely the men in his old battery would post his mail on, she thought. Then she realised they may be new people who didn't know him.

She stood and adjusted her dress, then reached down, picked up his tunic and began to dust the sand off it. Some folded papers fell from an inside pocket and began to scatter in the breeze. She dropped the tunic and raced after them, but it was over fifty yards before she'd caught them all. One sheet was covered in a child's block letters, the last words printed in red crayon, *LOTS OF LOVE DADDY*.

She glanced quickly at the other pages and gasped. The letter began with *My darling husband*, and ended, *Take good care and keep yourself safe for Alice and me. You're forever in our thoughts. Your ever-loving wife, Marion.*

Harry had started towards her and she quickly finished buttoning her dress. When he reached her he held his hand out for the letter, but she pulled it away and brought her free hand round in a sweep that connected with his face. He staggered and fell.

'You two-timing cad. You're married. A father. You took advantage of me. I thought you loved me.'

He had struggled to his knees, but she swung her hand with all her strength, slapping him again. Harry sprawled in the sand, shaking his head, his legs wide. She stepped forward and kicked him in the groin. The nurses' shoes may not have been very elegant, but they were ideal for that, she thought.

'I'll write to your wife and tell her what a despicable husband she has.'

For a moment a look of horror replaced that of pain, but he was still gasping from her kick and unable to speak.

Vicky rushed away, the letter clutched in her hand, tears streaming, but when she reached the esplanade she slumped onto a seat and wiped her eyes. They would be red and she couldn't go back to the hospital until she'd recovered. Harry would want that letter back, but she could see no sign of him. She hurried away.

She knew that she wasn't the first woman to be tricked in this way, but it was no consolation.

Number 3 ACCS, Nine Elms, Poperinghe,
Thursday, 4 October 1917

The Australian CCS had been relocated, and the intake of wounded was light. They were working with Number 44 British CCS accepting patients on alternate days. Lucy had a night off duty, but, although exhausted, she'd had little sleep.

A little before midnight the first squadron of German planes had appeared overhead and dropped bombs, which had landed close. Just how close she couldn't work out, but they sounded as if they were exploding next to the tent and she wished it was sunk and sandbagged like the tents had been at Brandhoek. The bombardment lasted four hours as more *jastas* of German bombers arrived to take their turn.

The German shelling of Poperinghe screeched overhead without a break and added to the noise of the night. Other shells landed closer to the CCS. Once again a battery of howitzers had been set up not far behind the CCS and, as usual, the German shells ranged indiscriminately as they searched for their position.

At 0500 hours the battery opened up with a drumfire barrage, and rent the pre-dawn with a continuous cacophony of sound. There must be a stunt going in, Lucy thought and after fifteen minutes she gave up all hope of sleep.

Vicky's bed was empty. She'd returned to the CCS on Monday and had been assigned to the resuscitation ward on nights, helping men recover from the shock of their wounds before they were sent on to the theatre or one of the wards. Since she'd been back, she'd been withdrawn. All her former vitality had disappeared and Lucy was worried about her.

When dawn broke Lucy, Vicky and three other sisters went to investigate the bombing, leaving the home sister to prepare breakfast. An empty field between the Australian CCS and Number 44 was pockmarked with huge craters, yet their hospital had escaped with no more than a smattering of tears in the fabric of a few marquees.

'Do you think they were aiming for us?' one of the sisters asked.

She had only arrived in France a couple of weeks earlier and was new at the CCS.

'I doubt it,' Lucy said. 'They'll have been trying to silence those things.' She pointed across to some trees where the muzzle flashes of the guns were bright in the morning gloom. 'I do hate them being so near. It only stands to reason Fritz will try to silence them.'

'They'll be gone soon,' Vicky said.

'Not soon enough for me,' Lucy said. 'Let's get back, I'm starving.'

At one of the wards they passed on their way back to the mess a British officer, a captain, talking to the ward sister near the entrance.

'… I don't know what's happened to the other bottles I sent, but to make sure you received this one, I've brought it myself.'

The captain hurried away to a truck where orderlies were unloading medical supplies. The ward sister stood clutching a bottle of cognac. Confusion was strong in her face as she stared at the officer's retreating back.

'Whatever is the matter?' Lucy asked.

The sister snapped out of her reverie. 'I feel such a fool.' She read the label and nodded towards the officer. 'That's the quartermaster. For the last couple of weeks I've been requisitioning brandy with my daily supplies and they've been sending this cognac up. I didn't know what it was, so I kept requisitioning more brandy. Yesterday I ordered another bottle and put a note for the QM with the requisition asking him to make sure I got it this time. Come and have a look.'

She led them to the store at the end of the ward and opened a cupboard. One shelf was crammed with bottles of cognac.

Lucy laughed. 'Don't worry about that. Your patients should be cheerful for a little while.' As soon as the words were out she felt contrite. 'That sounds awful. What I meant was it'll do them good. They've nothing else to be cheerful about, especially when they're brought in here.'

They'd finished eating and were savouring the coffee when one of the sisters said, 'That's an ambulance.' She rushed to the door. 'They're offloading patients. Why are they bringing them here? I thought it was our turn for a rest day.'

'It's supposed to be,' Matron Kenny said. She placed her cup by the washing-up bowl and started towards the door. 'There must be a reason, so rest day or not, we'll just have to cope, but there are enough nurses on the day roster to cope. Thanks for offering to help, but I don't need you.'

Lucy and Vicky returned to their quarters. 'I can't say I'm sorry Tubs didn't want us,' Lucy said. 'I've been on night duty so long I've got so used to sleeping during the day that I hardly slept last night. I'm going to turn in.'

The British guns were still firing, but the roar of their discharge was constant so it was not disturbing.

'I think I'll do the same,' Vicky said.

It was mid-afternoon when Lucy was woken by a sister from a surgical ward. The British guns were silent and the sound of a passing motor ambulance seemed loud in the silence. 'I have a visitor asking to see you,' the sister said. 'A gentleman.'

Lucy sat up in bed and rubbed her eyes. 'Who is it, Jenny?'

'I didn't ask. He's waiting over by my ward. Shall I tell him you'll come?'

'Yes, do that, Jenny. Do you know what he wants?' Lucy asked as she swung her feet onto the duckboards and began to dress.

'He came to see a mate who'd been shot. When he discovered that man had moved on he asked for you. I'll tell him you'll be along in five minutes, shall I?' Jenny crossed to the doorway, where she turned and waited.

'Yes, of course. It might be a little longer.' The sister slipped through the tent flaps.

Adam was lighting a cigarette outside the entrance to the ward when Lucy arrived. He offered the packet to her. 'Cigarette?'

'No, thank you. I don't smoke.'

He pushed the packet back into his pocket. 'Thanks for your letters,' he said. He'd had no letters while he'd been in hospital and she had felt sorry for him so had written to him once a week since he'd returned to duty. 'I get so few from home. The mail from America is erratic and Pa's not a great correspondent. For the last six months he hasn't answered any of my letters. Grandpa writes occasionally, but he never has much to say.'

'Thanks for yours too. Don't you have a girl back home?' Lucy asked. Adam shook his head. She was about to ask about his mother when she remembered she'd been killed in a Zeppelin raid, which was why he'd joined the British army.

'How about coming for a little walk?' he asked.

'I'd love to, but I can't be long. I'm on duty tonight.'

Adam took her hand. 'I think the rail tracks will be easier walking than those log roads. They get really churned up with all the horses and wagons.'

'I wish they didn't use horses. It's not fair on the poor animals,' Lucy said.

'How else are they going to move stuff around?' Adam said.

'They have all these motor trucks. Can't they use them?'

'They're not as reliable as horses, and they get stuck as soon as they leave the corduroy. Horses are still the best for moving the field guns,' Adam said, as they began to climb the low embankment. She slipped on a loose stone and Adam grabbed her. He pulled her close to his side and his arm circled her waist. For a moment she resisted. She didn't need any help, but it was pleasant. Together they started along the railway towards Poperinghe.

'You're looking pleased with yourself,' Vicky said when Lucy joined her in the nurses' mess for their evening meal. She was frowning. 'I hear you spent the afternoon with an airman.'

'Who told you that?' Lucy asked. For a moment she was annoyed, but so close to the front the sisters had little to relieve the unremitting drudgery of attending to wounded men. Any break in the routine would attract attention. She wondered why Vicky was looking so worried.

Vicky nodded towards a large sister sitting at the end of the table. 'Jenny saw you going off along the railway with an airman.' She pursed her lips. 'You have to be careful with these officers.'

'We just went for a walk,' Lucy protested, but she could feel the warmth rising in her face as the memory of his goodbye kiss flooded back. 'I felt sorry for him. He's American and so far away from home.'

'Not as far away from home as we are,' Vicky said.

'I suppose that's true, but there are a lot of us. He's the only American in his squadron. He feels left out of things when the other pilots talk about home. America is so different to England and he knows nothing about the places they mention. His father doesn't write very often and his mother's dead.'

'So he's lonely. Well, that makes it all right then.' Vicky raised her eyebrows. 'These airmen have a reputation, and an American too. There's no way you can check what he's telling you. It could just be a load of cobblers. You be careful.'

Vicky's admonition rang in her head as they walked to their quarters. Adam obviously liked her, why else would he search her out? But Vicky was right, she knew nothing about him, other than what he'd told her, and even less about his background. He'd been the perfect gentleman, except for that kiss. She should have pushed him away, but by the time she'd recovered from her surprise, she'd been enjoying it.

They sat in silence for several minutes, side by side on Lucy's bed before Vicky took a deep breath, as if she was steeling herself for a difficult task.

'I made a fool of myself.'

Lucy waited in silence, wondering what Vicky found so difficult to say, but after her caution she guessed it involved a man.

'There was this captain in the artillery who was in the next room to me.' Vicky hesitated, staring through the flaps of the tent.

For a moment Lucy held her breath, fearful that she'd been right.

'After your letter about Lex he was very kind and we became friends. He was charming and I fell for him. I really loved him and thought he loved me too. When he was due to go back to the front I wanted to show him how much I cared for him and I let him… well you know.'

'Vicky… You made love?'

Vicky nodded. 'Several times.'

'You're not pregnant?'

'I don't think so, but I'm not sure. I hope not. I'd be sent home and everyone would know. I'd be so embarrassed.' Vicky took a deep breath. 'He was a cad and had been stringing me along with lies. A letter fell out of his pocket after the last time. It was from his wife and daughter. I was so angry I threatened to write to his wife, so I kept the letter.' Vicky wiped her eyes and sniffed. 'I feel such a fool. I don't want you to make the same mistake. There's no way to know if these men are telling you the truth… You won't tell anyone will you?'

'Of course I won't. We're friends. Even if we weren't, I wouldn't spread gossip about something like that. And you're not a fool. It's easy to fall in love with someone who's been kind.' Lucy wrapped her arms about her and gave her a hug. 'Did you write to his wife?'

They drew apart and Vicky said, 'Of course I didn't. How could I do that to the poor woman? But what if I am pregnant? What will I do?'

'We'll cross that bridge *if* we come to it. When will you know?'

'The curse is due in a couple of days.'

Number 3 ACCS, Nine Elms, Poperinghe, Tuesday, 9 October 1917

'Our boys and the Kiwis have been involved in a stunt over at Poelcappelle,' Bob said when he joined Lucy in the theatre. He donned his gown and began to scrub his hands as he talked. 'The conditions are terrible. Since the rains returned everything is covered in thick mud, but hopefully the losses won't be as high as the Menin Road. I heard the preliminary figures in the mess during dinner. The Tommies and our boys had over 20,000 casualties, but that will rise. It always does.' He dried his hands and pulled on his gloves as they crossed to the operating table. 'The Polygon Wood attack was almost as bad, we incurred around 17,000 in that stunt. All those men dead or wounded, yet the Boche are still there. It seems so futile.'

'We can't be busier than last night,' Lucy said. 'Do you know how many wounded the ambulances brought in?'

'Not yet, but in the previous twenty-four hours the CCS received over three thousand patients. We only saw the worst cases. The less seriously injured went straight onto the hospital train.'

A man with multiple shrapnel wounds was placed on their table, and they set to work at once. Like Malcolm Rigby, Bob had studied under Joseph Lister at Kings College Hospital in London, and had taken his system of antiseptic surgery seriously. They both insisted that every member of their teams scrubbed their hands before each operation and despite some initial scepticism, everyone now wore a facemask as a matter of routine.

They were attending to their fifth patient when Lucy noticed a persistent drone high overhead. 'Sounds like Fritz is paying us another visit,' she said.

Bob paused for a moment, his head cocked to the left as he concentrated. 'I don't think he's as high as usual, and there's only one of them. He seems to be heading south.'

'That makes a change,' Lucy said as she dressed the wound. When she'd secured the bandage she placed the instruments in the steriliser, stood back and signalled to the orderlies.

Two of them lifted the patient onto a stretcher and William, the AAMC orderly who was attached to their team, began to wash down the table. 'Why don't you grab a cuppa, Sister,' he said. 'For the moment all the incoming wounded are going to 44. When they've got their quota we'll take the next batch.'

'Good thinking,' Bob said. 'You'll keep an eye on the steriliser for Lucy?' William nodded and Bob glanced to the anaesthetist as he took hold of Lucy's elbow, leading her from the marquee.

The anaesthetist shook his head. 'Count me out. I'm going to grab a minute to catch up on some letters.'

In the open they paused, watching the flashes of anti aircraft shells as they exploded almost overhead, bright bursts of light amongst the searchlights probing the darkness. 'There it is. They've picked it up.' Lucy pointed to the illuminated fuselage and tail of the plane. The black crosses were stark against their white backgrounds. More lights locked on to the plane and shells began exploding around it. 'It's so big,' she said.

'I've heard that the Boche have a new bomber made by Zeppelin, a huge thing. They have a squadron stationed at Ghent,' Bob said. 'It could be one of them.'

Lucy watched the plane drone on through the ring of explosions. 'It's not dropping any bombs,' she said.

'If it is one of those Zeppelins, it's probably returning from a raid and has nothing left. I was told that they're intended for targets in England, not local raids.' The bomber eluded the searchlights and vanished into the dark sky. The guns fell silent.

Bob became quiet for a moment, then said, 'He was lower than usual, I wonder…' His voice tailed off as a finger of flame burst into the darkness to light up one of the engines, which was suspended between a pair of wings. The engine became engulfed in flames, which grew and began playing across the upper wing. 'They must have hit the blighter,' Bob said. 'I don't think he'll make it back to base.'

The blaze spread and the plane began to lose height. Burning pieces began to fall, tracing their descent with showers of sparks. The wing crumpled and the plane dropped, trailing flames until it disappeared beyond the horizon, and they heard a distant explosion. She shuddered. 'That's awful. I know they're the enemy, but I can't think of a worse way to end your life.'

'Maybe so, but don't waste any sympathy on them. They're the ones dropping bombs on innocent civilians and wounded men in hospitals,' Bob said, taking her elbow again and steering her towards the kitchen.

'When's all this killing going to stop, Bob?' she asked.

'When the Kaiser comes to his senses, I guess.'

'It can't be just the Kaiser. Not just one man.' She lifted two cups from the table and began to pour their teas.

Bob added sugar to his tea and said, 'You're right. He's just the figurehead.' He pulled out a chair and beckoned Lucy to sit. 'There'd been trouble for years, especially in the Balkans. It was a complex situation.' He paused, staring through the open doorway, his head cocked to one side. 'Is that a plane? I can hear engines.'

'It sounds like a truck,' Lucy said. After a few seconds she added, 'I think it's an ambulance.'

They returned to the theatre as two orderlies were lifting a man with a skull wound onto their operating table. A piece of shrapnel had sliced a section from the crown, but it was still attached by a strip of skin. Bone fragments fringed the edges of the hole.

'Reminds me of a boiled egg with its top sliced off,' Bob said. He took his time examining the patient's head. 'The cortex seems fine, but he needs specialist care. All we can do is extract the fragments.'

Lucy had freed the severed piece of skull and washed it in saline solution. 'This is almost complete. Do you think we could fit it back?'

Bob shook his head. 'They may be able to do something with it back at one of the base hospitals. I don't have the expertise to do more than patch him up, and I'm worried that his injuries will be aggravated on the way back to base. How are we going to protect his head?' He studied the wound. 'It's a pity we can't use a tin hat. What we need is something to keep the bandages from rubbing on the cortex.'

'We could bridge it with paper-mâché.'

'I wonder if that would be strong enough,' Bob said. 'We'd need a form and it would take too long to dry.'

'We can use strips cut from medical cards to make a form. They'd be stiff. We can use sticky paper to hold the strips together. Then we can run the bandages over it and build a shell using plaster of Paris. That sets quickly and it would make a sort of skull cap.'

After a few seconds Bob said, 'That would work. At least it's worth a try, and it should be strong enough to give him some protection if he gets a knock. I'm not sure about working plaster of Paris over the hole, though. The powder could get through to the cortex.'

'Not if we make up a sheet of it on a tray, bandages impregnated with plaster, and place it in position while it's wet. Once it's set we can build up a thicker layer.' Lucy stared at the patient's head. 'There'd be no powder anywhere near his skull.'

'I can see why Malcolm Rigby thought so highly of you. You have a refreshing way of approaching problems. I suspect part of that is because your thinking isn't influenced by conventional ideas taught at medical school.' Bob glanced across to her, his eyes twinkling. 'Let's get on with it.'

18

Number 3 ACCS Nine Elms, Poperinghe,
Wednesday, 10 October 1917

Lucy probed for the fourth shell fragment, hoping it was the last piece. It was deep in the man's thigh and she withdrew it with difficulty. After checking that no major vessels had been damaged she closed the wound, but was still wrapping the dressing when the order came to light the lamps. William was adjusting the wick when the generators fell silent, the electric lights in the operating theatre went out and they were left with the barely adequate illumination from the hurricane lamps.

The orderlies were carrying the man to the resuscitation marquee when Lucy became aware of the drone of aircraft engines. Almost as soon as she'd noticed it the sound disappeared. The Fritz pilots often did that as they made their final run and now that she had no patient to absorb her attention her fear mounted. It was 0235 hours.

The anti-aircraft fire was another sound she hadn't noticed while she'd been concentrating on her work. The archies were in the compound next to the hospital and she was astonished that such a loud noise could go unnoticed, but when she was working, concentrating on the surgery consumed all her attention.

By the time she returned to the operating table with freshly sterilised instruments, a new patient was laid out and Bob was beginning his examination.

'Amputation, I'm afraid. His foot's beyond saving,' he said, then added, 'Bring that light closer.'

Bob was sawing at the bone when a loud explosion split the night. The sound was followed immediately by a blast that billowed the side of the marquee and ripped the pegs from the earth so the canvas flapped. Rain splattered across the theatre as the ground trembled and Lucy stumbled, struggling to keep her feet in the rush of hot air. She coughed as phosphorous fumes invaded the theatre.

Five more blasts followed, but they were further away and their force had diminished by the time it reached them.

A team of sappers arrived and began to secure the marquee wall. 'Put those bloody lights out,' came from outside the marquee and an irate sergeant stormed into the theatre. 'What the hell do you think you're doing showing lights while Fritz is about?'

'Sergeant, this is an operating theatre and we can't work in darkness,' Bob said when the man reached them. 'We are all well aware that our lights attract the attention of the enemy, but it's a risk we can't avoid.' Bob looked up from the leg for a moment. 'We have no alternative. If that was you on the table would you want me to stop?' He resumed concentrating on the amputation.

'Sorry, sir.' The sergeant saluted. 'I can see you've turned them down a bit, but can't you turn them down a touch more?'

'No, Sergeant. They're lower than we'd like as it is,' Bob said as he passed the saw to Lucy.

'Sir,' the sergeant said. He saluted again, turned and rushed out of the marquee shouting at the men securing the flapping canvas, 'Get your bloody fingers out.'

They soon had the side fixed in position, but it was riddled with holes. The sergeant reappeared. 'We can't do anything about the holes, sir. They'll have to wait until daylight.' For a moment Lucy wondered if the man was making a point, but Bob ignored him. After a few seconds the sergeant saluted and left the marquee.

When the orderlies brought their next patient one of them said, 'Fritz hit one of the wards. The one with the prisoners in. He killed twenty-four of them and most of the others were wounded.' After they'd placed the man on the table he became thoughtful. 'That must be bloody rough. Bombed by your own side when your enemy is taking good care of you.'

The bomb craters had been filled before Lucy came off duty. The rain had stopped and a watery sun was struggling with the clouds as she made her way to her tent thinking of the efficiency of the sappers, and of the sergeant who had wanted them to turn the lamps down. He'd only been carrying out his orders, and she wondered what had made him change his mind. Was it just blind obedience to a senior officer, or had he seen the sense in Bob's words?

Vicky was sitting on her bed, a broad smile filling her face. 'I've started. I never thought I'd be so happy to see the curse.' She stood and hugged Lucy. 'I'm so relieved.'

'Of course you are. So, are we going to see the old, happy Vicky from now on?' Lucy asked.

'I can't say. Everything is different.'

'Nothing's different, except you've had a scare and learnt a lesson. Just relax. I'm the only one to know what happened, so cheer up.'

Passchendaele, Thursday, 11 October 1917

So much for a rest, John Mitchell thought. The five days at Dickebush were all they'd had out of the line, yet they'd been promised two weeks. No wonder some of the men were grumbling. It was a surprise they weren't all whinging.

Enemy flares brightened the sky in the distance and their machine-guns sprayed bullets, but John was far enough away from the front to ignore them. In fifteen minutes or so it would be a different proposition, but for the moment he was grateful for the darkness. It was a pity it hadn't been dark when they'd moved up through Ypres two days earlier.

The city had been destroyed, just a burnt and crumbling shadow of its previous splendour. The famous Cloth Hall was nothing more than smashed walls. The cathedral was in a similar state, but it wasn't the ruined architecture that saddened him. He shuddered at the memory of the march along the corduroy roads past Hell Fire Corner and Birr Crossroads.

The strip of corduroy had been narrow and shell torn, and as usual slippery and bordered with the bodies of horses and mules, interspersed with shattered hardware. The stench of blood and torn guts would stay with him forever, and it didn't pay to dwell on what mingled with the mud they trudged through. The bodies of a few dead men lay with the animals. They had been so recently killed that the working parties had not yet been able to carry them away.

John shuddered again as the whine of a shell passing overhead brought his mind back to the present. They were getting close to the line and occasionally enemy machine-gun bullets whistled past. A flare went up and he propped, shutting his eyes against the sudden light. The company propped behind him, each man standing rock still, afraid some sharp-eyed German observer would notice a movement and alert the gunners to their position. The flare faded and blackness reclaimed the night.

They moved forward again. The only sounds to break the silence were their laboured breathing and the slurp of sloppy mud as they dragged their boots from the morass they were crossing.

The sky was beginning to lighten in the east. He halted the men and moved on alone, through a recently contested area. A party of stretcher-bearers passed to the rear with a wounded man as John made contact with the guide from the British regiment they were relieving. After a few words he returned to the company.

Soon they were following the guide, strung out in single file, each man close behind the man in front so he could touch him. John tried to pick out landmarks, but that was difficult in the dim light. He knew the old hands would be doing exactly the same and made a mental note to instruct the new reinforcements about the importance of being aware of the layout of the ground. It could be the difference between returning to your own positions safely instead of blundering into a Fritz outpost.

The Australians moved on along freshly laid duckboards. Ahead, the front line was harassed by artillery and machine-gun fire. Within a few yards they were crossing ground that had only recently been captured. The pungent odour of cordite lingered in the air. The morning was brighter now and John could make out huddles of dead as the numbers of casualties increased. Frequently they stepped aside for stretcher-bearers carrying wounded to the rear.

The duckboards ended and they began to follow a low bank that was about chest high. Machine-gun fire from the German trenches sprayed the lip of the bank and their guide crouched. The Australians copied him. John worried about the new reinforcements. Despite their training some would be unsure what to do. For most this was their first stunt, and for too many it would be their only one. He fell back to counsel them.

John returned to the lead and heard a German command, which carried clearly from the enemy trench. Although he'd picked up a few words of the language he couldn't understand what had been said, but the firing stopped. The company left the shelter of the bank, abandoned their single line to double across a quagmire of mud in an open group. They had covered no more than fifty yards when John heard a salvo of shells falling towards them and flung himself prone. A series of splashes told him that the rest of the men were following his example. Explosions threw up mud behind them and he wondered if anyone had been injured. As silence returned they clambered to their feet to resume their rush.

The guide whispered, 'We're almost at the line, sir. A sap starts about twenty yards ahead.' The leading platoon bunched up as they reached the sap, each man forced to wait for the man ahead to move clear before he could drop into the shelter of the trench. The remaining platoons closed too, so that the company huddled in the muddy tract. John chivvied the men at the front, urging them to hurry. If Fritz opened up now, they'd be sitting ducks.

When they reached the end of the sap a young officer, a second lieutenant, joined them and pointed out the dispositions of the men they were relieving.

John turned to Lofty and whispered, 'Pass the word back, take cover until you have the order to come forward. He beckoned to the lieutenant in charge of the first platoon, and they squelched off following the young officer to find the commander of the company they were relieving.

Lofty felt a hand on his ankle as he lay in the mud peering towards the position they were to move into. He turned his head to see that Muscles was crawling up to his side. 'What's wrong?' he whispered.

'Don. He bought it. Copped it in the guts.' Muscles said just as quietly. 'Bearers have him.'

That's a bugger, Lofty thought, and wondered how seriously Don was wounded. At least the bearers would have him back at a CCS as soon as possible. He stared into Muscle's eyes. 'Bastard,' he mouthed, the sound no more than a sigh.

He turned back to watch his front, trying to block out his rising fear. He had to remain calm. The men depended on him, especially the new reinforcements.

The platoon lieutenant tapped Lofty on the shoulder and pointed ahead. Lofty scrambled to his feet and passed the order back. Soon the section was moving forward with the other sections following. After fifty yards or so, he found the first short length of disconnected trench and ordered Muscles and two of the new reinforcements into it. He led the remaining men on, detailing three or four to occupy each foxhole as they reached it. They'd have plenty of digging before they had them joined up.

Ahead Lofty could hear muffled whispers and the sounds of boots in the mud, and a dark shape loomed up. Other shapes followed as the British unit they were relieving began to file past in the growing light. 'Good luck,' a few of them murmured as they disappeared, but most of them passed in silence, their faces rigid and their eyes blank.

By breakfast time they had the foxholes linked, but the day was gloomy under thick clouds. They were still working to deepen the trench when shells began flying high over their heads, to pound the enemy lines. Flames flashed and blazed along the German trench like an out of control bush fire.

'That'll stir Fritz up a bit,' Muscles said.

Minutes later a company of Australians arrived to drop into their new trench.

'What the bloody hell are you lot doing here?' Lofty said.

'We're the first wave of the attack,' a man told him. He sat down on the fire-step and lit a cigarette. 'Just having a breather before we move up to the start line.'

The creeping barrage had moved forward as the first wave had charged the final few yards to the German trench. The shells were falling well ahead, smashing into the enemy rear lines, but the German guns were taking their toll on the Australians. Walking wounded were making their way back, some helped by German prisoners. One of the wounded men dropped into the trench at Lofty's side.

'That's me done for mate. I'm buggered if I know how I made it this far, but I can't go on. I'll have to wait for the bearers.' The thigh of his trousers was saturated with blood.

Lofty called for bearers, then rummaged in the man's pocket for his field dressing before he slit his trousers to expose the wound. He broke the top off the man's iodine ampoule and splashed the liquid liberally over the raw flesh, then bound the field dressing around his thigh. The man stiffened to lie rigid and white-faced as he worked, but no sound escaped from his clamped lips. When he'd finished the man exhaled and said, 'Thanks mate. That bloody stuff must be good. It gees you up a bit.' A trickle of blood escaped from his bottom lip. 'Have you got a fag?'

Lofty lit a cigarette and gave it to the wounded man as a German shell exploded a few yards away, covering them both with mud. The man peered up when the air cleared. 'Sorry, but I didn't even get a drag. Can you spare another one, please?' He held up two fingers with a mud-sodden cigarette clamped between them. 'Bloody Fritz has no respect for anything.'

Number 3 ACCS Nine Elms, Poperinghe,
Thursday, 8 November 1917

'What's so important about this Passchendaele place?' Lucy asked when she returned from the steriliser. 'It's been a month since this stunt started. How many more wounded will be brought in?'

'You might well ask,' Bob said. 'Passchendaele was no more than a village, now it's a heap of rubble, but there's a high ridge that dominates the area and that's what they've been fighting for. The Canadians and our boys finally captured it a couple of days ago, but it's been another bloody fiasco. From what I hear in the mess we've lost about two hundred and fifty thousand men.'

Lucy was stunned at the magnitude of the numbers. She shivered. 'What? In one stunt? They must be exaggerating.'

Bob sighed and shook his head. 'You've seen how many men we've operated on. Think of all the other casualty clearing stations. They've been as busy.' He turned back to the patient. 'Scalpel.'

At first she had to force herself to concentrate on the operation, but soon she was absorbed in her work, determined they wouldn't lose this man. They removed the last piece of shrapnel and she dressed the wound. As the orderlies carried the man away, her mind returned to the losses.

'Two hundred and fifty thousand men. That's a quarter of a million in less than a month. How can they know?'

'They'll be close. The Intelligence Corps has had plenty of practice. They say that the Boche has lost even more. Now that we've finally captured the ridge it should be over.' He paused, rubbed his eyes and took a deep breath. 'Unless of course the Boche stage a counterattack. They estimate that during the final phase, one in four of our casualties drowned in the mud.' Bob shuddered. 'I can't conceive how that can happen. You'd think they'd be able to scramble out of the holes.'

'Mud can be a problem,' Lucy said. 'If they panic they'll just sink deeper. The only way out is to lie down and sort of crawl, but city boys won't know that. Once they start to struggle they soon lose their strength and if they're already weak from wounds they'll have no chance.'

Bob studied her and frowned. 'It sounds as if you've had some experience.'

'I've seen cattle trapped at water holes. It's an awful sight. Usually they're too far gone to help, so all Dad can do is shoot them, but he still has the carcass to deal with. If he doesn't get them out they foul the water hole when it fills again.' She fell silent, wondering who'd pull the human carcasses from these muddy holes.

The orderlies lifted another patient onto the operating table and laid his tunic neatly over a box at the side of the instruments trolley. Lucy saw the major's crowns on the epaulettes, but she didn't recognise the unit flash at the shoulder. She picked up the patient's notes. Major Quentin Denison, Australian Army Veterinary Corps. The name seemed familiar, but she put the matter from her thoughts to concentrate on preparing for his operation.

Number 3 ACCS Nine Elms, Poperinghe, Friday, 9 November 1917

It had become Lucy's habit to visit the recovery wards each evening before she started her duties in the theatre. She found that following up on the patients she'd helped increased her sense of purpose. To see them regaining strength gave her a lift for the rest of the night. Sometimes a patient had died while she'd slept, and that saddened her. She knew her visits cheered the men, and that made it easier to work through the difficult times.

After the turmoil of the last four weeks the night was remarkably quiet. Only an occasional gun fired towards the German positions. Almost nothing was being fired in reply and Lucy found the relative silence unnerving. She glanced at her watch as she entered the first recovery ward. It was 1915 hours, too early for the Fritz bombers.

In a screened area she found Major Denison sitting up in bed, his right shoulder swathed in bandages and his arm in a sling. Again she wondered where she'd heard his name. It could be any time since she'd arrived in France eighteen months earlier. She moved to his bedside. 'How are you feeling?'

'Not as perky as I normally do, but heaps better than I did yesterday.' He eased his arm. 'Are you going to be looking after me tonight, Sister?'

She shook her head. 'Not tonight. I helped last night. Tonight I'll have other people who'll need my services. I work in the theatre. I like to check up on the people I meet on the operating table, but you won't remember that.' She smiled and leant across to tidy his blankets.

When she straightened up the major said, 'I don't remember last night, but I have the feeling I've met you somewhere. It'll come to me.'

Lucy glanced at his tunic, which was draped over a hanger hooked onto a length of cord near the bed head. 'I see you're in the Veterinary Corps,' she said. 'What does that entail?'

'I'm in charge of a hospital for injured horses and mules. So in a way we're in the same business.'

'Horses… Did you travel around the Northern Territory in 1914, buying horses?' she asked.

He looked up, recognition brightening his face. 'That cattle station… Aughton Park, wasn't it?' Lucy nodded, surprised he remembered the name. He held out his left hand and they shook. 'Quentin Denison.'

'Lucy Paignton-Fox,' she said and they shared a smile.

'I remember the owner walked with a limp and he had no horses to spare. Those in the paddock were fine animals, but they were all he had. Well, that was his story. I didn't believe him, you know, but I could see that I would never find where he'd hidden the rest. I checked up on Elands River, so I understand how he felt about the army and horses. The slaughter of those animals must have been a terrible thing to see. Was he your father?'

Lucy nodded. 'It wasn't only Elands River,' she said. 'The stallion that sired most of those horses saved his life. He was on a drove across the Gibson Desert when some Aborigines attacked while he and the stockmen slept. One of the horses woke him so he was able to defend himself, but one of his stockmen was killed. It was a bad time.'

'How can he be sure which animal it was?' Major Dennison asked.

'It could only have been the stallion, Monarch. He has a special bond with that horse. He'd lost all the cattle because he couldn't find water, but Monarch showed him where to dig for it several times, so he could get enough for the men and horses. They smell the water.' Lucy paused, recalling how Monarch would follow her father like a dog. 'If you'd tried to requisition any of his horses, especially those with Monarch's blood, I don't know what he would have done, but you'd have failed.'

'I had armed men with me. Five trained soldiers.'

'But you didn't know the country. You'd never have reached Timber Creek.'

'There would have been a search. The army wouldn't let an incident like that pass without an inquiry,' Major Denison said. 'Your father would have found himself in big trouble.'

'I don't think so,' Lucy said. 'It's easy for strangers to get lost in the bush and do a perish. But there are other ways too. Crocodiles don't leave much in the way of evidence.' She fell silent and her face paled as the memory flooded back of her mother shooting Barney, the young Aboriginal, then pushing his body into the waterhole. The crocodiles had made short work of his corpse. She wished she could forget, but some things remain forever.

'Sister, what's wrong?' Major Denison asked.

'A memory I wish I didn't have.' She remembered her mother's slap after she'd questioned her. Thank goodness she had died and Dad had met Dorothy.

'Can I do anything to help?'

'It's something I have to work out for myself. Most of the time it's no problem, but…' She shrugged. 'Dad would never have let you take any of his horses.'

'I could see he valued them,' Major Denison said. 'I've a soft spot for horses too. Now I've seen this war I realise how he felt. It's terrible what we put the animals through, but I can't stop it. I can only try my best to repair a little of the damage.' He eased himself backwards in the bed and scowled. 'The saddest part of my job is shooting the animals I can't help. When you next write to him, give him my regards and tell him he was right.' His grin returned. 'You can tell him too that he'd done a good job of eradicating that poison weed. I couldn't find any on my way back to Timber Creek.'

19

Number 3 ACCS Nine Elms, Poperinghe,
Saturday, 10 November 1917

'Do you mind if I go to the resuscitation ward?' Lucy asked Bob. 'I might be able to help Vicky. This waiting around with nothing to do is more wearing than being busy.'

It was four days since the Australians and Canadians had finally captured Passchendaele and the number of wounded being brought to the CCS had dropped dramatically. It had been over an hour since their last patient and for the moment the theatre was empty.

Bob lifted his head from the report he was reading. 'That's fine. I'll send William if I need you.'

Lucy found Vicky massaging the legs of a mud-encrusted soldier. 'Can I do anything?' she asked.

'If you'd refill the hot water bottles that'll be a big help. Once he's warmer his circulation may improve. Then you can give me a hand to clean this mud off him.'

After she'd refilled the bottles, Lucy brought a bowl of warm water and began to sponge the man's face. 'He could be a ghost,' she said.

'He's been lying out in a shell hole for at least a couple of days with a lump of steel in his stomach,' Vicky said. 'His pulse is almost non-existent.'

A doctor had joined them as Vicky was talking. 'Don't waste any more effort on him. He won't make it,' he said.

'I think he's clinging to life, Doctor. I'd never forgive myself if I didn't try to save him,' Vicky said.

The doctor frowned then bent over the man with his stethoscope. When he straightened up he said, 'You could be right, and we've nothing more urgent for the moment.'

'He'd recover if we gave him a blood transfusion,' Lucy said. She though about Malcolm's article.

'I'm not going to waste my time on that sort of thing.' The doctor frowned and started to walk away, then he turned back. 'That procedure is too complicated for a CCS. We'll stick with the saline.'

'I helped in a transfusion last year, when I was in Number 5. It wasn't difficult, but it needed two doctors and me.'

'And did the patient survive?'

'No. The blood was incompatible.'

'My point exactly,' the doctor said and left.

'Do you think it would have worked?' Vicky asked. She hadn't stopped massaging the man.

'If we matched the blood I think it would, but I can't force the doctor to do it. I think he's scared to try something different.'

Two hours later Vicky became excited. 'We've won. His pulse is stronger. We need to get him to the theatre. Where's the doctor?'

The man's pulse strengthened and his breathing became less laboured, although he didn't regain consciousness. The wound began to bleed again when the orderlies transferred him to a stretcher. Lucy accompanied them to the theatre and directed them to the operating table, then she dressed and scrubbed-up ready for the surgery.

'Are you touting for business now, Lucy?' Bob asked, and grinned. 'I've seen some things in the army, but this is the first time a nurse has gone searching for patients.' He donned his surgical overalls, moved to the basins and began to scrub his hands.

Lucy laid out the instruments and said, 'We should get started, Bob. He's very weak and the sooner we get that shrapnel out of his stomach the sooner we can stop the haemorrhaging.'

'Very good, Sister.' Bob laughed. 'I'm so glad I have you to advise me on procedures.' He returned to the operating table, tugging on his gloves, and began to examine the patient. 'You say you've spent hours fighting to get his pulse back?'

Lucy nodded. 'He was so cold and plastered in mud when they brought him in that the doctor didn't think he'd pull through, but Vicky was determined to save him. She said it was a miracle when he improved.

'A couple of hours' resuscitation,' Bob said and pursed his lips. 'We'd better not lose him then.'

Half an hour later Bob and Lucy watched the orderlies carry the man away to the recovery ward.

'You did a good job, Lucy, you and Vicky. It makes you feel good when things turn out so well. Two days lying in a muddy hole with a lump of shell casing in the guts. She's right, it was a miracle. By all the textbooks he should be dead. It's an even bigger miracle that he didn't drown.'

Lucy shuddered as the memories of the mud she and Lex had crossed came flooding back. Most of the mud in the shell holes had had the consistency of thick gruel.

'You think he'll be all right now?' she asked.

'Too early to say, but he's got a good chance, as long as there's no infection. Far better than he had lying in the mud. He must have a strong constitution to last so long without help.'

'He's Australian,' Lucy said. She felt an affinity with the man after expending so much effort fighting to restore his pulse. It was an empathy that never had time to develop during the normal theatre work.

'That explains it, then. Do you know, I never realised that nationality would make that much difference,' Bob said and dodged as Lucy pretended to slap him.

Number 3 ACCS Nine Elms, Poperinghe,
Monday, 12 November 1917

Lucy turned in her blankets, and snuggled down, trying to get back to sleep, but Vicky's voice cut through her sleepiness.

'Are you awake?'

'I am now,' she said, peering up at her friend. 'What's wrong?'

'With all these guns I can't sleep. I have to get away from this place for a break. Come for a walk with me, please?'

'I may as well, now you've woken me.' Lucy sat up and rubbed her eyes. 'What's the weather like?'

'It's stopped raining.'

That's an improvement, Lucy thought as she slipped out of bed and began to dress. She checked her watch and saw it was 1442 hours. She'd slept for over five hours, oblivious to the sound of the guns that Vicky complained about, but now the edge had been taken from her tiredness they'd prevent her getting back to sleep. Three days earlier, to the nurses' dismay, the guns had been installed close to the hospital. Now they fired sporadically and the intermittent discharges were more noticeable than a constant barrage. She grabbed her respirator and steel helmet and joined Vicky, who was waiting at the flap of the tent.

'Let's see if we can find a truck we can hop on,' Vicky said.

They passed the ambulance station and started along the corduroy road that led between their CCS and the Canadian CCS a little to the north.

'Did you hear about the two Fritz officers we had in the ward last night?' Vicky asked.

Lucy shook her head. 'What about them?'

'Once their wounds had been treated they'd been interrogated, but they wouldn't say anything. Late in the afternoon all the patients on one side of my ward were moved out and the two Fritz were brought in. I'd just gone on duty when they placed another patient in the bed between theirs. His head was so heavily bandaged that all you could see were his eyes, mouth and ears. I was told he had serious head wounds. The MO said I was to check his pulse every fifteen minutes, but not to worry about anything else.

'I thought it was a bit odd, but I still had over twenty patients to attend to, so I didn't give it much thought. His pulse seemed quite normal. Far stronger than I would have expected, and there was no sign of bleeding. Each time I went towards his bed I could hear the two Fritz chattering away in German, but they stopped as I approached. Sometime after midnight they fell asleep and the next time I went to check the man's pulse he grabbed my hand and asked for the MO.

'The MO arrived with two orderlies and a stretcher. I was told to go with him to the reception tent. When I removed his bandages he wasn't wounded at all.' Vicky stopped and raised her steel helmet, rubbing her forehead. 'These damn things are heavy.'

'So, he was spying on the Fritz?' Lucy said.

Vicky nodded. 'It was the intelligence officer who'd been interrogating them. He was so excited about what he'd learnt he rushed off to report.'

'Did he say what it was?' Lucy asked.

'Of course he didn't. You don't think they'd tell us anything like that.' Vicky turned to watch a truck labouring along the corduroy road heading for the front line and waved to the driver.

'Hop up,' the man said when the truck stopped. They scrambled into the cab and he said, 'What is it with you sisters? Always wanting to hop on for a ride towards the line? I would have thought the CCS was close enough to the front for anyone.'

'It gives us a change of scene. It's so depressing to see all the fresh wounds as the men are brought back,' Lucy said. 'It doesn't worry us when we're busy, but when we're off duty it plays on our minds.'

She shuddered at the sight of the mangled bodies of the horses that were intermingled with the wreckage lining the rim of the road. The conversation she'd had with Major Denison three days earlier intruded, but she forced the memory to the back of her mind, concentrating to hear what the driver was saying over the noise of the truck.

'I've not seen a truck like this before. What make is it?' Vicky asked. She was sitting in the centre, next to the driver, with Lucy squashed against the door.

'A Dennis, a damn good lorry. Fast too. It can do fifty-five miles an hour.' The man braked and changed into a lower gear to negotiate a section where a shell had ripped a gap in the corduroy. 'But this is fast enough for these roads,' the driver said. 'It takes a bit of stopping when you've a load on.'

'What are you carrying?' Lucy asked

'About two tons of wire and stakes with a few shells. Mostly shrapnel for the eighteen pounders, and I've about fifty thousand rounds of .303 for the men in the line. I prefer this to the high explosive I've been carting for the past week: 9.2-inch for the howitzers. If I'd had that on board I wouldn't have stopped to pick you up. There must be a stunt coming up judging by all the stuff we've been bringing up.'

About six hundred yards ahead, Lucy could see a detachment of field artillery. She counted a dozen guns and limbers hauled by horses. Vicky had fallen silent and had her mouth clamped in a tight line. The guns must have reminded her of the artillery officer. Lucy squeezed her hand and was rewarded with a smile.

Shells began to fall along the corduroy road and the driver accelerated. The truck bounced over the logs so that Lucy and Vicky had to brace themselves against the dashboard. Ahead they saw the road disintegrate in an eruption of mud and a flash of flame as a shell found its mark. More shells hit the road and the logs of the corduroy were scattered. Shattered trucks and damaged guns mingled with the logs.

The driver slowed to walking pace, picking his way around a truck that was lying on its side, its chassis twisted with the rear axle hanging by one spring, dangling onto the logs. He worked past the wreck only to find a few yards ahead that a crater and torn timbers completely blocked the road.

As the driver switched the engine off Lucy looked ahead to the guns and saw that several had been hit. The shelling stopped and the sounds of explosions were replaced by screams of pain and fear from the horses. A party of men ran towards the damaged guns. As soon as they reached the wreckage, a couple of them began to cut the horses free while the rest started to lever the damaged guns and limbers off the road. Lucy could see one of the horses thrashing around on the corduroy, its entrails spread at its side. It struggled to lift itself to its feet, its front legs straight and braced, but it was twisted unnaturally with the back legs stretched out, both to the same side.

She said, 'Dad, you were so right.'

'What's wrong?' Vicky asked.

'Those horses. We shouldn't be using animals in war.' She was about to blurt out the story of her father hiding the horses, but pulled herself together. 'Why doesn't somebody put the poor beasts out of their misery?'

She leant behind Vicky and pulled the driver's rifle from the securing clips. As soon as she was out of the vehicle she opened the bolt and unclipped the magazine, checking it was loaded, then set off at a run, scrambling across the blockage on the road.

'Hey! Bring my rifle back,' the driver called.

When she reached the horse with the broken back and saw the extent of its wounds she steeled herself, took aim between its eyes and squeezed the trigger. She reached the next horse that stood holding a splintered leg, squealing with pain. She shot it as the driver reached her with Vicky hard on his heels.

As Lucy handed his rifle to him the driver said, 'I didn't expect that. Where did you learn to fire a rifle?'

'Guns are necessary in the bush. You never know when you have to put an injured animal down, but this is awful,' Lucy said.

'Well, you did better than I would have done. I'd have probably missed. I've never fired the damn thing, except in training,' the driver said.

'Poor animals.' Lucy stared down at the last horse she'd shot, shaking her head.

'Never mind about the animals. The men have to put up with the shelling, and so do we,' Vicky said. 'Don't forget Lex and all the men who've been killed.'

Lucy's head shot round towards her friend. 'I'm not likely to forget Lex, or the men. Come on, Vicky. There'll be wounded men in that lot. We're here so we've work to do.'

Lucy said to the driver. 'Thanks for the ride. We'll get a lift back with one of the ambulances.'

Cambrai, Tuesday, 20 November 1917

Adam peered down at the battlefield, searching for a suitable target for his next run. He'd give Fritz strafe, he thought, thinking of the German phrase for these airborne attacks. *Gott bestrafe England.* They'd see about punishing England.

He circled slowly, examining the battlefield where he could see the British infantry behind lines of tanks, advancing towards the barrage. From this height they looked like toy soldiers. The infantry must have been pleased about the tanks—what a difference they made. He remembered the times he'd hopped over to attack the Germans without any protection except for the shelling, and knowing that it had to stop before they closed with the enemy trenches. He could see that the tanks were doing a better job of protecting the men, and there were hundreds of them. Where had they gotten them all from?

A series of rapid flashes came from ahead of the advancing men and he saw a German machine-gun post dug in at a shell hole. He pushed the stick forward and began his dive. His height dropped quickly, but before he was close enough to open fire, a tank turned towards the German position, flames flaring from its guns, and the flashes from the shell hole stopped abruptly. Adam pulled out of his dive and checked for enemy planes. The sky was clear and he circled again, watching the battlefield below.

Several Germans in the crew at the machine-gun post had fallen, but two men started back towards their lines, one of them stooping with the gun across his shoulder, the other staggering behind carrying the tripod, an ammunition box and the can of cooling water. The Germans had barely covered five yards when more flashes of flame spewed from the tank and they dropped. The tank moved inexorably on to drive over the machine-gun position. It continued without faltering and one of its tracks flattened the machine-gun as if it was made from Plasticine.

Adam eased the stick back and began to climb, searching for another target, still thinking about the tank below, fascinated by the ease with which it had dealt with the machine-gunners. He saw a second tank attending to another German machine-gun and wondered who had come up with the idea. And why do they call them tanks? They didn't look a bit like any tank he'd seen.

The tanks had suffered so much criticism since they'd been introduced. It was true the early ones had been unreliable, often breaking down before they'd reached the start line, but they'd improved. Adam was irritated by the negativity. It wasn't as though the designers had had the luxury of time to test them thoroughly before they were handed over to the men who'd use them. But the Mark IVs were showing their worth.

The creeping barrage moved forward and the leading tanks reached the first German trench. They stopped for a moment to release their fascines, then they drove across the causeway that the bundles of brushwood had created. As they crossed they sprayed the trench with machine-gun fire and German troops abandoned their positions in panic. Most of the survivors surrendered, but a few raced back towards their second line, straight into the shelling that had moved on ahead of the advancing British.

The second German trench was where his bombs would be most useful, Adam thought. He checked the sky. Behind him he could see three more Camels from his squadron, but there was still no sign of German aircraft.

As he turned to the east he thought of the latest rumour circulating at the breakfast table, that the Royal Flying Corps and the Royal Naval Air Service were to be amalgamated. The bearer of the buzz even had a name for the combined service, the Royal Air Force. That officer often came up with rumours that turned out to be correct. This time though, he lost credibility when he mentioned the date for the inauguration of the new service—April first next year. He'd protested vigorously that he was telling the truth, but no one took him seriously any longer.

In the distance Adam saw a battery of German artillery and turned towards them, pleased to see that the three Camels were swinging into line behind. As an ace with eighteen confirmed victories to his credit, it was natural that the less experienced pilots should follow him, and since he'd been promoted to lieutenant, he had some authority.

The Camels climbed steadily and by the time he was over the German guns he was at sixteen thousand feet. He levelled out and checked his companions. The other Camels were lined up behind him, but there was still no sign of enemy planes. He shivered, despite his sheepskin lined thigh-boots. At this height it was cold, and he wished the leather coat was lined with sheepskin too.

Adam felt uneasy, but pushed the nagging worries behind him

and began his dive. He released his four twenty-five pound bombs at the first gun, but he'd left it late to turn away and felt the blast buffet the Camel. More blasts followed, but he was clear, and climbed back to five thousand feet where he circled, watching and waiting for the other three pilots to complete their runs. The gun he'd targeted was wrecked and by the time the other Camels had joined him, two more guns had been demolished. The ground around another was pockmarked with craters. That gun seemed to be intact, but, judging from the frantic activity, the bombs must have inflicted casualties.

Without the drag of the four bombs, the Camel was noticeably more responsive, but he was getting low on fuel. The four planes flew west in a group at a little over ten thousand feet. On a road below them Adam saw a squad of German troops carrying boxes. He waggled his wings to attract the attention of the other pilots, gave them a wave then, with an elaborate gesture, pointed to the road.

He peeled off from the group and his speed built as he dropped. The altimeter was showing two hundred feet when he levelled out and began his run. The Germans were already scattering, most leaping into a drainage channel at the side of the road as he approached. He lined up on the drain and pressed the triggers of the twin Vickers.

At the end of his run he swung right and began to climb. He could see the second Camel halfway through its strafing run with the other two still diving, spaced out to allow the plane in front to get clear before beginning to fire. He thought about a second run, but noticed six observation balloons about a mile away. Eliminating those observers would be more helpful than giving a few foot soldiers the gee-up. He began to climb.

The four Camels approached the balloons in line abreast. As Adam swooped towards the nearest, two dark shapes dropped from the gondola, falling swiftly until white canopies blossomed above them. He dismissed them, lined up on the balloon and fired a long burst, watching the fall of shot. Every fifth round was tracer, and he grinned with satisfaction as the burning bullets vanished into the balloon, which erupted in a flash, the fabric folding over itself as it began to fall. He skimmed over the blazing wreck and lined up on the next balloon.

This balloon too burst into flames and he flew on. He glanced behind and was pleased to see that the other Camels had accounted for the remaining balloons.

As he began to climb a burst of tracers flashed across the nose of his Camel. Instinctively he turned to the right, glancing over his shoulder, automatically correcting the inherent dive as the plane spun round. They'd been jumped by a *jasta* of Albatros fighters. He'd no time to count, but there were well over a dozen and they were diving in a concerted attack.

One of the Camels began to spin. Adam swung round towards the attackers. They were outnumbered at least four to one, but they had to meet the German attack, and each pilot was in his own fight for survival. Briefly he pressed his hand against the pocket with the bullets the nurse at the CCS had given him.

The distance between his Camel and the diving Germans decreased rapidly. He lined up on the nearest enemy, flying through a storm of bullets and fired a burst in return. To his surprise he escaped without being hit. Then he was clear of the enemy planes, climbing above them and able to take stock.

Below the *jasta* he could see the spinning Camel. In the distance he could see another Camel with flames licking along the fuselage. The fourth Camel had also come up through the *jasta* and was climbing below him.

The German planes had pulled out of their dive, except for one, which had smoke trailing from its engine. Now he could see them all he counted. 'Sixteen, plus the damaged one,' he breathed and clenched his teeth. He levelled out at twelve thousand feet and circled until the other Camel joined him. For a few seconds they flew side by side and Adam pointed towards the British lines, jerking his finger to emphasise that he intended to return to the airfield. The other pilot gave him the thumbs-up. They turned west, making for British territory.

The Albatros had spread out, no longer the cohesive body they had been, although they were still a formidable array. Adam could see the damaged Albatros was well separated from the others, flying lower and slower. He guessed it was about three thousand feet below the *jasta*, which itself was still a couple of thousand feet below him.

He glanced at the instrument panel: 0920 hours. Just ten more minutes of fuel left under normal circumstances, but he'd been pushing the plane hard. It would be too risky to mount an attack, even against a damaged adversary. Then there were the other Albatros in the *jasta*.

A few sporadic shots came from the German reserve trench, but the markers fell short. He could see the enemy troops frantically digging, trying to reinforce the trench. He glanced behind. The pursuing planes had levelled out, but they were no closer than before. They were no further behind either. The other Camel was now well ahead.

The German second line was under artillery fire and he flew over it without attracting any shots. Thirty seconds later he passed over the tanks and breathed a sigh of relief, grateful to be over British territory. He flew on, searching the ground for suitable landing spots as he went. When the engine began to splutter he could see a grassy field ahead, a pasture full of cows, and he dropped lower, circling once. The cattle panicked and rushed to the edge of the field as he touched down. The plane bounced and he had to correct a lurch to the left on the uneven grass. The engine gave a last gasp and cut out as he rolled to a stop.

'Sorry to disturb your breakfast, ladies,' he said to the cows as he walked away from the plane. At least it's in one piece. That's an improvement, he thought.

20

Number 3 ACCS Nine Elms, Poperinghe,
Saturday, 24 November 1917

The home sister met Lucy as she walked across to the nurses' mess. 'You have a visitor. He was asking how he could find you, but when I told him men weren't allowed in the nurses' quarters he looked so disappointed I took him to the kitchen.'

'Who is it, Maud?' Lucy asked. She wasn't in the mood for socialising, but she was becoming curious. The home sister had said 'he', but she couldn't think of anyone… unless John Mitchell had come over from the lines for some reason.

'I never thought to ask,' Maud said.

That's strange, Lucy thought. Maud was usually so inquisitive. 'I suppose I may as well find out what he wants, but I'll need to wash and tidy up first. I was on my way for some warm water, but if he's in the kitchen… Can you bring some for me, please?'

Ten minutes later Lucy entered the kitchen to see a solidly built man dressed in flying clothes sitting at the end of the table, talking to the home sister. She felt thrilled and wished she'd taken more care with her dressing.

'Adam. What are you doing here?'

'That's a fine way to greet a chap who's flown halfway across France to see you,' Adam said and grinned. 'Come and sit down. The sister has made a pot of tea. Can I pour you a cup?'

'Thank you,' she said as he stood and pulled a chair out for her. 'I thought your squadron had been posted south. How on earth did you get permission to come all this way? You did get permission, didn't you?' She realised she was being rude, but she was flustered. 'How are you?'

She glanced across to Maud who had turned her back and was

busy peeling potatoes for the evening meal. She'd have to be careful what she said. By the time dinner was over every sister in the CCS would know she'd had a visitor, but there was no reason they should know the gist of their conversation.

'I'm well,' he said. 'And I'm really pleased to see you again. How are you?'

'I thought you were down near Cambrai.' He nodded and she rushed on, her voice betraying her anxiety. 'You're not injured, are you?'

'Of course I'm not, and permission didn't come into it. I'm just a messenger boy. The generals needed an urgent package taken to St Omer and the usual courier was ill, so I volunteered for the run. I wanted to see you and it was too good a chance to miss.' He reached for the ashtray and stubbed his cigarette out. 'I'm on my way back. The CO would have torn a strip off me if I hadn't taken the opportunity to check up on a pilot from our squadron. He was left in this CCS before we moved south, but he was transferred to Étables. When the matron checked she was told he's on his way to Blighty.'

'Wouldn't the CO know what was happening to one of his men?'

'Of course, he knows the pilot's in dock, but he won't know about Blighty. Not yet anyway. Sometimes it can take a while before that sort of information reaches a unit.' He drank the last of his tea. 'I worry about you up here, so close to the fighting. I wanted to make sure you were safe.'

Lucy could feel the warmth spreading up to her face, which annoyed her, but she was pleased he was interested enough to care that she was safe. 'You don't have to worry about us.'

'I can't help being concerned. Don't forget, I was here when those bombers came over. And I think of you every time I feel those bullets in my pocket.'

'You still have them?' Lucy said, suppressing the desire to give him a hug. That really would cause tongues to wag.

'Of course I have. They're my good luck charms. I worry about you. Every man in the unit is concerned about you nursing sisters being so close to the front, but you're the one I care about. You're someone special. It's not right they put you so close to the fighting.'

'It's where we're needed,' Lucy said. The heat had left her face and she was more in control of her emotions. She took the empty cups across to the sink. That he worried about her and said she was special gave her a comfortable feeling. Her hands trembled as she rinsed the cups. She'd never experienced this emotion before, but she tried to keep her voice normal. 'The men in the front line are fighting and dying for our freedom. What we're doing is nothing in comparison.'

'I know the Fritz bombers are still coming over. And by the look of those craters they're shelling you as well?'

'Sometimes,' Lucy said. She wanted to play it down, but there was no point in denying it completely. After seeing the shell craters he'd never believe that.

'Sometimes? I can see it's a bit more than sometimes.'

Lucy tried to deflect his attention from the CCS. 'What about you? You pilots are more at risk than anyone.' She wanted to be alone with him, somewhere they could say things without being overheard. The other sisters would be abuzz if they went off together, but they'd make a meal about his visit even if they didn't. Let them, she thought. There was nothing she could do to stop them, but while they were gossiping about her they'd be leaving some other poor soul alone. 'Let's go for a walk. I need to get some fresh air before I go on duty.'

'That will be lovely,' he said. 'Where would you like to go?'

'We don't have a lot of choice. It's either the railway line or the corduroy. It doesn't matter which.'

'We'll take the railroad then. There won't be as much mud.'

Number 3 ACCS Nine Elms, Poperinghe,
Wednesday, 12 December 1917

John Mitchell looked up from the book he was reading as two sisters entered the ward. One of them was familiar, but it took him a few seconds to place her. She was one of the two who'd come up to the line that time when the other sister had been killed. He tried to think of their names, but failed. That was no surprise. There had been so many men whose names he couldn't remember. This sister had been in the group he'd escorted from the south when they'd first arrived in France, the one from the cattle station in the Northern Territory. Strange how he could remember that yet he couldn't recall her name.

'How are you feeling, Captain?' the sister asked.

'I feel as if a train hit me, but I expect I'll live. Fritz can't get rid of me that easily. And the name's John.' He reached out with his left hand and the book slipped. He scrabbled for it, but with his right shoulder and arm strapped up he was clumsy, and the book fell to the floor. He gasped with pain. 'Damn it. I feel so helpless with all these bandages.'

The sister from the cattle station retrieved the book and said, 'You make sure you do live. We can't waste all this medication.' She smiled and perched on the edge of the bed with the book clutched in her hand.

The other sister placed a thermometer in his mouth. When she removed it she picked up his record card and made a note of the reading before she took hold of his left wrist to check his pulse. After she made another entry she replaced the card and moved along to the next bed.

The sister with the book remained. 'You'll feel a bit battered for a few more days, but it will gradually wear off as the bruising heals. Your shoulder will be sore for much longer, but if you work with your remedial masseuse I'm sure you'll be able to do everything you used to do.' She reached forward and placed his book on his locker. 'Your shoulder movement may be a bit restricted, but not enough to hold back a bloke like you. You'll probably have to go to Blighty for a while.'

John's eyes widened. 'You think I have a Blighty? That'll be good, but I'm not so happy about the shoulder. You're not trying to set me up for bad news?'

'I'm being honest with you. They have better facilities for rehabilitation in England, but the decision isn't mine. Whatever they decide, I'm sure you'll be fine in the end.'

'I hope you're right about that. I'd hate to be a cripple.' He frowned again, trying to recall the sister's name, but he gave up and said, 'I'm sorry, Sister, I remember your face, but I can't remember your name. I feel bad about being so rude.'

'You're not being rude at all, John. Why you should remember my name? Don't worry about it. I'm Lucy. Lucy Paignton-Fox. How come you were wounded? I thought the fighting in this area had ended early last month.'

'Fritz bomber. We'd been pulled out of the line for rest and reinforcement. Queer thing fate. I go through all these stunts, even the hell of Pozières and then this Passchendaele, and get nothing more than a scratch, only to cop this when we're out of the line.' Now that he'd mentioned Passchendaele he fell silent, his thoughts running over the horror.

'Are you all right? You've gone pale.' She sounded concerned. 'Can I get you anything?' He didn't answer and she hurried away.

She returned with a bottle and a small tumbler. 'This will help,' she said, filling the glass with amber liquid. 'It's Cognac.'

John shivered, but pulled himself together. 'Sorry,' he said. 'Memories.' He took the offered glass and drank. 'Thank you. Those memories are raw. I lost the last of my old platoon in that Passchendaele stunt. Lofty Mathews and I had been together for years… since before Gallipoli. We were privates together.' His head drooped and again he fell silent, frowning, thinking of the mateship that had existed in the platoon: Lofty, Don, Ted and young Muscles. He swallowed. If only he could cry it might help. In the trenches staying alive had been the main thing, there had been no time for tears. Staying alive and killing Fritz. He lifted his head and said, 'They were more like brothers than men under my command. Real good mates. Now they're all gone and I'm left on my tod.' A single tear trickled down his face, but after breathing deeply he regained control. 'Good men, every one of them. Sorry, I didn't mean to bore you with my nightmares, Lucy.' He drained the glass.

As she refilled it she said, 'You're not boring me. Talking about it may help and I do know something of mateship. It's the same for us nurses, although probably not so strong.'

'I don't know about that. I remember the time you and that other sister came up to the line because she was worried about her fiancé.

You'd only come to give her moral support. That's mateship.' Her fiancé had been new to the platoon and he hadn't known him well. He remembered the event as if it was five minutes ago and tried to recall his name. Dev… something like that. Then it came to him… Devlin. 'When Fritz dropped into the trench and killed him she was like a wild animal.' He almost added that he'd probably died because he was thinking of her safety instead of concentrating on the enemy, but it would not be appropriate. 'She was only a little woman, but the way she wielded that spade…' He shook his head slowly. 'You were so different, so calm, caring for the wounded. You inspired the men and their opinion of you sisters has been sky high ever since. It was high before that, but that clinched it. I'm glad you weren't anywhere near that Passchendaele stunt though. That was…' He broke off, closed his eyes, screwed his face and swallowed, then breathed deeply.

'We knew it was bad from the casualties,' Lucy said and gripped his good hand. 'Try to relax. Let the tears come. No one will think you're less of a man.'

John continued as if Lucy hadn't spoken. 'It was as bad as any stunt I can remember. And for what? I know I should be positive, lead by example and all that, but by the time we finally took the ridge, us and the Canadians, the village was nothing but rubble, not worth a brass razoo.' He shook his head in disbelief. 'When's it all going to end? I wish someone could tell me that.'

'I wish that too at times, but at others I think it's as well we don't know. It could go on for donkey years. Wouldn't that be awful?' She reached forward and refilled his glass. As she replaced the cork she said, 'That's your last. We don't want to get you drunk.'

He smiled and lifted his eyebrows in mock surprise. 'Why not?' Then he became serious again, his face filling with sadness. 'I don't think it will go on for years. Fritz must be running short of men. Some of the prisoners we're capturing are just young boys, and they're so poorly trained. They should still be at school, still be in short pants, not trying to fill an army uniform. Their rifles are longer than some of them are tall.'

A tear trickled down his face. 'Poor little bastards. They're shitting themselves, and who's to blame them.' He was worked up and didn't apologise for his language. 'Children in the front line, that's almost as bad as bombing hospitals, but that's Fritz for you. We'd taken a mob of prisoners during Passchendaele, a lot of them were these boys, and a corporal who can speak a bit of German heard a Fritz officer telling them that they'd be tortured. They must have believed the rubbish because I could see they were terrified. The poor little buggers cringed every time one of us went near them. When the corporal told me what was going on, I took the Fritz officer aside. The Fritz are dead keen on this officer-to-officer nonsense, especially for prisoners. He wasn't so keen on it by the time I'd sorted him out. He'd have had difficulty eating for a few days.'

'What if he complains to someone? You could be in trouble.'

'Oh he complained, all right. He squealed like a pig in a slaughter house, but it didn't take long to convince the arrogant sod that he was being unreasonable.'

'Isn't hitting prisoners against the regulations?' Lucy asked.

'As far as I know all the Hague Convention says is that prisoners of war must be treated humanely. If a boy tells lies, his father will usually chastise him, but this Fritz was no boy. He was bigger. So was the chastisement.'

John became thoughtful. 'Just poor bloody boys. Fifteen years old at the most. They're like gangling puppies, not an ounce of muscle on them. Those who've been killed look like babies lying in the mud.'

'So young?' Lucy said. He saw the revulsion in her eyes. She fell silent for a moment, then she said, 'I never realised that Fritz was so desperate.'

'He's that, all right. We're better off for reinforcements, particularly now that the Yanks have joined in. They're not a lot of help at the moment, too few of them, and they don't have any experience. They'll need a few months before they'll be up to scratch, the ones who are still alive, that is. It'll most likely be the end of next spring before there'll be enough of them to do anything useful. I wish the bastards had come in earlier though, instead of sitting on the fence until they saw which way the wind was blowing.'

'You think they did that, sat on the fence until they saw who was winning?' Lucy asked.

'Looks that way to me,' John said.

'But Americans have been fighting with us all through the war. They have a lot of medical teams over here. Whole hospitals sometimes.' She thought of Adam. 'Some of them joined the British army.'

'I'll give you that, but the American army wasn't over here. It seems to me their politicians were happy enough to make money from selling us what we needed, but that was as far as they were prepared to go.'

He saw Lucy raise her head, listening, and he became aware of the drone of aircraft engines in the distance.

'What are you going to do when all this is over, John?'

'I suppose it'll be back to stock work, but it'll take a while to settle after this lot. I don't know if I want to go back to Gidgealpa. It's a bit far from anywhere, and I don't think there'll be anyone who'll understand.' He reached across and rubbed at the bandages at his right shoulder. 'They'll have a new head stockman anyway. He won't want me around.'

'Lean forward,' Lucy said. He did so and she fluffed up the pillows. 'Why not give the Northern Territory a go? I know Dad would like a white bloke to help him run the station. Now he's older he finds mustering is getting harder each year and he'd appreciate someone he can discuss his ideas with. The Aborigines are no use with the planning. They just agree with everything he suggests. He lost a leg in the Boer War so he'd understand how you feel. I'm sure you'll get on okay.'

'It would be a good idea to start somewhere fresh. You sure he won't mind?'

'Of course he won't. I'll write to him. Mum was a nurse in the Boer War so she knows what it's like as well. You'll have no trouble fitting in. You have a piece of paper?' She wrote the address, then said, 'It's south from Timber Creek, that's west from Katherine. There's a steamer from Palmerston,' she broke off. 'I keep forgetting, they've changed the name. It's Darwin now. That's the easiest way to get to Timber Creek. Just ask the copper at the depot for directions to Aughton Park. There's only one track from the north.'

The noise of the aircraft engines had become louder. 'Is that Fritz?' John asked.

Lucy nodded. 'Every night about this time he pays one of the hospitals a visit. Fortunately we've had no intake today, so the theatre's not working. That's why I'm in the wards. We should put the lights out.' She leant forward to the hurricane lamp. 'Do you mind?'

'Go for it. No point in giving the bastard an easy target… Sorry, forgot myself,' he said and flushed.

The aircraft droned closer and John said, 'Don't you have a shelter to go to? Somewhere you'll be safe from the bombs.'

'We have a dugout, but we don't use it unless the CO gets windy and orders us to go down. We can't scuttle into a hole and leave the patients to fend for themselves,' Lucy said.

'You should use it every time he comes over.'

'How can we abandon a patient on the operating table? If we did, he'd be dead by the time we got back and Fritz would have won,' Lucy said. 'If all the patients were down in the dugout, it would be different.'

John could see how determined Lucy was. 'Well, if you won't go to the dugout, at least get under my bed. That'll give you a bit of protection.'

Lucy grinned and said, 'Get under your bed? Well, what an invitation, but I must decline. Our job is to take care of you, not the other way round.'

The sound of the planes grew faint. 'They'll probably fly on to St Omer and dump their bombs there. They quite often do that on nights like this, when there's no moon and they can't find us,' she said and relit the lamp.

'Where are our fly boys?' John asked. 'They should be doing something to stop him.'

'How can the pilots see him? Anyway, he's very high. That's why the archies didn't open up. It's not easy when the moon's bright. When it's as black as this, the pilots would have Buckley's,' Lucy said.

'But Fritz is up there now. If he can do it, why can't our boys?'

'St Omer is a large town,' Lucy said. 'So he'll find plenty of lights to guide him. He doesn't care what he hits. Whatever damage he does disrupts something.'

'You're right,' John said. 'I shouldn't be so critical. I'm aware of the airmen's difficulties. It's just that I feel so helpless lying here in bed.'

He fell silent and his eyelids drooped. 'Sorry, Sister. I feel knackered. Can you help me down before I fall asleep, please? It's that cognac you fed me.'

She helped him to lie down, tidying the blankets and straightening the pillow. 'You'll feel better after you've had a good sleep.'

Number 3 ACCS Nine Elms, Poperinghe,
Tuesday, 25 December 1917

The nurses' mess was abuzz, and in the background a gramophone played a carol repeatedly. They had few records and 'Silent Night' was the only carol. It'd be worn out by lunchtime, Lucy thought, but so what? Hearing the same tune over and over was tedious, but she said nothing. The other nurses seemed to find some solace in the words.

The mail had arrived a couple of hours earlier. That was the best Christmas present they could have had and, like her, most of the other nurses were still reading their letters and cards. She'd open her parcel later.

Sergeant Tom Sorrell had appeared with four of his men during the morning. They had brought a small fir tree, which they were now dressing with the help of five nurses, using homemade decorations.

Someone had asked, 'Where did you get the tree?'

'Santa Claus,' Tom had said with a wink, and the question was dropped. They must have pinched it, Lucy thought, but he would probably say they'd only borrowed it. What did it matter? It's just a tree and it's Christmas.

She pulled out the letter from Adam and began to read it again. It would have been good if he was here, she thought. It would be better still if her father and Dorothy and her grandparents were here too… No it wouldn't. She wouldn't wish this on anyone, least of all those she loved. If only she could be home with them. She hoped they were enjoying the day. She glanced at her watch. It would be almost over for them, but here the sisters still had Christmas dinner to enjoy.

Tom and his men had brought a couple of geese with the tree and they were now in the oven. They'd saved the feathers and had two pillow slips filled. After lunch they'd run a sweep so that two of the sisters would have new pillows.

'Captain Mitchell ordered me to make sure you sisters had a good feed for Christmas,' Tom said. 'When we saw these geese we thought they looked lonely, so we brought them along to spend Christmas with you ladies. We knew you'd be able to take proper care of them.'

They'd take proper care of them, all right, Lucy thought, and wondered where the soldiers had found them. Found them before they'd been lost, of course.

Tom's eyes twinkled and he added, 'Turkeys would have been better, but you can't expect to find turkeys in France.'

The home sister chivvied them up, fussing like a mother hen, bullying them to take their places at the table.

Lucy grabbed Sergeant Sorrell's hand. 'Come on, Tom. You can sit next to me. I want to hear how John Mitchell was before he left. He was rather down in the dumps when he was here. Hardly surprising with that shoulder wound. My name's Lucy.'

'Pleased to meet you, Lucy. Captain Mitchell told me to look you up. I was going to do that after dinner.' He offered his hand and they shook. 'He was depressed when I saw him too,' Tom said. 'The railway line had been bombed, so the train couldn't get through and they'd taken all the wounded off at St Omer until they sorted it out. Then the hospital train had to wait until the backlog of supplies was cleared. It's more important to get supplies up to the front than get people out.'

'That's hardly fair,' Lucy said. 'The men on that train are all wounded and need to get to safety. They've done their bit.'

'The men at the front need food and ammunition, and a few more blankets wouldn't go amiss in this weather. Supplies have to be given priority. If they haven't got what they need we'll have a lot more men wounded. A lot more dead too. Don't worry yourself. The wounded are just happy to be out of it for a while and they're in good hands.'

'I suppose that's true. How did you manage to get to see him?'

'The CO had requisitioned a car, but he was called away. As I'd taken Sergeant Mathews's place, he sent me along to check that Captain Mitchell was okay. I'd only met him a few hours before he was wounded and the CO thought it would be good if I found out a bit more about my platoon. He thinks a lot of Captain Mitchell.'

A nurse, who was helping the home sister, placed bowls of soup in front of them and the conversation lapsed for a while.

'We all think highly of John,' Lucy said. 'When we first met him he was a sergeant.' She passed her plate along to the end of the table where they were being collected. 'How was he?'

'He was upset because he was unable to tell me much. The company had lost so many men. Sergeant Mathews's platoon had suffered worse than most. That had been Captain Mitchell's platoon before he was promoted. Only one man was still alive and he'd escaped unharmed, Brigham Young. It's strange the way these things happen.'

Tom paused and leant back as a sister served their main course. When she moved on he continued. 'They've promoted Brigham to corporal, which will be a big help to me. I'm new, so I don't know anyone other than Brigham. Neither did Captain Mitchell. That's him over there, the big man with two stripes on his arm.'

'Brigham Young. Is he a Mormon?' Lucy asked.

Tom shook his head. 'In the army Brigham is often the nickname for anyone named Young. Didn't you know? Captain Mitchell told me about the sisters here, you in particular, and he told me where to find the geese.' Tom grinned. 'Brigham says he was always a resourceful chap.'

'It sounds like he hasn't changed,' Lucy said. She thought back to the train journey north. Then her thoughts moved on to their conversation in the ward after Passchendaele. Mateship. 'I know he was feeling the loss of his men. He blamed himself.'

'That's nonsense. From what Brigham has told me they'd have lost a lot more men if it hadn't been for Captain Mitchell. I'm not surprised the men respected him. They thought the sun shone out of his…' He flushed. 'Sorry. Forgot myself, but you know what I mean.'

Lucy laughed. 'Don't worry, I've heard it all before. He still thought of them as his mates despite his promotion. It'll take time, but he'll get over it. Or maybe just learn to live with his memories.' She put a slice of goose in her mouth, chewing thoughtfully before she continued. 'I'm so pleased he's gone to Blighty. I don't think he'll be back. His shoulder was in a terrible mess and it was touch and go for a while. We thought at first we'd have to take his arm off. I can't see him ever having full movement again, so he won't be back fighting. They'll most likely put him in a supply unit or something.'

'From what I hear he won't take that lying down. If he's not fit for active duty, the most sensible thing would be to send him to a training unit. That way he'd be doing something useful, passing on his skills.'

The home sister called them to be quiet and pay attention. 'I've put some threepenny pieces in the pudding, so be careful. I don't want anyone choking on bits of silver.'

'With all you nurses to watch out for us, we're jake,' one of the men said.

'Don't you bank on it,' Vicky said. 'We're all off duty so we'll have to send you to the theatre. It won't take long for the surgeon to open you up. We can't afford to lose threepence from the mess funds.'

Laughter greeted this and when it subsided another man said, 'You're all heart, Sister.'

21

Number 3 ACCS Nine Elms, Poperinghe, Thursday, 25 April 1918

For the past week, the Germans had bombed the Australian CCS twice every night. Each time the Gothas departed within five minutes, but they dropped a terrifying number of bombs in that short time.

The CO addressed all the sisters in the mess on the morning after the third night of raids. Matron Kenny looked angry, but resigned, at his side.

'It appears that the Boche have decided to disrupt all our hospitals. The raids are so heavy we cannot ignore them, but as he's so punctual we can take action to alleviate the danger. Major Simmons will organise the surgery so that, unless there are complications, all operations will be completed before the German planes are overhead and no new surgical procedure will start for thirty minutes. That will allow us to extinguish all lights and permit the theatre staff to go to the shelter.' The CO raised his head and surveyed the gathered nurses, then continued. 'The other sisters will also take shelter before the bombers arrive. Therefore, my orders are for every sister to proceed to the dugout on my signal and remain there until the all-clear.'

A buzz of conversation spread amongst the nurses.

'You do mean the off duty sisters, sir?' a nurse asked.

'I said EVERY sister. Every includes those sisters on duty.'

'What about the patients?' another nurse asked. 'We can't leave them.'

'You can and you will,' the CO said firmly. 'The wounded will have to take their chances and a number of orderlies will be on duty in the wards for the period the sisters are in the shelter. If you nurses are wounded there's no one else to care for the patients, and who is going to tend to your injuries? The orderlies do their best, but they don't have the necessary skills. Do I make myself clear?' He examined the assembly and waited until the murmurs had subsided. 'Are there any more questions?'

A few sisters shook their head and mumbled 'No'. The rest just stood in abject silence, their eyes downcast.

'Good,' he said. 'That's all, ladies.'

'I don't think it's right,' Vicky said as she and Lucy walked back to their tent. 'We'll be safe, but the men won't be and they've already been wounded. They'll think we're cowards.'

'I don't like the idea of leaving the patients either, but what he says makes sense,' Lucy said. 'And I think you're wrong about the men. You know as well as I do, they worry about us. Right now I need to get to bed. I'm so tired that if I don't get some sleep I'll collapse.'

Number 3 ACCS Nine Elms, Poperinghe, Saturday, 27 April 1918

The hospital wasn't the only unit to take advantage of the Germans' punctuality. The newly established Royal Air Force was ready to pounce on the bombers when they arrived. A squadron, or sometimes two, would wait high above the hospitals and attack the German planes before they began their runs. Later they'd harass the survivors as they turned for their bases.

'It's time you went to the dugout. We're finished here for the moment,' Bob Simmons said.

Lucy glanced at her watch as she hurried along the duckboards: 0150 hours. When she heard the drone of aircraft engines she stopped and craned her neck, examining the sky. Adam would probably be up there somewhere, she thought, and crossed her fingers. His squadron had been moved north a week earlier.

In the light of the full moon she could see silhouettes of planes, stark black against the sky. They were too high to make out their markings, but from their formation she could tell they were Fritz bombers. She counted fourteen. A couple of nearby anti-aircraft guns opened up, which confirmed her thoughts.

As she watched, five smaller silhouettes appeared, closing rapidly with the Germans in a shallow dive. Lucy saw flashes of flame from both flights of planes, and streams of tracers laced the sky. For a moment exhilaration coursed through her body as the RAF planes threaded their way through the massed bombers, but it was soon replaced with apprehension. The RAF planes veered to their right, beginning to climb as soon as they had clear air space. One of the bombers blazed and began to lose height. Another bomber flamed and tilted, then began to spin out of control.

The rest of the bombers continued in their formation.

Searchlights flared, brighter than the full moon. One caught and illuminated a bomber, and more searchlights locked onto the plane. The anti-aircraft guns began to fire and she could see the shells bursting around the plane, but it flew on. More planes were lit up and the anti-aircraft fire increased.

The RAF fighters returned and the guns fell silent. Another bomber dropped out of the formation, flames spreading along a wing.

'You beauts,' Lucy said, and became aware of the irony. She was trained to save lives, but here she was rejoicing in the death of these men.

The bombers were now overhead and explosions ringed the CCS. Debris from the anti-aircraft shells was adding to the danger.

'For Christ's sake, Sister, let's get you into that dugout. Come on.' An orderly grabbed her arm and she snapped out of her inertia. She recognised Ralph, one of the men who was always so courteous and helpful. They began to run, but a bomb exploded ahead of them. A wave of hot air hurled Lucy from her feet to dump her in the mire at the side of the duckboards.

She scrambled onto her hands and knees, her ears ringing and the smell of burning cloth pungent, making her cough.

'Are you all right, Sister?' Ralph asked, the concern strong in his voice.

'Yes. Yes.'

'Come on then. Hurry,' he said, pulling her to her feet, and they scrambled over the wreckage of duckboards, past the smoking cra-ter, rushing as best they could towards the safety of the dugout. They were still threading their way through the damaged duckboards when she heard a whistle…

Lucy shivered, and pain shot through her body. Although she was lying on her back, she felt dizzy and could hear nothing, other than the ringing in her ears. Small fires were burning around her and she could see men rushing towards her. They had hurricane lamps, which added to the light from the moon and the flames and threw faint shadows along the ground.

Some of the men were fighting the fires and others began to drag the duckboards aside. She was surprised that they could work without making any noise, but the ringing in her ears was loud. Acrid smoke drifted over her and she coughed, gasped and tried to roll onto her side.

Something beneath her back was twisting her at an awkward angle, and she was in agony. It was soft with a hard centre and when she grabbed it, it was sticky and covered in a coarse material. She renewed her efforts and managed to roll onto her left side, gritting her teeth against the increased pain as she struggled to raise her torso and drag it free. When she eased herself down she saw she was gripping someone's ankle. Above the knee the leg looked as if it had been mauled by some wild beast and she struggled to suppress her horror. She thought she'd become inured to the sight of severed limbs, but this bloody, torn and shredded flesh made her stomach churn. She tried to hurl the leg away, but it was heavy and she was weak and it fell with the mangled thigh inches beyond her reach.

Her back still hurt, but less than before. The bloody stump taunted her and she struggled onto her hands and knees to move further from it.

'Help,' she called, but not one of the men turned towards her. 'Help.' She became frustrated at her lack of strength.

She tried to crawl away, but the soil crumbled as she scrabbled to drag herself up a slope and she realised she was in a bomb crater. Her pains increased and she collapsed in a spasm of coughing, clasping her arms around her chest to try to reduce the pain. She became aware of the taste of blood in her mouth. It was cold and she shivered, coughed again and saw one of the men fighting the fires turn to look in her direction.

'Help,' she called, and this time he rushed towards her, his mouth opening and closing as if he was shouting, but the sound was feeble. All she could make out was 'Stretcher' and 'Blankets'. Strong arms grasped her and a vicious pain stabbed through her body.

Lucy heard a faint female voice say, 'Thank goodness…' It was light and she squinted, trying to work out where she was. She was uncomfortable lying on her side, and her whole body ached. A cool cloth wiped her face and she opened her eyes, recognising Alice, one of the day shift sisters in the postoperative ward.

She tried to roll over, but her back flared in agony and gentle hands restrained her. Alice said something, but Lucy couldn't make out her words. The sister leant forward with her mouth close to Lucy's ear and repeated, 'Stay… You're in no… doctor.'

Lucy watched her hurry away. She had a vague memory of an explosion, but could not recall anything after that until she found herself in the crater.

Alice returned with Bob Simmons.

'Thank God,' he said. 'I was worried about you.' His voice, normally deep and resonant, was almost a whisper. He spoke slowly, but Lucy still struggled to hear. 'You were caught by a bomb on your way to the shelter. I've removed six pieces of shell from your back. One piece had passed right through your body piercing a lung. Luckily it missed all the other vital organs.'

'A lu… lung?' Her mouth was dry and she had difficulty forming the words. Alice held a glass of water to her lips and Lucy sipped.

'That's right. We've inserted a drain, but I'm worried about pneumonia.'

'My top was torn open,' Lucy said. 'The men saw me naked?'

'Being naked is the least of your worries, young lady. Be grateful they found you when they did. I don't think you would have lasted much longer. You could have only been in that crater for a few minutes, but you'd lost a lot of blood. It'll be a while before you recover, so I'm sending you to a base hospital. You'll need long-term care.'

Lucy thought of the hundreds of men she'd seen naked over the last three years. They'd been no more than patients. She remembered the orderly who had been helping her across the tangle of duckboards. 'How's Ralph?' she asked.

'Ralph?' Bob asked, frowning.

'Yes. We were together and he must have been wounded. Do you know what's happened to him?'

'I've no idea. They brought no one else into the theatre. You say he was with you?'

Lucy struggled to stem her tears. 'I found a leg…' She shuddered and winced. As she recovered she said, 'If you've not seen him in the theatre, he must be dead.'

Bob half turned to stare towards the ward's entrance. 'If that's the case he could have been buried. I'll ask.'

'Thank you. He must have shielded me from the blast.' She shuddered again, screwing her eyes tight, but was unable to prevent them flooding with tears.

South of Poperinghe, Friday, 3 May 1918

Captain Adam Hayward saw the glint of sunlight and turned his S.E.5a towards it. His squadron had been re-equipped with the new planes at the end of March and he'd been promoted at the same time. His mother would have been so proud. He was glad he'd resisted the pressure to transfer to an American unit. After all, he was half British and he'd lost touch with the States. His father hadn't replied to any of his letters for over a year and he wondered what had happened to him. He'd always been closer to his mother, but it would be good to know how his pa was. He'd write again tonight.

This dreaming was no good. He'd have to concentrate on his flying… and Fritz.

After the Camel, the S.E.5a was so docile and inherently stable that it was easy to fly, but he missed the vicious turn to the right that made the Camel so good in a dogfight. At first he'd missed the second Vickers machine-gun, although the Foster mounted Lewis gun on the upper wing allowed him to fire upwards. When the Fritz fliers were above him that was a huge improvement. Now he'd become familiar with it, he thought it a beautiful plane and was delighted with its performance. None of the rotary engines used in the Camels could compare with the Wolseley Viper, and with a top speed of one hundred and twenty the S.E.5a was faster by twenty knots. At altitude its performance was superb. No German plane could match it.

Below, he thought he could see an airstrip. He checked his watch: 1820 hours. Plenty of time before dusk. In his mirror the other three planes on patrol with him were lined up in echelon, their twenty-five pound Cooper bombs in silhouette, two under each wing.

He dropped a couple of thousand feet. It was definitely an airstrip and he could make out bombers in their sandbagged parking bays, their black crosses clear through the netting that had been draped over them. He became angry, thinking of Lucy, wondering if these were the planes that had bombed the Australian CCS. Now he was lower he could see the flattened grass of the airstrip between the two lines of parking bays. It stood out as clearly as if it had been marked with paint. At the end of the strip he could see one of the bombers being readied for take-off. A second Gotha moved down the flattened grass towards it.

A lorry towed a trailer loaded with bombs along the line of parking bays. The bastards were reloading, but he'd sort that out. He knew there'd be other airstrips and other Gothas. For the moment there was nothing he could do about them, but he'd do his damn best to prevent this *jasta* flying tonight.

The news in Vicky's letter had devastated him. His lips thinned. Lucy—almost killed by a Fritz bomb. Vicky hadn't said how seriously she'd been injured, only that she'd been sent to Blighty.

He squinted at the Gothas below and pushed the stick forward, beginning his dive towards the ground. The S.E.5a was a strong plane, and that increased his confidence. In his mirror he saw his three companions following.

He lined up for the end of the runway, an approach that would take him over the first of the sandbagged bays. Lines of tracers, like sparks from a grindstone, flew to meet him, but too angry to be afraid, he lost height, gaining speed, aiming the nose at the Gotha in the bay. At a little over six hundred feet he dropped his number two and three bombs and pulled back on the stick.

'That's for Lucy,' he called as the plane lifted when the bombs dropped away.

He swung to the right and saw the earth at the entrance to the bay erupt. He cursed, readjusted the angle of his dive so the Gotha at the end of the strip appeared over the plane's nose. The bomber that had been taxiing down the strip had joined it. Adam lined up on the planes and released the two remaining bombs.

This time, as he turned away to avoid the blast, he saw the two planes engulfed in dirt and flames.

Free of his bombs he began to climb, circling as he gained height so he could check on the damage he'd caused. A rent appeared in his upper wing and he became aware that the anti-aircraft guns were now firing. Below he saw men rushing towards a group of smaller planes parked in the end two bays.

Although he'd missed his first target, the crater at the mouth of the parking bay would prevent it moving out and, with luck, the shrapnel would have done some damage. At the end of the strip both Gothas were burning fiercely, one leaning on its port wing. The second S.E.5a was climbing and the third had finished its run and was beginning to climb too. Two more planes were wrecked, and a third flashed into flames as he watched.

The lorry with its trailer of bombs was halfway across the strip when the last S.E.5a released its first two bombs. The trailer erupted in a ball of fire with the lorry flung aside like a discarded toy. The RAF plane swung round in a wide turn to begin its second run, but its nose dipped and it began to spin. The plane fell rapidly and hit the ground.

The anti-aircraft fire was heavier and for a moment Adam felt scared, but he still had work to do. He could see a huge crater had been carved across the centre of the airstrip. That would prevent bombers using it until it had been repaired, but a fighter plane was taxiing from the end bay.

He lined up, heading along the strip towards the taxiing plane. It was an Albatros D.V, and he eased the angle, aiming for the fighter as it gathered speed. Two more Albatros fighters were close behind it.

At less than one hundred feet, Adam pulled out of his shallow dive, lined up on the leading plane and fired a long burst. The tracer rounds smashed into the cockpit and he saw the pilot slump. The Albatros slewed to the right across the strip. A wing dropped, struck the grass and crumpled, so that the plane spun round to be side on to the plane behind. He saw the rudder of the second Albatros move to the left, but the pilot was too late and the plane piled into the first.

Two explosions rent the air as he lined up on the third German plane and he saw earth thrown up from one of the parking bays to his left. He fired a long burst at the third Albatros, which had slowed and was veering to the left to avoid the wreckage that littered the runway. His tracers hit the engine cowling, then the cockpit. He smiled with satisfaction as the plane careered into a sandbagged parking bay.

His companions were now strafing the Gothas. He began another run and saw that the flames had died down at the two he'd destroyed. Two more bombers were wrecked. He turned his concentration to his flying and picking his own target, ignoring the fire from the German guns.

Another Albatros emerged from the end bay, the side of the fuselage and the expanse of wings too good a target to ignore. Adam fired another burst, but bullets began striking his plane and he jinked to the right, levelled out and increased speed before climbing again.

He was on his sixth run, concentrating on finding another target, when he realised he hadn't seen his number two for some time. The machine-gun fire had slackened, but the anti-aircraft fire was still heavy. He flew low along the line of sandbagged bays, where at least six Gothas were likely beyond repair. One of the engine nacelles on another bomber had collapsed and it lay at an angle on the lower wing. Most of the others would be damaged in some way too, so those planes wouldn't be going anywhere for some time.

The gauge showed he was getting low on fuel, so it was time to turn for home, but he wanted to make one final check on the damage they'd caused before leaving.

A quick glance at his watch showed it was 1855 hours, over two hours until sunset. He climbed to make a high level run over the airfield. His tally, he was certain, was two Gothas and three Albatros, and probably a fourth. The other pilots would have their own claims, but an overall report would interest the CO. The machine-gun fire started again, but he increased his altitude and the tracers began to fall short. He could see no other S.E.5a and hoped the other pilots had turned for their base. Like him they'd need to refuel.

Now that he was the only British plane over the airfield all the anti-aircraft fire was concentrated around him. While the action had been furious, he'd been detached, but now the shell fire terrified him. Some bursts were close, but he forced himself to continue with his slow reconnaissance run.

Adam confirmed the six damaged Gothas he'd seen previously were total write-offs. They included the one he'd thought was just a probable. The one with the dropped engine nacelle would need at least new wings and the fuselage was extensively holed. That was likely a write-off too. The remaining five bombers were all holed, but whether they could be repaired was not something he could confirm. All the Albatros fighters that he'd fired at were definites, as were two within a parking bay at the end. Three more seemed undamaged.

Three Gothas and four Albatros, he thought. They brought his total to forty-one. He accelerated, ignoring the shell bursts that ringed his plane to fling showers of shrapnel in every direction. He was no longer over the airstrip when a shell exploded alongside his plane and a shard of hot metal sliced along his right forearm. More shrapnel lodged in his leg and something large smashed into the back of his seat, driving him forward away from the squab and over the controls. Something thumped the back of his head and he gasped. The plane began to dive. He struggled back into the seat, hauled on the control stick and levelled out.

As soon as he had the plane flying level, he checked his instruments. The oil pressure and water temperature were fine, the engine was running smoothly and the flaps and rudder were working as they should. He set the course back to base.

The seat squab stuck into his back so he was forced to twist at an uncomfortable angle. He eased himself forward and felt along the squab. The left hand side was bent forward and beneath the thin padding he could feel a sharp point. He reached behind to find a splinter of steel wedged firmly into the frame. It was hot and, after a futile attempt to free it, he abandoned his efforts. He needed to concentrate. His head throbbed and he reached up to press his hand against his helmet. When he pulled it down it was sticky with blood. He was becoming dizzy. For a moment he thought he would vomit, but he fought the nausea, breathing deeply, and his stomach settled. He fished his field dressing from his pocket and wrapped it round his forearm. It was difficult to secure the tapes, but he managed a knot of sorts and the dressing stemmed the worst of the blood. He ran his hand over his right thigh and felt the small shrapnel scraps that were wedged in it. They were not causing much pain so it would be best to wait until he was back at base and let the medics sort them out.

His head worried him more. He couldn't feel anything lodged in his skull, but the throbs were vicious. Blood saturated his neck and shirt and he was having difficulty focusing.

The needle of the altimeter climbed steadily. At fifteen thousand feet he levelled out. A flash in his mirror caught his attention. He checked more carefully and saw it was a reflection from a plane. An Albatros was climbing behind him. Three other planes followed, but he was too far ahead for them to catch him. He put the plane into a shallow dive and opened the throttle. All being well he'd be on the airstrip in ten minutes or so.

His neck wobbled as if it was rubber, and again he felt nauseous. He breathed deeply trying to control the reflex. Vomit was the last thing he needed in the cockpit.

The German planes fell further behind, but he was getting weaker and concentrating was becoming difficult. The controls grew heavy and he wondered if he would have the strength to manoeuvre the plane for a landing when the engine began to misfire. For a moment he panicked before he remembered the reserve fuel tank, which held enough for fifteen minutes. That was plenty to get him back to base.

He turned his attention to the wireless that had been fitted four weeks earlier. The new equipment was useful when directing artillery fire, but while he could speak to gun crews, they couldn't speak to him. But if he could get a message to one of them they might be able to use their field telephone to pass it on to base.

A few minutes later he saw a gun battery and picked up the microphone. For a moment he couldn't remember what to do, but when he felt the switch on the side the instructions flooded back. He pressed the button and passed the message, repeating it twice, wondering if they'd heard him. A gunner climbed into the open where he waved a flag and Adam waggled his wings in thanks.

22

West of Poperinghe, Friday, 3 May 1918

'At least he's got the machine back in one piece,' the driver said as he pulled a lorry to a halt at the side of the S.E.5a.

His passenger, another airman in the ground crew, leapt from the cab. 'The archies have had a good go at him though. Cop a gander at the size of those holes.' He pointed to the tear in the fuselage behind the cockpit. 'Why the hell isn't he getting out?' He grabbed a pair of steps and hurried to the plane, clambered up and peered into the cockpit.

An ambulance pulled up beside the lorry and a sergeant medical orderly rushed out. He ran to the plane as the airman turned and called, 'Bloody hell. He's all shot up.'

The sergeant shouted, 'Out the bloody way then. Let me up there.'

The airman jumped down. 'He looks like he's bought it. There's blood everywhere,' he said as the sergeant hurried up the ladder and reached across the cockpit coaming.

The sergeant felt for a pulse. 'He's alive, but we can't hang about. He's leaking like a bloody colander. Got another ladder?' His partner, an airman medic, had moved to the foot of the steps and was holding a folded stretcher. 'Open that up and let me have it. Then get up the other side.'

The ground crew returned with a second pair of steps and the medic scrambled up. 'That head wound worries me,' he said as he helped the sergeant wedge the stretcher in position.

'That's two of us, but we can't check him out while he's in the bloody cockpit. Give me a hand, but be careful.' They eased him from under the protruding breech of the Vickers machine-gun, up and back from the seat, and over the fairing behind the cockpit. 'Thank Christ he's unconscious. Why the hell did the designers put this bloody hump here?' The sergeant slapped the fairing.

'If he hadn't been out when we started, he would be by now,' the medic said as they lifted Adam over the hump and onto the stretcher. 'Shit!' he screamed and wobbled on the steps.

'Just look what you're bloody doing,' the sergeant barked. 'I told you to be bloody careful. I don't want you falling off and dropping matey here. He's got enough bloody problems.'

'It's damn hot.'

'What is?'

'This soddin' exhaust.'

They straightened Adam on the stretcher and strapped him in.

'Get your ladder round here.' While the medic repositioned the steps the sergeant called to the ground crew. 'You blokes give us a hand to lift him down, and be bloody quick about it.'

They eased the stretcher to the ground and into the ambulance.

'Do you think he'll live?' an airman asked.

'Stuffed if I know,' the sergeant said. 'We can only hope. It's difficult to believe he brought that machine down with those wounds. Bloody good landing too.'

A second ambulance arrived and a doctor rushed to the side of the stretcher. After a brief examination he said to the sergeant, 'Get that head wound bandaged. We'll have to get him to the sickbay for a more thorough examination. I'll give him an anti-tetanus when we get there.'

1st Australian Auxiliary Hospital, Harefield, England,
Sunday, 12 May 1918

'Lucy, wake up. Wake up.'

Slowly she dragged her eyes open, trying to control the spasms of shaking that racked her body. She was disoriented and bathed in sweat. Her heart was racing and her head ached. The two beds at the far side of the small ward were out of focus and the window a blur.

'Lucy. Are you all right? You were screaming.'

She felt cool hands on her forehead and her shaking eased. She was still breathing quickly, but her heart palpitations subsided and her focus cleared.

'You were thrashing about like someone crazy.' The nurse leant across her bed and straightened the blankets. 'If you don't lie quiet you'll aggravate your shoulder.' Lucy recognised Annette. She was older than most of the nurses, one of the few who'd spent time in a casualty clearing station.

Lucy dragged a deep breath. Slowly her breathing returned to normal. 'That dream again, Annette. I was back in that bomb crater with arms and legs falling all over me.'

'Amputations?' Annette brushed hair back from Lucy's forehead. 'I can understand. It was awful the number of limbs we took off.'

'Not amputations. These were just mutilated lumps of flesh piling up all round me, ragged and dripping with blood.'

'What was piling up round you?' Lucy raised her head to see a young doctor whom she hadn't met before. Matron Reeves glowered behind him.

'Limbs, doctor. Ragged limbs, as if some animal had ripped them from bodies. It's the same nightmare I keep having. Doctor Jameson knows all about it.'

The doctor listened to her heart and as he hung his stethoscope back round his neck he said, 'I'm not going to disturb Doctor Jameson on a Sunday afternoon for something so trivial. It was just a bad dream. There's nothing wrong with you. Pull yourself together.'

'Pardon?' Lucy said, wondering if she'd heard correctly. The doctor ignored her, turned and hurried from the ward.

'You heard the doctor,' Matron Reeves said. 'Doctor Jameson is too easy going. If you don't get a grip and stop wasting the doctors' valuable time, I'll report you for malingering.' She smirked and hurried after the doctor like a well-trained spaniel.

Lucy watched them disappear. For a moment she was speechless with astonishment. 'Malingering? How could she say that?'

'Take no notice of her. You're not malingering, Lucy,' Annette said. 'I've seen so many men with exactly the same symptoms. It's shell shock. I'll let Doctor Jameson know, but I can't do so until I'm off-duty.'

1st Australian Auxiliary Hospital, Harefield, England,
Monday, 26 August 1918

Lucy sat in a deck-chair on the lawn outside her ward in the morning sun, reading the *Daily Chronicle*. The news was all good. The Germans were being pushed back in Flanders and France. Bulgaria had agreed to the Allied terms for an armistice and General Allenby had the Turks on the run in Palestine. Surely the war couldn't last much longer. She lowered the paper. Peace, how marvellous that would be, but she wondered how she'd cope with life in a civilian hospital after the trauma of the last three years.

A RAF officer approached across the lawn. A blond curl had escaped from his cap and Lucy noticed his uniform was new. For a moment she refused to accept the evidence before her eyes.

'Adam.' She dropped the paper and stood, her heart racing. 'It is you. Why didn't you write and let me know you were coming?' She rushed towards him and he gathered her in an embrace.

'It's so good to be with you. How are you?' He kissed her. 'The docs refused to give me any leave. Made a big song and dance about my skull being fragile. Claimed I needed time to recover from my head wound. This morning was the first time I've been allowed out, and they'd given me no warning. I came straight away. I've been so wanting to see you.'

'Me too. I did love getting your letters and knowing you were safe.' She snuggled her head into his shoulder. 'I can't believe you're here in England.'

'I'm here all right.' He tilted her chin up and kissed her again. 'You didn't say how you are.'

'I start convalescence leave tomorrow. Three weeks, then I'm back here on light duties for six months or so. After that, I don't know.' She stepped back, examining his face. 'What about you?'

Adam pulled her close again and placed an arm round her shoulder. 'We're being watched.' He nodded in the direction of an open French window where two sisters where standing with huge smiles on their faces.

'I don't care,' Lucy said. 'Don't change the subject. How's your head?'

'Fine. Firing on all cylinders. Say, are you allowed out? We could go for a walk. Maybe have lunch somewhere.'

'I'd like that. I'll have to let the ward sister know, but I'm sure there'll be no problem.' She led him across to a bench near the French window. 'You'll have to wait here. I won't be long.'

She returned five minutes later. 'I have to be back by 1730.' She pulled him to his feet and kissed him.

'The sisters said there's a pub on the canal where they serve a good lunch. Shall we give that a go?'

'I'm happy with that. You say a canal? It'll be interesting. I've never seen a canal before, except from the air over in France. Does it have a name?' Adam asked.

'The Grand Union.' She took his hand and they started towards the gate. It was less than a mile to the canal and they turned north along the towpath.

Ten minutes later they saw the pub on the opposite bank, about one hundred yards beyond an arched brick bridge. Lucy stopped at the top of the bridge, watching a pair of heavy horses pulling a mower around a diminishing stand of hay.

'These fields are tiny,' she said. 'Each one can only be a few acres, and the hedges waste a lot of space.'

'I don't know whether they're small or not. What are yours like in Australia?' Adam asked.

'The home paddock is over three miles by two. Some time ago, Dad started fencing another. He'll have finished it by now.'

'Why so big?' Adam asked as they left the bridge.

'We need plenty of room for the horses,' Lucy said. 'Keeping them in a paddock means we don't need a horse-tailer to watch out for them.' Now that she'd mentioned the horses she felt a pang of home-sickness and fell silent.

'Lucy, what's wrong?' Adam asked. When she didn't answer he drew her to him and gave her a hug. After a moment she sighed and raised her head.

'Just homesick. Talking about the horses…'

Adam bent and kissed her. 'If the newspapers are right, it won't be long now before you're back there.' He led her towards the pub, his arm round her shoulder, and left her while he ordered drinks and two ploughman's lunches.

They ate in silence until Lucy said, 'Here's a boat coming along.' She pointed to the horse towing the boat. 'Just look at that stallion, he's magnificent.'

The powerful black stallion stopped without any command that she could hear, and a man in a peaked cap leapt ashore with a line. He slung a loop round an iron bollard on the quay and raced to the stern where he took another line from a plump woman wearing a colourful apron, and secured that too. The barge surged to a stop and swung into the bank. After he'd adjusted the lines the man walked up the slope to the lock. He closed the top gate on the near side and began to wind a handle, then crossed over to the far side, closed the other gate and wound another handle.

'I see what he's doing. I'll give him a hand,' Adam said and ran up the slope to the lock.

Three children were playing on the barge. A young girl, four or five years old Lucy guessed, was talking to a couple of dolls in the cockpit while two boys, a little older, were chasing around the cabin, heedless of the danger of slipping. The decks at the sides could not have been more than six inches wide.

The woman stepped ashore carrying a nosebag and the stallion lowered his head as she approached. A white blaze ran down its nose and white feathers covered all four feet. Its coat glistened in the sunlight as if it had been burnished. The stallion was another reminder for Lucy of Aughton Park and she felt another pang of homesickness.

She stood and, with her drink and a piece of bread and cheese, walked to the lock. The water level inside was dropping and after a few minutes it matched that on the downstream side. The boatman swung the bottom gate open and began to wind the handle to close the drain valve. Adam copied him, pushing on the horizontal beam on his side and the boatman called across.

'Thanks mate. You're a real toff.'

The man crossed the lock, cast off and led the horse forward while the woman steered the barge into the lock. He secured the boat again, then closed the lower gates.

Now the boat was close, Lucy could make out the details of the colourful decorations. Bright flowers and swirling patterns covered the sides of the cabin, which extended about fifteen feet ahead of the cockpit. Buckets and pots painted with the same patterns were displayed on the spotless cabin roof. M.V. & J.N. Jones was painted in an arc on a panel at the rear of the cabin, and a series of low box-like structures covered with tarpaulins filled the deck ahead.

As soon as the water in the lock was level with that upstream the man opened the upper gates, slipped the ropes off the bollards and jumped aboard the boat. He coiled the ropes, placed them neatly on the deck then leapt back to the lock side.

'Need everything ship shape. The missus can't stand an untidy boat,' he said to Adam and walked to the horse.

Lucy stroked its neck and talked softly to it as it chewed on the feed in the nosebag. She turned at the man's approach. 'This is a magnificent animal. I've never seen a horse as large as this. It must be over eighteen hands. Is it what you call a shire?'

'He's almost nineteen hands. Where do you live if you've never seen a shire horse?' the man asked.

'Australia. We don't have shire horses, well not where I live, they're too heavy. We use Clydesdales.'

'By the way you're handling him I guess you know about horses. Do you have any at home?' the man asked.

'A couple of hundred at the last count, but there could be a few more by now.' She gave the horse a final pat on its neck and moved away. It was a quiet animal and its mane fluttered in the light breeze. The feathers on its feet were coarser than those of the Clydesdales, but they were free of knots and tangles.

'A couple of hundred. I'll be buggered.' He called across to the woman, 'Did you hear that, Jane? Two hundred bloody horses.' He turned to Lucy. 'They'll take a bit of feeding. What the hell do you do with so many? Are they all Clydesdales?'

'Most of them are stock horses, saddle horses, and feeding them's not a problem. Dad has a cattle station,' she said, smiling at the man's confusion. 'It's like a big farm where we breed cattle. We don't need that many horses most of the time, but when we muster they work hard and cover a lot of miles. With a big mob it means we can spell them.' As an afterthought she added, 'We like horses.'

'You bloody well must,' the boatman said and shook his head. 'Two hundred bloody horses. Well, we've got a schedule, so we have to go. Thanks for your help, mate.' He clicked his tongue and the horse started forward. As the boat moved out of the lock the man hopped back aboard and waved to them.

Lucy watched the boat and stallion disappear round a curve in the canal and her homesickness intensified. She hadn't realised how much she missed the station. During her training she'd been too busy, and there'd been even less time to think of home at the CCS. It would be the same when she went to medical school. Visits to home would be rare, and too short by far. It dawned on her that it would be like that for the rest of her life. There were too few people to justify having a doctor in the bush. Even Katherine was too small. Palmerston—Darwin she corrected herself, it would take a while before she got used to the name change—could only support two doctors. She'd only see the station during holidays. She'd never get to know the horses, and she'd be a stranger to the Aborigines.

Adam placed his cup back in the saucer. They sat in a small cafe in Harefield with Lucy staring dreamily into the distance. She looked happy and he didn't want to spoil her mood, but he had to tell her.

'I have enjoyed the afternoon, Lucy, but it's almost time for you to be back,' he said.

'It's been lovely and I'd like to do it again.'

'So would I, but I don't know how I can manage it. I have to go up to Sheringham to see my grandfather. Since Ma and Gran were killed he's not been too good. He's living with Aunt Rose, Ma's sister, but she says in her letters that he hardly eats, just sits there doing nothing.'

'Can you get across tomorrow?' Lucy asked.

Adam shook his head. 'Not possible, sorry. I'm leaving the hospital and there are a lot of things I have to do as part of the discharge routine. It'll take all day.' He saw the disappointment in her face.

'Where are you going?' she asked.

'It's embarkation leave. I'm posted back to France. I do want to see you again, Lucy, but I don't know how I can arrange it. I have to spend some time with Grandpa. Aunt Rose thinks he'll not last much longer.'

'How long is your leave?'

'Just ten days. I wish there was some way to see you, but Sheringham's too far away to get across for a day. I'll write to you. You did say you were coming back here.'

Lucy nodded. 'Why do you have to go back to France?'

He tried to make light of it. 'They need every man. The war's almost over.'

'That's not fair. I haven't seen you for months, worrying if you're okay, then after one day you say you're going back to the fighting.' She propped her elbows on the table and buried her face in her hands.

Adam pulled a chair to her side. 'It won't be for long. Fritz is on the run. You must have seen the news.' He placed an arm round her shoulders, but she shook it off.

'They're still fighting,' Lucy said, sniffed and pulled out her handkerchief to wipe her eyes. 'I was so happy today, but this has spoiled everything.'

'Hey, I'm a soldier and I have to obey orders.' To see her so upset made him feel awful. After a couple of minutes he could see she was calmer. More in control of herself. 'Lucy.'

She swivelled on her chair to face him. 'What now? I know you have to obey orders, but it was a lovely day and this has come as such a shock. There must be some way you can get across.'

He wondered how he could comfort her. 'We're both on leave, but I have to spend time with Grandpa. That's a responsibility I can't avoid. Why don't you… Would you… We could both go.'

She straightened her back. Her face filled with alarm. 'Go with you to Sheringham?'

He nodded, too choked to speak. She sounded shocked and he cursed himself. It was a disappointment, but he couldn't blame her. He shouldn't have suggested it.

'We'd be together for the whole ten days,' Lucy said. Her face had softened and it was as if she was thinking out loud. 'And you'd be able to see you grandfather.'

'I'm sure Aunt Rose will put you up and I know Grandpa will like you. We could go for walks and things. They used to have a picture theatre, but I don't know if it's still open. Please come.'

'I'd love to come,' Lucy said. 'I really would.'

'People will talk. They'll say things,' he said.

'Let them. I don't care. I love you, Adam. I know you have to go back to France, so I want to be with you as much as possible before you leave.'

He felt he would burst with happiness. 'I love you too.' He drew her close so she almost slipped from the chair and he had to wrap his arms round her to prevent her falling. He tilted her face and kissed her. His mind was in a whirl. She loved him.

Mons, Flanders, Monday, 4 November 1918

Adam peered down from the S.E.5a as he flew over the ruins of Ypres thinking about the latest rumours. This morning at breakfast the mess had been abuzz, but these days it was like that every morning. He tried not to listen, but it was impossible to ignore the excitement. The Boche were falling back on every front and speculation ran riot as to how much longer the war would last.

Strange how the officers always referred to the Germans as the Boche, yet to the other ranks they were Fritz. The only exceptions seemed to be those men who'd come up through the ranks like himself.

But speculation wouldn't win the war. They had to keep Fritz retreating and his part in that was to harass the lines of withdrawing troops, and destroy the supply convoys. He glanced ahead to his three companions. They were flying in echelon, with him bringing up the rear.

For a while he managed to concentrate on his task, but the memories of his leave kept intruding. He'd never known such joy. That Lucy had agreed to be his wife made him so happy, but until this war was over their wedding would have to wait. So, let's hurry it up, he thought.

The ten days had been marvellous. The walks on the beach and that little teashop with the homemade cream cakes that Lucy loved so much. And just four days before the end of his leave she'd accepted his proposal. That night she'd slipped along the passage and into his bed. From the way Aunt Rose kept glancing at them she must have known. She'd been pleased when they'd told her they were engaged and for the rest of his leave she'd turned in early and they'd had most of the evenings to themselves.

At lunchtime, while the plane had been rearmed and refuelled, he'd grabbed a sandwich in the mess and been told that a new offensive had been launched. Early in October the British had retaken Cambrai and four days earlier the last of the Hindenburg Line had been rolled up. So much for it being impregnable.

The Americans too had had some success around the Argonne. It was embarrassing that they'd waited so long before joining the Allies, but what could one expect from politicians? At least they were here now and he no longer had to make excuses for them.

Not that he thought of himself as American anymore. He'd been fighting with the British for so long that he felt he was one of them. But he was one of them, he thought, thanks to his mother. It had been over eighteen months since he heard from his father, and that had been just one paragraph with no news. Even when he'd written to him after being wounded, he'd heard nothing. Finally, after his last letter, he'd had a reply from a priest telling him that his father had been ill with consumption and had died after a long spell in a sanatorium. No one realised he had a son and his property had been sold to defray his medical expenses, but there was still monies outstanding. The bill for the priest's services was enclosed.

It had been a shock, but typical of his father to keep his troubles to himself. Now his only family was Aunt Rose and Grandpa, so after he'd married Lucy he'd be going with her to Australia. He'd decided to name Lucy as his next of kin and had talked briefly to his colonel at breakfast. As soon as he came off-duty, he'd fill out the paperwork.

He should stop daydreaming, he thought. He'd have to do his bit to boot Fritz back to Fritzland. He dropped down below the cloud, following the rest of the squadron, and turned his attention to the ground.

This was only the second day he'd been back in the air since he'd returned and the easy fluency with the controls had disappeared. It was as if he was learning to fly all over again and he was grateful to be piloting a S.E.5a and not a Camel. His head was aching as it had yesterday at this height, making it difficult to concentrate. He hoped his reactions would improve as he re-familiarised himself with the machine. The ground organisation was different too. He no longer had a dedicated mechanic and although he'd asked the workshop to fit a mirror, he was still waiting. One more detail he'd have to chase up once he was back at base.

Below he saw the British troops digging in to the west of Doornik. The Germans' trench was a little further ahead. A German convoy of artillery and lorries was approaching from the east, intermingled with squads of infantry that were strung out along the road. He remembered the smart squads that the Germans used to bring up. What a change! These units were rabbles, but they still carried weapons and parade ground smartness had no correlation with the ability to fire a rifle. He put the plane into a dive, selecting a gun and limber for his target. German troops scrambled into the ditches at the side of the road and a couple of machine-guns began a desultory fire in his direction. Compared to the barrage he remembered from May, this was nothing to get excited about. He released his first two bombs, swung left and pulled out of the dive as a massive column of flames and earth threw the gun aside. When the dust cleared he could see nothing was left of the limber and a huge crater cut the road.

Adam gained height and turned for his second run. Again he selected a gun and limber. This time the explosion was smaller, although he could see that the gun carriage had been shattered. The limber was lying on its side, still intact.

Instead of climbing he flew along the road, machine-gunning the German troops cowering in the ditch. He was so low he could see the terror in the faces of the men. The other planes had turned for home. He could see that his strafing wasn't very effective and so he abandoned it. The Cooper bombs were more useful for this work.

He started to climb to follow the other planes, which were already in the distance. He was at five thousand feet when he felt bullets hitting the plane. He swung round in his seat, cursing the lack of a mirror, and saw three Albatros fighters diving onto him. The leader, who was the pilot firing, was less than one hundred yards away, and above him. The other planes moved to the sides and opened up so that he was engulfed in their crossfire.

He put his plane into a shallow dive and opened the throttle wide. The Albatros were no match for the S.E.5a when it came to speed and a quick glance over his shoulder showed that he was drawing away. It was time to go for height. He eased the stick back and turned to the right. The three Germans were way behind and he began to relax, feeling his old skills returning.

Now well above the enemy planes, he levelled out. With plenty of ammunition and plenty of fuel it was too good an opportunity to miss. Another kill would quieten the tongues of the youngsters in the squadron. Most of the pilots were fresh men who had joined while he'd been laid up. Men? More like boys, he thought. They were polite and respectful to his face, but when they thought he wasn't around they were not so charitable. 'Past it' and 'Over the hill' were just a couple of the phrases he'd overheard.

Past it indeed. He'd see about that. He'd show them he was still capable of taking on Fritz.

Adam could see the three Germans below. They were game, climbing towards him. They must have known the Albatros was an inferior plane, but they were still coming. The airspeed indicator was showing one hundred and twenty knots. Flat out.

At three hundred yards, he lined up the ring sight of the Vickers machine-gun on the nearest enemy and squeezed the trigger. His first burst fell short, but the tracers in his second burst hit home and the Albatros spun to the left, its nose dropping. Adam felt the old elation as he drew the stick back and watched the plane begin to fall, spinning out of control.

The other Germans had abandoned the fight and were heading for their base. Away to his left, below the stricken plane, he could see British tanks with infantry digging in around them. He turned for the airstrip to refuel and reload, relieved to be over British territory and safe.

'Forty-two,' he breathed, then jerked and gasped as he felt the burn of bullets striking him under his left armpit. He swung the plane right and turned his head to see a solitary Albatros diving towards him from the clouds, tracers flashing as its Spandau spewed rounds at him. In the distance, beyond the German lines, he could see the planes he'd attacked.

The wounds in his chest restricted his arm movement and he struggled to ignore the agony as he fought to maintain control. The S.E.5a started to dive and pick up speed, then he realised it was no longer being hit. He glanced over his shoulder and saw that the German pilot had abandoned his attack. He levelled out and eased back on the throttle. At the lower speed the plane was easier to control, but breathing was difficult.

He reset his course for the airstrip. A few minutes' concentration and he'd be on the ground, but the controls were getting heavier and his reactions were becoming slower. The landing would not be easy. His thoughts drifted to the Albatros. That would give the new boys something to talk about.

It was a good tally. Forty-two…

23

1st Australian Auxiliary Hospital, Harefield, England,
Monday, 11 November 1918

Lucy eased her back, breathing deeply. Her chest was still sore and all this bending and tugging was not her idea of light duties. There were easier tasks she could be doing that would have made better use of her nursing skills, but the matron refused to let her administer to the patients or work in the dispensary.

As her breathing returned to normal she listened to the church bells in the town. For some reason they'd been ringing for almost an hour. She'd never heard them before. And why today? It's Monday.

She moved to the next bed and began to tuck the blankets in, careful to leave the patient room to move his feet. It had been four weeks since she'd started on the ward. Four weeks of unhappiness. After the relaxed comradeship at the casualty clearing stations everything about this hospital was stiff and formal. So many regulations that seemed irrelevant. She remembered them from her training, but in the CCS patient care was the overriding focus.

Lucy finished remaking the last bed and glanced out of a window, across to the town, wondering why the bells were still ringing.

Matron Joan Reeves walked into the ward. 'You've no time for daydreaming, Sister Paignton-Fox,' the sour-faced overweight woman said in an imperious tone. She pulled the blankets out from the last bed Lucy had tidied. 'These envelope corners are a disgrace. A child could get the blankets tighter than this. Remake them, and when you've finished, make sure the beds are properly aligned. We've no time for sloppy work here. You're not in a CCS anymore.'

Lucy looked along the beds. She could see nothing wrong with the corners or the alignment. A couple of beds might have been further forward by an inch or so, but what difference would that make? 'My shoulder is still sore and my chest hurts. This is too heavy for me.'

'There's nothing else I can trust you with. You had no real nursing experience in France.'

Lucy's mouth fell open and for a moment she was speechless, then her anger flared. 'No real nursing experience. I spent night after night in the operating theatre, sometimes for more than twenty hours, often under fire from the Fritz guns and bombs. There was no time to waste with pointless rules. And you have the gall to tell me I've had no real nursing experience. What would you know about real nursing? You spent the whole war here in Harefield. You'd have fainted at the thought of doing a blood transfusion.'

The matron puffed herself up, her bosom thrust out and her eyes glaring. 'Don't you dare speak to me like that. I was warned about you, but I'll not allow you to disrupt *my* wards. This is a real hospital, not some makeshift lash up where nurses make eyes at the surgeons. We do things correctly at Harefield. We respect the regulations.'

Again Lucy was momentarily lost for words. Warned about me? What the devil did she mean? But she wasn't going to be insulted by this pompous woman.

'Makeshift lash up? In the CCS we saved men's lives. They are the real hospitals, not like this follow-the-rules over-regulated establishment.'

'It's time you started to pull your weight and get on with your work.'

'I'm still recovering from my wounds, still regaining my strength. I'm supposed to be on light duties. If you care so much for the regulations, find me some less physical tasks.' She had difficulty controlling her anger. She'd be in trouble, but so what? The matron couldn't do anything to her. 'If you don't like these envelope corners, do them yourself.'

'Don't you…' The matron's face turned red and spittle formed at the corners of her mouth. 'Rhonda Morgan was right. Be outside my office at 1400 hours. I'll deal with you then. This isn't France. Your standards are not acceptable at Harefield. You'll have to buck your ideas up when you return to a civilian hospital after the war ends. My office, 1400 hours. Don't be late.' The matron gave Lucy one final glare then stormed from the ward.

'Good for you, Sister. It's about time someone told that miserable cow a few home truths,' a man said. 'If you need a witness just let me know. Sergeant Haslam's the name. I heard everything.'

'Thank you,' Lucy said, her smile reinforcing her thanks. A friend of the Moron. That explained a lot. Regulations… What about the patients? This hospital was so regulated that at times it seemed as if it was a machine set up to stifle initiative. The doctors too were quite different to those she'd worked with in France and Flanders. They were aloof and arrogant, refusing to allow the nurses to make any suggestions or decisions about medication, and some of them seemed to delight in making life difficult for her. At times she had the impression that the patients were an irritation that interfered with the smooth running of their lives.

She thought back to the young doctor who'd refused to send for Doctor Jameson after her nightmare. He was typical. Most of the doctors were young and none had served in France, but they were all conscious of their status in the hospital hierarchy. And unlike the CCS, where care for patients eclipsed everything else, the animosity and arrogance of most of the doctors here at Harefield had come as a surprise.

If this was how life in a civilian hospital will be, Lucy was not sure she wanted to be part of it. Even when she became a doctor she doubted she could be civil to people like the Moron, or this wretched Matron Reeves.

Most of the sisters were friendly, but it was the friendliness of strangers. A few were actively hostile, as if they resented her for having experience in a CCS. Or was it because she'd been offered the opportunity to go to medical school?

Dorothy hadn't said anything about attitudes of this sort, but perhaps hospitals were different in her day. After all, it was a generation earlier. The way Dorothy had cared for her father, and her stories, had been the trigger that had stirred her to become a nurse. Now she thought about it there had always been some gentle pressure behind the stories. The encouragement had strengthened when she'd been offered the opportunity to become a doctor.

She thought about the future. As a doctor she'd spend the rest of her life in the company of people like them. She shuddered at the thought, feeling the strength drain from her legs, and sat on a bed. How terrible that would be. Her mind raced as she recovered, thinking over the last few years. She'd no pull of vocation. In the CCS she was doing something essential, but she'd had her fill of blood and amputations. Being a doctor was Dorothy's dream. Lucy had been trying to repay her for her devotion to her father.

She smiled, remembering the trip to the canal with Adam and the magnificent shire horse. Her thoughts moved on to Aughton Park. She'd been thinking of the station so much lately. The idea of only visiting home during her holidays filled her with sadness. But she was going to be married as soon as the war was over. That thought cheered her. She'd have no time for medical school.

Her reverie was broken by an excited nurse who rushed into the ward. 'The war's over. We've won. We've won. It's all over!' She grabbed Lucy's hands, dragged her to the centre of the ward and began to dance circles, pulling Lucy round with her. 'The war is finished.'

Patients who were able sat up, some faces registering disbelief, others grinning like imbeciles. Sergeant Haslam slipped out of bed and hobbled across to the sisters. He had only one leg and struggled to control his crutches.

'That true, Sister?'

She nodded.

He stood swaying. For a moment Lucy thought he was about to fall and pulled free from the sister to reach out to steady him, but he grabbed her and gave her a kiss. She helped him to a chair. As he propped his crutches at his side he said, 'Bloody hell…'

'It's over, Muriel?' Lucy asked, staring at the nurse who'd brought the news. For a moment she was unable to accept the simple statement.

'We've won. The Kaiser's gone and the Germans have surrendered. We've won. We've won. It's all over!' Muriel couldn't contain her excitement.

Lucy sat on an empty bed, her face buried in her hands as tears of relief streamed down her face. She thought back to the CCS. After all these years, all the bombs and all the shells. The fighting might be finished, but the war would never be over for her. She'd never be able to forget the hundreds of operations and the rows of graves that emphasised the failures. She glanced across to Sergeant Haslam. For the men with amputated limbs the war would be with them for the rest of their lives too. They'd always be disadvantaged.

Muriel grabbed Lucy's hands again and went to pull her to her feet, but she hesitated. 'Why are you crying? The war's over.'

'Have you ever nursed in a CCS?' Lucy asked.

'No, I've spent all my time here since I left Egypt. What difference does it make? Nursing's nursing.' Muriel's eyes widened and she stepped back. 'I'm sorry, you were wounded. I forgot. Sorry. Was it very bad?'

'Those sisters are bloody angels,' a man in a nearby bed said and sat up. 'Bloody heroines, the lot of them. There's a lot of us wouldn't be here if it wasn't for them. It's wrong to have nurses so close to the fighting, but we were glad to see them when we were in strife.' He slipped the left sleeve of his pyjama jacket off his shoulder and waved the stump of his arm in the air. 'Saved my life, for one. Even if I'm not all here anymore. Bloody angels.' He paused and Lucy saw him staring at the look of horror on Muriel's face. 'Sorry, Sister. You nurses here do a good job and we're grateful, but you don't have the same conditions as the sisters in the CCS. They shared our problems, the mud, the bombing, the shelling.' The man drew a deep breath, and Lucy could see he was trying to control his emotions. 'That bloody gas. It's wrong to expose women to those things, but we were glad they did though, when we needed them.'

The man pulled his jacket back over his shoulder, slipped down under his blankets and turned onto his side, his back towards them.

'Too bloody right, mate,' Sergeant Haslam said. 'Angels, every one of them. Better than angels. They were real flesh and blood and we were glad to see them all right.'

Muriel glanced at him, then turned to Lucy. 'You didn't say. How bad was it?'

'It had its moments,' Lucy said. There was no point in trying to explain to Muriel. She hadn't been there. She'd think she was spinning a load of bull. 'It had its moments,' she repeated. 'But we had a job to do and got on with it. Everyone was focused on taking care of the wounded. There was no time in the CCS for anyone forever spouting regulations like this matron.' She thought back to Matron Morgan. Her nickname had been so right.

They were halfway through lunch when an orderly walked into the dining hall. 'Mail up, ladies,' he called and walked along the tables handing out letters.

Lucy received three. One from Aughton Park, which, as usual, was in Dorothy's writing. A fat envelope was from Vicky. The other was addressed in a hand she didn't know and she could feel something hard inside, something that slipped around. That can wait, she thought and eagerly opened the letter from home. She read slowly, giving each word time to develop fully before moving on to the next.

Everyone was well and sent their love, and the simple note appended to the bottom in her grandmother's ill-formed letters brought tears to her eyes. *Lots of love from Grandpa and Gran.* She knew how difficult the old lady found writing. She'd never been to school and had been taught to write by her grandfather who had had little schooling himself. The few simple words meant so much and she felt an overwhelming desire to be home.

A short note from her father was tucked into the three pages from Dorothy. He'd discovered that the CCS had been close to the front and was worried, but had refrained from saying anything until her wounds had healed. Now he urged her to stay in England and not go back to France. She smiled at his final words. *You're the future, Lucy. I love you. Take good care.* It was unlike her father to show so much emotion and the desire to be home became stronger.

At least her dad would be relieved now the war was over. He'd be happy too when she told him she was getting married.

Vicky's letter was full of gossip. Robert Simmons had left the CCS and the surgeon who'd replaced him was terribly good looking, and single. So many nurses were requesting to work in the theatre that Tubs had threatened to send anyone else making that request to Étables.

She turned to the third letter. When she opened the envelope a small gold St Christopher and chain fell out and she felt chilled. It was the one she'd given to Adam before he'd left to go back to France. She weighed it in her hand, her mind blank. She recovered and turned to the single sheet, ignored the address, and began to read.

Dear Sister Paignton-Fox,

It is with much distress that I write to advise that Captain Adam Hayward was wounded on November 4th in an action over Mons. He did not recover consciousness after surgery and passed away during the night. Earlier that day he had told me that you were going to be married and was ecstatic. He intended to change his next-of-kin details, to replace those of his father with yours, after he'd returned from duty. We had talked about it, but as he had not done so officially, my hands are tied, at least for the moment. I've bent the regulations as far as I dare and return this St Christopher that you gave to him. I thought it more appropriate than including it with the rest of his personal belongings. He had also told me that his father had died, so I foresee no difficulties in acceding to his request, but it will take a short time before everything is finalised and his personal belongings can be forwarded to you.

He was well respected in the squadron and will be missed. He was a brave man, with 42 confirmed victories. I shall be recommending him for a medal. I am honoured to have served with him. You can be very proud.

Yours sincerely,

A D Howell, Lieutenant Colonel, RAF

Lucy let the letter slip from her fingers and pushed her chair back. She was dry eyed, struggling to control herself as she rushed into the garden. Once she was screened by a hedge she sank to a seat and burst into tears. Adam… dead?

Very proud… She'd sooner be very married.

She felt a hand on her shoulder and looked up. It was Annette. 'You dropped the letter, and this.' She held out her hand with the St Christopher. 'I'm sorry. I saw what the letter said.' She sat and wrapped her arms round Lucy, pulling her close.

Lucy's sobbing intensified as she remembered the last days with Adam. Her world was shattered. Her future was… What future? It was all gone. All she had to look forward to were empty years. She'd been so happy. Now the future seemed bleak, but perhaps not. At least she'd have something to remember him by, something no regulation could prevent.

1st Australian Auxiliary Hospital, Harefield, England,
Friday, 29 November 1918

It was just before lunchtime when Lucy knocked on the door of the matron's office. 'Come.' The command was curt and imperious. Lucy entered and walked up to the desk.

This was the first time she'd met the matron since she'd been suspended from duties on the eleventh. The news of Adam's death had spread like wildfire and the CO had been with the matron when she'd reported at 1400 hours. The CO had offered his commiserations and he must have had a restraining influence because the matron, although not offering sympathy, had been civil. Lucy had been relieved from all duties for an indefinite period.

Matron Joan Reeves lifted her head. Her lips quivered, which set her jowls shivering. 'Yes, Sister Paignton-Fox. What do you wish to see me about? Make it brief, I'm very busy.' She glowered up at Lucy, placed her pen in a holder and closed the lid of the heavy glass inkwell at the side of the desk blotter.

'I've been thinking about my future. Since you told us that this hospital will be closing at the end of December, there'll be more nurses than the army needs. I'm resigning and going home.'

The matron sat back, her eyes flashing anger. She lifted her hand and caressed her double chin. 'You are not free to resign. This isn't a civilian hospital. Until the army decides to discharge you, you will remain subject to military discipline.' She smirked and Lucy saw the hatred in her eyes. 'I have decided that you are to be posted to France.'

'The war is over and…' Lucy began, but the matron interrupted.

'That has no bearing on the situation. We still need nurses in France and you have been posted there. That's the end of the matter. Dismissed.'

'I'm not posted anywhere. This is my resignation.' Lucy placed an envelope on the desk in front of the matron. 'The war is…'

Again the matron cut her off. 'You'll do as you're told, Sister Paignton-Fox. It's time you learnt a little discipline. Didn't you hear what I said? You are not free to resign.' The matron pushed the letter back towards Lucy. 'You have experience of nursing in France and you'll do as you're to—'

'SHUT UP,' Lucy shouted, her voice raised over that of the matron who fell silent, her face registering astonishment, and her eyes blinking above the fleshy bags. 'I said the war is over.'

'Enough. You'll be disciplined. And this time the CO will not interfere.'

Lucy reached across the desk, picked up the glass inkwell and tapped it on the desk top. The sharp rap was loud in the small room and the matron cowered, pushing backwards in her chair, as if trying to move as far from Lucy as possible, but her chair moved just inches before it crashed into the wall.

'The war is over and I signed on for the duration. My service has ended,' Lucy said. She picked up the letter and pushed it into her pocket. 'It is not necessary for me to resign. This letter was just a courtesy. I became a civilian on the 11th of November and as such you have no authority over me. You check my service documents and you'll find everything is as I say.'

The matron recovered and sat forward, her mouth working as if she was arranging the words before she spoke. Finally she said, 'That is no longer applicable. You'll do as you're told.'

There was one certain way to get home and Lucy almost voiced her thoughts, but it was none of the matron's business. Besides, it would involve the indignity of medical examinations to prove her claims and it would leave the matron in command. She wasn't prepared to allow that. But there was a better way. She was still holding the ink-well.

'You stupid old *vache*,' Lucy said, remembering one of the French insults she'd learned. She flung the ink-well down onto the desk top. The impact flipped the lid open and black ink sprayed across the starched white bosom of the matron's apron. That was not intentional, but no less satisfying. Despite her anger, she smiled as she left the office.

On her way to her quarters she stopped at the main entrance and said to the woman manning the reception desk and switchboard, 'Do me a favour, Gladys. Can you telephone for a taxi for me, please? Urgently. I'll be back in a few minutes. It's an emergency and I have to get into town as quickly as possible.'

Her packing took less than five minutes. As she returned to the entrance a taxi was pulling up at the bottom of the steps.

'Thanks, Gladys,' she called as she hurried through the door.

The driver took her case and held the door as she climbed into the rear. 'Where to, miss?' he asked.

'Watford. The railway station.' They turned onto the main road and she asked, 'When's the next train to London?'

'You're cutting it fine, miss, but I think we'll make it if I get a move on. You'll need to look sharpish getting your ticket.'

1st Australian Auxiliary Hospital, Harefield, England,
Saturday, 7 December 1918

It was 0930 hours and Lucy had just arrived. She'd returned to Harefield on Friday evening with the documentation from the army, but had spent the night in a hotel. The interview with the Australian High Commissioner had been most satisfying. Now she was dressed in civilian clothes as the adjutant escorted her into the CO's office.

She crossed to his desk, pulled a chair from the side and sat, placing her handbag and a folder on her knees.

The colonel fiddled with the papers on the desk in front of him. 'You've caused a bit of a stir, Sister Paignton-Fox.'

Matron Reeves sat at the CO's right hand side, a little further away from the desk. She scowled.

'In what way?' Lucy asked as if she had no idea what he was talking about, careful to avoid the honorific. She could see the papers were her service records.

'Matron tells me that you have refused a posting to France. That's not acceptable. I have no wish to discipline a nurse who has such an impeccable and outstanding record,' the CO said. 'I have made allowance for your recent bereavement, but that is no excuse for your conduct. However, in view of your circumstances I'll ignore your absence-without-leave and give you one more chance to accept the posting to France.'

Lucy shook her head. She suppressed the automatic reaction to call him sir. 'Colonel, before you say another word I think you should read this.' She opened the folder, removed an envelope and pushed it across the desk.

'What's this all about?' the CO asked, but he made no effort to reach for the envelope.

Lucy removed a slim file from the folder and placed it on the desk beside the letter. 'If you read the letter, you'll find out. It is addressed to you,' she said and smiled. 'It's from the Chief of the Army. I have been asked to deliver it by hand. The High Commissioner did not wish to risk delays in the post. I understand it's an order. The other documentation contains the details of my discharge.'

The CO picked up the envelope. He read quickly, frowned, then reached for the file.

'When you've complied with the instructions I'd like my service records returned. They are my property.' She sat back, watching Matron Reeves who was red-faced, glaring in fury.

When Lucy had reached London she had booked into Claridge's Hotel and immediately cabled her father, telling him what had happened and asking him to telegraph money for her passage back home. The next week had been a blur of activity. She'd received a telegram from her father every day, keeping her informed of the progress.

She hadn't expected events to move so rapidly or in the direction they had taken, but this outcome was much more satisfying than simply walking away. It was fortunate that her father had been in Darwin and had called at the telegraph office to send a business telegram shortly after her cable arrived. He was well known, and the telegraph clerk had given him a copy of the cable, even though he'd already retransmitted it to Katherine.

Immediately her father had visited his solicitor, who had served with him in the Boer War. As soon as he'd read her cable he contacted an eminent King's Counsel in Melbourne, then he'd phoned the local member of the federal parliament, who was attending to his political duties. The KC and the MP acted at once.

The KC discovered that there were other nursing sisters due to be released from duty at the end of hostilities, but were still serving. It was a couple of days before they had assembled the information and the MP could appraise the Prime Minister. The government had reacted quickly.

The CO placed the file carefully on his desk, lining up the bottom with the lower edge of his desk blotter. 'I have to telephone the Australian High Commission in London for further orders.'

Lucy pushed the telephone closer to the CO's left hand. She knew what his orders were, but it was important that the order came from a senior officer.

'Please wait outside, Sister… Miss Paignton-Fox,' the CO said. 'I'll call you when I've determined what course of action I have to follow.'

'As the telephone call concerns me, I want to ensure that everything you say is correct,' Lucy said. She nodded towards Matron Reeves. 'And to be certain that no one has an opportunity to distort the facts.'

The matron snorted with indignation. 'How da—' The CO glared at her and she choked her words back.

'Very well, Miss Paignton-Fox,' the CO said. He picked up the telephone and rattled the rest. After a few seconds he said, 'I need this Whitehall number. Please get it for me, but before that I need to speak to the hospital administration.'

The CO quickly explained the situation to the major in charge of the administration and instructed him to make arrangements for Lucy's travel home. 'Let me know as soon as you have the details,' he said.

A few minutes later the phone rang again. The colonel picked it up. When he finished listening he sat back, looking Lucy in the eyes. 'You have influential friends, Miss Paignton-Fox.'

'Not true, Colonel. I have a father who has good legal advice. He was an officer in the Boer War, but has a low opinion of many of the senior commanders. After seeing all the wounded that came through the CCS, I share that opinion. Those memories haunt me. For two and a half years we saved men's lives, but were unable to help so many others. Now I'm expected to take orders from that.' She pointed to the matron. 'She wouldn't last five minutes.'

'Please, Miss Paignton-Fox.' The CO held up his hand and turned to the matron. 'You may leave, Matron. I'll see you back here at 1100 hours.'

He waited until the door had closed behind her. 'Miss Paignton-Fox. I was unaware of what was going on. It is remiss of me. I should have known, but pressure of work…' His voice trailed off and contrition filled his features. 'Please accept my apologies.'

The telephone rang and the CO picked it up. He listened for several minutes without interrupting. 'Thank you, Major,' he said and put the receiver down. Lucy went to speak, but he held his hand up again. 'It seems there are other sisters in the same position as yourself in this very hospital, but I'll attend to that matter on Monday. Admin advise that a passage has been booked for you on a steamer, which leaves from Southampton on Tuesday evening. Unfortunately it won't dock in Sydney until the New Year, so you won't be home for Christmas. Travel warrants and accommodation vouchers will be ready in the registry immediately after lunch.' The CO sat back and folded his arms. 'I wish you the very best of luck for the future, Miss Paignton-Fox. And with your experience in the CCS, I'm sure I shall be calling you Doctor Paignton-Fox in the not too distant future.' He stood and reached out his hand. 'Goodbye, Miss Paignton-Fox.'

Aughton Park, Northern Territory, Monday, 27 January 1919

Lucy leant on the rail of the yard, feeding carrots to Monarch and Princess, and stroking their noses. They'd become much greyer around the eyes and muzzle while she'd been away, but that was understandable. This was her first morning back home and the station was as trim as she'd remembered it. She breathed deeply, savouring the smell of horses and grass. Even the smell of cattle was not unpleasant. It was so good to be home, and tomorrow was her birthday. This was the best present she could she have, but it would take a while before she was used to the humidity again.

'You'll make those horses fat.'

'G'day, Dad.' His arm went round her shoulder and she leant against him, revelling in the human contact with someone she loved. 'Does it matter if they get fat? Surely you're not still working them.'

'No way. You're a bit long in the tooth these days, aren't you, Monarch?' Charlie said. He reached out to pat the horse's neck and Princess pushed along the rail so she was within his reach too. 'All right, girl. I love you just as much.'

'Did John Mitchell write?' Lucy asked.

Charlie nodded. 'I told him there's a job here if he wants it. You sure he'll be okay?'

'He's a very competent man, Dad. He was a sergeant when I first met him, but he was commissioned in the field. When I last saw him he was a captain. All his men thought the world of him.'

'So he's a good soldier. It's what he's like as a stockman that concerns me.'

'He was head stockman at Gidgealpa before the war, so he must know cattle. I'm sure you'll get on very well.'

Charlie smiled at her. 'I was just teasing. The army has been a bit tardy with his release so he won't be here until the end of the wet. Just when will depend on his discharge and passage.'

It would be April, or maybe May, before the rainy season ended and the tracks became passable, Lucy thought as she fed the horses another carrot each. So June would be the earliest John would be here. It would be good to see him again and she wondered how he'd recovered from his wounds. The scars of losing his mates would take longer to heal. Maybe she could help him with that, and maybe he could help her come to terms with Adam's death.

'Give me a couple of those carrots. I don't want you stealing all their affections,' Charlie said. 'I still ride them occasionally. I think they enjoy it, but they're only short rides and I wouldn't put them to a gallop.'

'How old do you think they are?' Lucy asked.

'They have to be at least thirty. It was '92 when I caught them and Monarch must have been four or five at least as he was the stallion. Princess must be as old. Let's see, that makes… Thirty-one? Thirty-two? That's a fair age for a horse, so they won't last much longer. I'll miss them.'

'Me too, Dad, but they won't be entirely gone.' She looked across the yard to the new foal suckling from its dam. 'That's one from Monarch's line, isn't it?'

Charlie nodded. 'Indirectly, yes, but it's been a few years since he sired a foal.'

Dorothy had joined them while Charlie had been speaking. Her arm crept round his waist and she laid her head on his shoulder. 'Don't be sad, Charlie. They've had a good life, better than they'd have had in the wild. They'd have been dead years ago if you hadn't caught them.' She lifted her hand and caressed the back of his neck.

Her father gazed down at his wife.

Lucy saw the love in his eyes and thought of her news. She had to tell them soon and this seemed an opportune moment. 'Dad. There's something I have to tell you,' she said.

'I'll leave you then,' Dorothy said.

'No don't go, Mum. It's something you have to know too,' Lucy said with alarm. Her father may need Dorothy's support. 'I met a wonderful man. He was a pilot with the Royal Flying Corps.' She took a deep breath. 'We were going to be married, but he was killed just days before the war ended.'

Charlie stepped towards her, concern strong in his face. 'Lucy. What can I do?'

'Wait a minute, Dad.' She took another breath. 'We loved each other so much. I'm going to have his baby.' She saw the horror flash across her father's face, but a moment later it faded and the concern returned.

He reached out to her and drew her close. 'My poor, Lucy. Did you think I'd be angry?' She nodded. 'It's a shock, I must admit, but how can I be angry with you for doing what I did?' he said. 'Do you want to tell me about him?'

Lucy was so relieved she began to cry, crushing her head into her father's shoulder. 'I do love you so, Dad.' She pulled away and wiped her tears. 'Later. I'll tell you later.'

Dorothy stepped forward and hugged her, their cheeks touching. She whispered, 'I'd guessed that airman you wrote about was someone special. Don't you worry about a thing.'

'What do you think Gran and Grandfather will say?' Lucy asked.

'Your grandfather will be fine, so will your grandmother, but it may take her a while to get used to the idea. Would you like me to talk to them?' Charlie said.

Monarch pushed his head into her back and she turned to caress his neck. 'Thanks, Dad, but I must be the one to tell them,' Lucy said. 'I'll have to tell Betsy One as well. She'll be delighted.'

'When is the baby due?' Dorothy asked. 'We need to make preparations.'

'It'll be early June,' Lucy said.

'What are you going to do about your studies? Having a baby is going to make it difficult,' Dorothy said, her eyes glistening as she blinked the tears away. 'We'll look after the baby for you, but you'll have to put your studies back another year.'

'I won't be going to medical school, Mum.'

'But you had such good reports. And you did so much when you were in France.' Dorothy failed to keep the disappointment out of her voice. She took hold of Lucy's hands. 'You'll feel different once you've recovered.'

Lucy shook her head. 'I've had my fill of doctoring. It was one thing when the men were risking their lives, but the hospital in England showed me what it'll be like in peacetime. And I never want to see another operating table.' She fell silent, thinking of Morgan the Moron, Matron Reeves and the arrogance of so many of the doctors at Harefield.

'Lucy. It's such an opportunity. Don't waste it,' Dorothy said.

'It's not the life for me, Mum.'

'What would you like to do?' Charlie asked.

'Can I stay home, Dad? Help you run the station.' Her hand moved to her waist. 'I'll need to learn everything, so I can teach my son as he grows.'

Charlie wrapped an arm around her shoulder and drew her close, his face wreathed in a smile. 'It might be a girl.'

Glossary

Albatros:	A make of a series German fighter planes produced by the Albatros Flugzeugwerke.
Anzac:	1 — Australian New Zealand Army Corps [acronym]. 2 — A member of the armed forces from Australia or New Zealand.
archie:	An anti-aircraft gun.
batman:	An officer's servant. Usually a private soldier.
camouflet:	An explosive charge used to cause the collapse of an enemy's excavation.
cannula:	medical; a short hollow needle that can be inserted into a body cavity or vessel to permit the withdrawing or injection of fluid. It terminates in a flexible section to allow a syringe to be connected.
charger:	A metal clasp that assembles ammunition to ease the loading of a weapon. For the Lee Enfield rifle it held five rounds. In use it slipped into a slot at the rear of the breach and allowed the five rounds to be pushed directly into the magazine, speeding reloading. When all the rounds had been forced into the magazine, the charger fell free. A second charger would then be inserted to allow a further five round to be loaded, bringing the magazine to the full capacity of ten rounds. A charger is frequently confused with a clip, which remains in the magazine until all the rounds have been fired.
chat:	A body louse.
CO:	Commanding Officer.
corduroy road:	A road constructed by laying logs, or sometimes planks, transversely across muddy areas to improve access to and from the front lines.
drum fire barrage:	A heavy continuous artillery barrage.

fascine: A large bundle of brushwood, or an assembly of timber, carried on a tank, which could be dropped to bridge a trench.

fire bay: A looped section of trench that projected towards the enemy lines.

fire-step: A raised portion of the floor of a trench that allows the occupying troops to see over the parapet and aim at the enemy.

Flamewerfer: A German flamethrower. It needed a crew of four or more.

haybox: A food container with the inner and outer separated by insulating material, which traditionally was straw. The forerunner of the modern icebox.

home sister: A nurse who was responsible for the nurses' mess, buying the provisions and preparing their meals.

housewife: A small roll of sewing kit issued to the British and Commonwealth troops.

jasta: A German air force squadron.

Kaiserheer: The Imperial German Army.

khamsin: An oppressive hot wind that blows from the southern Sahara Desert through Egypt for about seven weeks in the early months of the year.

knocked up: To be physically exhausted.

Lewis gun: A light machine-gun used by the British and Commonwealth armies in World War I and for some years afterwards.

Maconochie stew: A tinned meat stew complete with vegetables supplied to the British and Commonwealth troops in World War I. Produced by the Maconochie Brothers.

Maxim: The basis design of the medium and heavy machine guns used by both sides in World War I.

Minenwerfer: A German trench mortar. These were produced in three sizes: heavy, medium and light.

Mullaka: An Aboriginal term of respect, used in Australia's Northern Territory. The pronunciation and English spelling varies slightly between Aboriginal groups.

parados: A raised section at the rear of a trench built up with earth, which may be in sandbags, to improve the protection.

parapet: A raised section at the front of a trench built up with earth, which may be in sandbags, to improve the protection.

Pickelhaube (plural pickelhauben): A helmet with an ornamental central spike that was common for many German World War I units during the early years of the war.

pip: A stylised star that was part of the identification of an officer's rank, worn on the epaulets.

punkah-louvre: A spherical adjustable outlet set into a ventilation duct.

in the rattle: To be in trouble.

remedial masseuse: A nurse trained to provide mobility recovery. The forerunner of a physiotherapist.

ringer: An experienced Australian stockman.

sap: A communication trench in World War I, leading from the rear positions to the front line.

Spandau: A German government arsenal. Also the name of a machine-gun manufactured there.

Stahlhelm: The German World War I steel helmet that replaced the Pickelhaube. Often called a coal-scuttle by the British and Commonwealth troops.

Stielhandgranate: A German hand grenade mounted on a handle, often called a stick grenade.

stunt: An attack.

Sturmtruppen: German storm troops.

the real Mackay: Variation on the real McCoy. The genuine article.

Tommy: A British soldier.

traverse: A section of a trench that connects two fire bays.

Author's Note

Nursing Fox is my homage to those brave young women who served on the Western Front during World War I.

Although they performed a crucial role, the nurses of the Australian Army Nursing Service are rarely mentioned in accounts of that conflict. It was impossible to cover every theatre of the war, so I opted to concentrate on the Casualty Clearing Stations in Flanders and France. They were the locations where the nurses were continually in the greatest danger. They shared the horrors with the fighting troops, and were routinely shelled and bombed. For the nurses, conditions on the Western Front were totally different to those they experienced while caring for the wounded from Gallipoli.

While vitally important to Australia, Gallipoli does not feature strongly in this story. Other than for a few isolated incidents, the closest the nurses came to the fighting at Gallipoli was on the hospital ships evacuating the wounded to Imbros, the infamous Lemnos, Egypt, or perhaps Salonica. The major hospitals were in Egypt, and seriously wounded men would be taken to Alexandria, from where they were sent on to hospitals further south.

Lucy and her friends are a composite developed from the nurses' records. Until the Australian Casualty Clearing Stations were established in 1917, the Australian nurses served in British Casualty Clearing Stations. While I have no evidence that the nurses were transferred between hospitals, it seems logical that this did happen. Some nurses did undertake simple operations. Some were gassed. The nurses did visit the front lines so it could be possible for some of them to be there during a German attack. At times the nurses worked in steel helmets and at others they worked while wearing their respirators. The nurses would also hop onto trucks for a change of scene. The locations of many of the CCS are now the sites of war cemeteries.

Of the 2,139 nurses who served overseas in the AANS during World War I, twenty-one died during their service. Three hundred and eighty-eight were decorated, seven awarded the Military Medal. A further one hundred and thirty Australian nurses served with the Queen Alexandra Imperial Nursing Service, four of whom died.

It is fact that a party of Australian nurses arrived in France on 1 April 1916, landing at Marseilles. They then travelled north by train, but the journey was a shambles. The food halts were so disorganised that the nurses had nothing to eat until they arrived at their destination, Rouen. But I wasn't about to let that happen to Lucy and her friends, so I introduced John Mitchell and a party of Anzacs.

The dates and locations of the various Casualty Clearance Stations are factual, as is the bombing and shelling, but the story, my characters and their reactions are fiction.

These days blood transfusions are a routine procedure, but they had only been introduced a few years before World War I broke out. They were major operations, far too complicated for use in a CCS. However, in 1916, three Canadian medical officers introduced the syringe-cannula method to the Royal Army Medical Corps. One of the officers, Major Robertson, published a paper on the method in the *British Medical Journal* during the summer of 1916.

I was unable to write about the nurses without mentioning the men they cared for in their hospitals. The Anzacs allowed me to illustrate the appalling conditions that the men experienced and the indifference of many of the senior officers to the casualties. John Mitchell and his mates allowed me to show the Australians' disregard for the British Army's rigid hierarchy.

The dates and locations of the battles are, like those of the Casualty Clearance Stations, also factual, but the story, the battle scenes and my Anzacs' reactions are all figments of my imagination.

The death toll in World War I was on a huge scale. The total military casualties, both sides combined, were over eight million killed and twenty-two million wounded. While machine-guns and rifles contributed a significant proportion to these casualties, the majority were caused by artillery fire, resulting in shrapnel wounds being the most common reason for men to be hospitalised at a CCS. The artillery fire also shattered the drainage system on the Western Front with the result that the ground became a morass.

World War I was a time of rapid development in aviation so it was important to have the correct aircraft at the dates given. The British Army and Royal Navy operated their own aviation arms, the Royal Flying Corps and the Royal Naval Air Service respectively. Initially men joining the RFC as pilots had to hold a civilian pilot's licence, issued by the *Federation Aeronautique Internationale*. It was called a ticket. Many instructors ignored this ticket, treating the pilots as if they were new to flying. The requirement for a ticket was dropped in July 1916 as it limited recruitment, and from summer 1916 the RFC made periodic appeals for men to transfer from the infantry. The RFC and Naval Air Service were amalgamated to form the Royal Air Force on 1 April 1918, but officers continued to use army and naval ranks until 4 August 1919, when, as a result of large reductions in manpower, the army and navy refused to allow this practice to continue. In response Sir Hugh Trenchard, Chief of the Air Staff, then a major general, created new ranks specific to the RAF. These ranks were adopted by the RAAF when it was formed.

Parachutes were issued to observers in the balloons, but not to aircrew. The senior officers thought that if parachutes were issued, the pilots would abandon their aircraft rather than continue in combat. The Germans were the first to review the situation and issued their aircrew with parachutes early in 1918. The British followed suit in September 1918. The French and Americans never supplied parachutes to their aircrews.

The Royal Australian Air Force was not established until 31 March 1921.

At times the writer can leave myth in the story for greater effect. One myth in *Nursing Fox* concerns the Mills grenade. Superficially it looks like a small pineapple, but while the segmentation aids fragmentation, the main purpose is simply to provide a better grip.

For readers not familiar with army structure and ranks, here are basic lists of structure and ranks used in the Australian Army during World War I. Since World War I there have been changes to cater for developments in operational methods and technology.

Australian Army Structure WWI			
Organisation	**Manpower**	**Consists of**	**Commander**
Army		Two or more corps	General
Corps	30,000 or more	Two or more divisions	Lieutenant General
Division	10,000 to 20,000	Three brigades	Major General
Brigade	2,500 to 5,000	Four battalions	Brigadier General
Battalion	550 to 1,000	Four companies	Lieutenant Colonel
Company	100 to 250	Four platoons	Major or Captain
Platoon	30 to 60	Four (Three) sections	Lieutenant
Section	9 to 16		Sergeant or Corporal

With the rank structure there are several slight variations for specialised units, such as artillery, but basically the ranks are as follows. They were modelled on British practice. The modern rank structure has differences that have developed over the one hundred years since World War I. It is still developing. An example is the rank of Staff Sergeant, which is currently being phased out.

Other ranks	**Commissioned Officers**
Private	Second Lieutenant
Lance Corporal	Lieutenant
Corporal	Captain
Sergeant	Major
Staff Sergeant	Lieutenant Colonel
Warrant Officer class 2	Colonel
Warrant Officer class 1	Brigadier General
	Major General
	Lieutenant General
	General
	Field Marshal

Sometimes a unit may have a honorary appointment at the rank of Captain General. This is common in the British army and is frequently someone within the extended Royal family.

A Lieutenant Colonel is referred to just as Colonel.

In the Australian and British services, Lieutenant is pronounced

Left-tenant, whereas in the American services it is pronounced Loo-tenant.

In the British system a Warrant Officer Class 2 (WO2) is commonly called a Quarter Master Sergeant (QMS) and a Warrant Officer Class 1 (WO1) a Regimental Sergeant Major (RSM), but they are both Warrant Officers. Normally in a battalion there would be one RSM, called Sir by junior ranks. Each company would have one QMS, often simply called "Q" by experienced soldiers, but otherwise QMS or Sergeant Major.

A Quartermaster would be in charge of the stores, and would normally be a commissioned officer. It is a position, not a rank.

The designation Sergeant Major, or Company Sergeant Major is also a position and not a rank. In a company it is a post usually filled by a Warrant Officer 2 (QMS), but will be the role of a more junior non-commissioned officer in a smaller unit.

Acknowledgements

My greatest thanks go to the nurses of the Australian Army Nursing Service during World War I, who left a legacy of their experiences when they returned home from that conflict.

I also have a debt to those anonymous people who compiled an extensive record of the dates and locations of the CCS hospitals throughout the hostilities. This allowed me to ensure that the dates and locations of the various CCS are correct.

For the battles I relied extensively on H P Willmott's, *World War I*, published by DK Publishing. Other sources were used to verify facts, but they are less comprehensive and too numerous to mention.

I am grateful to my friend Molly, who read the manuscript and corrected my misunderstanding of medical matters. I also thank my fellow members of the Blackwood Writers' Group, Rob S, Rob B, Kon, Jason, Jenny, Steve, Michael and Andrew, who provided valuable comments. I must also thank my American friend, Julia Brown, who read the manuscript with her eagle eye and corrected my errors at a distance, bringing a female perspective to the manuscript. I also thank my editor and publisher, Michelle Lovi, for her help and understanding.

All the errors and mistakes are my own.